THE REMAINS OF GLORY

The Remains of Glory

Dean Urdahl

NORTH STAR PRESS OF ST. CLOUD, INC.
St. Cloud, Minnesota

First edition: August 2017

Printed in the United States of America.

Published by
North Star Press
19485 Estes Road
Clearwater, MN 55320

www.northstarpress.com

Dedication

To my wife, Karen, for her valuable assistance.
To Grandchildren Kateri Urdahl and Eli Urdahl
and thanks to North Star Press

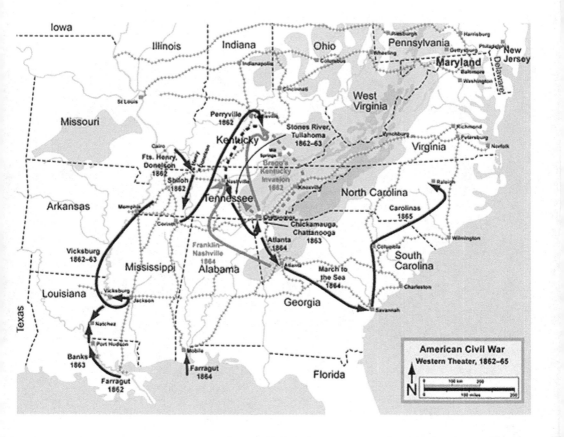

American Civil War
Western Theater, 1862–65

Foreword

THE CIVIL WAR IS THE GREAT defining point of American history. We measure our nation's story up to and from that great event. That's why it is so important we understand what was happening during America's most trying time.

The war was generally fought in two theaters, the East and the West. It seems that most attention is given to the East. That's where Gettysburg was. It's where Lee and Jackson seemed invincible in many battles such as Fredericksville, First and Second Bull Run, Chancelorsville, and the Penninsula Campaign. It's where Lee surrendered to Grant.

Many historians emphasize the Eastern theater, and the Western theater is sometimes glossed over unless particular attention is being given to a certain battle. What I did in *Three Paths to Glory* and now in *The Remains of Glory* is to follow specific men and regiments as they fought the battles of the West in Kentucky, Tennessee, Louisiana, Georgia, Missouri, and Alabama.

While *Three Paths to Glory* covered 1861 to early 1863, *The Remains of Glory* traces the war in the West from 1863 to 1865. It was my intent that these two volumes give a comprehensive, readable account of what happened in that theater of the war. Hopefully, readers of both books will have a deeper understanding what happened in the West during the Civil War.

The story of Jimmy Dunn continues as the Fifth Minnesota battles through the wars with the Native Americans to fight in the Red River campaign and other conflicts leading to Nashville.

Tod Carter of the Twentieth Tennessee shows another side of the war as his story spins to a battle in his hometown of Franklin, Tennessee.

We follow Clint Cilley of the Second Minnesota. He became a staff officer, the only Minnesotan at the bloody battle of Franklin.

This is a work of historical fiction. The fiction is primarily in the dialogue. The events and battles have been thoroughly researched and described in a highly accurate manner. The characters depicted are also well researched.

May this story give the reader a deeper understanding of the courage that caused these men to follow paths leading to great sacrifice. Both sides were convinced they were right. Both sides were prepared to give everything to prove it.

A New Campaign

ARCH 1864. FOR NEARLY three years, America had been split in two. Like two bare-knuckled prize fighters, the North and South had pounded away at each other. Torn and bloodied, neither fell. But after seeing its resources depleted and wasted away, the South no longer expected to record a knockout. Its only hope was to drag the fight to a stalemated finish.

Like a sea of whitecaps, thousands of dusky, once-white tents spread away from the Big Black River east of Vicksburg, Mississippi. They were shelter halves, home for Union soldiers since the first of the year. Each soldier carried half a tent. When matched with a partner, they provided shelter for the two men and little more.

The Fifth Minnesota had spent much of the winter encamped there. On February 12, nearly the whole regiment had enlisted for another three years with the promise of a thirty-day furlough as an incentive. The drudgery of camp life had been relieved when General Sherman had included the Fifth as part of a campaign into central Mississippi. They were to break up Confederate lines of communication and paralyze rebel forces on the Mississippi River in order to free up Union troops moving on to Atlanta.

Many of the Minnesota companies were organized primarily by county. Company B had started with seventy-eight from Filmore County, including fifty-five from Chatfield and twenty-three from Preston. Prominent local men with names like Gere, Marsh, and Bishop had all become Union officers.

Back in camp, they awaited news of a reorganization and orders for a new campaign. Private Jimmy Dunn from Chatfield stood before his tent and stretched out his five-foot-eight frame. The sun was sliding toward the western horizon as salt pork sizzled in a frying pan resting in a cook fire. Jimmy ran his fingers through his thick, curly brown hair, trying to smooth it and fighting a battle he had lost many times before.

1

"Ain't no girls ta look purty fer," Will Hutchinson, a young private, called. "And yer not clerkin' in yer dad's hotel, neither."

"Never can tell, Will. I might go visit in Vicksburg. They got some nice rebel gals there."

"What about goin' ta Georgia," Will continued. "Lotsa Georgia peaches there."

Jimmy paused, his youthful face sobering. "To tell the truth, Will, I'd like ta go home, back to Fillmore County. There's a pretty blonde Norwegian gal there waitin' for me. Her name's Lucy."

"That don't sound like the Jimmy Dunn I knew back in Chatfield. You could hardly wait ta git into this war. But yer over twenty now, I s'pose old age is gittin' to ya."

Jimmy smiled ruefully and warmed his hands over the flickering fire. "War gets old. 'Sides, we had to fight a war before we got sent here."

Will stared into the fire and flipped over the salt pork. "We lost a lotta friends in the other war. Damn Indians."

"They thought they had good reason ta fight," Jimmy replied. "We didn't exactly give 'em what was promised in the treaty that took their land. Still, it wuz a waste and hundreds died."

Will added, "We lost twenty-four Fillmore County boys at Redwood Ferry. Me and you were jest lucky they didn't git us."

"I know, Will, then they finally sent us here to fight at Vicksburg. I thought the war would be over before we got here."

Will stuck a fork in a slab of pork and slowly gnawed off a chunk. "And there's still lotsa war left."

"Too much, Will, too much war is left."

"And where will we be?"

"Wherever Gen'r'l Grant decides. I think we'll know soon. At least many Minnesota boys are here."

"Not all," Will countered. "The Second, Third, Fourth, and part of the Fifth have been in the war since '62. Now the Sixth and Seventh have joined us here, but the Eighth and Ninth are still fightin' Sioux in Dakota or pullin' fort duty on the Minnesota frontier."

"And the First is pretty much done."

"Not much left of 'em after Gettysburg," Will mused.

"Well," Jimmy concluded, "I just hope we git word soon where we're goin'."

* * *

GENERAL WILLIAM TECUMSEH SHERMAN surveyed the large living room with its rich carpet, full drapes, shining dark woodwork, and fine furniture. Then he gazed amiably at the handsome, mustached, dark-haired officer sitting at the polished table across from him. "General Banks," he began, "you have a lovely home here."

"A cotton speculator had it. He joined the rebel army, and we moved his family out," Banks explained. "How was your trip from Vicksburg?"

"A good trip. The *Diana* is a comfortable steamer, and fortunately the Mississippi is now unobstructed by rebels. I did stop in Natchez to deal with a friend of mine from my days as head of the Louisiana Seminary of Learning. He had joined the rebel army and was a prisoner of war in the Natchez jail. He was my professor of language and a fine man. I brought him down here to New Orleans with me. I want you to arrange an exchange for him. I'll give you the particulars later."

"Of course, General Sherman. I'll see that it's done."

"General Banks, I'm here to make sure we understand each other. We are to implement a plan that neither General Grant nor I advocated."

"It was not my preference, either. Originally I was to surround Confederate forces by taking Mobile."

"You're the commander of the Army of the Gulf, highest ranking general in the West. Only Grant outranks you, General Banks. Steele and I are department commanders. You have great responsibility. Still, President Lincoln and General-in-Chief Halleck call the shots, and they want a campaign up the Red River. They want Shreveport, and they want Texas cut off from the Confederacy."

Banks's face brightened. "We have the opportunity for a glorious victory. It's unfortunate you can't be with us."

Sherman's face flushed, almost matching his red beard. "It was my desire to lead this campaign. General Grant has other uses for me. But this campaign has serious flaws. Its troop movements are very complex. Don't be afraid to convey reservations to Halleck."

"General Halleck is proud of his plan. I'll do the best I can with it."

Sherman sighed. "You've spent most of your life in politics, not soldiering. You need to know the difference. Have you really ordered Commodore Porter to load barges with cotton while you bring speculators up the river on a steamboat?"

Banks bristled. "Depriving the Confederacy of revenue from cotton is paramount to our victory."

Sherman rejoined, "And the fact that you can make cotton buyers rich won't hurt your political ambitions, either."

This time Banks reddened. "Any ambitions I have certainly depend upon the path President Lincoln takes. Remember, I was speaker of the house."

"So you won't challenge Lincoln for the Republican nomination."

"That is not my current plan."

Sherman smirked. "I wonder if your current plan could change with a big military victory."

"That's enough," Banks's voice rose. "I—"

Sherman raised his hands palms up. "I agree, that's enough. I didn't come here to argue politics with you. I'm here to make sure we have a perfect understanding of what you are to do. General Grant's concerned there be no misunderstandings."

Banks shook his head. "Grant commands the military division of the Mississippi, and your Department of the Tennessee and Steele in Arkansas are under him. As you noted, I command the Army of the Gulf. I'll answer to Halleck, not Grant."

"Grant will soon command all Union armies. Then you'll answer to him. How many men do you have?"

"Twenty thousand."

"Just so's we have it right, you're to take your troops from New Orleans to Alexandria on a route up the Bayou Teche. There you'll be met with 10,000 of my men under A.J. Smith. They'll be coming down from Vicksburg. You've got them only a month. I'll be needing them in Georgia. You will march up the Red River toward Shreveport with the support of Admiral Porter's fleet of gunboats."

Sherman paused. "And of course his cotton barges. General Steele, with 7,000 men, will come down through Arkansas and rendezvous with you near Shreveport."

"I've a letter from General Steele," Banks countered. "He has political concerns with elections in Arkansas. He wants to make sure Union supporters are elected and suggests he only make a demonstration on Shreveport due to his responsibilities in Arkansas. General Steele wants to be excused from this campaign."

Sherman snorted. "Tell him to push on to Shreveport with all he has."

Banks considered a moment and replied, "They have fortifications at the mouth of the Red River."

"You will take them and move up the river, destroy the Confederate Army under Taylor, take Shreveport, occupy east Texas, organize pro-Union state governments in the region, and, yes, confiscate cotton bales."

"It will be nearly impossible to occupy this territory without a major influx of resources," Banks countered.

"Live off the land if you need to," Sherman responded. "I'm prepared to do it in Georgia."

"When do we put all this into motion?"

"Within a week, General Banks, and remember you have Smith's men only for a month. Today is March second."

"I do have an obligation," Banks informed him. "In two days we have a banquet here commemorating the installation of a pro-Union government. I urge you to attend."

Sherman shook his head. "Banquets are out of place when the war demands every hour and minute of our time. You have too many such events. I hear they call you 'Dancing Master Banks' in light of the balls you hold. No more. After March fourth, General Grant demands your full attention to this campaign."

Indignantly, Banks shot a hot glare at Sherman. "We hold New Orleans and southern Louisiana. When we march we will take the whole state, including their new capital of Shreveport. You and Grant don't need to worry."

"I'm sure General Grant will be reassured," Sherman replied with a tinge of sarcasm.

As General Sherman left New Orleans, the gala celebration commemorating the inauguration of a civil government for Louisiana was beginning. Fireworks painted streaks of red, white, and blue across the night sky as booms and crashes echoed onto the river. Sherman gazed from a boat railing at the shoreline scaffolding crowded with spectators and shook his head in disgust.

By March fourth, he was back in Vicksburg to meet with General Andrew Jackson Smith of the Sixteenth Corps. Sherman rode stoically through the town. His eyes took in the wreckage of what had once been a great city. The siege and bombardment ordered by Grant had demolished buildings and caused the people of Vicksburg to dig into bluffs or find caves for shelter.

"Brave," Sherman muttered to himself, "but stupid."

Some buildings were largely untouched. Sherman dismounted before one and strode through its entrance. Seated at a rough table in the sparsely furnished large room was a slight, middle-aged officer.

Andrew Jackson Smith rose and snapped to attention. Sherman gave a brusque return salute and motioned for Smith to sit down. He then took a seat across the table from him. Smith was a veteran officer born in Missouri, forty-nine years old with receding gray hair. He had a short, bushy, white-speckled beard and peered at Sherman through wire-rimmed glasses. His look and demeanor were almost professorial.

"Well, Whitey, I just received a communication from Grant," Sherman said. "They've revived the rank of lieutenant general for him. He'll be heading east soon. It had been my hope to lead the Army of the Tennessee up the Red River, but I'll be headed into Georgia. You will lead my Sixteenth Corps up the Red."

"How many men will be assigned to me?"

"You'll have two divisions from the Sixteenth and one from the Seventeenth. I'll transfer men from Hurlbut and McPherson to you. Kilby Smith and Mower will command under you. Ten thousand total for thirty days. Then I want you back to join me on the Atlanta Campaign."

"What are the logistics?"

"I just came from Banks. He's overall commander. I sent him a written message conveying how far I feel authorized to go in accordance with my orders from General Grant. I want no misunderstanding. East Texas must be cut off from the Confederacy.

"You'll depart Vicksburg on March tenth, conveyed by Admiral Porter's flotilla, and land near the outlet of the Atchafalaya by the twelfth. Mower's division will march by land up the Red River and capture Fort DeRussy, below Alexandria.

"With Porter's fleet, you'll then proceed to Alexandria. Banks should rendezvous with you on the seventeenth. He's coming up from New Orleans. Steele is coming down from Arkansas to meet you."

An expression of alarm flashed over Smith's face. "I was under the impression you would command the expedition. Porter was, as well. Let me assure you that the admiral will be very disappointed."

"I don't make the command decisions. Grant and Halleck do. This is how it will be."

"There's some complex maneuvering going on, General. I hope all are up to it."

"They better be," Sherman snapped crisply. "Banks signed on for this. He's risen beyond either of us in command, and he has no military training. Now he's dealing with cotton buyers."

Smith sighed. "We have many political generals."

"Well, Smith, no one will ever say that about you. You've been career Army since West Point, and you've done well wherever we've sent you. You spent years fighting Indians in the West. Even Grant and I took time in civilian life."

Smith shook his head ruefully. "My men don't seem to have a home. We get moved from army to army either detached from the main army or under independent command. We've become our own small army." He chuckled. "Some are calling us the lost tribes of Israel."

"Then be like Moses and lead them to the promised land. One more thing, blast it! This veteranizing business. Grant says I have to make sure everyone gets his thirty days off for re-enlisting. In the middle of a war, in the middle of a campaign, we have to send boys home to Mommy. Do you have any furloughed?"

"Mine have already gone through it. We are ready to fight."

"Godspeed, General Smith. I'll see your whole army in thirty days."

* * *

THE SECOND MINNESOTA soldiers had all largely re-enlisted or become "veteranized." They had been furloughed back home to Minnesota and were scheduled to return to Chattanooga before moving further south. But not Captain Clinton Cilley. The hero of Chickamauga and former professor at a seminary in Wasioja, Minnesota, had resigned from the Second to permanently join the staff of General John Schofield.

Colonel James George, returning from sick leave, would command the Second Regiment with Judson Bishop, a newspaper editor from Chatfield and second in command. In the first week of March the regiment traveled by rail through La Crosse, Wisconsin, on the way to Chicago. Ringgold, Georgia, was their destination. Along the route, they were joined by other regiments returning from furlough. The train cars overflowed with soldiers and supplies.

But the Fifth Minnesota regiment was in the First Division of the Right Wing of the Sixteenth Corps, poised to head for the Red River.

Prison Camp

FEBRUARY 1864. CAPTAIN TOD CARTER huddled next to a cast-iron wood-stove in the center of a large barracks that accommodated about 250 men. Rows of bunks, three tiers high and wide enough for two men, ringed the stove. Men slouched in their bunks, huddling and shivering beneath thin blankets. Some milled around between the rows of bunks or in the center of the room near the stove. The wind howled like a pack of hungry wolves and blew wisps of snow through cracks in the walls.

Outside, the wind whipped snow crystals like little daggers across the frozen bay where Johnson's Island, the prison camp, was itself imprisoned in a mausoleum of ice.

Tod held his hands over the stove and felt a warm tingle in his fingers. "The blood's moving again, Johnny," he remarked to a thin man beside him. Tod was thin, himself. His dirty gray uniform draped over his shoulders like a coat on a rack. He stood about five-foot-ten with light-brown, nearly blond hair. Normally trimmed at his ears, his hair had grown shaggy. His face, while thin, was handsome and intelligent with bright, blue eyes. In another month Tod would mark his twenty-fourth birthday.

Johnny smiled. "Sure would be nice ta be home. That twenty-below stuff 'bout did me in." He blew a moist cloud into the frosty air.

Tod shook his head. "There'll never be another New Year's Day like that one. At least not one I'll ever see. Once we get out of here, I'm never going north of the Mason-Dixon Line again."

Johnny lowered his voice. "There's talk they might try ta break us outta here. Get us across Lake Erie to Canada. It's only a few miles."

"It might as well be hundreds," Tod replied. They were prisoners of war, 3,000 Confederate officers on an island in Lake Erie. A fifteen-foot-high wooden fence surrounded twelve barracks and the 128th Ohio Volunteer Infantry made sure the prisoners didn't go anywhere.

A bald, full-mustached man on crutches clumped close to them. His left pant leg, empty at the knee, was pinned up.

Tod saluted. "General Trimble, can we get you anything?"

"A left leg would be good. I couldn't help but overhearing your conversation. I thought you might be interested in knowing I think some of us will be moving out soon. To another prison in Maryland. You two may be going, too. Where are you from, boy?"

"Franklin, Tennessee. I'm in the Twentieth Tennessee."

Johnny grinned at Trimble. "He's a smart one, General, a lawyer at twenty-two. He wrote a newspaper column for the *Chattanooga Rebel*. They call him 'Mint Julep.'"

"I've read your work. You're a talented writer. At the Battle of Mill Springs there was an officer named Carter, Moscow, I think."

"My big brother," Tod explained. "He was shot in the leg there, then captured. In August of '62 he was exchanged and went home to help manage our family farm at Franklin. My little brother, Francis—'Wad,' we call him— was at Mill Springs, too. He's in the Twentieth Tennessee now."

"A real military family," Trimble noted.

"Moscow was in the Mexican War, too. He was a colonel. But with his bad leg . . ." Tod reddened as he glanced at the General's empty pant leg. "Well, he could do more good at home."

Trimble smiled slightly. "Don't worry, boy, he did his part." He glanced around the crowded, stuffy room. "We all have. Where were you captured?"

"Mission Ridge, at the battle outside Chattanooga. The Minnesota boys charged up the side of the ridge, and we couldn't stop them. Our cannons were too high and couldn't point down at the right angle. Those Yankees ran right over us. Six thousand were captured. The only good thing to come of it is that General Bragg lost his job."

"Replaced by Joe Johnston." Trimble acknowledged, "A very able commander."

"Are we really leavin' here? When?" Johnny asked.

"Soon, I think. Even in a prison camp, rank has privileges. They tell me things."

Johnny grinned broadly. "Maryland'll sure beat Ohio. By maybe fifty degrees."

As General Trimble slid his beaten body away, Tod leaned close to Johnny. "I won't be going to Maryland," he mumbled softly.

"Why not?" Johnny asked incredulously. "It's sure better than here."

"I've got a plan, Johnny. I'll fill you in later. But I'm not going to Maryland, and I'm not going to stay here."

"Where ya goin', Tod?"

"Home."

To Red River

ON MARCH 10, 1864, TRANSPORT SHIPS began churning the dark waters of the Mississippi River south of Vicksburg. General Andrew Jackson Smith's Sixteenth and Seventeenth Corps had launched the Red River Expedition. Ten thousand men crowded into the boats. The two corps included ten regiments of infantry, two batteries of light artillery of the Third Division, the Sixteenth Corps, and six regiments of infantry and one battery of light artillery from the Seventeenth command of General Kilby Smith. Another five regiments were commanded by General Joseph Mower with the First Division.

Two blue-clad officers stood alongside a deck railing and peered into the murky water below. Lieutenant John Bishop seemed fixated by the large sidewheel, which spun and bit into the wide river as it drove the vessel south.

"Funny how folks get fascinated by moving water, isn't it?" Tom Gere observed.

Bishop gazed back at the twin smokestacks of the twenty boats trailing his. The smoke spewed into the fading light of the evening sky, leaving black smudges like ink smears blending into the horizon. "Ten thousand men," the young lieutenant muttered to the even younger adjutant. "I hope it's enough."

"Well," Gere replied, "any more and we'd need more boats. We've got near 500 on this one, and the boys are packed in pretty tight."

"Tom, what do you hear? Your brother Will is our lieutenant colonel. He talks to Colonel Hubbard. Got any news we don't know?"

Gere rubbed his smooth chin, then slightly tugged the brim of his kepi cap that covered dark, slightly shaggy hair and shaded bright-blue eyes. "A little." His handsome face flashed a slight smile. "It seems none of our officers trust each other. Porter agreed to lead his flotilla up the Red River and support us because he thought Sherman was going to be in charge of the expedition. Then Grant decided old Cump should march into Georgia, and Banks was given the command. Porter's worried Banks won't show or that he'll make a mess of things. That's one reason we're here. Porter doesn't like political generals. Everyone trusts that General Smith will do the job."

"It'd have been nice to have him in Minnesota. He knows how to fight," Bishop replied.

Gere's youthful face grew pensive. "Too many good men died in that war. I can't believe it's already two years ago."

"I was almost one of them," Bishop nodded. "If Jimmy Dunn hadn't been behind me, I would have been."

Gere chuckled. "Put his rifle right under your armpit and shot an Indian aiming a rifle at you. Quite a shot."

"We lost twenty-four friends and comrades that day."

Gere nodded sadly. They both knew the twenty-four he mentioned were just boys from the Fifth. The Dakota had killed over 250 settlers in the Minnesota River Valley that day alone, nearly 800 before it was over six weeks later.

Bishop spat into the river below. "All because we couldn't keep a treaty and pay them like we promised."

Gere shook his head. "The money showed up the day the killing started."

"Three months late! The Indians were starving. It was too late by then."

"I wonder, John," Gere considered, "what would it be like if there hadn't been an Indian war in Minnesota. The Fifth, all the boys from Filmore County, would've been sent to fight the rebs two years sooner. How many more battles . . . how many more would be dead?"

"God knows, Tom. I hope this ends soon. It's almost three years."

"The Red River Expedition is supposed to bring the end sooner. Cut Texas off from the Confederacy. Take Shreveport."

"It's all-out to end it, Tom. We're here in the West, Grant's moving into Virginia, and Sherman's going into the Deep South. We're hitting them on three fronts at the same time. The rebs can't hold out much longer. They don't have the men or the materials. Have you heard from your brother Beecher?"

"Just a quick note. He and the Second Minnesota are heading into Georgia with Sherman. Clint Cilley, the teacher from Wasioja . . . he's been transferred. He's on General Schofield's staff now."

"I heard Cilley was big at Chickamauga. He rallied the troops on Snod-grass Hill and helped make Thomas the 'Rock of Chickamauga.'"

"My brother was there, too," Gere smiled. "He said Cilley did pretty well for a math teacher. He'll get a medal for sure."

* * *

CRAMMED IN NEAR the stern of the boat, Jimmy Dunn and Levi Carr were also contemplating the future of their army. Jimmy ran his fingers through his tangled mop of dark hair and peered across the river into the growing dimness.

Levi scrunched up his face like he'd just swallowed a lemon and followed Jimmy's gaze. "What ya tryin' ta see? I don't see nothin'."

Jimmy looked solemnly at Levi. "I heard maybe there's rebs, or Indians hidin' along the bank ready to shoot us." He paused and uttered a low "Oooooh, ewwwww, maybe even ghosts." Then, like a cackle from a sur-prised chicken, he broke into laughter.

"This ain't no funny business," Levi countered. "They jest might be out there, all three, rebs, Injuns, *and* ghosts."

Jimmy sobered. "I expect yer right, Levi, but only about rebs. We'll run into them fer sure."

"Do ya think we'll be out here long, Jimmy?"

"Who knows? It shouldn't take much to mop things up. I heard Banks is comin' up from New Orleans ta meet us on the Red. Steele be comin' down from Arkansas. Porter will have a fleet to escort us up the river. That's three armies and a fleet ta take down Dick Taylor. My money's on us, and in short order. We got near twice as many men."

"Yer always the optimist, Jimmy. I'd sure feel better if Sherman was in charge and not Banks."

"Me too, but 'Old Cump,' got other orders. Anyway, we do have General Smith."

"And a plan worked out by 'Old Brains' Halleck and Father Abraham hisself."

Jimmy grinned broadly. "And nothin' can go wrong, can it?"

"I hope yer right. I wish we had more Minnesota boys with us. They're good fighters."

Jimmy ticked off on his fingers, "The First is about done, finished after Gettysburg, the Second's with Sherman, the Third's up in Little Rock on garrison duty, the Fourth's garrisoned in Alabama—they'll prob'ly wind up with Sherman. The Sixth fought in the Dakotas with Sibley and are stuck up north at Fort Snelling. We got the Seventh garrisoned in St. Louis, after fightin' Indians, too."

"Ain't you a walking text book on regiments," Will Hutchinson, sitting on Jimmy's right, proclaimed. "Is the Eighth still up north, still watchin' over Minnesota?"

"Ya gotta keep yer ears open, Will," Jimmy smiled. "That's how ya learn things. When I clerked in my dad's hotel, I heard more than I ever needed ta know. And yes, the Eighth's up north, but they're headin' inta the Dakotas with Sully."

"Finish up, Jimmy," Levi chuckled. "How about the Ninth and Tenth?"

"The Ninth's in St. Louis, too, guardin' the town just like the Eighth's guardin' Minnesota. The Tenth are done fightin' Indians. I think they're marchin' off ta Memphis. Maybe someday all the Minnesota boys will get together in this."

Will wondered aloud, "Should they make us one brigade all from Minnesota?" Then he grinned broadly. "With General Jimmy Dunn as brigade commander. How'd that suit you, Levi?"

"Right down to the ground." He slapped Jimmy on the back.

Jimmy laughed. "Well, they could do worse."

Will shook his head. "And they will."

Escape

RUMORS AT JOHNSON ISLAND were correct. In the spring of 1864, a portion of the Confederate officers imprisoned in Ohio were transferred by train to Baltimore. Captain Tod Carter was among them.

Tod felt fortunate. He was heading south, escaping the frigid temperatures. As he bounced over the rails, he counted himself lucky he wasn't stuffed in a boxcar, as prisoners often were. Two rows of double seats ran through the passenger car. Tod had taken a seat on the window side. A guard walked down the aisle between the rows.

He gazed into the inky blackness of the night and thought of home, of Franklin, Tennessee. Brother Moscow was there, exchanged from a prisoner of war camp, and now helping run the family plantation. He knew his younger brother, Wad, was still with the Twentieth Tennessee. Tod hoped to soon be with him. Gradually, a plan begin to form in the young soldier's mind.

Johnny Williams, his friend from Johnson's Island, sat next to him. "Ya think we'll get exchanged when we get to Baltimore, Tod?"

"Some will, but I've heard rumors Grant might end the exchanges. He thinks it helps us more than the Union. They can replace their prisoners from their big population. We can't."

"I sure hope we get exchanged before they end it."

"What we need to do, Johnny, is win some battles."

"Not much to cheer about since Chickamauga. We need more like that."

Tod nodded. "Another Chancellorsville or Fredericksburg wouldn't hurt, either."

Johnny's face lit up, and he reached into a front pocket, from which he procured a creased, wrinkled scrap of newspaper.

"Tod, I wrote my folks I was with you. They sent me this, the writings of Mint Julep." The young man read, "The *Louisville Journal* dubs the little affair at Fredericksburg the most disastrous and disgraceful defeat of the war. From various sources I learn this defeat had a very depressing influence upon the spirits of the enemy. General Lee is a skillful diplomatist. It is the only dignified and profitable means to negotiation for us. Their honor is the instincts of policy, and their patriotism, the romantic affection of a buzzard for his carcass. We fight them with shot and steel, and they fight us with shot and stealing.

"So," Johnny smiled at Tod, "when we gonna hear from ole Mint again?"

"Soon, I hope."

"Did you ever write about Sam Davis?"

"No, I never had a chance. I was captured at Missionary Ridge about the time Sam was arrested for being a spy."

"Sam was no spy!" Johnny proclaimed. "He was a courier and more true to his friends and our cause than anyone I ever knew."

"The Boy Hero of the Confederacy. Mint Julep will write about him someday. They hanged Sam because he wouldn't turn on his friends."

Johnny shook his head. "To think, the man they wanted was in the cell next to him and he wouldn't tell."

"We've got a lot of heroic boys fighting for the South, Johnny."

"Watcha gonna do when it's over, Tod?"

"My law practice was just getting going when the war started. I'll go back to Franklin and take it up again."

"People say you were a great lawyer already."

"I tried to do my best. Listen, Johnny." Tod leaned closer and spoke in a whisper. "I've got an idea. I'm getting out of here. The window is open next to me. I'm going to rest my feet out the window and my head on your lap. I'll pretend to sleep. At some point the train will have to slow for a big curve. When it does, help push me out the window. Make sure the guard isn't looking."

"What . . ." Johnny began.

"Shhh." Tod put his finger across his lips. "Just do it. I'll greet your folks for you."

"You sure about this?"

"For *amor patriae*, the love of country."

"All right, I'll do it for you."

Tod stretched out, his feet poking through an open window and his head on Johnny's lap. The train continued to slice through the black night. After about a half hour the train slowed dramatically as it came to a curve. Tod peeked back. No guard in sight.

"Now!" Tod commanded as he leaned forward. Johnny shoved hard into his friend's back, and Tod slid through the open window and into the night. He thudded beyond the track bed and tumbled hard into the grass beyond.

Scrambling to his feet, Tod tried to unscramble his brain to get his bearings. He saw a faint light glowing in the distance. A loud screech ripped through the night air as braked wheels slid with a shower of red sparks over the tracks.

"They'll be coming for me," Tod muttered. "I've gotta find somewhere to hide."

He turned toward the distant light and moved in that direction. About halfway between the tracks and the light, he paused to listen. Behind him, a distant clamor revealed that Union soldiers were on his trail. As he took a step forward, a sharp click sounded just before him.

"Hold! Boy, that's far enough!" A voice sounded from the frosty stillness of the night. Tod froze. The sound of footsteps, more than one person, approached. As his eyes adjusted to the blackness, Tod made out the figure of a man holding a musket at the ready. What looked to be a woman stood behind him.

"What you doin' out here? They after you?"

"Yes, I was on the train, and they're after me."

The woman walked around Tod and slid up a cover on the side of a lantern she held, careful to keep her body between the light and the sounds of searchers behind her. Tod blinked in the sudden light as it washed over him.

"He's just a boy, Simon."

"A rebel boy, I gather from what's left of his uniform. We could just wait here for the pack chasin' him to git here. Whaddya think, Martha?"

"Simon," the woman persisted, "he's not much older than our Billy. He's escaped from the train. They'll beat him, or worse. If this were Billy and he was in the South, what would we want to see happen?"

"You a prisoner?"

"Yes, sir, being transferred from Johnson's Island, Ohio. I jumped from the train."

"We heard the brakes squeal. That's why we're out here."

"Simon, I've read about them. The prison camps are horrible. The death rate . . ." Martha's voice trailed off as she pleaded with her husband.

"All right, boy, this is your lucky day. Martha, lead the way down the path. Block the light. I don't want it seen. Follow her, boy. I'll walk behind, with my gun cocked."

"Thank you, sir," Tod gratefully replied. "Please don't trip."

The three continued down a well-worn path leading to the farmstead ahead. An oil lamp burned in the window of a sturdy brick house. As they entered the farmyard, Martha gestured to a large wooden building. "In the barn?"

"No, they'll search there for sure. We can hide him in the house and do a better job keeping him out of sight."

When they entered the dimly lit home, Tod got his first clear look at his benefactors. Both were middle-aged and plainly dressed. The man was sturdy, with a dark beard. The woman was slender, dressed in gingham with her hair disheveled as if she had arisen from bed without combing it.

Simon placed his musket in a corner and extended his hand to Tod. "Name's Dudley. This is my wife, Martha. We farm here."

Tod grasped the proffered hand. It was large, hard and strong. The young man matched the firm grip. "I'm Tod Carter, a captain in the Twentieth Tennessee."

Martha nodded a tight-lipped smile. Simon removed a rug from the wooden floor, revealing a trap door beneath. "We'll waste no time. Soldiers will be here soon." He lifted the door open. "There's a dirt floor down there, not much else. But you should be safe."

As Tod started down a ladder into the cellar, Martha commanded, "Stop!" She handed the young soldier a loaf of bread and a mug of water. "You must be hungry."

Tod smiled up at her gratefully. "Thank you, ma'am."

The Dudleys looked down as Simon began to lower the trap door. "This isn't the first time, boy."

"Where am I?"

"Northern Pennsylvania. This house is on the Underground Railroad. The spot you're in hid many an escaped slave. Kind of ironic, isn't it?"

With those words hanging in the air, the door swung shut.

At the Mouth of the Red River

GENERAL SMITH'S FLEET OF TRANSPORTS steamed down the Mississippi to their rendezvous with Porter's fleet near the mouth of the Red River on the Louisiana side of the Mississippi. At midnight on March 11, Smith, in the lead transport, sighted hundreds of lights down the river. He turned to General Joe Mower, one of his division commanders. "Either that's a bunch of real bright fireflies, or we are at the Red, and Porter is waiting for us."

"General," Mower answered, "I believe the admiral is ready for us. There must be a hundred boats over there."

There were ninety vessels all told, including Smith's transports and an assortment of Porter's heavily armored ironclads, lightly armored tinclads, and more transports, as well as tugs and pump boats.

A flare burst up from a ship and showered light into the darkness above them. *Must be the* Black Hawk, Smith reasoned, *Porter's flagship. The admiral is saying hello.*

He turned to an adjutant. "It's late, but get me a launch ready. We'll go visit. No sense delaying."

In minutes Smith, Mower, and General Kilby Smith, the other division commander, were in a launch boat as it was rowed between their transport and Porter's ship. Soon they scrambled up a rope ladder tossed down the side of the flagship, and, as they climbed onto the deck, they were met by Rear Admiral David Dixon Porter.

Heavily bearded, his brown hair parted on the right, the fifty-one-year-old was of medium height and weight. He extended his hand to his visitors and urged them to his cabin. "Welcome to the *Black Hawk*, gentlemen, pride of the largest flotilla in this war." The three followed him into a small cabin lit by a single kerosene lamp.

Porter motioned for the soldiers to sit at a small table. As the yellow lamplight cast yellow flickers and shadows, Porter began. "It's late. I'll keep this short. General, you can transport your troops and move into Simmesport, a little town four miles up the Atchafalya.

"We've been here a few days and have had a chance to do some reconnaissance." He motioned to a young man who stepped from the shadows. "This is Lieutenant Frank Church. He leads my marines. And this," he gestured to another, "is my lieutenant commander, Randolph Breese. Deliver your report, Lieutenant Church."

The young marine saluted and addressed the generals. His handsome, boyish face was tense with responsibility. "Sirs, we face Major General Kirby Smith, and Dick Taylor, his commander of the Western District of Louisiana for the Confederacy."

"Son of President Zachery Taylor," Mower interrupted. "He fought Banks in the Shenandoah with Stonewall Jackson."

"Yes, sir, and we have reports he and Smith aren't always on the best of terms with each other. Let me tell you what we've discovered. Smith has about 30,000 men divided into three equal groups. Taylor has ten, maybe another 5,000 available. They've built an extensive array of fortifications on the Red River, some even upstream in Arkansas.

"Upriver, about halfway between the mouth of the Red and Alexandria, is Fort DeRussy, an earthen fort on the right bank of the Red. It's about a hundred yards square and the strongest of their fortifications. They have ten cannon there. Sixty miles south of Shreveport, they've fortified the bluffs of Grand Ecore."

"General Smith," Porter inserted, "this will be your first big test. We need to take Fort DeRussy and any other outposts in the way. I believe it best we act in conjunction, with you in the rear by land, and the Navy by river. It's thirty miles from Simmesport to DeRussy. That's where we'll enter the Red River for the rest of the expedition.

"I received a communication from General Banks yesterday. He's been delayed by heavy rains and will not be able to join us at Alexandria until March seventeenth at the earliest. I hope to God he gets there. I had misgivings."

"I know, Admiral Porter," A.J. Smith replied, "but our task is to offer you the support you need, with or without Banks."

Porter sighed. "I accepted this mission when I thought Sherman would lead us. He assures me that, should Banks falter, you will be there."

"And I will, rest assured, Admiral."

"If we can coordinate this correctly, they can't stop us. Banks up from New Orleans with 20,000; we go up the Red with 10,000. We meet at Alexandria and then head to Shreveport in the northwest corner of the state, where we meet up with Steele and 15,000 more. This is the most formidable navy and army force ever assembled in America. We'll crush them and make Halleck very happy. We will cut off Texas, occupy east Texas, confiscate cotton, and capture Shreveport with its armories, foundries, and shipyard, while countering the French threat in Mexico, all just as our esteemed leaders want."

"Grant had other plans," Mower commented.

"But Grant isn't general-in-chief, nor is he the president. So right plan or not, we do what we're ordered and we make it work."

* * *

THE NEXT DAY, Smith's Sixteenth and Seventeenth Corps proceeded up the Red River to the mouth of the Atchafalaya River and Bayou. The rest of the fleet continued up the Red. From there, with transports, Smith's force moved down the Bayou to Simmesport, arriving at about 5:00 p.m. Thirty miles away was Fort DeRussy.

The beginning of the campaign was not auspicious for Porter and his navy. As they embarked on March 12, the *Eastport*, Porter's largest ironclad, became wedged in a sandbar at the mouth of the river. Several hours later, freed from the obstruction, the ironclad and the rest of the fleet moved four miles up the river to Simmesport, where Porter and Smith established a supply base. The next day they would move on Confederate fortifications, the army by land, supported by the navy from the river.

Porter's force included the finest Union vessels in the West. Thirteen ironclads of varying sizes and armament were the admiral's vanguard. *Essex*, *Benton*, and *Lafayette* would join *Choctaw*, *Chillicothe*, *Ozark*, and *Louisville*. *Carondelet*, *Eastport*, *Pittsburg*, *Mound City*, *Osage*, and *Neosho* completed the ranks of the ironclads. Four tinclads bolstered the flotilla's firepower with twenty-seven more weapons. They were *Cricket*, *Gazelle*, *Signal*, and *Juliet*.

Also cruising the river were *Lexingtron*, a stern-wheel timberclad with three years of service on rivers, and three tinplated steamers: *Covington*, *Ouachita*, and *Fort Hindman*, came along with the steamer *Benefit*.

The tinclads were shallow-draft vessels and ideal for the Red River. However, they were not heavily armored enough to withstand the fire of field guns from the shore. Thus, the deeper-draft ironclads were necessary against fortifications and heavier riverbank weapons. All movements and orders for the squadron would come from Porter aboard his flagship, the *Black Hawk*.

After months of being largely inactive, the Fifth Minnesota and Jimmy Dunn were poised to fight again.

* * *

HUNDREDS OF MILES AWAY on March 17 in Nashville, Tennessee, General Ulysses S. Grant was in his makeshift office in a confiscated house. Before him was a breakfast of sliced cucumbers, his customary morning fare. His good friend and confidant, William Tecumseh Sherman, sat across the table.

"Two messages this morning, Cump. The Red River Expedition is underway, for one."

He paused and stroked his full dark beard. Sherman, his short red beard and hair flecked with gray, waited expectantly. Grant coyly covered his mouth with his right hand to cover a smile and remained silent.

Finally Sherman blurted out, "All right, what's the other?"

Grant removed a folded piece of stationery from his front pocket and laid it on the table, carefully smoothing it out. He didn't read it but simply answered, "It seems that General Halleck is now President Lincoln's chief of staff for military affairs. I am to be the general-in-chief of all armies of the United States."

Sherman abruptly rose to his feet and extended his hand. "Congratulations, Sam. It's about time."

Grant shook the proffered hand and said quietly, "I guess it's my time."

"By God! Look what they put you through to get to this. Halleck demoting you after Shiloh, McClelland lording over you, the press and others calling you a drunk and a failure even when you won. Finally, some justice."

"You always stuck by me, Cump."

"You were with me when they said I was crazy, and I was with you when they said you were a drunk and I'm still with you. What changes do you plan?"

"For one thing, I won't be a Washington commander. I'll be with the troops. Other plans in place will remain. Mead will command my Army of the Potomac, but I will be with them in Virginia. You will continue into the

South, destroy Joe Johnston and take Atlanta. We have Banks with the Army of the Gulf in Louisiana and Texas. After he takes Shreveport, he's to move on to Mobile. We'll hit them on so many fronts they won't have enough men to cover them all.

"Your role is the key one, Cump. I'll be engaged in an all-out effort to take Richmond. I want you to advance on Atlanta. That will tie down Confederate armies that could otherwise be used to help Lee in Virginia."

"You won't change the Red River plan?"

"No, though I would have concentrated on Mobile, and gone through North Carolina. I don't see the advantages of the expedition. Large numbers of troops are needed for the campaign in the East, and we'll have men tied down in Louisiana in action of little military consequence. But Halleck, 'Old Brains,' has convinced the president. Even with Halleck's demotion, I believe Lincoln wants the strategy carried out. Politics, cotton, and Halleck's insistence can't be countered in this instance."

Sherman chuckled. "Lincoln called Halleck a first-rate clerk."

"Halleck is a fine administrator; he's not a fighter. But as chief of staff in Washington, he'll provide a valuable service to me. He gets to review all the reports that come in and report their conclusions to me. I don't have time to read."

"Well, Sam, we've got a fighter now: you. The bottom rung is on top."

Return to Tennessee

TOD CARTER HAD BEEN MUNCHING on bread and sipping lukewarm water while listening intently for any telltale noises that the search for him had neared his hideaway. It hadn't taken long before a sharp rap on the door of the house signaled the arrival of Union troops.

Footsteps toward the door were followed by voices, which were muffled but understandable. "Sir, I'm Captain Roberts, 128th Ohio. We're looking for an escaped rebel prisoner. Have you seen him?"

"Can't say I have," Dudley replied. "When did he get away?"

"Within the hour. We saw tracks between here and the railroad tracks. His and a couple of others."

"Well, my wife and I have been in bed sleeping. It's the middle of the night."

"We need to look, sir. Sorry, but I've already sent men into the barn, and we have to look through the house."

"You don't believe me?"

"It's . . ."

Tod strained but couldn't make out what the captain was saying. Then he heard, ". . . here in the house. You might not have woke up."

Footsteps seeming to be those of several people sounded from above. Tod looked up. As light filtered down through cracks between the floorboards, dust particles were illuminated like little flecks of snow. Sounds of moving furniture, the clumping of boots going up stairs and shouted instructions all carried to the young man below.

Then it was quiet again, and he heard the captain's voice. "All right, he's not in the house or on your property as far as we can tell. If you see him, contact the sheriff in town. The prisoner was wearing a scruffy Confederate uniform. In case he's managed to find a change of clothes, look for a skinny young man, fair complexion, and sandy blond hair. He's well-spoken and educated. If he uses Latin on you, he's our man, for sure."

"We'll be sure to notify law enforcement if we see him."

"Then we'll be on our way. He's out there somewhere."

Listening as the door opened and closed, Tod continued to wait in the darkness. In a moment, the light above extinguished, and he heard a harsh whisper. "Stay put, boy. We'll bring you up when we're sure they're gone."

Time crept slowly for Tod. He dozed off a couple of times, but it was cool on the cellar's dirt floor. Then he heard footsteps above, and the trapdoor opened. He emerged like a gopher from his hole, examining his surroundings. A single lamp was lit and sat upon a round wooden table in the center of the kitchen. Martha Dudley stood by a black iron woodstove. The smell and crackling sounds of frying bacon enveloped the room as warmth wrapped around Tod like a welcome blanket.

"I can't thank you enough, Mr. Dudley, Mrs. Dudley. You likely saved my life."

"Glad to help you, boy," Martha replied softly.

Tod gazed at a duerreograph picture on the wall. Even in the shadows and soft yellow light, the image was plain. It was of a young man dressed in the uniform of a Union soldier.

"That's Billy, our son," Simon Dudley said. "He's with Grant."

"He's why we helped you," Martha explained. "You're about the same age. You even resemble him in some ways. If things were reversed, if it was Billy escaping from a southern prison, we'd want someone to help him. You're both just boys in a terrible war."

"Now sit down and eat," Simon directed. "We need to get you out of here before sun up. I checked, the train's gone. What's your name, boy?"

Tod slid a chair from the table and sat down. "I'm Tod, Tod Carter from Franklin, Tennessee. Captain in the Twentieth Tennessee."

"Pretty young for a captain," Simon observed as he sat across from Tod. "Billy's a private."

"We all serve in different ways."

"For different causes, too," Simon concluded.

"Are you a farm boy?" Martha asked as she heaped eggs, fried potatoes, thick bacon, and bread on the young man's plate.

"My family operates a farming business. I'm a lawyer."

"Awful young for that, too, ain't you?" Simon rejoined.

"I guess so, but I think I'm doing all right."

"I bet you are!" Martha agreed.

"Your family have slaves?" Simon asked pointedly.

Tod forked in some food and shifted uncomfortably. "About a couple dozen, I suppose. They're well treated by my father. No beatings, well fed."

"You just work them in the fields all day."

"Some are field hands. Others work in the house, cure meat, work in our cotton gin or the kitchen."

"But they can't leave, they aren't free."

"We treat them well," Tod repeated.

"Yes, but—"

"Now, Simon," Martha interrupted. "This isn't the time to argue slavery or the war. Let the boy eat. It all will be decided soon. The war's going against you, Tod," she said softly.

"Maybe now. Things have a way of changing."

"Well, that may be, but I doubt it. But speaking of changing," Simon continued. "On the chair in the corner are some of Billy's clothes. Put 'em on, we'll burn the rags you got on. You'll never get through Pennsylvania wearing them."

Tod shoveled more food into his mouth and wiped the plate clean with a slice of bread. Then he rose and gathered up the clothing. Martha pointed to a side room. "You can change in there. I left a basin of warm water and a cloth for you to wash up some."

"Thank you, ma'am." He looked at Simon. "Thank you both. I can't tell you how in debt to you I am."

Tod went into the side room and closed the door behind him. A few minutes later he emerged, his face scrubbed, hair combed back and looking fresh in clean clothes.

Martha handed him a satchel. "It's just some bread and dried meat. To tide you over some."

"Thank you, Mrs. Dudley." He looked through the window to the east. The horizon was a blurry pink smear in the twilight of morning. "I'd better leave. It'll be getting light soon."

"Take care, boy, er, Tod." Simon clasped the boy's hand.

Tod smiled. "*Cura te ipsum*, take care of your own selves, both of you. I'll never forget this. When it's over, I'll repay you."

"Just be alive when it's over," Martha said solemnly.

Tod smiled, nodded and walked off into the dim light of early morning.

He knew his regiment was in Georgia and decided to take a somewhat circuitous route through Pennsylvania to the Ohio and then Mississippi rivers to Memphis. Once in friendly lands, he could head to Georgia. It would be a long walk. Tod hoped to find work on steamboats to pay his way.

After a few hours he rested beneath an oak tree, its leafless branches just sprouting buds. The ground was damp and spongy. Here and there green grass greeted the growing power of the March sun. Tod found a dry patch where he could sit and eat lunch. Reaching into the satchel, he pulled out a small loaf of bread and was shocked to find several gold coins inserted into the top of the loaf.

"The Dudleys," he whispered gratefully. "I can make Memphis within a week. God bless good people."

Fort DeRussy

THE SIXTEENTH CORPS HAD DISEMBARKED at Simmesport on the Atchaflaya Bayou on March 12. There the Minnesota Fifth Regiment assigned to the Second Brigade, First Division, awaited orders for their next move.

Jimmy Dunn, Levi Carr, and Will Hutchinson went into camp with the rest of Company B at about 5:00 p.m. Shelter halves were set up quickly and cook fires ignited. The three young men impaled salt pork on bayonets and held them over the fire while coffee percolated in a pot.

Jimmy smiled. "We eat like kings, and look like paupers." He gazed at his friends with their faded, tattered uniforms. "'Cept for you, Will. You got somethin' new." He motioned at the new, bright yellow sergeant stripes on the young man's shoulders.

"A whole new uniform would look better," Will said laconically.

Levi countered, "At least it looks like we bin doin' somethin'. A nice pretty uniform this time of the war means you ain't been doin' much. Sure not fightin' any."

"Just movin' on up," Will grinned.

"The boys have bin doin' that," Jimmy agreed. "Tom Gere to first lieutenant and now an adjutant for Colonel Hubbard. His brother Will started as our captain and got promoted to lieutenant colonel of the regiment; McGrew was a sergeant at Fort Ridgely, and now he's our captain."

"Don't forget John Bishop," Levi reminded him. "He was our sergeant at Ridgely and now he's our lieutenant."

Will stirred the fire. Little red embers amid smoke drifted upward. He took a chomp of salt pork from the end of his bayonet and chewed thoughtfully. "Remember, a lot of those promotions only became possible 'cause we lost some good men fightin' Indians. Men like Captain Marsh and First Sergeant Russ Findley."

"Well, speak of the devil!" Jimmy exclaimed. "Look who's here!"

The three stood to attention and saluted as Lieutenant Tom Gere strode into camp, Jim McGrew and John Bishop at his side. Gere returned their salute and raised his voice. "Gather around, men! I've got news for you."

Several dozen men in dirty, faded blue uniforms assembled around the young lieutenant. "Regimental headquarters has just been briefed by General Smith. Colonel Hubbard sent me to brief Company B.

"Tomorrow it all begins. We will move out on the Fort DeRussy road to capture or disperse any parties of the enemy and any fortifications between here and the fort. We will then proceed by land to Alexandria. The fleet will follow by water. At Alexandria, we will be joined by General Banks and his command."

"Where we gonna wind up?" Sam Fauver asked.

"The goal is Shreveport, new capital of Louisiana. We're gonna put a dagger in the Confederacy right here and cut the West off from them. I was proud to fight with you against the Sioux in Minnesota and to serve with Company B here. I know you'll do everyone proud again."

"What about the rest of the Minnesota regiments?" another young soldier called.

"The Sixth, Seventh, Eighth, Ninth, and Tenth will all join us eventually, but not likely here. The Second is on its way back from leave in Minnesota and will join Sherman in Georgia."

"What about leave for us?" Jimmy wondered.

"When we get done with this, you'll get your month."

Jimmy laughed. "Why, you mean next week, then. Just let us at 'em!"

Gere smiled. "That's all right by me. Any words, Captain?"

McGrew, who had commanded an artillery battery at Fort Ridgely, was to the point. "Finish your mess and get a good night's sleep. We start early tomorrow."

* * *

BUGLES SOUNDED before dawn. After a quick breakfast of bacon and coffee, two divisions of Smith's Sixteenth Corps were on the march, commanded by Joe Mower. A division of the Seventeenth Corps was held in reserve.

Jimmy Dunn marched alongside Levi Carr. "Doesn't look much like home," Levi muttered. "Damp, spongy, mossy grass."

"At least it's green," Jimmy remarked, "and there are trees around."

"Scrub trees, Jimmy, oaks and pines. These oaks are nothin' like ours."

"I'll grant you they're a little stunted."

"No snow in the winter, at least."

Jimmy wrinkled up his nose. "How do they get rid of mosquitoes and their malcontents? That's what keeps Minnesota clean. Snow and freezing weather. Ya gotta be hardy and of strong character to live there."

"I s'pose they just have ta put up with things the way they are."

"Well, Levi, we're here ta help 'em see the light."

Three miles from the landing, in the fork of the Yellow Bayou and Bayou Des Glaize, the two divisions encountered a brigade of Confederates in the process of building an earthen fort. Company B moved into attack position with the rest of their division.

The Confederates abandoned their position and fled down the road. A pursuit over two miles by the Union troops netted six captured wagons and twenty prisoners. After Mower and his staff questioned the captives, General A.J. Smith met with Mower.

"Joe, we've learned what we can from the rebs here. We have no cavalry to give pursuit. Take your command back to the landing. I'm going to disembark the rest of my command, and we'll all proceed by land to Fort DeRussy. Our transports will accompany Admiral Porter to the fort."

At nine o'clock that night, Smith's force left the landing. They then bivouacked for the night four miles from Simmesport. It was a short night. At 3:00 a.m. on the fourteenth, Smith ordered an advance on Fort DeRussy.

As Company B moved along the dark road, a dull glow rose in the distance. "Hey, Will," Levi called to Hutchinson, "that's not the sun comin' up. It's the wrong direction."

"Unless I miss my guess, those are bridges on fire. The rebs are tryin' to slow us down."

Sergeant Hutchinson was correct. General Smith sent men on ahead, and they successfully extinguished the fires over two bridges before they were seriously damaged. But farther ahead, on reaching Mansura, the Union Army found the bridges across Bayou Des Glaize had been destroyed.

A scout reported to A.J. Smith, "General, a division of rebs has marched out from Fort DeRussy under General Walker. They're dug in with Scurry's Brigade about five miles west of here, where they think we'll have to cross."

"Well, we'll just have to bridge here at Mansura."

"How are you going to that, General? There aren't any bridges."

"We'll outmaneuver them. We can take material from an old cotton gin I saw and, by crossing companies at the same time on a ferry boat, the whole command can cross before Walker is aware of the advance. General Smith," A.J. said, turning to his other division commander, Kilby Smith, "stay to the rear of my column, keep well closed up and watch carefully my left flank and rear."

The movement put A.J. Smith's men across and left Walker and his command behind on the left. The way was clear to Fort DeRussy. Smith called a halt about a mile from the fort and conferred with his commanders. "General Mower, advance the First and Second brigades of the Third Division. Form a line of battle with skirmishers out front. The Third Brigade will be behind in support. Kilby Smith will cover our rear from any attack Walker might make once he figures out we're past him.

Colonel Hubbard wondered, "General, what are the particulars we face?"

"Fort DeRussy is mostly earthen, a hundred yards square with ten casemented, protected cannon. They're protected by metal plates backed by oak. It appears that most of the troops have been pulled out. They have three to four hundred to oppose us."

At 6:30 p.m., the order to charge was given. A couple of Union cannon shots preceded the rush to the fort. Within twenty minutes, the parapet was stormed and the Confederates surrendered.

Captain McGrew reported to his company. "A fine day, lads. You marched twenty-six miles, fixed bridges, crossed a bayou, attacked a fort, captured 319 rebs and ten pieces of artillery, not to mention the ordnance. All at the loss of only three men and all done before sunset. Hot work! Tomorrow you boys will be on transports on the Red on the way to Alexandria to meet up with General Banks. General Kilby Smith and the Seventeenth will stay behind in DeRussy."

Tod Finds His Regiment

BY THE END OF MARCH, Tod Carter had reached Dalton, Georgia, where General Joe Johnston, commander of the Army of Tennessee, now encamped his troops. Thousands of dirty white tents were spread before him as Tod scanned the area for Tennessee regiments, looking particularly for a guidon signifying Company H, Twentieth Tennessee.

A soldier had pointed out the right direction, and, after a short time, Tod found the boys from Williamson County. His brother Wad, younger by three years, was squatting in front of a fire baking sloosh, a combination of cornmeal, lard, water, and eggs mixed together, wrapped around a ramrod and baked over a fire.

Wad squinted through the bright sunlight trying to make out the figure coming toward him. Something seemed familiar. Then it hit him. He threw down the rod, food and all, and rushed toward the figure. "Tod!" he shouted. "Tod, is that you?"

Wad ran into Tod's outstretched arms, and the two heartily embraced. "How?" Wad marveled. "We heard you were in prison in Ohio. Moscow said they were going to transfer you."

"I escaped off a train. I'll fill you in later. You look good, little brother, maybe a little skinny."

"I need more sloosh. Come over to the fire, I've got some cooking."

Wad handed Tod another ramrod with the concoction wrapped around it. As they sat by the fire cooking their food, other Company H soldiers gathered around to greet Tod.

Jim Cooper warmly clasped Tod's hand. "I thought you were gone for sure."

"Not when I have friends like you to get back to." He pointed to Cooper's shoulder. "Another stripe. It's Sergeant Cooper now."

Cooper smiled. "They ran out of people to pin stripes on."

"We thought you wuz dead fer sure," Phil Boxley said. "At Missionary Ridge yer horse swam the river and came into camp in full rig without you."

"My horse! Rosencrantz is still alive!"

"Sure is. I've made sure he was cared for," Wod assured Tod.

Another soldier remarked, "We heered the Yanks got ya."

Joe Canada enthusiastically pumped Tod's hand. "Great ta have ya back! We missed Mint Julep, too!"

Tod stood up and shook hands all around with a broad grin plastered on his face. "It's a blessing to be back with you. Mint Julep says he's happy, too."

The men laughed and slapped Tod on the back. "Tell me," Tod asked, "what's up hereabouts? Any changes?"

Sergeant Tom Giles answered, "Well, quite a lot. We're fightin' Yanks all over the place but things ain't been goin' so good. We're holdin' our own, though. Joe Johnson took over for Bragg after Chattanooga. Now we be in Hardee's corps, Bate's division, Smith's brigade, and Shy's regiment. Right down to Company H and Captain Tom Caruthers. Welcome home!"

"Where are we going?" Tod asked.

"Well," Giles pondered and spat a brown stream of tobacco through yellow-stained teeth, "since it looks like Sherman's headed to Atlanta, I 'spect we'll be headin' that way, too."

"Any other news?"

"Frank Flein went fishin'," Jack Pinkerton said.

Everyone laughed. Tod asked, "So what's so funny about fishing?"

"He musta caught a real big one," Henry Short called, "'cause he never came back."

Sergeant Giles straightened up. "Boys, we fergot somethin'. We got all worked up at seein' Tod here, but, remember, he's still a captain assigned to Gen'r'l Smith, even though he's dressed like a northern farmboy. Now, let's pay proper respect. He's the gen'r'l's aide-de-camp."

"With quartermaster duties, too," Wad proudly announced. "General Smith has total confidence in Tod. He delivers personally any messages the general needs delivered, keeps track of troop positions and writes out anything Smith needs written."

The men laughed. Jim Cooper added, "We all knew that aide-de-camps were important. Sounds like we should bow down," he grinned, "or at least salute our long-lost friend."

Everyone around stood at attention and saluted Tod, who solemnly returned their salute. Then he chuckled. "You weren't far off, Sergeant, on that comment about my clothes. I'll report to General Smith presently and make sure he still wants me. But for a little while I'd like to catch up on family with Wad here."

The men drifted away, but Nathan Morris brought a plate of burned greens to Tod. "Here ya go, sir. Try these. They're not half bad."

Tod looked down at the food. "What is it?"

"Turnip greens."

Wad explained, "Nathan calls them that, but he makes them out of briars and 'buck bushes.' But he's right, they aren't half bad."

"Thank you," Tod called as Nathan slipped away. Then, slurping greens and chomping on sloosh, the two brothers sat down to talk.

"Have you been home lately?" Tod asked Wad.

"It's been a few months, but I was able to stop by."

"How are things going?"

"Moscow's still there, helping run the farm. The cotton gin's operating and producing. Oats, corn, wheat, and Irish potatoes are still being harvested, but not like before the war."

"Family still growing?"

"Let's see," Wad paused to think. "You and me are gone, Moscow was gone and now he's back, James died before the war, but Sallie and their two children have come to live in Franklin. Mary left her husband in Texas and came back with her four young ones. And Sarah, Annie, and Frances are all at home, too. Then there's Moscow's family. After his wife died and he enlisted, his four children moved in with Pa."

Tod thoughtfully considered, "I count sixteen children, grandchildren, and other relatives living on the farm. It's sad, though. Pa sure could use Ma right now."

Wad solemnly shook his head. "What's it been, twelve years now?"

Tod nodded. "Even without Ma, the family's still strong, Wad, and the land's still Carter land. In twenty years, Pa's gone from business and surveying to become a prosperous farmer."

"It's all in danger, Tod. The Yankees still have Franklin'."

"I'll get home, Wad, and when I do, it'll be to drive the Yankees off our land, like Jesus did the money changers in the temple."

"Old Joe's taking us south first. We'll be heading to Atlanta."

"Things finally caught up with Bragg after Chattanooga, didn't they?"

"Tod, I don't think anybody liked him anymore. He was too hard on the men. You were here for the shootings." Bragg had ordered boys killed for looking crosswise at him. His generals had signed a petition asking Jeff Davis to remove him, but he wouldn't do it until the rebel army lost at Chattanooga. "After that," Wad went on, "Joe Johnston took over the Army of Tennessee. He moves a little slow, but he's a good general, and he cares for his men."

Tod stood up and stretched. "Well, Wad, it's great to see you and catch up. I suppose I'd better report to General Smith, get back in uniform and do my job.

"And a good job it is. Quartermaster's assistant. You don't even have to fight."

"If they let me choose, I'd be in the ranks with you. I just hope I still have a position."

"I wouldn't worry," Wad smiled. "There's always a place for Mint Julep."

"Fine, take me to Rosekrantz first. I've missed my horse almost more than you." Tod laughed and playfully touseled his brother's hair.

Alexandria

A.J. SMITH ORDERED KILBY SMITH to remain behind and dismantle Fort DeRussy while Joe Mower and two divisions, the First and Third, boarded transports to travel upriver to Alexandria.

Jimmy Dunn and the rest of Company B took their places and prepared for a voyage that would last through the night. Arriving on the sixteenth, they were a day earlier than the planned arrival of General Banks and his army.

The troops disembarked, marched into Alexandria and went into camp. General Mower, with a cadre of staff including Colonel Hubbard and Tom Gere, walked into the heart of the town.

"Seems kind of quiet," Mower muttered. "Some people going about their business, but still quiet."

A small group of well-dressed men approached the soldiers from down a mostly deserted dirt street. A tall, mustached man spoke to General Mower. "I'm mayor of this heah town, sir. This is our council, and we are at yer service. We trust that our town will be spared any, uh, depredation from your army."

"Mr. Mayor," Mower responded, "Alexandria will be our base of operation. Other Union forces will gather here. I understand you are not unfamiliar with Union armies in this area. Our troops will be respectful while we are quartered here."

"Banks first came heah a year ago. Yankee troops have been heah off and on since. Our Confederate soldiers and you fellas kinda take turns."

"Well, Mayor, we've heard that Dick Taylor's been around here lately."

The mayor hesitated and eyed his council. "Well . . . he was hereabouts. Now he's gone. Went north, toward Shreveport."

"When?" Mower asked sternly.

The mayor shuffled his feet and hesitated. "A few hours ago. He had six steamers and loaded on all the public property he could for Shreveport."

"Looks like most of your town went with him," Mower observed. "This town is supposed to have 600 people. Where is everyone?"

The mayor sighed. "I gotta admit that some of our people are a little apprehensive of you fellas and left town. Some are at home, inside their houses, and . . ." he gestured, "some folks are still goin' 'bout their business."

Mower followed his gesture, then replied, "Cooperate and cause no trouble and this town will be safe. But there will be engagements nearby. I'm pretty sure of that."

Another officer hurried up to Mower and took him aside for a brief, whispered conversation. Mower turned back to the mayor. "It seems General Taylor was in a bit of a hurry. I'm told three artillery pieces and supplies of ordnance have been found in this city."

"We can't be held responsible for what an army brings in or leaves behind, General."

Mower's eyes bored at the mayor as if drilling into steel. "If there's anything more, you better tell us where it is."

* * *

THE FIFTH MINNESOTA went into camp with the rest of Mower's division. They were impressed at what they found. "Will ya look at this?" Levi called out to Jimmy. "This here camp has foundations from before, even wood platforms to tent over."

"Almost like bein' at home," Jimmy agreed.

"Get yer half out, Jimmy, I got a good spot here."

Jimmy unrolled his tent half and assembled his shelter with Levi. In short order, camp was set and a fire started. As the two friends sat back, Levi pulled a corncob pipe from his pocket and stuffed some tobacco into the bowl. He fished a smoking stick from the fire and held it to his pipe, sucking deeply until he was rewarded with a puff of rich tobacco smoke. Then he leaned back against a small tree in the warm spring sunlight. "Ahh, Jimmy, my boy. This is fine. I feel like a fat cat sunnin' itself."

"More like a fat pig ready for slaughter. We're in a war, ya know."

Both men chuckled. Jimmy gazed into the distance and spied an older black woman overburdened by a load of laundry and trying to hang it over clotheslines to dry. Watching as the woman struggled with her task, he rose to his feet.

"I'll be back shortly," he told Levi as he walked toward the woman.

It was just a little short of a hundred yards to the clothesline, and in a few moments Jimmy was there. The woman looked up at him. He saw fear flash through her eyes, and she stepped back away from him.

"Don't worry, ma'am, I don't mean no harm. Do you need some help?"

"Ah kin do it. Don't need no help."

Jimmy smiled. "I know you can do it. But ain't two hands, er . . . even four hands better than two? Let me help ya."

"Help yerself, Ah cain't stop ya," the woman said grudgingly, a trace of a smile almost distinguishable on her lips.

Jimmy took a damp pair of pants and draped them over the line. "You a slave?" he asked.

"Yessir."

"Mr. Lincoln freed slaves, you know."

"Not me."

"Well, you will be soon."

Jimmy helped the woman until the lines were full of clothes. Then he went back to Levi.

"You don't hafta do that, ya know. Hell, I remember you helpin' the laundresses at Fort Ridgely, too."

Jimmy grinned, the freckles wrinkling up on his cheeks. "I know. I just feel like it now and then."

The young man reached into his knapsack and removed a wrinkled sheet of paper. He carefully unfolded it, as he had many times before, and began to read.

"Anything in that letter ever change?" Levi smirked.

"Nope," Jimmy smiled sheepishly. "Lucy still misses me every time I read it."

Levi laughed. "Never gits old, does it?"

"Nope, but I sure hope I get another letter soon."

"Every mail day is like Christmas. But we're not likely to git letters while we're on campaign."

"More for when we get back, Levi."

* * *

On March 18, Admiral Porter's fleet, buoyed by transports carrying A.J. Smith and the rest of the Sixteenth Corps, steamed into Alexandria. General Smith found that General Banks had not yet reached their rendezvous point. Admiral Porter discovered an even more vexing problem: low water and a double rapids north of Alexandria would make passage by his vessels very difficult.

Smith's and Porter's forces went into camp to wait for Banks as they scouted the area around Alexandria and planned future moves. But the admiral had another interest to occupy his time as they awaited Banks: cotton. The war had led to shortages in cotton in the North and in Europe. Speculation in the fiber could lead to fortunes.

President Lincoln had given in to political pressure and issued permits to speculators to accompany the Union Army into Confederate territory to procure cotton.

Porter brought his top subordinates onto his flagship. "I want you to send out men to look for cotton in Alexandria. Molasses and sugar, too, but primarily cotton. I don't care if it belongs to the Confederate government, your run o' the mill rebels, or even loyal citizens. Have the bales stamped 'USN' and bring 'em to the wharf. Oh, if they aren't already stamped 'CSA,' stamp that on them, too. They look more legitimate that way. Captain Church, your marines will oversee the process. Do it now. Bank's delay gives us an avenue. He's bringing cotton speculators with him. We'll beat them to it. This is a windfall for us. Lucky we still operate under the old prize law. Fifty percent of the value of captured property goes to the captors. In this case, the navy."

"Five percent to the man in charge," Church smiled. "General Banks will not be happy."

Porter smiled sardonically. "Spoils of war."

* * *

GENERAL DICK TAYLOR, commander of the Western District of Louisiana of the Confederacy, had left Alexandria as the superior forces of A.J. Smith and Porter approached. He had moved twenty-two miles up the Red River. There, meeting in a clearing with his two most trusted officers, General Alfred Moulton of the Louisiana/Texas Infantry and General Hamilton Bee, he planned his strategy.

"Smith," he referred to the commander of the Trans-Mississippi Department, Edmund Kirby Smith, "is at Shreveport, and we have orders to stop the invaders."

"They've already laid waste to much of central Louisiana," Moulton noted.

"It'd be easier to stop them if Smith sent us more men. What do we have, 9,000, if Walker gets here?"

"They already have more than us, and two more armies are coming," Bee added.

Taylor rubbed his knuckles and grimaced.

"Hurtin' today, Dick?" Moulton asked gently.

"I hurt every day. At least I can walk. This stuff had me laid up pretty good a few months ago."

"Rheumatoid arthritis can be a devil, I know. My father had it," Bee sympathized.

"But your father was an old man. I'm thirty-seven," Taylor grumbled as he rubbed his dark, full, medium-length beard.

"What do you think we should do?" Bee wondered.

"My orders when I took this job were to command all troops south of the Red River and keep the enemy from using our rivers and bayous. Then they told me to recruit Louisiana boys and send them to Lee in Virginia, just retain what I needed. 'Keep the Mississippi open,' they say. 'Use artillery on the streams.'"

He slapped his gloves in disgust against his thigh. "Then let me do it the way I know how and give me men to do it. I told Smith all these fortifications on the river wouldn't work. The Yankees had Fort DeRussy in half an hour. When Grant was after Vicksburg, the time was ripe to march on New Orleans and retake it. But no, Smith ordered us to march up the river across from Vicksburg. We accomplished nothing and Vicksburg was lost anyway. 'Defend the citizens of Louisiana,' they tell me. How? They don't give me men to do it!"

"We may only have 9,000, but they're good men, and Tom Green is coming from Texas with more. He should be here any time. Remember, Walker's coming from Arkansas," Moulton rejoined.

"Yes, yes, you're right, Alfred, and that's why I'm going to make our General Smith unhappy again. He wants us to delay here. I don't know what he wants us to wait for."

Taylor paused and dropped his hand on Moulton's shoulder. "We've been a good team, old friend. Throw in Green, and between the three of us we've confused, frustrated, and delayed Union efforts to take the Bayou Teche region. Now we have a chance to really kick 'em in the ass. When Banks comes, this time we're not going to wait for him and we're not going to retreat. Gentlemen, we are going to go *stop* him."

"Where?" Bee asked.

"Mansfield."

Waiting for Banks

GENERAL MOWER'S DIVISION, including the Fifth Minnesota, had arrived at Alexandria on March sixteenth. A.J. Smith and Porter reached there late in the afternoon of the eighteenth. Hoping to rendezvous with Banks's command, Smith found the commander of the expedition was still en route from New Orleans.

On the nineteenth, an advance guard of 100 cavalry rode into Alexandria, and the next day General A.L. Lee led his cavalry division into the town. He and Banks's chief of staff, General Stone, who had just arrived by river, were greeted in camp by Smith.

"How soon until General Banks and the rest of the army gets here?" Smith asked.

"The general's coming by boat," Lee answered. "He should be here within a few days. The rest of the army, led by General Franklin, is about two days behind him."

"He's taking his sweet time of it. My divisions are supposed to report to Sherman by April fifteenth."

* * *

GENERAL NATHANIEL BANKS slowly blew a stream of cigar smoke as he gazed at the foamy water being churned by the paddle of his ship, the *Black Hawk*. The ship was primarily a transport, but his army was marching by land to Alexandria. His passengers were dozens of friends, business associates, and speculators, all intent on making their fortunes in cotton.

A light haze of cigar smoke hung over the large cabin like a soft veil. The clinks of whiskey glasses, laughter, and men's voices smothered out the sounds of the water outside. A stocky blond man sidled across the room to Banks. "Can't you just smell the cotton out there?"

"Well, Mr. Butler, there certainly should be enough for everyone."

"Money to be made, thanks to our president."

Banks smiled. "He was drawn somewhat reluctantly to our cause. Treasury Secretary Chase opposed any permits pertaining to cotton."

Butler drew a folded sheet of paper from his pocket. "The result is this: 'All military and naval commanders will give to the bearer protection and safe conduct from Cairo to Red River, and up said river, and its tributaries, till he shall pass beyond our military lines, and also give him such protection and safe conduct, on his return to our lines, back to Cairo with any cargoes he may bring.' Cargoes, that means cotton. It's signed 'A. Lincoln.'"

"It almost puts the army and navy under the authority of you speculators," Banks replied. Then he chuckled, "I'm glad we all have the same goal."

Rush Plumly, another speculator, approached Banks and Butler. "There should be enough for all of us," he gestured at those in the crowded cabin. "Miss Wellington did her job well obtaining permits."

Banks reddened and placed a finger across his lips. "Shhh, Miss Wellington used her wiles and talents to obtain many permits for you gentlemen to bring out cotton. She was well paid for her work, but speaking of it will not serve our purpose."

Butler grinned slyly. "Word is you benefitted from her peculiar talents, General."

Banks snapped, "Spreading rumors is not seemly, Mr. Butler!"

Plumly cleared his throat. "This war has been hell on business for us. We hear of England suffering with half a million textile workers jobs at risk when the South cut off cotton to them. What about Massachusetts and New England? Our mills suffered just as much. Almost all of our cotton was coming from the Confederate states."

"And allowing you to obtain cotton from Confederate agents and plantations will keep revenue from cotton sales out of Confederate government hands."

"And into ours," Banks smiled, "and break the rebels in the process."

"Grant opposes this," Butler noted.

"Grant should stick to his cigars and whiskey," Banks rejoined. "Lincoln signed the permits. I command a territory under martial law, and I'll do what I think best to hamper the Confederacy."

"And line a few pockets. The more cotton a loyal man can control, the more likely to get a pass," Plumly continued.

Banks looked over the room. "The docks at Alexandria are loaded with cotton. Cotton plantations line the Red all the way to Shreveport. I see a lot of men on board getting rich."

Plumly smiled. "That is the essence of why we're here, General. We thank you and President Lincoln, and," he nodded knowingly, "Miss Wellington."

A man named Mansfield quieted the crowd and shouted, "General Banks has provided us with a great opportunity. The closer we get to Alexandria, the more cotton fields we see. Three cheers for Nathaniel Banks!"

The room erupted, "Huzzah! Huzzah! Huzzah!"

"Banks for president!" someone shouted.

The forty-seven-year-old general grinned like a Cheshire cat.

Banks Arrives

J IMMY DUNN GLEEFULLY MARCHED into Alexandria with his comrades of
the Sixteenth Army Corps on the morning of March 22. Marching between the ranks of blue-clad soldiers were 262 Confederate captives. All,
Union and Confederate alike, were grimy, wet, and mud-splattered. Jimmy
called out to other Union troops watching their arrival.

"While you boys were loafin' around here, we were out helpin' ta win
the war!"

Levi Carr echoed, "Ol' Jeff Davis has a couple hundred less fools with
him today."

General Mower rode at the head of the column and found A.J. Smith
near the river wharf. Smith smiled broadly and saluted Mower. Mower dismounted and returned the salute.

"It looks like you were successful," Smith observed. "Give me a synopsis
of your report."

"General Smith, we did as ordered. You sent us to confirm that a portion
of Dick Taylor's command were in the vicinity of Henderson's Hill on Bayou
Rapides. After about twenty-two miles, we found that the enemy was indeed
in the area of Henderson Hill with both infantry and cavalry. At nightfall I
sent two regiments of infantry, one section of the battery, and the Sixteenth
Indiana Mounted Infantry on a detour to the left, under cover of darkness.
The rest of the command remained in the enemy's front.

"Then," Mower laughed, "we got lucky. A reb courier was coming down
the hill with dispatches for Dick Taylor. He walked right into us. It was raining hard, and he looked like a drowned rat. We managed to, ah . . . obtain
the countersign from him. The papers he had showed that they had one regiment of cavalry and one battery of artillery on the hill.

"We moved forward and completely surprised their whole force. They were sitting around their campfires. They found shelters from the rain and were singing, eating, some sleeping. We didn't even fire a shot. So, there they are." He pointed to the assembled gray-clad men to the rear. "The Second Louisiana Cavalry, men, horses, and equipment, along with Edgar's battery, all four pieces of light artillery and their crews."

"Great work, General Mower," Smith said in praise. "Near thirty miles of marching through rain and mud in twenty-four hours. Your Minnesota boys know how to fight."

"Rain, sleet, or snow," Mower agreed. These boys are up to it. Banks here yet?"

"No, but I'm expecting him any time now. He's late, and we need to get moving."

* * *

ON MARCH 24, the steamer *Black Hawk* paddled into Alexandra with General Banks and his business friends on board. The general puffed himself up like a peacock and strutted down the gangplank to the wharf. A.J. Smith was there to greet him.

"Welcome, General," Smith said. "We're ready to move out. Where's the rest of your army?"

"Marching along the river. They should be here in a day or two." He paused and gazed down the long wharf. Suddenly his face turned crimson. "Those stacks there!" he gasped. "Are they cotton bales?"

"Yes, sir, Admiral Porter has been bringing them in."

"Where is Porter?" Banks demanded.

"In the cabin, over there by the river." Smith pointed to the location.

Clamoring down the plank behind him were Banks's friends and cotton speculators. "What's going on here?" Mansfield demanded with spittle flecking from his mouth. "Those are cotton bales, thousands of them!"

"That's our cotton!" Plumley cried.

"Stay calm, gentlemen," Banks gestured with his palms down. "I'll take care of this."

Leaving all in his wake, the general strode brusquely toward Porter's headquarters. Ignoring any military protocol, he burst into the admiral's office and confronted Porter, who was seated at his desk. Captain Church, his marine commander, stood beside him.

"What have you done?" Banks demanded. "There are thousands of bales of cotton stacked on the wharf. I see they're stamped 'CSA' and 'USN.' What does that stand for, 'Cotton Stealing Association of the United States Navy'? Do you realize what you've done? I have dozens of businessmen with me who hold permits signed by President Lincoln, and you have confiscated or stolen all the cotton! This is outrageous! There will be great consequences to the treasury of this nation if you continue your indiscriminate confiscation!"

Porter smiled benignly up from his desk. "General Banks, good to see you. I doubt if the treasury would see much cotton money anyway with all of your friends, permits or not, tramping all over the hinterland."

"You wouldn't have gotten away with this if I was here sooner," Banks proclaimed.

"That's just it," Porter responded. "You should have been here sooner. You only have Smith here until April fifteenth, then Sherman wants him and his men back. I've got enough problems with the river."

"What's wrong with the river?" Banks asked. "It was just fine coming up from New Orleans."

"The Red is too shallow. Sherman said it would come up but it hasn't. There are two sets of falls above the city. The rapids are only one mile apart with only a twenty-foot-wide channel between them. My tinclads with shallow draft can negotiate the rapids but there aren't enough to adequately support your army."

"I need your entire flotilla, Admiral."

"It will be near impossible to get the bigger ships over the rapids and down again."

"It must be done."

"We'll try, General."

"Good. And one more thing: we're not done with you about the cotton."

"Good luck to you, General," Porter smiled.

As Banks stomped out of the room, Porter turned to Church. "Double the guard on the cotton and see that more men are sent into the countryside on 'rescue' missions for more cotton."

"What about Banks?"

"Beat him to it."

Once on the wharf, Banks was surrounded by angry cotton speculators. "What is Porter doing?" a red-faced man shouted.

"This is our cotton!" another exclaimed. "We have permits for it!"

"Gentlemen," Banks's voice rose. "Porter has taken advantage of our delay and is lining his own pockets. But we aren't done yet. I'll organize details to patrol the countryside and search for more cotton, either in fields or bales. You may accompany them. Porter has been ordered to get his fleet above the falls. That should take his time, men, and attention away from cotton."

But the competition over cotton had just begun. Over the next few days, the army and navy both scoured surrounding territory in search of the white fiber. Then each stole from the other. Jimmy and Levi watched as soldiers broke into a warehouse in Alexandria and hauled out bales of cotton.

"Pretty bold o' those boys ta steal in broad daylight," Levi observed.

Jimmy nodded. "I heard some of Banks's men sayin' it just ain't right. The navy is supposed to be concerned about things on water. Cotton is on land and so it should be a prize for the army, not the navy. That's why they're takin' it."

"Poor Banks," Levi added. "What little cotton Porter ain't already got the rebs are burnin' so nobody gets it."

"Ya know who comes out ahead on this, Levi? The rebs. Taylor's getting reinforcements while Banks and Porter fight over cotton."

"At least Gen'r'l Smith is keepin' us out of it."

"Yep," Jimmy agreed. "Our gen'r'l wants ta fight before Sherman calls us back."

"Well, Jimmy, we ain't goin' nowhere until Porter gets his boats over the falls."

"Levi, the water isn't coming up any and it might drop even more while these boneheads are stayin' put and fightin' over cotton."

* * *

ON MARCH 26, the last of Banks's troops arrived. Major General William Franklin rode at the head of his men. They looked splendid as they crisply marched into Alexandria. Shiny bayonets glistened in the afternoon sun. Buttons sparkled on clean, blue uniforms. On both sides of the street the men of Smith's Sixteenth Corps watched. Their uniforms were mud-splattered, dirty, and badly worn.

"Don't they look purty!" a man shouted from the sidelines.

A man in ranks turned his head and growled with an arrogant sneer, "Prettier than you, you dirty mud suckers."

Tom Gere turned to John Bishop. "They look a little stuck on themselves, don't they?"

"Captain, we've been fighting Indians and rebs for three years and they've been sitting most of the time in New Orleans."

Gere shook his head and gazed at his men. "I'd rather have these men, worn and dirty, than pretty boys who don't know what a fight is like."

"I think they'll all learn about fighting soon enough."

For three days, Porter's sailors toiled with tugboats and ropes as they strained mightily to move the fleet over the rapids north of Alexandria. The admiral sent up his heaviest ironclad, *Eastport*, first. The vessel became lodged on rocks and could not be budged.

Porter and Church watched. "Well, Captain, the men are putting their backs into it."

"Yes, sir, but all the sweat and grunts won't make any difference if the river doesn't rise. We need water to move that boat."

Providentially, after three days, the river did rise slightly, just enough for the sailors to force the *Eastport* past the falls. A hospital ship followed, struck the lower falls and sank. Porter commanded, "We've got twelve ships that draw less than six feet. Send them on up."

"What about the rest?" Church asked.

"We'll have to keep them back. The troop transports can make it, so Banks should be happy."

As the fleet moved up the river and past the falls and rapids, Banks's men were busy searching for cotton while Banks organized an election in town to choose delegates for a convention of the newly formed state administration.

A.J. Smith met with Banks in a house in Alexandria that he had converted into his headquarters. "I have a dispatch from General Grant." Smith handed a sheet of paper to Banks. "He wants to dispel any notion that our time here is at your disposal. We are to report to Memphis by April fifteenth to join Sherman."

"We'll move soon, General Smith, tomorrow. On April first, the civilian vote will be held. Admiral Porter has finally managed to maneuver his fleet above both falls, and I will be ready. I'm certainly disappointed Grant won't extend your time with me. But it shouldn't take two weeks to whip Dick Taylor."

"I hope so, General Banks. Between waiting for you, the cotton squabble, and the problems moving on the river, we've wasted far too much time."

Banks's face flushed crimson. "General, we *will* move. This has been a complicated campaign to coordinate. Remember that you are not in command. I am."

The next day, cannons boomed and flags waved high like a Fourth of July celebration as hundreds of Unionist voters filed to the polls. On April 2, Porter changed his flagship to the tinclad *Cricket* and ordered his flotilla to Grand Ecore, upriver, to rendezvous with Banks. A.J. Smith's army, loaded into thirty transports, followed.

That evening, Banks left 3,600 men to guard Alexandria while his army marched upriver, following Porter's squadron. The general penned a message to Halleck before he left. It read: "I will be in Shreveport by the tenth of April and will pursue the enemy into the interior of Texas. I am convinced Taylor will not fight us."

The Red River Expedition, with all its pieces in motion, was finally underway.

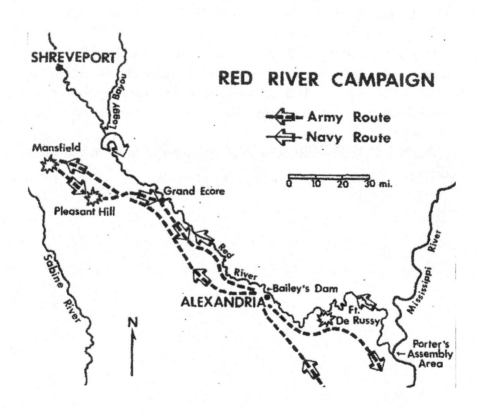

RED RIVER CAMPAIGN

⟵ Army Route
⟵ Navy Route

0   10   20   30 mi.

SHREVEPORT

Bayou Pierre

Mansfield

Pleasant Hill

Grand Ecore

Red River

Bailey's Dam

ALEXANDRIA

Sabine River

N

Ft. De Russy

Mississippi River

Porter's Assembly Area

Battles in the Bayou

ON APRIL 1, FRANKLIN'S CORPS camped in an area between Natchitoches and Grand Ecore, where he awaited orders from Banks. At noon on April 3, Porter reached Grand Ecore. He met onboard his flagship with his marine commander, Frank Church.

"Captain," Porter requested, "report on the status of the squadron."

Church consulted a folded sheet of paper. "*Eastport* is grounded, *Chillicothe* is still on the way. The four turtles, *Carondelet, Louisville, Pittsburg,* and *Mound City,* are sitting off the bank. Our three river monitors, *Osage, Ozark,* and *Neosho,* have gone above Grand Ecore with the gunboats, *Fort Hindman, Juliet, Cricket,* and *Lexington.* Two of General Smith's transports are aground."

"Send tugs to pull them off," Porter ordered.

"I think the river is rising a little," Church commented.

"Good, we'll wait here for Banks."

"What do you want the men to do?"

Porter considered, then smiled. "Collect more cotton."

The next day, Banks arrived on the scene. In disgust, he met with Porter. "My maps are horrible, misleading," he complained. "I had trouble following the roads."

"I have a pilot on one of my vessels who is a native of this area. He knows the roads and the best routes."

"I'll send my chief of staff, General Stone, to speak with him," Banks said. He looked down at the riverbank and saw stacks of cotton bales being loaded onto Porter's boats. Banks shook his head. "You just had to go after more cotton," he said belligerently.

"Gotta do something while we wait for you," Porter smirked.

Within the hour, Banks sent Stone to the *Mound City* to meet with the pilot of the boat. The plump, gray-haired boatman met the general onshore. His assistant pilot stood alongside.

Stone got right to the point. "General Banks says you know the best routes to Shreveport. What do you suggest?"

"Well," the pilot scratched his stubbled chin, "ya could go across the river and follow it, but ya travel through some tough country, bayous and such. I'd advise ya ta go inland. Ya have ta take a road west ta avoid Spanish Lake. That'd take ya ta Pleasant Hill and Mansfield and then up to Shreveport directly north o' there."

"We'll be leaving the fleet, with its gunboats."

"They won't be that far away and after Loggy Bayou ya'll come tagether at Shreveport. 'Sides, if ya wuz marchin' on t'other side o' the river, you'd git slowed down so much the fleet would git way ahead of ya."

"Thank you," Stone replied. "I'll tell General Banks."

As the chief of staff walked back to report, the assistant pilot commented in a low voice to his pilot, "Across the river are good, wide fields on all sides and plenty of water and other provisions. You're sendin' 'em across a dry stretch, a tangled forest with no water nowhere."

The pilot smiled and placed his index finger over his lips. "Shhh. I own land across the river, and my fields are filled with cotton. I don't want no Yanks stealin' my crops. They kin git to Shreveport without takin' from me."

* * *

DICK TAYLOR AND HIS Confederate forces had retreated from Natchitoches as Banks's forces moved upriver under the protective escort of Porter's fleet. From a distant wooded hill, Taylor watched with General Hamilton Bee as the Union troops moved below.

"Ham, what in hell are they doing? Banks has left his gunboats and is off the river. His whole army is marching down a narrow road through thick woods. They could be sitting ducks."

"They're fools to march through a tangled woods," Bee agreed. "Away from the river, no wells to speak of. Scouts tell me there's about 20,000 of 'em. Kilby Smith and the Sixteenth Corps are with the fleet on the river. Their cavalry is out front, then Banks and Franklin next. Look there, the baggage train. A.J. Smith is way back with his two corps."

"We've got about 9,000 troops on hand, Walker's Texas boys, Mouton's Infantry, along with Green's Texas Cavalry and Vincent's Louisiana cavalry."

"They still have us over two to one, General, even with Governor Allen's volunteer militia."

"We've got 5,000 more troops coming in. I've sent for the divisions of General Churchill and General Parsons. They've been camped at Keachi, 'bout halfway between Mansfield and Shreveport. They'll be here tomorrow afternoon."

"I thought General Smith wanted you to delay, not fight here."

"Kirby Smith is at Shreveport. The Yankees are destroying whatever they find. I'm not going to sit and watch them lay waste to all of Louisiana when we can do something about it. There's a clearing at Sabine Crossroads, three miles south of Mansfield. For some time I've been thinking that it's an ideal spot to make a stand. The clearing is about a half mile wide, stretching across the road about three quarters of a mile with a ravine in the middle. When Banks comes out of the woods, we'll hit him in the open. Get the men ready. I'll deploy them in the morning. By midday tomorrow, Banks will be in the trap."

* * *

BANKS'S PROCESSION was strung out for miles. Cavalry and the Thirteenth and Nineteenth Infantry Corps led the way, followed by the supply wagons. Bringing up the rear was the Sixteenth Corps with A.J. Smith.

"Close up, boys," John Bishop commanded the Fifth Minnesota. "We don't wanna get too spread out. Not in these woods."

"Watch yer step, too," Jimmy Dunn called. "There's ruts everywhere."

"Gittin' thirsty, Lieutenant," Levi Carr shouted. "Canteen needs a fill."

"There must be wells in the town ahead," Bishop replied. "Mansfield."

"When we git there?" another man shouted.

"Tomorrow."

Groans echoed from the ranks of the sweaty, grimy soldiers.

"This road twists like a long snake," Jimmy mumbled to Levi.

The cry of a distant animal sounded. "It's a howlin' wilderness," Levi answered.

"So tonight we camp in woods. Thousands of us."

"Ya know, Jimmy, we'll have a time findin' enough space in that jumbled mess ta put two halves together."

"Let's hope it don't rain, Levi."

* * *

TAYLOR KEPT RETREATING before Banks's tortured advance. On the night of April 7, his army reached the clearing at Sabine Crossing. He met with a courier and handed him an envelope. Turning to his friend, General Mouton, he explained, "Just covering my butt a little. It's another request to Kirby Smith to let me fight. He won't be able to say I didn't ask."

"The men are ready," Mouton announced. "We've assembled in lines on the far edge of the clearing. Banks will come out of the woods about three quarters of a mile from us."

"Banks won't make the spot until afternoon tomorrow. Our men are like cats waitin' for the mouse to come out of the hole." Taylor looked up into the sky. "I think it'll be warm tomorrow. I know it'll be hot for Banks."

* * *

THE BOYS OF the Fifth Minnesota endured a hot, dry night. Most didn't even attempt to fasten their shelter tents and instead just spread their bedding on the forest floor and slept there. To avoid mosquitoes, many stretched their blankets over themselves from head to foot. But even then the tough, long needles of the insects occasionally pierced through the woolen blankets.

"Damn!" Levi's muffled voice grumbled as he swatted his hand at his thigh. "These are the starvin'est critters I ever seen."

"I don't see 'em," Jimmy answered. "I just feel 'em."

Levi chuckled. "Call 'em 'no-see-ums,' that's what they are."

"Levi, I think they're bigger than we got back home."

"Maybe, Jimmy. Hungrier fer sure."

"Hold onto yer blood, you'll need it if we run inta rebs."

"Don't worry 'bout rebs. They're runnin' ta git away from us."

"I don't know, Levi, word is they're up ahead."

"And when they see us comin', they'll run some more."

* * *

AT DAWN THE NEXT morning, April 8, Union cavalry trotted out front, followed by Franklin's division. The army unfolded like a big accordion, leaving the Sixteenth Corps in the rear awaiting space to move. Due to the narrow road and the length of the train, the Fifth Minnesota stepped out hours after the first cavalry brigade pranced ahead.

At Sabine Crossing, three miles south of Mansfield, Taylor peered over the clearing from the edge of the woods. He turned to General Mouton.

"Al, I want your division to form up on the east side of the clearing. When Walker arrives, his division will form on your right. Green's cavalry will feint into the clearing and then fall back. I want two of his brigades to move to your flank and his third brigade to Walker's flank. At the right time, we charge."

* * *

NATHANIEL BANKS RODE alongside William Franklin, commander of the Nineteenth Division, as they wound through the thick, green pines. The sun, reaching its highpoint, glared where it escaped the protective cover of tree branches.

Ahead of the generals rode the cavalry of Albert Lee. Banks peered ahead as a rider thundered up to him from the front. "General Lee's compliments, sir," the rider announced. "There's a clearing up ahead with a whole passel of rebs waitin' for us!"

"I'll join you," Banks answered. "General Franklin, move them up. No delay."

A few minutes later, Banks joined Lee on the edge of the clearing. He squinted in the bright sunlight and viewed a long gray line on the perimeter of the clearing across from them. A red Confederate crossbar flag fluttered in a slight breeze. Men moved along the front.

Banks looked at a small hill to the south. "Lee, take your men and occupy that hill. It's good ground, high ground. I'll send Landram's division to join you. General Ransom has the Thirteenth Corps; his Third Division is under Bob Cameron." Banks pointed. "I'll have them spread out here, on the opposite edge of the clearing. We've got more men. We'll keep moving them up."

The next two hours were like a chess match as the two commanders moved their men into position and watched each other from across the clearing. Taylor hoped that Banks would be rash and charge across. Instead, Banks waited for more of his troops to move up the road as Taylor maneuvered his forces into place. At four o'clock, the Confederate general was satisfied. He actually had a temporary numerical supremacy over Banks, whose men were not all in position.

On the left, whether by design or a miscommunication, the Confederate force began a slow, in-echelon advance into the clearing. Taylor reacted in surprise. "What in hell! Who ordered that?" he demanded. He paused, then turned to an aide. "Can't stop it now. It's begun. Get to General Mouton, tell him to charge."

The aide galloped his horse down the line to where Mouton was leading his men forward. "General Taylor's compliments, sir," the aide directed. "He says to charge."

Mouton straightened in his saddle, removed his saber, extended it toward the Union line and shouted, "For Louisiana! Charge!"

The gray line surged forward. Fire erupted from both sides with a withering crescendo. Mouton on horseback, sword extended, towered over his infantry. About a hundred yards away a Union rifleman turned to another soldier. "Look at that," he pointed at Mouton. "Have you ever seen a more perfect target?" He slowly sighted his rifle and squeezed the trigger. Mouton straightened in his saddle and clutched his chest. As blood trickled between his fingers, the Confederate general slid from his horse. A soldier alongside the horse caught the falling officer and guided him to the ground. But Mouton was dead.

Brigadier General Polignac instantly rode in to fill the void. The French nobleman shouted, "Our General Mouton ees killed! Follow me. We fight for our general!"

The line plunged ahead with renewed vigor. Tears of grief and rage stung the eyes of a horde bent on revenge. "Follow Prince Polecat!" a man screamed, unable to pronounce "Polignac." "Kill Yankees fer Mouton!"

But a stream of murderous fire blasting from a solid line of rifle barrels halted the rebel charge. Courage and revenge weren't enough to match the hail of death facing them. The charge was repulsed, leaving behind a third of their division.

Meanwhile, to the west of the road, Walker's division of Texans wrapped around the Union position and folded it in on itself. General Ransom rode through his ranks, desperately encouraging his men. "Hold firm, boys!" he shouted. "Show 'em what you're made of. Hold steady!"

Then Ransom grabbed his shoulder and tumbled from his horse. As the wounded general was carried from the field, his men panicked and ran to the rear as if the hounds of Hell were chasing them. Hundreds were captured by the pursuing Confederates. The first Union line had collapsed.

Far to the rear, the Fifth Minnesota, with the rest of the Sixteenth Corps, heard a distant rumble. Jimmy Dunn called to Lieutenant Bishop, "What's that, Lieutenant? I kin hear thunder, but there's no clouds."

"I just came from General Smith. The rebs have opened up on Banks up ahead. Old A.J. sent word to Banks that he's ready to pass around the supply wagons and bring us on ahead to help. So be ready to move out fast."

"Fast?" Levi questioned. "On a road packed tight like a tin of sardines and a jungle on both sides, there ain't nothin' fast gonna happen. How far ahead are they?'

"Ten miles anyway. I'm not sure. Just be ready."

Ahead, at the battlefront, Cameron attempted to form another battle line after Ransom's disintegrated. The onrushing rebels forced the second Union line back as well. General Franklin took a ball in the shoulder but remained in his saddle and feverishly tried to rally his men.

Blazing rifle shots erupted out of thick black powder smoke from both armies as Franklin's and Cameron's men grudgingly fell back over several miles down the road they had traversed earlier. Hot, sweaty, and bloodied, the Union soldiers prayed for relief.

Their prayers were answered when the retreating soldiers encountered a third line of defense across the road. General Emory's division of the Nineteenth Corps was strung out over the road and woods. Once Cameron's force passed through, Emory's men held firm and repulsed several charges launched by Taylor's men.

The sky turned pink and then faded to black as nightfall ended the battle. None of A.J. Smith's Sixteenth Corps were called to enter the fight. They went into camp two miles from the little town of Pleasant Hill after marching twenty-one miles from Grand Ecore.

The Next Day: Pleasant Hill

THAT NIGHT EACH SIDE TOOK STOCK of the eventful day. Taylor stood in flickering, buttery light from a campfire surrounded by his officers, Walker, Green, and Polignac among them.

"You achieved a great victory, General," Walker claimed in the fire's yellow glow.

Taylor nodded sadly. "We lost General Mouton. We may have won, but this is a very sad day and very costly to our cause."

A young officer approached Taylor with the assuredness of someone with important news. He handed his general a note. "It's from General Smith, sir."

Taylor took the slip of paper and held it toward the glow of the flames. He read the note, then shook his head. A small smile tugged at the corners of his mouth. "General Kirby Smith informs me that my request to attack is denied. We are to continue to delay at Mansfield."

He turned to the waiting officer. "Just tell General Smith this: 'It's too late. We won a battle.'"

The young man saluted and departed. Taylor asked his aide, "What are the causalities?"

"It looks like about a thousand killed or wounded. But we've made quite a haul in Yankee property. We took twenty cannon, 156 wagons, and a thousand horses and mules."

"We've been fortunate, gentlemen. I'm told that Churchill and Parsons have arrived with their divisions to reinforce us. Where has Banks gone?"

"Scouts say he's retreating. It looks like they might camp a little less than twenty miles south, near Pleasant Hill."

"Then we'll go after him." Taylor looked at his officers. "He shouldn't be hard to find."

Meanwhile General Banks, along with Franklin, Ransom, Lee, Cameron, and A.J. Smith, met to assess the day's battle. He turned to Charles Stone, his chief of staff. "What were our losses, General?"

"I don't have the all the exact totals yet, but we had considerable losses in cannon, wagons, and horses. Over 500 wounded and over 1,500 missing, we presume captured. It looks like 113 killed."

William Franklin winced as he sat on a camp stool, his wounded right leg stretched out before him. Concern flashed across Banks's face.

"General, are you badly hurt? Are you fit to command?"

"I'm still able to command. My boys fought hard today."

"They were brave boys. It was a great victory."

"Victory?" Smith questioned incredulously.

"Militarily, we held the ground," Banks snapped. "Our third line held. We only retreated because we ran short of water."

"Really?" Smith countered. "Even way back where we were, it sure looked bad. Men, horses, wagons, all racing past us to the rear."

"It was strategic," Banks corrected. "With the thick woods I could never engage all my forces."

Smith rejoined, "It was more like a poorly arranged line of march left most of your army stuck on a narrow road."

Banks swallowed hard. "General Franklin, at first light move the rest of the baggage wagons to Grand Ecore. General Lee, your cavalry will provide the escort, along with the Thirteenth Corps."

"You want to retreat further? You want to reduce our force. We need to finish the fight!" Smith demanded.

"Tomorrow you and the Sixteenth will get your chance. The Thirteenth has had enough. Ransom is wounded."

The general flexed his arm. "It's okay, General Banks. I can still lead my men."

"You'll lead them to Grand Ecore. General Smith, see to your men. I expect a visit from General Taylor in the morning."

* * *

THE FIFTH MINNESOTA was encamped the night of April 8 about two miles from the small town of Pleasant Hill. Will Woodard and Will Hutchinson joined Jimmy Dunn and Levi Carr around their cook fire. They munched hardtack as slabs of salt pork sizzled in a fry pan.

"Slice me off a piece of sowbelly," Hutchinson asked.

Levi chopped a hunk off with his knife and tossed it to his mess mate.

"Did'ja hear what they're callin' us?" Woodard wondered.

"Fine lookin' Yankee heroes," Jimmy laughed.

"No, they say we be wanderin' all over. That Smith ain't attached to any army fer long. So they say we're like the lost tribes of Israel. We're the 'Gorilla Guerillas.'"

"Smith's Guerillas," Jimmy smiled as he bit into a slice of salt pork, ignoring the juice that ran down his chin. "I like the sound of it."

"Well," Levi countered, "we won't be for long. We'll be part of Sherman's army."

A lone figure approached out of the fading daylight. "Boys," John Bishop suggested, "it's gonna be a short night. If I was you I'd get some sleep. Taylor's comin', and we're gonna be in the front tomorrow."

"So Banks finally decided he wants to win," Levi pronounced.

Jimmy opened his arms expansively. "If ya wanna do yer best, ya gotta use yer best."

Bishop shook his head. "Let's hope you're all feeling as chipper tomorrow night."

* * *

AT 2:00 A.M., reveille sounded and the Sixteenth Corps was ordered into line of battle. The corps was assembled where the road passed near Pleasant Hill. A long line of Union troops formed up through the large open field. The position of the Fifth was well toward the right of the line and somewhat in reserve.

Colonel Hubbard addressed the men of the Fifth Minnesota just as the horizon turned into a pinkish blur. "We are here to check the advance of Taylor's rebs," he proclaimed. "Conserve your water. This is barren, sandy country. Not much water, not much forage. Just a lot of scrubby pine trees.

"We will meet them here, in this open field. The town over there," he pointed to a slightly elevated center of the field, "is Pleasant Hill, though that little mound it sits on is hardly worth the name of a hill. It looks like there's about fifteen houses and a few stores. That semi-circular belt of thick pine timber is on the Shreveport side. They'll be coming from there. The town will be on the edge of the battle. Do Minnesota proud. Hold this ground!"

With cries of "Huzzah" ringing in the early morning air, the Minnesota boys took their position and waited. The sun rose higher and time weighed heavily as the Union troops continued to wait for something to happen.

"I'd just like ta see somethin,'" Jimmy mumbled to Levi. "I'm gittin' bored."

Levi gazed up at the blazing ball in the sky that was nearing its highesr point. Then he peered across the clearing. "Look, Jimmy, somethin's movin' over there."

Jimmy shaded his eyes and squinted. "Rebs. Just checkin' us out, I think. Somethin's gonna be happ'nin' soon, mark my word."

A couple of hours later, sharp fire blasted from across the open field. All through the afternoon a steady *pop, pop, pop* rained shot in intervals at the Union line. Then at about 5:00 p.m., Walker's Texas troops and the command of the dead general, Mouton, hit the Union right hard.

A.J. Smith trotted his black charger before his troops and glared fiercely as if his eyes and sheer will could halt the attack. "Give 'em hell, boys!" he commanded as his troops opened up on the charging rebels. A sheet of lead ripped into the attackers, dropping many dead in their tracks as the Union right held.

But on the left and center, many Union positions were overrun by Churchill's and Parson's fresh forces. The Union line was bent back. Reinforcements rushed up to bolster the Union line and pushed the Confederates back.

Will Hutchinson shouted above the din, "They're fallin' back! We beat 'em!"

"Not so fast," Lieutenant Bishop cautioned. "Taylor's massing his men back there. They'll be comin' again. Stay primed and ready."

Jimmy bit the end off of a cartridge and placed it into the muzzle of his rifle. He took a quick look down the battle line. His comrades' faces were blackened by gun powder and streaked by blood and sweat, yet Jimmy swelled with pride as he sensed the strong, quiet determination that shone from their faces. They stood rooted like fence posts. They would not be moved.

"Bring it on, Dick Taylor!" he shouted. "We're ready fer all you've got!"

They came again and were driven back. Then Taylor sent his boys again, and again and again. Each time, fierce fire drove the gray line back. Finally Smith sensed the time was right. He galloped back to his reserves and screamed, "Now, come on up! We'll hit 'em with everything we've got! The whole corps!"

Smith hurled his army into Taylor's force like a cyclone and broke it into pieces. The Confederates swept back in disorder and retreated into the woods beyond the clearing. They left dead, wounded, and artillery in their wake. It had all lasted two hours.

The jubilant Union forces went into camp that night convinced that their victory would be followed up the next day by pursuing Taylor's army.

Jimmy glowed with pride and satisfaction. "We'll finish 'em off tomorrow, sure thing."

"Old A.J.'s got fire in his belly," Levi agreed. "We'll chase 'em all the way ta Shreveport if we have to."

At 2:00 a.m., the Union troops were roused from their slumber. With eager anticipation they formed into ranks, ready to hunt down Taylor. To their shock, the first order was, "About face!"

"What?" Jimmy questioned. "That way is Grand Ecore and Alexandria, back where we came from. Taylor went the other way. To Shreveport."

"Wait," Bishop urged. "Old A.J.'s on his way to Banks. He'll set things right."

Smith galloped his stallion to the front, where Banks had his headquarters. He encountered the commanding general as he finished his mess. General Franklin stood by Banks's side, leaning heavily on a crutch.

Smith wrenched his horse to a stop and leapt to the ground. "General Banks, what are you doing? We just won a battle and you've ordered a retreat."

"General Smith, you fought a great battle. God bless you, your men saved the day. But my force was badly crippled at Mansfield. General Franklin's wound has incapacitated him, and I've replaced him with Emory. Also, we have a severe shortage of drinking water. Even the rain water in the cisterns of Pleasant Hill is depleted. We've lost about 150 men dead. We must retire to Grand Ecore."

"They lost nearly ten times our dead. What about Porter's fleet upriver? What about our dead? We need to bury them."

"The good people of Pleasant Hill will see to your dead. Porter can take care of himself."

Smith's face turned redder than a ripe tomato. "I have a division under Kilby Smith with Porter. You want to leave them?"

"That's why I'm not worried about Porter. He has your men to protect him."

"Are you crazy besides being a coward? We are leaving them in dire circumstances!"

Banks puffed up indignantly. "Watch your step, General Smith. You are on dangerous ground. I am doing what I believe right for my command. This whole campaign was a farce. Even Steele agrees. There will be no rendezvous with his army. They turned around and went north. Thus, our plan to take Shreveport has fallen apart. The river is too low, the terrain a twisted mess. I don't have Steele, and Sherman wants you back. We had no business being sent here in the first place."

"Especially when Porter beat you to the cotton."

Banks glared at Smith. "You are dismissed. Leave me now and report to your men."

As Smith stomped away, Franklin caught him from behind. "General Smith, General Banks is right. You are on dangerous ground. It would be wise to temper yourself."

"This is a travesty," Smith snapped. "General Franklin, you are second in command. Take over and turn this army around."

"General Smith," Franklin responded, "I'm going to pretend I didn't hear that. What you are proposing is mutiny. It would lead to dire consequences for you. Besides, I am physically unable to lead an army."

Smith sadly shook his head and mounted his horse.

* * *

NORTH OF PLEASANT HILL, Dick Taylor regrouped his army. He was met by General Kirby Smith, commander of the West Louisiana District of the Confederate Army.

"General Taylor," Smith admonished. "You were given explicit orders to delay any attack. Your orders led to a disaster at Pleasant Hill."

Taylor glared indignantly at his commanding general. "General Smith, we won decisively at Mansfield. At Pleasant Hill our gallant boys were repulsed by a much larger Union force. But we inflicted such damage on Banks that he is retreating back down the Red. The Yankee invasion of Louisiana has been stopped dead in its tracks and the enemy is leaving, to devastate this land no more. Texas and Louisiana have been saved. Now is the time to take back New Orleans."

Kirby Smith's dark eyes burned as hot as fire embers. "We will not move on New Orleans. Our forces in Arkansas must be shored up. The Yankees may move on Little Rock. Steele is heading back that way. You will follow and harass Banks all the way back to Alexandria. I'll leave Polignac's division with you. I'm taking Walker's Texas division and Churchill's men to Arkansas to operate against Steele."

"You can't!" Taylor blazed at Smith. "That will leave me with barely 5,000 men! Your misguided strategy will cost us a great opportunity."

"You had your chance, General Taylor. You bungled it."

"I . . . *what!*" Taylor turned crimson as he took a step toward Smith. An officer placed a cautionary hand on his arm, and the general paused.

"General Smith, your incompetence will cost the Confederacy Louisiana and Arkansas. It is shameful."

Smith swallowed hard, subduing the rage rising within. "I will deal with your insubordination later. You have your orders. Keep after Banks."

Terror on the Red

PORTER'S FLEET CONTINUED an exhausting traverse up the Red River, thirty miles north of Banks. Low water repeatedly grounded vessels and caused delays as sailors worked to free them. Confederate engineers had made matters even worse by blowing up a dam, allowing the river to drain into the floodplain of Bayou Pierre. The Red dropped even more.

On April 9 and 10, thick smoke from burning cotton bales stung eyes and choked the men on board the flotilla. Occasional shots from rebel marksmen kept all on alert.

"They can't see us any more than we can see them," Frank Church complained to Commander Breese while on board the *Gazelle*. "What's the point?"

"General harassment, keeping our minds off the river. It's tough enough trying to avoid sandbars and snags. How was your escapade yesterday?"

"A fine day, Commander. Admiral Porter wanted my marines to scout the riverbank. We saw some reb cavalry, burning cotton, and a plantation. Now, the admiral wants as many horses as we can take and any slaves we find, too. There were no horses and only a couple of Negroes. They're on board. We found a shotgun, a rifle, a fine saddle, and some eggs. Porter was a little unhappy that we didn't bring back any horses. But he sends us ashore regularly to drive off snipers and look for cotton. I'm sure we'll find more horses."

From his flagship, Admiral Porter was grateful that they were finally reaching Springfield Landing, where he expected to rendezvous with Banks's army for the push to Shreveport. But it wasn't Banks who greeted Porter.

The admiral laughed in spite of himself at the sight before him. One mile above Loggy Bayou, halfway between Grand Ecore and Shreveport, a huge steamer, *New Falls City*, stretched across the Red River, blocking the whole fleet. It extended fifteen feet on either side of the river, broken in the middle with a growing sandbar filling out below.

"Will you look at that, Church," he told his marine captain. "That's the smartest thing I've seen the rebels do in the whole war."

"Look at the sign, sir." Church pointed.

A large sign was painted on a board and nailed to the side of the boat. It read: "Welcome to Shreveport. A ball will be held in your honor."

"Tempting, Captain, but that's one ball I don't think we'll get to. Do you see Banks anywhere?"

"No." Church shaded his eyes against the morning sun. "But there's a horseman on the road coming fast."

In minutes the horseman, a Union soldier, had left his lathered horse by the riverside and was on deck with Porter. Pausing to catch his breath, he handed the admiral a letter. "From General Banks, sir."

Porter ripped it open and quickly read the short missive. His face turned dark as if a thunderstorm had passed over it. He looked at Church. "Our political general," he spit out the words like little bullets, "has made a mess of things. Defeated at Mansfield, he managed to drive Taylor back at Pleasant Hill. Now he's heading back to Grand Ecore and orders us to follow. God knows what the rebels have in store for us down the river. Praise the Lord that Kilby Smith and his division are still with us."

He nodded to the messenger. "Tell your general it is my intent to meet him in Grand Ecore. We'll get there when we can, no thanks to him. Where's Taylor?"

"Going north, as far as we know. We licked him pretty bad at Pleasant Hill."

Porter seemed perplexed. "Just so I have this straight, Banks lost a battle, won a battle, and now he's retreating south while the army he beat is retreating north. Two armies going in opposite directions. Captain Church, we have been deserted."

Porter sighed and shook his head at the messenger. "It's a real wonderment. Get back to your army."

On the afternoon of April 10, Porter's fleet began the arduous task of returning to Alexandria by way of Grand Ecore. It took all afternoon for the squadron to turn around in the narrow channel.

Chillicothe struck a snag in the river and had to be pulled off by a transport. Occasional rifle shots zinged bullets into the boats. Church reported to Porter as his marines anxiously watched both riverbanks.

"Admiral," Church cautioned, "I don't like the looks of this. The banks of the river are higher than the pilothouses; we've already been taking some fire from rebs, and they've got cover from thick brush."

"Get sailors to move howitzers onto the hurricane decks," Porter ordered. "Work through the night if you have to. We'll blast our way down the river."

Church acknowledged, "We'll have to. They know Banks has left us and they're on us like a pack of hungry wolves."

"Prepare for the worst, Captain."

* * *

WORD HAD REACHED Dick Taylor that while Banks's army was marching to Grand Ecore, Porter's fleet was also reversing itself and struggling to move down the river.

He met with his cavalry commander. "General Green," Taylor said, nodding at the middle-aged, cleanly shaven officer, "Porter and his fleet are having a devil of a time trying to get down the Red. When they get hung up they sit like ducks in the river, and we have snipers worrying them a bit now. You captured a Union steamer last year; this should be old hat to you. I want you to harass them, capture the whole flotilla if you can. Cross Bayou Pierre, and you'll find that Kilby Smith's division is on transports. He'll give Porter some support. But you should be able to make 'em pray they never heard of the Red River."

Green's pleasant face broke into a grin. "No problem, sir. We'll chase 'em to Hell if we have to, just like Santa Anna at San Jacinto."

"You were with Houston there, weren't you?"

"Yes, sir, he put me in charge of the 'Twin Sisters.' It'd be nice to have those cannons today. But I do have a four-cannon field battery."

"General Green, you'd do fine with just cavalry, but the artillery will help. You've fought Indians, Mexicans, and Yankees all over the Southwest. You'll do us proud, like you always have. Just one thing: easy on the liquor. We need the clear-headed, well-mannered General Green."

Green chuckled. "Maybe just a touch of rum, to get my blood up a little."

"Discretion and moderation," Taylor admonished. "Discretion and moderation. Porter's fleet is moving south. Harass, kill and capture."

* * *

THE NEXT DAY, April 11, Banks's forces reached Grand Ecore at about the same time Porter's flotilla was finally turned and able to start south from Loggy

Bayou. Kilby Smith had lined the transports with captured cotton bales and brought his soldiers topside to spray the riverbanks with musket fire.

Green's Confederate cavalry galloped along both sides of the river and ripped shot from the banks at soldiers and vessels. A disillusioned Porter penned a message to Sherman. "Had Banks been victorious, as any ordinary general . . . we would have had no trouble at all, but he has led all hands into an ugly scrape.

"I did all I could to avoid going up this river with him, but he would have thrown all the blame of failure on me had I failed to go. I have risked a great deal and only hope for a rise of water."

The flotilla encountered a series of mishaps and accidents as they endured gunfire from both sides. They moved downriver with the speed of a giant caterpillar. From the decks, Porter's sailors fired at Confederate snipers.

"Keep it up," Church cried. "It's like hunting partridges with eleven-inch-wide shotguns!"

Church placed men on the hurricane roof. Then he coiled a large hawser, piled fence rails around it and then put his men's hammocks all over for a barricade. Next, the marine lieutenant climbed up into the lookout on top of the pilothouse.

As they rounded a bend, Confederates onshore opened up again on two transports just ahead of Church. *Zip! Zip! Zip!* Minie balls buzzed through the air from both the boat and the shore. Then a broadside from the *Cricket* dropped a blast into the midst of the rebels. Many dropped their guns and ran for shelter.

Lieutenant Church watched as one man ripped off his gray coat and ran. He took careful aim and fired his rifle. The distant target threw his arms in the air and collapsed.

Then more rebels crowded the shore, and with reckless abandon, gray-clad figures on the bank shot back. Some stood in full view and shouted insults at the men in the river as they fired their weapons.

Just before sunset, the *Emerald* ran aground abruptly, jarring the whole fleet to a stop.

* * *

TOM GREEN RELAXED by a campfire with his officers as flames illuminated their faces in the dark. Green took a pull from a bottle and smacked his lips. "Mmmm, nothin' like Louisiana rum." He passed the bottle to the officer sitting on a log next to him.

The younger officer asked, "What's the plan for tomorrow, General?"

"We'll keep on 'em until they get good and stuck. Then we'll charge into them boats and capture or sink a few."

Green took the bottle, savored a long swallow and smiled as he handed the bottle back. "Finish it off. I've got more. For now, I'm to bed. Big day tomorrow."

On unsteady legs, Green stumbled off to his tent. The young officer looked at a captain beside him. "You've been with him a long time," he noted. "I'm new to him. Does he get like this often?"

The captain laughed. "He's a very well-mannered gentlemen, as fine a lawyer or soldier as there is in Texas when he's sober. But when he's in good supply of old bust heads, he's all fight. I 'spect he'll take a pull or two tomorrow."

* * *

THE NEXT MORNING, Porter's fleet was underway again. Then the *Lexington* collided with a transport, *Rob Roy*, and staved in the wheelhouse. With bullets raining down, workers frantically made repairs. Near dusk, the *Chillicothe* ran aground and wouldn't budge. Her men labored to free her as echoes of gunfire thundered from down the river, where the rest of Porter's fleet was a tangled mess.

Below Blair's Landing, Green had timed his attack perfectly. The transport *Hastings* was being repaired and was tied to the landing. *Alice Vivian*, with her cargo of 400 horses, was grounded midstream, blocking the channel.

Emerald and *Clara Bell*, with hawsers attached, were trying to pull her free. A monitor, the *Osage*, had also grounded and the transport *Black Hawk* labored in assistance. Porter was still in the *Cricket*, upriver, looking for Banks.

From the shore, a battery of artillery fire slammed shrapnel and shot into the helpless vessels. Green, on horseback, took a swallow from his canteen, winced and wiped his mouth. This was the time, he knew it. He turned and looked at his cavalry assembled on the river bank behind him. "Men," he shouted, "the river's low and they're stuck. It's time to finish 'em off! Follow me! I'll show you how to fight!"

Sword in hand, Green spurred his horse, and man and animal bolted into the shallow river. His men followed with screams like a horde of banshees. From the beleaguered boats, rifle and cannon shot sent missiles at the advancing horsemen.

Green flew from his horse, the top half of his head carried away by a cannonball. *Lexington* came down and joined the fight on Green's battery. From their hurricane decks, *Rob Roy*, *Emerald*, and *Black Hawk* riddled the woods on both sides of the river with grapeshot and shrapnel.

Kilby Smith's infantry huddled behind bales of cotton and hay as they blasted shot into the distant cottonwood trees. Finally *Hastings* was freed and slipped back into the channel. The battle raged, with fire continuous and deadly. Gunboats worked down the river, pouring canister shot into Confederate positions over a two-mile stretch.

Osage was freed and rescued *Alice Vivian*. It was dark. For two hours, the roar of cannon and the rattle of musketry had never stinted. Only occasional flashes now disturbed the curtain of night that fell on the battle scene.

The fleet was free the next morning, the thirteenth, but only for a short time. *John Warner*, a transport, became grounded and caused yet another delay. Confederate artillery on the north bank opened up on the stalled fleet. Once again, Union gunboats patrolled the river and silenced the rebel guns.

Rob Roy broke a rudder trying to free *John Warner* and had to be towed away. General Kilby Smith turned to his staff officer and announced, "I've had enough of this. Send every transport that can make it on its own downriver."

"What about *John Warner*?" the officer wondered.

"Leave it. *Fort Hindman* can watch over it. Porter just arrived."

Porter wound through the grounded vessels and continued down to Grand Ecore, where Banks waited. Once on shore, Porter marched directly to the small house where Banks was headquartered. He strode into Banks's office, where A.J. Smith was also in attendance.

"General," Porter confronted Banks, "you have led us into a terrible mess. Much of my fleet is still stranded up the river, under attack by Green's cavalry and Taylor's army. Now Kilby Smith has sent his men here to you."

"Admiral," Banks asserted, "we all have problems. I've got nearly 25,000 men here. Their safety is my chief concern."

"And much of my navy is stuck on the river facing daily fire from rebels."

"I'll send a relief brigade to keep the rebs off your back," A.J. Smith offered.

"No, you won't," Banks countered. "I need you here and Sherman expects you to leave us in just a few days."

Porter steamed, "I don't care where it comes from. I need some help upriver."

"I'll see what I can do," Banks replied. "That's all I'll say."

Angry and frustrated, Porter left the room, followed by Smith. "Admiral," Smith remarked, "my division is detached. We have no permanent home in this army. I will immediately send a brigade to help you."

"Thank you, General. Your lost tribe would be most welcome. I only hope Banks can send help, too."

The next day, the Fifth Minnesota joined the rest of Smith's brigade in a march up the Red River to rescue Porter's fleet. But they were met by the transport, *John Warner*, newly freed from a shoal, and the rest of the fleet. By the fifteenth, Porter's entire flotilla was anchored off Grand Ecore.

Banks was in no hurry to leave the little town. Taylor and his 5,000-man army hemmed in the 25,000 of Banks. Desperate to keep Smith's division, he informed General Grant that he intended to renew his plan to attack Shreveport and needed Smith. He waited for a response.

Porter went to Banks's headquarters to meet him again. "General, what is your plan? We are ready, awaiting your orders, but the river continues to drop. I fear for my ironclads if we wait much longer."

"Admiral Porter, I am awaiting word from General Grant. As soon as I hear from him, I'll give you orders."

"General Banks, I can't wait. My fleet will be stranded here."

Banks held firm. "I need to hear from Grant."

"Then I'll meet you downriver. I can't wait."

On April 17, Porter sent his ironclads downriver. But danger followed like stink on a skunk. *Eastport* hit a Confederate mine in the river and sank in the channel. Porter journeyed on to Alexandria to obtain pump boats. Once there, he was alarmed at the low water level above the falls.

Knowing he was in dire straits, Porter dashed off a missive to Sherman. "General, I ask you to allow General A.J. Smith's corps to remain with us," he wrote. "My whole fleet depends on his staying here. His is the only part of the army not demoralized. You know my opinion of political generals. It is a crying sin to put the lives of thousands in the hands of such men, and the time has come when there should be a stop put to it. I fear Banks may go off on some new venture and leave me stranded above the falls."

After hearing from Sherman, Grant responded. "I will leave Smith's corps with Banks until the end of April, but only if Shreveport can be taken."

Banks continued to deliberate his next move, and a frustrated Porter sent a letter to Secretary of the Navy Gideon Welles. "I don't see why a fleet should not have the protection of the army as well as an army have the protection of a fleet. If we are left here aground, our communications will be cut off and we will have to destroy the vessels.

"I do not intend to destroy a rowboat if it can be helped, and if the proper course is pursued, we will lose nothing. I wish the department would give me its views without delay. I must confess I feel a little uncertain how to act."

Finally, A.J. Smith demanded to know what Banks intended. "Porter claims that no advance can be made until the river rises. Therefore, I have no intention of going back toward Shreveport. We'll go back to Alexandria," Banks told him.

"We're giving up!" Smith cried incredulously.

"Circumstances dictate that we return to Alexandria. You will be my rear guard."

"Good luck with your presidential ambitions," Smith offered sarcastically as he turned to walk away.

Armies on the Move

ON APRIL 9, 1864, THE SECOND MINNESOTA, fresh from furlough back home, rejoined the Second Brigade, Third Division, Sixteenth Corps of the Army of the Cumberland in Ringgold, Georgia. Colonel James Grant and Lieutenant Colonel Judson Bishop met with brigade commander Colonel Newell Gleason, successor to Colonel Van der Veer, as their regiment established their camp.

After the meeting of the officers, Grant and Bishop assembled their company captains for a briefing. They met in a well-trod open space while camp activity swirled around them on the sunny spring day.

Grant, formerly a lawyer in Wasioja, Minnesota, greeted his officers. "Gentlemen, Colonel Bishop and I have just come from brigade headquarters. Let me put things on the drum head for you.

"The rebs are only about twenty miles from here at Dalton, Georgia. There has been reorganization in the Union Army, but General Sherman is still running the show. He commands the Division of the Mississippi. Our good friend General Thomas leads the Army of the Cumberland; you've served with him at Mill Springs, Chickamauga, Chattanooga, and elsewhere. He's a great man.

"We will be part of an army of 99,000, and we'll be facing Joe Johnston's Army of Tennessee, which has about half the men we have. We will move into the heartland of the Confederacy toward Atlanta. We will occupy Confederate forces in Georgia so that they can't be spared to help Lee against Grant in Virginia. Any questions?"

"Sir," Captain Clint Cilley asked, "since this is a large army and will require tons of supplies, how will we maintain a supply line?"

"We will remain near the north-south railroad line. It will be the lifeline for our supplies and must be protected."

"Where's Forrest?" John Moulton of Company D wondered.

Judson Bishop, called by some the best-looking man in the regiment, smoothed back his wavy dark hair, then tugged at the moustache that drooped over the corners of his mouth. "We don't know for sure. He's been sighted in western Tennessee and even eastern Arkansas. Our boys in the Fifth out west with Smith might run into him. But he is a menace to our supply line, there is no doubt."

"When do we march out?" Cilley asked.

"That wasn't definitively revealed," Grant replied, then began to cough. He took a handkerchief from his pocket and covered his mouth.

"Let me finish that," Bishop concluded. "We think sometime in the next month. One third of our men are new. We'll take whatever time we have to drill and prepare."

Captain Loomis of Company F expressed concern. "Colonel Grant, how is your health?"

Grant pocketed his handkerchief. "Better, but I won't lie to you. I've had to take a couple of leaves, as you know. I'm fit to command, but my health is not 100 percent. I don't know if it ever will be again. But I'll lead this regiment as long as I'm physically able."

"Any other questions?" Bishop inquired. He waited and, when the men remained silent, he continued. "I do have another announcement. Captain Cilley, our young mathematics professor from Wasioja, will continue on detached duty with General Thomas. Lieutenants Couse and Thoeney will have added responsibilities. Now, see to your men."

* * *

ONLY SIXTEEN MILES to the south, General Joe Johnston met in his large wall tent with his corps commanders, generals William Hardee, Benjamin Cheatham, and John Bell Hood. Several division leaders stood behind them, including Cleburne, Polk, and Bate.

Johnston stood before the three corps leaders, who sat upon camp stools. Slender, of medium height, with a wide forehead and trimmed goatee, the fifty-seven-year-old general addressed his officers. "Sherman's army is growing and we must be prepared to move. We are what stands between the Yankees and Atlanta."

"They have twice the men we have," Cleburne noted in his Irish brogue. "I'm after finding a way to win this."

"We cannot allow ourselves to match forces in a pitched battle against Sherman," Johnston explained. "Our campaign will be one of feint and maneuver. If ever we find a Union force has become detached or isolated, we must be ready to pounce. That's how we win."

"What about supply lines?" Polk asked.

"Bishop," Johnston recalled the general's civilian profession, "Forrest will raise havoc in Sherman's rear and disrupt his supply line on the railroad. By the same token, our railroad line to Atlanta must be maintained."

"General," Hood asserted, "I prefer a more aggressive approach. Let's hit 'em hard before they get goin'."

"Rein it in, John," the commander cautioned. "That time may come, but it isn't now."

Hardee nodded at Johnston. "We have a very difficult task facing us, but, General, I'm thankful that you are in charge. You are our best hope in this type of campaign, and after serving under Bragg, I thank God every night that you've replaced him."

"Thank you. I hope your faith in me is justified. Remember, you must be nimble and flexible. Be ready to move and not fall into a trap."

He looked at the men sitting and standing before him: Hardee, the roughhewn professional soldier who had written a book on military tactics; Polk, the long white-haired Episcopal priest turned soldier; Hood, the brash, aggressive fighter who had lost the use of his left arm at Gettysburg and his right leg at Chickamauga. His friends called him Sam.

Then there was General Cleburne, a division commander under Hardee. Cleburne was an Irishman who had immigrated to America fifteen years ago and had become a lawyer devoted to the South. Handsome and trim with a short, dark chin beard and mustache, he'd earned the devotion of his men.

Johnston felt blessed to command these men. Their division generals, men like Cheatham, Bate, and Cleburne, were exceptional soldiers. It was true that a daunting task lay before him, but if there was any chance of success, it would be because of these men.

* * *

TOD AND WAD CARTER were joined by Lieutenant Tom Caruthers and Sergeant Tom Giles as they watched men at drill.

"The men are gettin' bored," Caruthers noted. "Marchin', drillin', and shootin' kin only go so far. Cap'n Carter, you're on Smith's staff. When we gonna do somethin'?"

"I guess when General Johnston thinks it's time. We have to match what the Yankees do. Sherman is putting together a huge army in Ringgold. When he moves it will decide where and how we move. It's like a chess game, but we only have half as many pieces."

"Do you like 'Old Joe'?" Giles asked.

"Better than Bragg," Wad interrupted. "He'll be easier on the men."

"Ya know," Tod began, "the men would have liked Bragg a lot better if he gave them a chance. He was doing what he thought was best. But he was too hard on the boys. Too many firing squads for infractions and too rigid when it came to other things. General Smith worked closely with him. He says Bragg couldn't control his temper and seemed to hold everyone else in disdain."

"Losing a half-dozen battles didn't help," Wad responded. "I've heard it said that he had the instincts of a drill sergeant but not the genius of a general. All he had going was that Jeff Davis likes him. At least now, if Johnston orders a man shot, it's because of a crime committed and not to intimidate the rest of the army."

"He didn't take advice from his officers very much," Tod agreed. "Hardee came to hate him."

"Now," Caruthers continued, "he's kicked upstairs to advise Davis and 'Old Joe' is our man."

"He sure dresses purty," Giles added. "Finest uniform I've seen and a star and feather on his hat."

"Bright sash," Wad continued. "Silver spurs. He'd make a perfect picture of a general for schoolbooks."

Tod watched as a blast of gunfire from a platoon of eight erupted at a distant target. "Johnston is a great general, but he'd be even better if we weren't losing so many men. Between battles and desertions, we're down thousands of men from where we need to be. Spirits are down and morale crushed."

"At least we git food," Giles noted. "The gen'r'l shaped up those commissaries that were lining their own pockets sellin' off our food. Bragg shoulda done somethin' 'bout them before."

"It sure helped us," Wad agreed. "Johnston will get the boys to feeling better. Whiskey and tobacco issued twice a week, sugar, coffee, and flour instead of meal," he said almost dreamily. "Ham and bacon instead of 'blue' beef." His face wrinkled in distaste.

"Don't forget new tents," Giles smiled. "Soon we'll be livin' like kings. He's even makin' sure we git paid reg'lar."

"None of it will make any difference if we don't find a way to stop Sherman," Tod countered. "The best general in the world can't win without sufficient numbers of men."

Tod looked over at Caruthers. "Captain, you're from Franklin, too. Did you know Sam Davis from Smyrna?"

"Just knew the family a little. They lived about ten miles from Franklin."

"I talked with him a couple of times before the Yanks caught him."

"He weren't no spy!" Giles exclaimed. "He was a courier. They had no bus'ness hangin' 'em."

"I heard all he had to do was tell who was in charge of the couriers and they would have let him go," Tod relayed.

Wad stared silently in remorseful remembrance. "He told them, 'No, I won't betray a friend to save my life.' Then they hanged him."

"I heard that his friend, Mary Kate Patterson, showed up but was too late to do anything," Tod said.

Caruthers nodded. "She got there just as they dropped Sam from the rope. Folks could hear her scream."

"Funny, isn't it." Tod commented. "She was a real spy."

"I heard she's took up with Sam's brother," Giles continued. "Ain't that a wonderment?"

"The real wonderment," Caruthers noted, "is what Johnston will do with this army and when'll he do it."

"For part of the answer to that question," Tod noted, "you'll just have to ask General Sherman. I hear he's waiting for more Yankee troops to arrive from the Red River. Then he'll come at us with over 90,000 men. He'll have us almost two to one."

Wad laughed. "If we weren't so much smarter, I'd be worried."

Battles on the River

GENERAL BANKS'S ARMY MARCHED back toward Alexandria, sending a messenger upriver to tell Porter. A.J. Smith placed a proper guard on each of his transports, ordering them to proceed down the river to Alexandria.

On the morning of April 21, Smith's army left Natchitoches and fell in behind the land column. The Fifth Minnesota marched with them in the rear of Banks's army to provide the force protection.

Jimmy Dunn shouted to his lieutenant, John Bishop, "Is this all we're ever gonna do? At Vicksburg we wuz on our own out front of the army leadin' the way, and now they got us on our own again, this time in back."

"They tell us to do what we're good at, Jimmy. Rear guard action of a retreating army is just like leading an advancing army, only backwards."

Jimmy shook his head as if trying to dislodge cobwebs. "Ya got me confused with that one, Lieutenant. I kinda got lost after 'what we're good at,' but I'll just let it go at that."

"Just keep lookin' for rebs, Jimmy. When we see 'em, we shoot 'em."

The Fifth continued the march. They were hot, dusty, and sweaty. The spring heat and the scarcity of drinking water weighed heavily on them. The regiment was frequently hit from behind by Taylor's forces. Each time Smith's Sixteenth Corps, with the Minnesota boys, had to stop, form a line of battle and drive the troublesome rebels back to allow Banks to make more headway down the valley. At Grand Ecore, Cloutiersvillle, and Cane River Crossing, sharp exchanges held Taylor's men at bay.

The army was worn down by the fatigue of continuous day and night duty, marching, skirmishing and fighting. They plodded into Alexandria on April 26, much relieved to be out of the wilderness that had nearly finished them. They went into camp and formed a line of battle to combat any Confederate advance.

Porter's fleet was not so fortunate. Unable to keep up with Banks's army because of low water and constant harassment from the Confederate marksmen on the river banks, they were stalled. The *Eastport* still blocked the channel. With pump boats, Porter's men labored for three days to raise the vessel. On April 21, she was finally dislodged.

Captain John Phelps, one of Porter's most valued boatsmen, could not find the leak in *Eastport* and built a bulkhead to contain the water. Pump boat *Champion No. 3* towed the big boat while Porter followed in a flatboat loaded with *Eastport*'s guns.

But fate was against the ironclad. The next day, she became lodged on sunken logs. Phelps worked his crew all night to get her off. On April 23, *Eastport* grounded again. Sailors spent two more days wrenching, winching, pulling and pushing to force the boat three more miles down the Red. Then she wedged solid again.

Phelps reported to Porter, "My pilots have taken readings, sir. She's stuck tight. There just isn't enough water to get her to Alexandria."

"Try one more day, Captain, one more time."

The next day, Phelps's crews endured musket fire from both banks as Confederates descended in hordes like hunters on a wounded duck.

"Where is Banks?" Porter cried to Captain Church. "How can he let us sit here and be riddled with shot?"

Within the day the answer came. "He's left us high and dry, Church," Porter told his marine commander. "Banks left Grand Ecore, and both sides of the river are in control of the rebs. He's gone to Alexandria, and we're supposed to fend for ourselves."

Porter went back to his flagship, *Cricket*, where he met with his skipper, Lieutenant Henry Gorringe. "I gave orders to *Fort Hindman* to try to dislodge *Eastport* one more time," he told Gorringe. "If that doesn't work, they'll have to scuttle her and blow her up. We have no choice; we can't leave an ironclad here for the rebs. We've got three tinclads and two pumpers ahead of us, and the mouth of the Cane River is close."

Suddenly the afternoon erupted with gunfire. From the shore a battery of six Confederate cannons poured grapeshot at *Cricket* and riddled the vessel with a shower of lead. Porter ordered his twenty-four pounder to open up on the shore batteries.

The skipper stopped *Cricket* in midstream, shouting, "Fire the guns and cover the boats astern!"

Alarmed, Porter snapped, "Get your every man available on deck and armed! We've got to hold on and push 'em back! And get this boat moving. We can't sit here like this!"

Shot ripped through the vessel and cleared the deck of sailors and soldiers. Porter ordered the gun crews to remain on deck and directed the fire of his gunners. A Confederate shell dropped onto a gun in the boat's rear, killing its crew. Another hit near the stern, wiping away the forward gun crew and exploding in the fireroom. Fire and smoke enveloped the crew as Porter clawed his way to the pilothouse.

Seeing the wounded pilot slumped over the wheel, Porter took the helm himself. Flames flickered around him and a hose crew desperately pumped water on the fire as the admiral maneuvered his flagship around a bend. The only two gun crews left shelled the enemy.

Gorringe pointed to the riverbank. "Look there, Confederate cavalry!"

Horsemen were guiding their mounts into the stream and plunging ahead into the muddy river. The lieutenant continued, "They're coming right for us. They mean to board!"

Rebel horses splashed near the *Cricket* in the shallow water. Kilby Smith's riflemen, behind barricades on the boat, fired desperately in hopes of driving the attackers back.

Engineer Charlie Parks urged the men on. "Make yer shots count, boys! Keep 'em off the boat!" Then he grabbed his head and tumbled to the deck.

A horseman leapt from his mount and grabbed the boat railing to hoist himself onto the vessel. A sailor blasted a shot of lead into his chest. Heavy fire from *Cricket* drove off the attackers. Nine defenders lay dead on the deck.

An eerie silence claimed the river for an instant. Then an enormous boom rolled down the river from above. "*Eastport*," Porter observed. "We blew her up." Suddenly the bank erupted again with cannon fire.

Balls and shot splashed all around the *Cricket*. Sounds of splintering wood alarmed all on board. "We gotta get outta here," Captain Phelps shouted to Porter. "I count at least sixteen guns over there!"

"Run 'em!" Porter commanded. "We can move faster than they can aim!"

Run the artillery they did. *Cricket* streamed past the batteries. But *Champion No. 3*, following the flagship, was hit, her boiler shattered. Scalding hot water sprayed a hundred black refugees rescued from upriver plantations.

Their agonized shrieks rose above the gunfire. With a gaping hole in the hull, the transport was grounded and captured near the rebel battery.

Next in line came *Juliet*, a tinclad, bound to *Champion No. 5*. Both vessels faced a cascading torrent of gunfire. A shell ripped into *Juliet's* steam pipe and tiller ropes. After the resulting envelope of steam subsided, *Juliet's* and *Champion No. 5's* pilots discovered that they were now facing upstream and the crew of the pump boat was trying to cut loose from the tinclad.

In a hailstorm of fire, *Juliet* captain William Maitland leapt onto *Champion No. 5* and climbed into the empty pilothouse. While navigating the boat, he had a line stretched back to the *Juliet*. With covering fire from *Fort Hindman*, *Juliet* towed the pump boat back upstream.

Fort Hindman, with Church on board, was obliged to run upriver out of range. Before they reached safety, Ensign Pool, standing next to the marine leader, was fatally struck by shrapnel. Church himself was flattened by a bullet in his leg. *Fort Hindman* moved out of range and waited through the night.

Meanwhile, *Cricket* cruised downriver seeking help. But below Crane River the flagship grounded, and for four desperate hours Porter's crew tried to get their boat afloat. Nightfall found them free of the shoal, but the sound of heavy artillery fire from downriver signaled another alarm.

Porter conferred with his captain. "Gorringe, that must be *Osage*. *Lexington* tried to run that battery earlier and had to retire with eighteen holes in her."

"What do you want done, sir? Should we order *Osage* back to assist the others?"

Porter considered. "No. Send her on to Alexandria. Get a message to Phelps upriver. He's to see that *Juliet*, *Fort Hindman*, and *Champion No. 5* get to Alexandria. God help us all."

As Porter fought his way down the river, above him Phelps frantically worked his crews to a fever pitch in making repairs. By nine o'clock the morning of the twenty-seventh, they were ready. *Fort Hindman* led the way with *Juliet* in tow, followed by *Champion No. 5*. But their trials and tribulations were far from over.

With a rebel battery just a half mile downriver, *Juliet* smashed into a snag and ripped a hole in her hull. Phelps had her towed back upriver, where she was repaired and then started back down. The Union Navy swept the woods with steady fire until they were about 500 yards from the Confederate batteries.

At that point, heavy fire burst from the riverbank. *Fort Hindman*'s tiller ropes were ripped away when a shell passed through the pilothouse. Shot and shell tore into *Juliet*'s upper works, disabling the tinclad. Powerless, the two vessels bounced back and forth between the riverbanks, barely missing the wreck of *Champion No. 3*. Providentially, they floated through the barrage to safety downriver, where the crews were picked up by *Neosho*.

Champion No. 5 was not as fortunate. All rebel fire concentrated on the transport. Her steering became disabled, and she drifted to the opposite bank. Once there, she was abandoned as her crew fled into the woods. With Lieutenant Church standing gingerly at a railing, the *Fort Hindman* successfully drifted past the Confederate gun battery. In the ensuing firefight, two shore batteries were put out of commission by shot from *Fort Hindman*.

Colonel Bailey's Dam

ATE ON THE TWENTY-SEVENTH, PORTER, aboard *Cricket*, steamed into the upper falls above Alexandria. He looked with disgust at his once-proud fleet, now gathered in shambles before him. Two ships, *Caroudelet* and *Mound City*, were wedged aground. Most of his other vessels were riddled with cannon and rifle shot. Deep scrapes were gouged along the sides of many. A few never made it. Porter called for a meeting of his officers.

They gathered on *Cricket*'s deck. Admiral Porter was relieved to see his top marine. "Lieutenant Church, how is your leg? We need you."

"I'll recover, sir. No bones were hit."

"Good. Banks is gone. He took Kilby Smith and his division with him, and I don't know what we'll do. The water by the falls is three feet deep. I need at least seven feet to move this fleet. We are high and dry with no army, and damn Banks is running the other way."

Porter turned to his skipper, Lieutenant Henry Gorringe, who stood next to Captain John Phelps and William Maitland. "Gentlemen, nothing looks good. We lost two pump boats and of course *Eastport*, the best damn ironclad in the fleet. *Cricket* was hit by thirty-eight shells and the whole fleet bears damage of some sort. Half my crew, twenty-five men, were killed or wounded. Another eighteen casualties from *Juliet* and *Fort Hindman*.

"Now, look at this channel. It's so narrow it doesn't even do the name justice. Here we have a rapids," he pointed. "Jagged rocks, three feet of water with another rapids downriver, ending at the falls above town. Now our whole shot-to-pieces fleet is gathered here with no place to go. We can't navigate past here."

"Can't we lighten the boats to get them over the falls?" Phelps wondered.

"Not enough," Porter responded.

Ensign Tom Quinn offered a suggestion. "We could blast a channel through the rapids."

"That might work," Porter agreed, "but it would take all summer. We have nine of the best vessels in the Mississippi squadron trapped above these falls. We have to get them below. I can see Banks abandoning Alexandria and forcing me to destroy the whole fleet."

"Can't you get help?" Maitland wondered.

"I've sent a message to Secretary Welles, suggesting that unless instructed by the government, I do not think General Banks will make the least effort to save the navy. Especially now that Grant has ordered Banks to attack Mobile."

"Who's that?" Phelps asked, pointing to an officer boarding the ship.

"I don't know," Porter replied. "I expect we'll find out soon."

A rugged, solidly built officer approached the group. He saluted and announced, "I'm Colonel Joe Bailey from Wisconsin, sir. I've been sent here by General Franklin to assist you. Here is my letter of introduction." He handed Porter an envelope.

The admiral flashed a sardonic smile. "And what can you do? Pick us up and pitch us over the falls?"

"Not quite, Admiral. I'm an engineer. I come from logging territory in Wisconsin, and I can build you a wing dam."

"A wing dam?"

"It will have an arm sticking out from either shore, leaving a small gap in the center, sir. This will be closed with a sluice gate until the water reaches a seven-foot level."

Porter grumbled. "If damming would get the fleet off, I would have been afloat long before now."

"My dam will get you afloat."

"How?"

"I'll use simple logging techniques. We will build a dam at the lower falls and leave an opening in the middle. Your fleet will stream through the spillway."

Porter rubbed his chin in thought. "It might just work, and I'm getting desperate. Have other engineers viewed your plan?"

Bailey laughed. "Just about every engineer in the army and navy has examined it, sir. It has been unanimously pronounced impossible and/or ridiculous. But I am chief engineer, and I tell you it will work. Besides, we have no alternatives. Do you have any lumbermen?"

"We have some Maine boys," Porter responded. "Get Banks and Franklin to back this and I'm all in."

On April 30, men from Wisconsin, Iowa, and Illinois, along with two regiments of black soldiers and lumbermen from Maine, assembled above the falls in Alexandria to begin Bailey's dam. It was 758 feet across the Red River, with the depth varying between four and six feet. A train of wagons and draft horses hauling equipment awaited the workers.

Bailey confidently explained to Porter as they stood alongside the river, "The sides of the riverbank are rocky and bare. The shallow, narrow channel in the middle runs at about ten miles an hour."

"Well, Colonel, my fleet's future lies in your hands. I pray you are successful."

All preparations were done by May 2, and the sound of axes swung by 3,000 men rang across the river from the forest like a staccato symphony. Logs anchored with stones, wires, and debris began to fill the river. Every man in the fleet became engaged in the construction of the dam, either by cutting logs, conveying stones and frames into position, or by floating logs to the dam.

Bailey, closely supervising, ordered a subordinate, "Take two of the most damaged barges and fill them with rocks. Get them onto the dam and sink them. It'll speed things up."

It worked, but almost too rapidly. The river rose so fast the barges broke loose. Porter quickly ordered two ironclads and two wooden steamers cut loose in time to grab the crest downstream. The four vessels rode the wave and flew down the river and past the falls unscathed.

Cheers from 30,000 voices erupted in a deafening cacophony of joy. Porter excitedly shouted at Bailey, "Great work, man! But the dam broke and I've still got a fleet above the falls. What's next?"

"We build another dam and do it again, Admiral."

It took until May 13 for the final three ships, *Louisville*, *Chillicothe*, and *Ozark*, plus two tugs to blast through the chute on a wild ride into the quiet water below. One man was swept off a deck to a watery grave below.

Soldiers on the riverbank cheered and bands played as the boats came to rest onshore. The last of Banks's troops came aboard and wasted no time escaping the Red River as they raced for the Mississippi.

Retreat

ON MAY 14, WITH THE LAST of Porter's fleet over the falls, the army was put into motion for the final exodus from the Red River country. Dick Taylor, with his little army of 5,000, was still dogging Banks every step of the way. The Confederates had possession of the roads over which the Union Army had to march.

When the army was about twenty-five miles from Alexandria at a little village called Mansura, A.J. Smith's Sixteenth Corps camped for the night. The Fifth Minnesota, under Mower, was with them. On May 15, they were ordered to Simmesport on the Atchafalaya Bayou.

The Fifth Minnesota marched far to the front. Jimmy Dunn, Levi Carr, and Will Hutchinson cautiously eyed the road ahead of them as they marched over prairie.

"I can smell 'em," Levi remarked to Jimmy. "Rebs are close. Things are too still. It ain't right."

"Ol' Dick Taylor ain't gonna let us get outta here easy," Jimmy agreed. "Look there, cavalry!"

Up ahead, a brigade of Confederate horsemen and twelve pieces of artillery opened up on the Minnesota boys. The rest of the Sixteenth moved up to join the Fifth and advanced forward to hit the rebels right, left, and center. Taylor's cavalry broke and retreated, taking their artillery with them.

Skirmishes with Confederate horsemen continued into May 16, when the boys in blue reached Simsport. Porter's boats were there, and a bridge was made of them to cross the bayou at Atchafalaya. The crossing was made on the seventeenth, eighteenth, and nineteenth of May. The Fifth Minnesota had been given its customary assignment: rear guard of the Union Army.

Smith met with Colonel Hubbard. "I want you to stay in line, protecting the crossing of the other corps. If the enemy attacks, use whatever force is necessary to drive them back."

"What's this place called?" Mower asked.

"Yellow Bayou," Smith answered as he left for the landing.

Shortly thereafter, Taylor ordered a mass attack on the Union line. Skirmishers were pushed back.

Jimmy Dunn, in the fore with his comrades, shouted, "They're comin', boys! Pick 'em off like shootin' squirrels!"

Lieutenant Bishop cried, "Forward!" and the Union line advanced. Jimmy and Levi raced ahead, firing and reloading as they charged. The rebels retreated nearly two miles across an open field and through a briar thicket. Dead trees were thickly interspersed on one side.

Beyond the thicket the Confederate Army gathered in force, far outnumbering Mower's command. Twenty pieces of artillery were leveled at the Union Army, which halted at the far edge of the thicket. Mower, his force concealed in the brush, formed up in line and brought his artillery up in close range.

They awaited a rebel attack. "Make sure yer loaded, boys," Bishop reminded his men. "And don't double load. Make sure yer rifle really fired the last time you shot."

In moments, fire and smoke blasted across the opening as the enemy batteries opened up, followed by a line of gray-clad men racing pell mell at the Union line. Mower screamed, "Fire!" at his cannon, and canister and case-shot swept into the charging rebels, cutting them down like a scythe cutting through grass.

"Fix bayonets!" Bishop ordered. Then, "Charge!" The Fifth Minnesota joined the rest of the Sixteenth in a mad bayonet charge, resulting in a terrible slaughter. Bayonets sliced, stabbed and ground into the rebel forces until they turned and ran for the safety of their artillery, back through the thicket and the field beyond.

But with amazing courage, the Southerners regrouped and charged into the Union troops again. Both sides endured fierce fire as the battle seesawed back and forth.

The fierce rifle fire from both sides set the thicket on fire and formed an impassable barrier for either army. General Mower moved his army back to the open field, formed a line and camped for the night. There was no further action. Taylor's pursuit of the Union army was over.

On May 20, the Sixteenth Corps, bringing up the rear, crossed the bridge and marched to Red River Landing on the Mississippi River. The

transports were waiting there, and Smith's army boarded with orders to proceed back to Vicksburg. They reached the city on May 23, having been on
the expedition for seventy-four days. The Red River Campaign was over. It
had been a failure.

Colonel Joe Bailey was proclaimed a hero. Nathaniel Banks, after failing
to follow up at Pleasant Hill and deserting Porter's navy twice, was virtually
relieved of command. General Edward Canby and Admiral David Farragut
replaced Banks in the campaign on Mobile. General William Franklin left
Red River wounded and disillusioned. He would never command again.

In Washington, hearings began on what became known as the "Red
River Fiasco." Porter testified that cotton killed the expedition, in addition
to stating pointed criticism of Banks. After a time of rest and leave, he would
be ordered to lead a fleet on the Atlantic coast.

On the Confederate side, acrimony between Kirby Smith and Dick Taylor led to Taylor's dismissal. But the Confederate Congress thanked him for
his defense of the Red River Valley and sent him to Mobile to command the
defenses there.

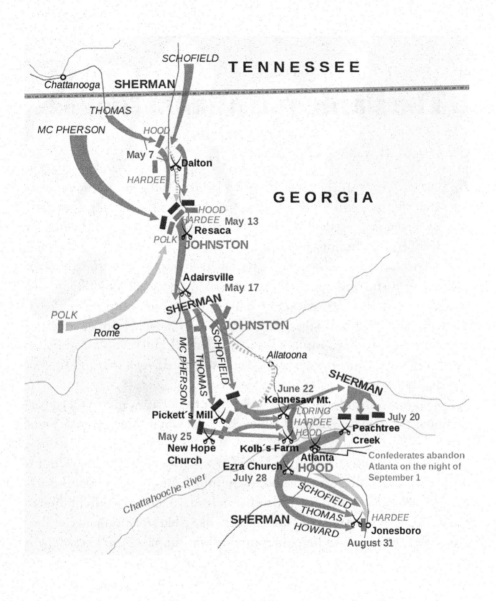

The Battle for Atlanta Begins

TOD CARTER WATCHED OUT from Rocky Face Ridge in northern Georgia. He stood with Twentieth Tennessee First Lieutenant Tom Carruthers as the sun receded to a crimson sliver in the west. The lieutenant asked, "Sherman's comin', ain't he?"

"General Smith thinks so. We've been here for months now. Grant's been moving on Richmond up in Virginia. Sherman's got near a hundred thousand men, almost twice what we have. It's time for him to move, too."

Carruthers pointed to the valley below. "They'll come from down there, and we hold the ridge, Turner's Gap, and Tunnel Hill. We'll be stretched mighty thin, but the boys are ready, Tod, well rested, well fed, and tired of waiting. We'll see how good a general we have."

"Old Joe's a smart one," Tom said. "I hear he doesn't want a pitched battle unless the time is right and he thinks we can win it. That means a lot of move and counter-move."

"General Smith tells me that Sherman will have some trouble with his supply lines. General Forrest has been sent into Tennessee to disrupt the railroad that Sherman is tied to." Carruthers added, "Sherman needs his line to the north. They have to hold Nashville. It's like a big storehouse to the Yankees. We depend on our line to Atlanta for our supplies. You know how it is, Tod, you're a quartermaster. So we move, protect and harass each other. We've got Wheeler's cavalry. He can give Sherman fits here."

"We don't have to beat the Yanks, you know," Tod continued. "Just string this out. An election is coming up north. I know we have support up there. People are tired of the war and want to see it over. Some there even believe that we're right. If Lincoln loses and a Peace Party man wins, well, they'll end it."

"So we just need to hold on, and Old Joe is the man who can do it."

"Can he pull the trigger?" Tod wondered. "I know General Johnston is good, but is he too cautious? General Smith says that President Davis has been prodding him, trying to get him to move on Sherman. But he won't, he says the time isn't right. You know, there's a story that Old Joe has a plantation with lots of good duck hunting. They say he's a crack shot but he never shoots his gun. The ducks are always too high or too low. The dogs are too close or too far. Nothing is ever just right."

"Well, Captain Carter, let's hope his cautious nature works, and he lets Sherman get so close that we can't miss."

* * *

SHERMAN HELD TWO COMMANDS, one as Division of the Mississippi chief and the other as a field commander with three armies under his direction. For months at Ringgold, trains from Louisville and Nashville had brought in enormous amounts of supplies. Nearly every train, boxcars loaded, also brought in veteran regiments on the rooftops returning from furloughs. On May 7, 1864, he gave the order to advance.

William Tecumseh "Cump" Sherman met the night before in a council of war with his top commanders. The generals of his three armies, George Thomas, John Schofield, and James McPherson, gathered in a small house in Ringgold.

Before them was the long, steep ridge upon which Johnston's army was entrenched. There were several openings in the ridge, including Buzzard Roost Gap, Dug Gap, and Snake Creek Gap to the south. Off the southern end of the ridge lay the town of Resaca.

Sherman peered closely at a map spread on the table before him. Thomas placed his finger on the gap in the mountains near the town. "Here, General, if we can flank them at this place, Snake Creek, we can cut the railroad between Johnston's army and Atlanta. The enemy will be forced to either abandon their strong position or attack. Then we'll have 'em."

"A reasonable approach," Sherman considered. "I really don't want a frontal assault. Tomorrow we move up to Rocky Face Ridge. But I won't just walk through their terrible door of death. Like boxers, we'll jab and feint. Thomas and Schofield, I want you to fix Johnston's attention to the left on the ridge—you'll engage them at Buzzard's Roost and flank them at Dug Gap. This is our diversion. McPherson, you'll swing wide to the right through Snake Creek to hit the railroad at Resaca, fifteen miles behind them. That's where we'll get them."

The Atlanta Campaign began the next morning with an attack on the rebel forces on Rocky Face Ridge. Sherman unleashed his pent-up thunderbolts as they hit from the valley before the ridge. Union cannon hurled shot and balls into the midst of the Confederate line. Rebel marksmen picked out battery gun crews and dropped them with long-range fire.

Tod Carter watched from his position alongside General Thomas Benton Smith. The handsome twenty-six-year-old boy general peered intently, removing his cap and running a hand through dark brown hair. Then he nervously tugged at his bushy mustache. The valley below was filled with blue-clad soldiers milling in the distance like hungry ants. Volley after volley blasted down from the ridge into the enemy below. Then rebel cavalry charged into the Union forces, driving them back.

"General!" Tod shouted at his commander. "They're swinging to the right around Dug Gap!"

"We're ready for 'em!" Smith returned. "General Johnston reinforced there! Cleburne's men just got there!"

As the battle raged, the third column under McPherson raced through Snake Creek Gap to the south to hit the railroad at Resaca while the assault at Dug Gap was halted. Then Sherman pulled back from Rocky Face Ridge and ordered his whole army through Snake Creek to join McPherson.

But McPherson overestimated the size of the Confederate Army before him and proceeded cautiously. Just short of the railway, he encountered fortifications that stretched all around the town. He halted his forces and dug in without taking the railroad.

Johnston, countering the Union maneuver, moved his whole army to Resaca. There he conferred with William Hardee, his corps commander, who asserted, "General, Sherman's whole army is coming through the gap. We're being flanked. They've got Dalton and the ridge. What's your plan, General Johnston?"

"We can't fight them here. We need to slip away to the south to defend the river crossing. We've got to be able to move."

* * *

ON THE NIGHT of May 12, Sherman descended on the town, expecting to deliver a knockout blow to Johnston. But the entire Confederate Army had disappeared from the town, leaving Sherman furious that McPherson had delayed.

Johnston was entrenched near Reseca, leaving the city to be taken. Sherman smashed into the Confederate lines but was repulsed. Hood hurried to Johnston and exclaimed, "The Union left is in the air. Sherman sent Sweeney over the river and he's unsupported! Let me hit 'em!"

"Do it!" Johnston agreed.

Hood's division courageously burst forward, but Sweeney's men blasted fire into them and drove them back in a sea of blood. The Union force dug in and was reinforced. McPherson rushed to Sherman and asked, "Should I move to cut off the rebels?"

"No, we've got them penned up, I think. I believe Johnston plans to make a stand here."

However, Johnston, realizing that the Union maneuvers had made his position untenable, moved his whole army south during the night. The morning of May 16 found the Confederate trenches empty.

It was a tactic repeated throughout the summer. Weeks of it left the Union general frustrated and upset that Johnston hadn't been cornered at Resaca.

Sherman complained to his officers, "We move south, then Johnston takes up a strong position. So we stop, deploy troops and reconnoiter. Then we flank him and he moves again, establishes another strong position and we do everything over again."

"We've been doing it for six weeks," McPherson agreed. "Adairsville, New Hope Church, Dallas, and Pickett's Mill. Every time we think we have him, he moves on."

"Well, Mac," Sherman admonished, "you missed the opportunity of a lifetime at Resaca. We had him if you moved quickly. We could have cut them off from Atlanta."

Chagrined, McPherson hung his head and mumbled, "I know."

* * *

TOD CARTER ACCOMPANIED his superior as General Smith joined other commanders in a conference with Joe Johnston. Their leader looked worn and fatigued, like a rag squeezed through a wringer. But his eyes glowed bright as he explained to his officers, "I've been waiting for Sherman to give us an exposed formation. We'd be fools to try to take his total army on. But if we could hit him piece by piece, it might work. Scouts tell me that his corps are now widely spaced. I want to pounce upon and destroy an isolated component of Sherman's army. I think the opportunity is about to present itself.

"Hooker is approaching Cassville from Adairsville with his Twentieth Corps," Johnston continued. "General Polk, you will attack the Union center. General Hood, I want you to swing around and flank the Yankees' left. If this works, it will cripple Sherman's army and be a tremendous boost to our morale."

Sherman, believing Johnston would continue to move south toward Kingston, pursued cautiously over a network of roads toward the town. He was determined to cut off the Confederate path of retreat and supply along the railroad.

On the morning of May 19, as Polk and Hood prepared to spring Johnston's trap on Hooker, plans went awry. Hood failed to attack as he spied Union troops approaching Hooker on the Confederate's left. These forces were not where they were expected to be. Hood withdrew to protect his flank after a brief skirmish.

Johnston realized that Cassville would not be defensible and ordered a withdrawal to the Etowah River. That night his army slipped away again. Sherman pursued slowly as the Confederates continued to retreat south. Before crossing the Etowah, Sherman ordered a halt to rest, resupply and plan.

The Union general tugged on his red beard as he surveyed the rough, mountainous territory before him. "This ground will either slow Johnston to a crawl or lead us into a spot where we can catch him," he observed to McPherson and Thomas. "I want the quartermaster to issue twenty days' rations and ammunitions. We're going to catch that slippery devil."

"How do you propose to do it?" Thomas asked.

"We'll abandon the railroad and swing around the Confederate left in a wide sweep. We'll move fast without tents or other baggage. If we can move quickly enough, we can get behind Johnston and force a retreat south of the Chattahoochee River close to Atlanta."

"It sounds doable," Thomas agreed, "but I'm bringing my tents. Let me know if you need one."

Johnston retreated across the Etowah, still looking for the right moment to attack. Sherman's men rested and waited. After Hooker was sent to flank Johnston, the Confederate commander ordered a defensive line stretching from west to east through three little towns: Dallas, New Hope Church, and Pickett's Mill.

A battle for position resulted with Sherman first trying to move around the rebel left and then the right. Fights occurred at each of the three towns with no conclusive results. Johnston continued to move the pieces of his army, always staying ahead of Sherman. Then the Union Army shifted back to its supply line, the railroad. The Confederates shifted along with them and moved onto Kennesaw Mountain.

Watching from the mountain were Joe Johnston and his corps commander, John "Sam" Bell Hood. Hood leaned heavily on a crutch as he peered into the darkness below. His left arm, crippled at Gettysburg, hung at his side. Most of his right leg had been left on the battlefield at Chickamauga.

A heavy beard hung from the general's thin face. It quivered slightly as he spoke in a low voice to Johnston. "We should hit them, Joe. We've been holding back too long."

"I know you're schooled in the offensive tactics of General Lee, Sam. Your attack ruined Rosecrans at Chickamauga. Lee made you a general after Seven Days. But that was a different time and place," Johnston replied. "What was right to do there isn't right to do here. We have to keep moving. Thank God we have cavalry to be our eyes so we know where and when. Besides, Sherman wouldn't be so foolish as to attack this position, and we certainly can't attack him."

"I wouldn't be so sure, Joe. I think old Uncle Billy might be paying us a visit soon. His supply lines are a mess back in Tennessee."

Johnston nodded. "Sherman has to worry about us in his front and also three hundred miles to the rear. Forrest was sent there to disrupt his support and to cut the railroad, and he's being successful. As soon as Sherman began his campaign on Atlanta, I ordered Forrest to move into middle Tennessee."

Hood laughed. "I believe he said, 'I'll put a real skeer in 'em.'"

"He's got 'em a lot more than 'skeered.' Sherman will send an army after Forrest. He can't let him roam free."

* * *

IT STARTED TO RAIN on June third in northern Georgia. It rained for eleven straight days, making Sherman's flanking maneuvers impossible over the quagmire created on the glutinous red mud roads. Union lines had extended beyond Confederate lines at Marietta, causing Johnston, fearing envelopment, to withdraw nearer Kennesaw Mountain.

"We've only covered a hundred miles in seventy-four days," William Sherman noted. "Johnston has now fallen back astride Kennesaw Mountain with an arc-shaped defensive line to the west of Marietta. I'm getting tired of this chess game."

Sherman peered into the drizzle from beneath a canvas canopy in front of his tent. He turned to his generals: George Thomas, Jim McPherson, and John Schofield. "They're dug in on that mountain with a line stretching out on both sides, to those lower mountains close by. They have a line out front. We're stalled here, just like Grant at Petersburg."

"We can't flank them," Thomas agreed. "We can hardly move the six miles back to the railhead for supplies."

Sherman grumbled, "Nearly two weeks of rain. That and this constant maneuver and entrenchment without a battle is dulling our fighting edge. A fresh furrow in a plowed field will stop the whole column and all begin to entrench." The general pounded his fist into his left hand in frustration. "We are on the offensive, and we must attack and not defend!"

"Still, no matter what," McPherson noted, "the firing never stops. My men ignore it now, unless they are called to direct action. It just seems part of daily life. Some segment of the army is always under fire."

"A lot of shooting and not many casualties."

Sherman contemplated and then stated decisively, "I think it's time to hit him straight on."

With surprise in his voice, Thomas noted, "That's what he wants, General. This whole campaign you've avoided a direct assault. Schofield and I demonstrate against rebel lines while McPherson goes around the left flank and threatens their supply lines. Maneuvering is working. Johnston's falling back closer and closer to Atlanta."

Sherman sighed. "Look, the roads are all muddy. We can't maneuver. The men are tired of constant and apparently pointless marching. We outnumber them. We can push them off the mountain. Hood's with Johnston now. He's reckless. Maybe they'll do something foolish."

Schofield and McPherson exchanged knowing glances. Schofield remarked, "Jim and I know Sam Hood pretty well. We were both in his class at West Point. I was his roommate."

"He was reckless," McPherson continued. "He received 196 demerits. Two hundred is the limit before expulsion."

"And," Schofield considered, "I believe he graduated forty-fourth out of fifty-two in our class."

Thomas added, "I was his artillery instructor. Hood is one to take chances, with little regard to his personal safely. War has carved him down pretty good—a Comanche arrow through his left hand in 1857 in Texas, loss of the use of his left arm at Gettysburg, and he lost most of his right leg at Chickamauga."

"How can he ride?" McPherson asked.

Schofield said, "I've been told they strap him onto his horse. He's got a cork leg attached to his hip. I guess an orderly rides behind him with crutches. But, amazingly, I'm told he can make twenty miles a day tied to his horse. I concur; he is reckless and a gambler."

Sherman pondered. "We'll use that against him. He was from Kentucky, wasn't he?"

"Yes," Schofield responded. "His dad was a doctor there. He disapproved of his son's military career. After he graduated, Hood was sent to Texas. He kind of adopted the state, considers it his home now."

"At least they don't have Polk," Thomas reminded them.

Schofield laughed. "Funny thing, Hood was always a bit of a hellion. It seems last spring that he found religion. Bishop Polk baptized him."

"I liked the old bishop," Sherman replied. "Too bad a cannonball put a hole through him. Just a wound putting him out of commission would have done the trick."

"Supplies are running short," McPherson noted, changing the subject away from Hood. "We're not in dire straits, but it's getting serious. As fast as we rebuild a section of railroad, Forrest rips up another. Both middle Tennessee and northern Mississippi are menaced by him. Johnston's supply lines shorten as he nears Atlanta, but ours grow longer."

Sherman snapped, "I've ordered an expedition out of Memphis to follow Forrest to the death, even if it costs 10,000 lives and breaks the treasury. There will never be peace in Tennessee till Forrest is dead."

Back Home

AFTER THE RED RIVER CAMPAIGN the Fifth Minnesota, with the balance of the Sixteenth Corps, had steamed up the Mississippi to Vicksburg and disembarked there on May 24. The regiment was resupplied with clothing and equipment and ordered back up the Mississippi.

As the men prepared to board a steamer, Levi Carter spat a brown tobacco stream on the wharf, spittle clinging to the stubble on his chin. "What gits me, Jimmy, is that they said if we re-enlisted fer three years we'd git a thirty-day furlough back home."

"Most of us re-enlisted," Jimmy Dunn replied, "and we get sent to fight more. Not home."

Will Hutchinson added, "Maybe the fellas got it right who're just gonna serve out their original three-year enlistment and go home."

"When we do go on furlough," Jimmy said, "those folks stay here and fight wherever Gen'r'l Smith and Captain Sheehan tell 'em. We'll be back home with warm beds and good food."

"Don't forget warm girls, Jimmy," Will laughed.

"And don't forget," Levi reminded them, "that right now there's no furlough set, and we're in the same boat with fellas who didn't sign up again."

"They'll get around to treating us fair," Jimmy said optimistically. "I know they will. There were two letters from Lucy waitin' for me, but I want the real thing."

* * *

THE FIFTH MINNESOTA advanced up the river and fought a spirited battle when they experienced a blockage on the river from the Arkansas side at Lake Chicot. The regiment lit into Confederates at their position commanding the river and captured the post while driving off its defenders. Back on the boats, the Union soldiers reached Memphis on June 10.

There, the Fifth Minnesota received welcome news: those who had re-enlisted were to be furloughed back to Minnesota for thirty days. A grand reception awaited them in St. Paul.

The regiment colonel, Lucius Hubbard, assembled the regiment on a flat plain near the river and spoke to his soldiers.

"Gentlemen, most of you signed up for three years. This summer your enlistments would have been up. But it's evident that the war will not be over this summer.

"Some of you are new recruits, and we welcome you. But it's a certainty that experienced, veteran soldiers are greatly superior to newly enlisted men who must be trained. The question of re-enlistment is a personal one. You either have already, or must now, make that decision for yourselves.

"Whatever decision you make, there will be no distinction or discrimination made, or permitted, regarding those in the regiment who choose to re-enlist and those who do not. With due consideration, each of you must decide for yourself. Your decision will be respected.

"Those who decide to not re-sign will serve out their term of service on a campaign led by Captain Sheehan." Hubbard's voice rose to a shout. "Those who re-enlist will go back to Minnesota with me! On June seventeenth, we'll board a steamer and head to St. Paul for thirty days at home!"

Hundreds of voices thundered in approval. Then the chant of "Huzzah! Huzzah! Huzzah!" rose from the ranks. When all was said and done, nearly eighty percent of the regiment had or would re-enlist.

"Nice job," Will Gere complimented his colonel.

"Thank you. I picked up a few thoughts after hearing Judson Bishop address the Second Minnesota. Always pays to listen to a newspaperman. I've found that, if they can write, they can speak."

* * *

ONCE THEY PASSED into Minnesota, the residents of the little towns along the river turned out to line the banks and cheer the troops as the steamer paddled by. The boat would steer closer to shore as they passed, and the welcome cries of the people wafted over the men on board. Some towns had assembled their community bands playing patriotic tunes.

Jimmy Dunn eyed the lush, green banks of the Mississippi with excitement as the regiment's steamer chugged past Fort Snelling on the way to St. Paul. Above the boat, high on the bluffs overlooking the confluence of the

Minnesota and Mississippi rivers, was the limestone-walled fort, the oldest standing building in Minnesota.

A cannon blasted in salute, and blue-clad soldiers lined the walls, echoing cheers into the valley below. Jimmy and Levi Carr waved happily at them.

"Whatcha gonna do, Jimmy?" Levi said.

"After we dock at St. Paul, I'll be goin' back down to Chatfield as fast as I can. I wanna get home."

"I don't think we can go right home. We gotta march down the streets in St. Paul first, and then they got some sorta banquet for us."

"Well, Levi, let's eat fast."

Bands played and folks cheered as the boys of the Fifth Minnesota marched to a large hall, where speeches and food abounded. Then the men were set free. For the next thirty days they would be unencumbered by officers, duty, or military protocol. They were home.

It took Jimmy and the other Chatfield boys a couple of days to reach their homes. Jimmy paused at the city limits, slicked back his unruly brown hair, swatted dust off his blue uniform and straightened it out as best he could. Then he continued into the little town, heading for the small collection of stores known as "downtown."

It didn't take long to reach the Chatfield Hotel, a solid brick building owned and operated by Jimmy's father. Three people rose from chairs on the hotel porch and rushed into the street to greet the young man.

Jimmy's mother wrapped her arms tightly around her son. The man, Jimmy's father, waited patiently, beaming as if a deeply felt wish had been granted. He clasped his son's hand firmly. "Welcome home, boy."

"Ma, Pa, it's great ta be home."

His eyes locked on a pretty, young, blonde-haired woman who stood expectantly to one side, smiling broadly.

"Lucy!" Jimmy exclaimed as he rushed into her waiting arms.

"I thought you'd never get home," the girl cried with tear-filled eyes.

"I got me thirty days," Jimmy grinned as he held Lucy close.

That night the Chatfield boys were fêted at a picnic in the town park. Local politicians burst with pride extolling the virtues of their local heroes. Norm Culver, a man in his mid-forties, took his place on a makeshift platform.

Culver had been a lieutenant in the Fifth. He had fought through the Dakota War with them and had aided in the defense of Fort Ridgely. He had resigned and returned home due to injuries in July of 1863 after the siege at Vicksburg.

Leaning on a cane, Culver nodded in appreciation as his mates loudly cheered his appearance. "Men of the Fifth Minnesota," he cried, "Chatfield men! It was my great honor to serve with you. Your exploits will be forever enshrined in the lore of Filmore County. We can be proud of how you fought to save the Minnesota River Valley from desolation. How you marched with General Smith in the Red River Campaign and defeated another reb army in Arkansas. I know that when you return to the South, you'll help bring this ugly war to the glorious conclusion I'm sure God has ordained."

He paused, then somberly continued. "There are other Chatfield boys who aren't with us. Will 'Beecher' Gere, a colonel and a staff officer, is still with A.J. Smith. But his brother, Lieutenant Tom Gere, is here!"

The men burst into loud applause and slapped Tom on the back.

"Our newspaper editor, Judson Bishop, may be colonel of the Second Minnesota, but we have his brother, John, now a lieutenant as well, in our midst."

Again cheers resounded before Culver continued. "Colonel Josiah Marsh might be a lawyer from Preston, but he's a Filmore County boy and leads the Ninth Minnesota. Of course we remember with sorrow his brother, John, your captain, killed at Redwood Ferry by the Sioux." He paused a moment. "If I've made this sound like a family affair, it is. We have many sets of brothers, cousins, and even fathers and sons fighting together to save our Union. You have done us all proud, because we here in Chatfield are your family.

"My brother Charlie is here. For two years, starting at age twelve, he served as your drummer boy. He was sent home with an injury, but he's with us now to help us remember."

A slender young man with a drum strapped around his shoulders limped up to stand beside his brother.

Norm Culver proclaimed in a lower voice, "Let us have a moment of silence to remember those who will never come home to Filmore County."

The assemblage bowed their heads and stood quietly and respectfully. Then the slow, measured tapping of a mournful drumbeat began as Charlie Culver slowly played the "Death March."

Lucy reached over and grabbed Jimmy's hand. She whispered in his ear, "Jimmy, you make sure you come home to me."

Jimmy gazed down at the tear-stained cheeks of the young woman at his side and whispered back, "A whole tribe of Indians couldn't kill me. Don't worry about rebs. Hell will have ta freeze over ta keep me from you."

"Don't take chances, Jimmy. You did at Redwood Ferry and you did at Fort Ridgely, too."

"They woulda killed John Bishop if I hadn't shot first, Lucy."

"I know, but, Jimmy, you don't hafta try to be everywhere and do everything. Promise me. Don't take chances you don't need to."

Jimmy forced a smile, "Sure, Lucy, I'll be careful." He suppressed further thoughts of danger as he leaned down, closed his eyes and tenderly kissed the top of her head.

Chasing after Forrest

SAM STURGIS SAT IN HIS TENT south of Memphis with his cavalry commander, Benjamin Grierson. A single lamp cast a yellow glow across the bearded faces of the two men. Sturgis gazed across a small round table at the former music teacher he was depending upon to help him stop Forrest.

"We've got a big task ahead of us. We're to keep Nathan Bedford Forrest occupied and destroy his cavalry. Sherman's depending on us. We are to proceed to Corinth by way of Salem and Ruckersville, capture any force that may be there and then proceed south, destroying the Mobile and Ohio Railroad as we go."

"Where are we going, sir?" Grierson asked.

"Tupelo, maybe Okolona. Toward Macon."

"I've got 3,300 cavalry. How many infantry do you have?"

"Over 4,000, I have Colonel McMillan in command of them."

"So we have about 7,000. Last I heard, Forrest doesn't have over 4,000."

"But they're led by a devil. Forrest will stop at nothing. Look what he did at Fort Pillow."

Grierson nodded. "He killed 500 of our men," he said somberly. Many had fallen to their knees in surrender and then were ordered to their feet and shot down. Many were Negro soldiers. It was like waving a red flag before a bull, and they had been slaughtered by the rebels. Witnesses said the river ran red with the soldiers' blood.

Sturgis spat angrily on the ground. "Forrest justified it in a report. He said Major Bradford had refused surrender and this should demonstrate to the people of the North that Negro soldiers can't cope with Southerners. Nothing has stopped Forrest since."

"General, the devil belongs in Hell. Let's send him there."

"Agreed. It starts tomorrow. In the morning I'll meet with Colonel McMillan. He'll command our division of infantry. Three brigades are included: Wilkin with 2,000 men, Hoge with 1,200, and Benton with 1,200 colored infantry."

"How many supply wagons?

"Two hundred fifty, and twenty-two pieces of artillery."

"My cavalry's ready. Horses are well rested, blast the ornery beasts!"

"You don't like horses, General Grierson?"

"I hate them. I was kicked in the head when I was a boy. Almost killed me."

"So, my cavalry commander hates horses. Now, isn't that something?"

"My nag and I tolerate each other."

"Get a good night's rest. You and your horse. We head out after Forrest tomorrow."

* * *

THE NINTH MINNESOTA, Lieutenant Colonel Josiah Marsh commanding, disembarked on the morning of June 1. They marched to the Memphis and Charleston depot and boarded a train for LaFayette, Tennessee.

Thirty officers and 635 enlisted men carried three days' rations in their haversacks. Knapsacks, blankets, and camp equipage were left behind. The train stopped six miles from LaFayette. From there, the regiment marched into town, where Sturgis was busy organizing for the expedition.

The Ninth spent a gray, drizzly day in camp awaiting assignment. The men of Company G sat near campfires or in their tents playing cards, writing letters, napping or just talking. A black-haired young man with a dark complexion laid down his hand of cards and proclaimed to the three soldiers with him, "Full house!"

"Tarnation, Chief, you won again!" Sergeant Andy Hubbard complained. "You got some secret medicine you're using?"

"Ojibway medicine," Roger Aitkin smiled.

"Well, bring it into battle with you. We can use the luck," Hubbard grinned.

"I'll ask my cousins to do the same. We have over two dozen Ojibway in the regiment. That should be enough good luck for the whole regiment."

"Okay, Chief, I'm game for that."

"Sergeant, I'm not a chief, you know."

Hubbard laughed, "You're all chiefs to me. Just don't take no scalps."

Aitkin reddened slightly. "We don't do that."

"No offense, Chief. Hey," he pointed to a soldier speaking to a nearby group, "ain't that Frank Merchant, Company K sergeant?"

"Sure is," Private John Kern agreed. "Now there's a real hero."

"They threw him in jail back in Jefferson City."

"He did what was right," Kern countered. "I met him, and he told me what happened."

Hubbard sobered. "We all heard stories about it. But if you got the story from the horse's mouth, don't keep it in. Tell us."

Kern took a breath and began. "It was back in November last year. Companies O and K were in camp at La Mine Bridge. A Negro came into camp, a slave. He said he'd traveled all night and that his wife and family had been taken from him by slavers. They were going to be shipped to Kentucky to be sold, and the train they were on would reach Otterville in an hour. He begged the men for help."

"What could they do?" another soldier asked. "Missouri's a slave state."

Kern answered, "They didn't care about that. This is a war to end slavery. Merchant said, 'I'm gonna help. Who's with me?' Forty men marched with Merchant to the depot. When the train pulled in, a squad of boys drew a bead on the engineer and told him to wait. The rest of the boys entered cars looking for the Negro family. When they found them, they told them to get out and head for the woods."

Hubbard interjected, "Too bad there was a high-ranking Missouri officer on board. I heard he drew his revolver and tried to stop Merchant and his boys."

"They got a little rough with him," Kern admitted. "The Negroes got away, the train left and the forty-one got arrested."

"We all know how it ended," Hubbard said. "The boys spent two months in the guard house in Jefferson City. Finally folks back home got wind of it, and Senator Wilkinson brought a resolution of inquiry to the U.S. Senate demanding to know why Minnesota soldiers were detained in prison for the offense of freeing slaves held by rebel sympathizers. That ended it, and the boys from companies O and K became heroes."

"They were good boys," Corporal Sam Horton nodded. "The Ninth is a great regiment. It's taken two years to get us all together, and it's about time."

"Ya know, Sam," Hubbard agreed, "yer right, but it's because we're so good they kept some of us guarding the Minnesota frontier, others chasin' Sioux in Dakota with Sibley and still others in Missouri and Kansas. They were afraid what might happen if they let such a great regiment all git tagether."

"They'll find out now," Roger Aitken concluded.

* * *

THE MEN OF THE SECOND MINNESOTA ate, slept, wrote letters, and played cards and chuck-a-luck. With the dull smattering of gunfire sounding in the distance, the men of Company C, Second Minnesota, huddled miserably around their shelter half tents. A light mist dampened their spirits as surely as if a wet blanket had been tossed over them. Kennesaw Mountain loomed in the distance through the mist.

Four privates gnawed on hardtack, knowing it was too wet to even attempt a cook fire. Dan Black mumbled to his comrades, "I don't think the shootin' has stopped fer a month."

Bill Bingham countered, "Not exactly true, Dan. Sometimes it stops for jest a little at night. The quiet wakes me up. Makes me nervous."

Mike Rohan slurped from his canteen and remarked, "Tell you what I'm tired of . . . all this chasin'. Ever' time I think we got Johnston cornered, he just slips away ag'in. Why don't he stand and fight?"

"'Cause we got twice the men he's got," Johnny Cartwright noted. "He's doin' all he can do. Drag this out and wait fer a chance at us."

"So we keep on," Black continued. "March four miles one day, six the next. Then sit in one spot fer a few more days. It'll all end sometime."

Rohan picked up his rifle and ran a cloth down the barrel to clean and dry it as Cartwright took a needle from a pouch and started stitching together a hole in the elbow of his blue uniform blouse.

"Watcha doin', Mike?" Black asked. "Yer gun will jest get wet again."

"Then I'll dry it again. At least the flash pan. The powder's gotta be dry."

Sergeant Bill Cassidy approached the four. "We got orders, boys. Tomorrow morning it's our turn in the front. It seems they want a line on that ridge up there." He pointed to a spot about 300 yards from the mountain. "We git ta dig a trench out there."

"Dig . . . in . . . this . . . mud!" Rohan spat out each word like it was a bitter pill.

"It's not our job to reason," Cassidy reminded him, "just to do. Now, make sure you've got forty rounds in your cartridge boxes and three days' rations in your haversacks. The supply and ammunition wagons are in the rear if you need them. Oh, and make sure you have your spades with you."

* * *

ON JUNE 18, the Second Minnesota moved in advance of Sherman's army. In a light rain they slogged over slippery red mud toward the ridge before the Confederate position. The rebels had withdrawn to a breastworks before the mountain and eagerly loosed artillery and rifle shot at the Minnesotans.

Each Union soldier lay prone on the earth, flat in the mud with a gun by his side and knapsack at his head. In that awkward position they began to dig, throwing the dirt up ahead and working toward the soldiers to the side. After about fifteen minutes the digging line would be replaced by another line of soldiers held in reserve.

In spite of the sporadic rebel fire, progress was made with no casualties. Suddenly a Union six-gun battery rushed into the fray, nearly running over the digging soldiers.

"Tarnation!" Dan Black shouted. "What is this for?"

The battery became a target, and Confederate cannon opened up on them. "What fool ordered this?" Bill Bingham exclaimed. "They got no cover and the rebs do. It's like they jest put a big target out there for the rebs ta shoot at and we're in the middle of it!"

After a few minutes the Union battery withdrew, leaving Lieutenant Jones of the Second dead and eleven soldiers wounded. The digging, suspended during the attack, was resumed. Once the new line was established, the Union troops' effective fire drove the Confederates back from their line to a new fortified line with Kennesaw Mountain in the center.

It was back to waiting. The Union camp spread out behind the entrenched breastworks. Several times a day, Confederate guns opened up from their mountain positions. Tod Carter watched with General Thomas Benton Smith as the Union soldiers scrambled and raced for the protection of their trenches whenever they saw a puff of smoke from Confederate guns.

Tod laughed. "Look at them scatter. It's just like putting a stick in an ant hill and stirring it up to make them run."

"Our guns cover their whole campground," Smith observed. "They huddle for cover like they all have girlfriends and mothers that they don't want to distress."

"We don't want them to get comfortable," Tod remarked.

"They'll be coming up here soon enough, Captain. I believe Sherman thinks he can take us. He doesn't like head-on attacks unless he is confident he has the advantage. He'll find how mistaken he is."

Nathan Bedford Forrest

THE TALL, WELL-MUSCLED OFFICER poked a stick into a campfire and gazed into the glimmering red sunlight fading into the western horizon. Bedford Forrest turned to his son, William, an eighteen-year-old captain. "We've been camped here a couple of days, Bill. The men needed rest, but we've gotta keep movin'. The Yanks will be comin' after us, and I never like to stay in one place long enough to be attacked. I met with General Lee yesterday—Stephen, not Robert. He had word that Grant's sent Sturgis to stop us. I expect his goal is Tupelo. Lee wants us to continue to raise hell in Sherman's rear and cut his supply lines. But Sturgis will outnumber us two to one. That could give us some trouble. We have to find a spot to block his advance."

"It don't make no difference, sir. They can't stop you," his son said.

People called Forrest the "Wizard of the Saddle." He had no military training, but was a plantation owner who dealt in land and slaves to make his millions. Even so, he went from private to general in three years, and had a reputation as a genius at war.

The elder Forrest chuckled. He brushed a hand over his wide forehead to his wavy, dark hair. The bushy black beard shook as he began to laugh. "I wuz fortunate. Don't be listening to too many folks or readin' too many newspapers. I'm not perfect or immortal, I just do what comes naturally. Don't over-think things, boy, jest do 'em."

"Like when we was chasin' that Yankee general, Streight?"

"He was tryin' to cut our supply lines. Foolish of him."

Forrest and his men had chased and harrassed Streight for sixteen days, finally catching them at Cedar Bluffs, Georgia. Forrest's forces had been out-numbered, but that hadn't made a difference—Forrest just paraded his men up and around the same hill, over and over. Streight didn't figure out they were the same boys, thinking they were going up against a force of thou-sands, so he gave up.

The general grimaced as he stood up from the fire and rubbed his hip.

"Sore?" his son asked.

"Jest a little."

"You gotta stop gittin' shot."

"Jest a couple of times."

"Sir, don't take such reckless chances. We need you. The South needs you. Yer jest forty years old."

"Then they should use me better. We coulda had Rosecrans after Chickamauga. We won the battle, but then Bragg let him escape to Chattanooga. I wanted to cut Rosecrans off. What the hell does Bragg fight battles for, anyway, if he don't finish 'em off?"

The two were quiet for a moment, and then William spoke again. "Sherman is on his way to Atlanta."

"So we have our task before us. The Yanks have a long supply line. All the way to Nashville. Ol' Cump needs it. So far we've bin givin' 'im fits, and we'll keep on doin' it."

"They'll be comin' after us," William responded, "and they'll do better than Streight."

"Yer right. Grant and Sherman will be sendin' better armies our way. Sherman depends on the supply lines we've bin rippin' up. He finally got movin' and he's zig-zaggin' all over north Georgia chasin' after Joe Johnston. But Sherman can't keep it up unless he's adequately supplied. It's our job to make sure he isn't."

The Battle of Brice's Crossroads

C OLONEL RUCKER," BEDFORD FORREST said to one of his commanders, "Sturgis is on the way. By the tenth of June we'll have him in the bag."

"How do you see it playing out, General?" Rucker asked.

"I know they greatly outnumber the troops we have at hand, but the road they'll march along is narrow and muddy what with all the drizzle and rain we've had this week. They'll make slow progress. The country's densely wooded, and the undergrowth's so heavy that, when we strike, they won't know how few men we have."

Then General Forrest tapped his chin in musing. "Their cavalry will move out ahead of the infantry. They should reach the crossroads three hours in advance. Yes, likely that long, I think. We can whip the cavalry in three hours. As soon as the fight opens, they'll send back to have the infantry hurried up. But what good will that do? It's going to be hot as hell, and coming at a run over five or six miles over such roads, especially just trampled by horses, their infantry will be so tired we'll ride right over them, too."

"It sounds good, General. You think the sun will shine tomorrow?"

"Colonel, tomorrow will be a bright day all around."

* * *

STURGIS HAD MADE SLOW but steady progress in pursuit of Forrest. His army slogged through heavy mud, some days making almost ten miles, other days barely five. On the eighth of June, scouts reported Forrest was near. Through much of the campaign the Ninth had brought up the rear of the column, often not getting into camp until 11:00 p.m.

On June 10, Colonel Marsh ordered his men to fall in at 7:00 a.m. They were to reach Wilkin's First Brigade and fall in behind the Ninety-third Indiana. The sun lifted their spirits as the week of damp, gray skies evaporated.

But trudging through sticky mud that sucked at their worn shoes while the sun grew hotter caused many to wish for the cool drizzle to return.

At 10:30 a.m., Grierson's patrol under Waring encountered rebel scouts on the bridge over Tishomingo Creek. The Union horsemen pursued the rebels as they galloped to the east past Brice's Crossroads.

Colonel Lyon's First Cavalry Brigade thundered into the pursuing Union force. Forrest shouted to Lyon, "Pin 'em down. Keep 'em busy! I need time ta move my boys up. Grierson's cavalry formed up at the crossroads a mile behind. We've got ta whip them here within three hours, before the infantry can git here!"

Grierson commanded Winslow's Brigade to join Waring in the fight in front of them. Forrest ordered Rucker's brigade and Johnson's force into the fray, and the battle line stretched out north and south. Both sides dismounted and fought on foot, with every fourth man holding three horses for the combatants. A fierce firefight raged along the line.

Grierson summoned an aide. "Tell General Sturgis to hurry up. We can't hold here long. We need to fall back to make a stand at the crossroads. We need his infantry!"

The messenger galloped to the rear as Grierson urged his cavalry to hold on. Sturgis was several miles to the west. His men were already fatigued from the tough morning march. Just after 11:00 a.m. the Ninth Minnesota received word that the cavalry was engaged some four miles ahead.

Andy Hubbard relayed the order. "All right, boys, ya might be tired, but there's a fight up ahead. Orders from Colonel McMillan himself. Double quick! Let's go!"

The regiment double quicked for three hours through muggy, hot air and boot-grabbing mud. The arduous trek left the lucky fatigued and wringing wet with sweat. The unlucky collapsed from exhaustion or sun stroke.

When they reached Brice's Crossroads, the infantry formed a line along the road. Grierson's beaten, done-in cavalry were allowed to pass through the line and retreat to the rear. As Sturgis's infantry took hold, Forrest ordered his dismounted cavalry to hit the flanks at each end of the Union line.

At first the Union infantry blunted the Confederate attack as they poured shot into them. As each regiment came up, they were formed in line of battle and ordered forward with no support on the flanks.

Marsh ordered his regiment to sit down and rest after reaching the battle line, but within five minutes the Ninth was ordered to take a position on the road to the right of the Union batteries, relieving the Ninety-third Indiana.

Privates Roger Aitkin and Fabian LeFebore struggled through dense undergrowth as they reached their position on the right. "Where are they, Rog?" LeFebore shouted. "I can hear 'em, but ya can't see more than a couple dozen yards in this stuff!"

"We'll see 'em soon enough. Here they come!"

The advancing rebels hit the Union right and formed a line directly before the Ninth. Captain Barret shouted, "Lie down and wait, hold fire until I give the order!"

The Confederates advanced cautiously until they neared the Union line. Then the Ninth unleashed a horrific volley that ripped into the rebel line, causing mayhem and driving them back. The rebels regrouped and tried to flank the Ninth.

Marsh screamed, "Charge into them, boys! Charge!"

A wild cheer emitted from hundreds of Minnesota throats as they smashed into the rebels, causing them to flee. The Ninth launched a frantic pursuit after them. But as soldiers dropped after being hit from behind, Colonel Marsh made a reluctant decision. He called to Barret, "Our own grapeshot is hitting our men the farther out we get. Bring them back to our original position!"

"But we're pushin' 'em back!"

"It can't last, Captain. We'll lose too many men! We've been ordered back to the road to support the left."

Meanwhile, Forrest ordered his batteries to unlimber and move on the Union center. "Concentrate fire!" he commanded. "I want canister shot. We'll hit 'em like one big shotgun!"

With a roar in the center of the line, Confederate cannons exploded with a blast of fire and smoke. "General," Colonel Alexander Wilkin cried, "we have massive damage in the center of our line! What do you want done!"

"Tighten the lines in a semi-circle facing east!"

In mid-afternoon, with the troops desperately holding on, word came to Sturgis that Forrest's men were attacking the bridge over Tishomingo Creek behind them. Sturgis made a fateful decision. He called to his officers, "They're closing in our front, and now they're trying to cut us off from behind. We've got to retreat."

"My boys still have fight in them!" Alex Wilkin shouted above the din of gunfire.

"Then cover our withdrawal, Colonel. Order a retreat!"

An orderly departure quickly turned into panic as the Union soldiers ran to safety. The Ninth followed behind them, carefully covering the retreat. The fighting became fierce as the Minnesotans stubbornly held on in 100-degree heat.

Forrest's men moved in, pushing the Union troops before them and capturing any who straggled. Two thousand seventeen boys in blue were wounded or captured, including 233 from the Ninth, most of whom had collapsed from exhaustion in the heat and humidity. Drenched in sweat, they were herded into captivity.

"By God, General Forrest!" Colonel Rucker exclaimed as he stared at the captives and the battlefield. "This all happened just like you said it was going to."

Forrest looked at his subordinate and smiled. "Sometimes I git lucky."

Behind Union lines, Wilkin summarized the battle with Colonel Marsh. "It was a disaster. The men were undersupplied and underfed, on half rations, then made to fight after running for three hours in this heat. I didn't want to order you to attack. But I was under orders to do so. I'm sorry."

Marsh shook his head. "My boys fought well, Colonel, and our Indians were among the best. You should be proud of them."

"I am. It was just all too much. I spoke with Colonel McMillan, and he's most grateful for the your efforts and that of your regiment. Yours was the only regiment he had left in reserve to drive the rebs back and re-establish his line. He told me the gallant work of the Ninth Minnesota under the heroic Marsh saved the army at that critical moment from utter defeat and probable capture. You'll be getting a written commendation from him. But the fact is, we didn't have a chance the way it all played out. This will go down as the best battle Forrest ever fought."

"And it should be the last one for the great General Sturgis," Marsh commented sarcastically.

Wilkin agreed. "It was like Forrest knew everything, just how it would all happen."

"He is the Wizard of the Saddle. But we deserved to have been led better."

Lincoln

THE PRESIDENT OF THE UNITED STATES sat glumly before a telegraph on the table before him. A heavy-set, thickly bearded man stood alongside. They were in the War Department headquarters, and Abraham Lincoln was with his secretary of war, Edwin McMasters Stanton. Lincoln held a strip of paper in his hand. He looked up at Stanton and muttered, "Sturgis made a mess of it. Forrest routed him at a place called Brice's Crossroads. When he gets to Memphis, he's resigning."

"We'll send him west," Stanton suggested. "Maybe he'll have better luck against Indians."

"I've got the melancholies, Mr. Stanton. Nothing is going right. Grant is grinding to a standstill outside of Petersburg, Sherman's playing tag with Johnson in Georgia, and now Forrest makes a fool of Sturgis.

"I just received this communication from Sherman at Kennesaw Mountain. He reports that the whole country is one vast fort, and Johnston must have at least fifty miles of connected trenches with abatis and finished batteries. He says they gain ground daily with continuous fighting and the lines are in close contact with a good deal of artillery.

"I swear, Stanton, it seems as fast as we gain one position, the enemy has another already. Sherman thinks Kennesaw is the key to the whole country, and he pledges to break the stalemate. I pray to God he can do it. We need some good news."

Lincoln reached into his tall, dusty black hat on the table and took out a folded sheet of paper.

As he opened it, he remarked, "I just received this from General Sherman. He writes, 'But Forrest is the very Devil, and I think he has some of our troops under cover. I have two officers at Memphis that will fight all the time—A.J. Smith and Joe Mower. I will order them to make up a force and go out and follow Forrest to the death.' He says more, but that's the essence."

"Mr. President, Smith's a very determined and capable commander. If anyone can stop Forrest, it's him. That's good news."

"Promising, but it hasn't happened yet." Lincoln paused as a sadness deepened over his lined, bronzed face. "Newspapers want me to call it quits. They say if I don't the Republican Party will surely face disaster in the November elections. I'm a dead goose to be sure. Salmon Chase, my own treasury secretary, is making noise about opposing me. How 'bout you, Mr. Secretary? Do you want to be president, too?"

"Hardly," Stanton replied. "Maybe a Supreme Court justice someday. But we have a war to win first. It can still be done. The rebels are just trying to string things along. Sure, they're fomenting opposition to you in the North, but McClellan can't beat you for president, and we'll be furloughing soldiers to let them vote. They'll be your salvation."

"No," Lincoln replied, his voice trembling. "I've had dreams. The army won't vote for me. Look at what I've put them through. All the dead, all the families without fathers. No, they won't be voting for me, Stanton."

"Mr. President, things will change. The Confederacy is running short of men, supplies, and money. They hoped to get France and England on their side, but you ended that possibility when you issued your Emancipation Proclamation. You turned this from a war to preserve the Union to a war to free the slaves. It's working, even if I didn't fully agree with your strategy."

"You may be right. But time's on their side. They just need to hold on, and not for years, maybe just till November."

"Time is on *our* side. We have the men and resources."

"But we'll lose the support of the people if they don't see hope of victory. A disillusioned people will not wait an indeterminable amount of time for success. They've waited long enough, and they want this war to end. I don't think we have a year. The best hope for the Union and for the election are with Sherman. His task is to tie up Confederate forces so that they can't help Lee and to take Atlanta. He's done the former. We must have the latter. Grant's future success and my reelection depend in large measure upon General Sherman. If he fails, I fear the election will surely be lost and McClellan will sue for peace."

"The end is coming, sir. We will prevail. Just take care of yourself. Washington is a Southern town, remember. You shouldn't take solitary rides to the outskirts of the district."

"I'll be fine," Lincoln chuckled. "I have you, my 'God of War,' to protect me."

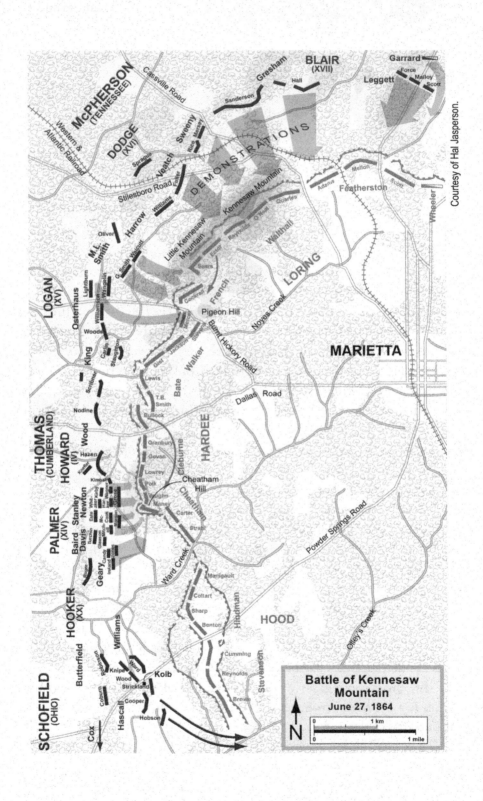

Battle of Kennesaw Mountain
June 27, 1864

Battle of Kennesaw Mountain

SHERMAN GATHERED HIS COMMANDERS behind Union lines with Kennesaw Mountain in the distance. They stood in a small clearing as Sherman began to rant. His glowing red face matched the red in his hair.

"It's been over two weeks since Forrest chased Sturgis back to Memphis and a week since the Minnesota boys tried to trench on the mountain slope! Enough of this side action! We've maneuvered for over two months and gone a hundred miles. That blasted mountain, all 700 feet high of it, is in our path. And the damn mud is still everywhere! The rebs dug in like gophers.

"That's it, gentlemen! We're taking that mountain. In three days, the twenty-seventh, we will feign on both flanks and launch a full-scale frontal assault. You'll have to go through dense thickets, steep and rocky slopes, and swamps. Once you get by that, you'll run into the rebs' trenches and abatis. But you can do it!

"McPherson, at 8:00 a.m. your army will feint on the northern end of Kennesaw. Logan, you'll take my corps and assault Pigeon Hill on the southwest corner. Capturing the hill will isolate Loring's corps on Kennesaw. At the same time, General Thomas, you'll launch a strong attack against Cheatham Hill in the center of the Confederate line. Schofield, strike their left flank. This is critical because it'll cause Johnston to thin out and weaken his line. We have great numerical superiority. We should overwhelm them."

"General," George Thomas asked, "you've always had an aversion to frontal assaults. Why the change?"

"Because I'm tired of toying around with Johnston and tired of being toyed with. I think we have the men and firepower to make this work. Besides, the mud makes it impossible to keep flanking. Atlanta's fifteen miles away, along with the intersection of four railroad lines crucial to supplying the Confederacy. Its capture will open the entire Deep South to Union conquest. It must be done. It may cost us dearly, but the results will surpass an attempt to pass around."

* * *

ON THE NIGHT of the twenty-sixth, the still of the darkness was an omen to both sides that something was about to happen. Captain Clint Cilley, adjutant to General Schofield and former commander of Company C of the Second Minnesota, stopped by the campsite of his former mates.

"Good to see you, Harry." he said, shaking hands with Lieutenant Couse.

"You're always welcome among friends, Captain," Couse returned.

"I just wanted to alert you. Thomas is going to hit the center. As part of Davis's division, I guess that means you could be in the thick of it. Keep your heads down."

"Thanks, Clint. Did you hear about Sergeant Wheeler?"

"No. He's a good soldier, time about up as I remember. What happened?"

"He was to be discharged on the morning of the twenty-third. The night before, we were sent out to relieve another regiment. Beautiful night, still, full moon. But the glimmer of rifle barrels could be seen in the moonlight. The rebs saw us. Next thing we saw was a bright flash, and then the ground opened up around us. Six were killed. We ran for the breastworks and endured a half hour of cannon fire hunkered down there. When it was over, we found that Sergeant Wheeler was one of the dead. In three hours it would have been over for him. I guess it was, anyway."

"That's a darn shame. What about Colonel Grant?"

"He took leave of us that next morning. He's never recovered his health. Judson Bishop's the Second's colonel now. You remember Mike Rohan and Bobby Dearmin? Their enlistments were up, too."

"Is General Schofield keeping you busy?"

"Just doing what a general's adjutant's supposed to do," Clint responded. "Publishing orders in writing, making sure orders get delivered to the right people, making sure camps get set up properly, letting the general know the needs of his men . . . just keeping records."

"No complaints from here, Captain."

"You'll do well with Bishop. He's a good man. Good luck, Harry. I've got to get back to General Schofield."

"Keep the general safe, Clint."

* * *

ON THE MOUNTAIN Tod Carter, aide-de-camp of General Smith, watched the movements below. Colonel Shy of the Twentieth Tennessee stood beside him. "Look, Lieutenant, you can just see them in the moonlight. They're movin' around plenty down there. Your men are well fortified. Dug in, head logs set, nearby trees cut and branches sharpened for abatis barriers, vines and tree limbs locked together. You're ready if they come."

"Captain, I 'spect we'll be plenty busy tomorrow, and it'll be a hot one. I kin feel it comin'."

"Have the boys ready. Hell's gonna break loose."

* * *

JUNE 27 DAWNED still and quiet with the sun soon blazing. Men on both sides waited and watched, their faces tense, apprehensive. The stillness was broken by the sound of a woodpecker hammering his beak into a hollow tree.

Then their world exploded. At 8:00 a.m., Union artillery unleashed a tremendous bombardment. Over 200 cannon burst smoke, flame, and shot into the Confederate works. In moments the rebels responded in kind, and Kennesaw Mountain blazed with fire.

From under the head logs, rebel marksmen poured hot shot at the advancing Yankees. One young blue-clad soldier scrambled up the mountainside only to be cut down ten yards from the Confederate line.

As his Union compatriots fell back, a young man cried wretchedly for help. "Water, water, for God's sake. Please give me water!"

A rebel sergeant grabbed a canteen and climbed past the barricade to hand the grateful boy the container of water. He started back to his battle line when a Yankee, hidden behind a tree, fired a shot into the good Samaritan's back.

His enraged friends poured shot back down the slope. The wounded boy, maybe sixteen, begged, "Let me climb up there. I don' wanna die here!"

"Crawl over here and we'll help ya over the log head!" a man yelled.

The grievously wounded boy struggled up the slope and painfully reached up for help when he finally made it to the earthen wall. Two rebels reached down and began to pull him over when more shots zipped from below, riddling the Yankee's body.

"Damn you," a rebel soldier screamed. "You're little more than murderers!"

An infantry assault followed a half hour later. Logan's corps hit the southern end of Little Kennesaw Mountain at the spur known as Pigeon Hill, near the points where small streams divided Johnston's center from his two wings. Rebel soldiers behind breastworks poured fire into the Yankee soldiers as they struggled through thick brush and steep rocky slopes. To the right, Union troops were forced to advance through a knee-deep swamp. Short of the Confederate breastworks on the south end of Pigeon Hill, the boys in blue were cut down by enfilading fire on both sides.

Fighting centered on the spur as Union soldiers launched attack after attack. Shy's Tennesseans continued to pour shot into them. They fell before the rebel line in stacks like cordwood. To the left, some of the troops managed to reach the abatis after scrambling over and around rocks. But most didn't make it and sought refuge behind rocks and trees where, drenched in sweat and streaked with blood and dirt, they returned fire.

Two miles to the south, Thomas's troops were behind schedule. At 9:00 a.m., 9,000 men advanced against the Confederate center. Rather than the usual broad line of battle, they came in columns against the Confederate divisions of Cheatham and Cleburne as they attempted to mass power against a narrow point. Farther to their left, Wagner's Union brigade wrested through dense undergrowth but was unable to break through the abatis and fierce rifle fire.

Above, the sun scorched the earth. Temperatures reached 100 degrees in what shade there was as Yankees fell back from the breastworks to regroup.

Davis's command slashed into the center. The Second Minnesota was held in reserve and saw little active action. Colonel Daniel McCook raced down a slope to a creek and crossed a wheatfield to charge up a hill defended by Cheatham. The colonel reached the Confederate parapet, slashed his sword and screamed, "Surrender, you traitors!" An instant later, he was cut down. Ferocious hand-to-hand fighting continued at an angle in the line. Once again, the dead fell in piles.

An eerie calm settled over the battlefield as the Union soldiers stumbled down and away. Tod Carter gazed over the destruction before him. He surveyed the dead and wounded Yankees but was alarmed when he viewed his own men in various stages of collapse all around. Broken and exhausted, drenched in sweat and blood, they sought any shade they could find. Some were on their hands and knees, vomiting.

A young private looked up at Tod. The boy's face was black from gun powder and marked by white streaks from sweat. His lips and tongue were parched and cracked from want of water. His voice a harsh croak, he whispered, "Sir, do ya got any water? Jest a sip?"

Tod swished his canteen. There wasn't much more than a sip in it, but he knelt down and dribbled what was left down the boy's throat.

Union assaults had failed at all points along the Kennesaw line except on the far right, where Schofield's demonstration on the rebel left put two brigades across a creek without resistance.

In the rear, Sherman conferred with Thomas. "Hit them again. Our loss is small, compared to some of those battles in the East!"

"General," Thomas replied, "one or two more of such assaults would use up this army."

The battle ended on the afternoon of June twenty-seventh. For five days the two armies faced each other at close range until a truce was called because of the sickening stench of the dead. Soldiers from both sides dug trenches and lowered the dead into them.

Sherman commented to Thomas, "This wasn't my first frontal assault. But it will be my last. I began to regard the death and mangling of 3,000 men as a small affair, a kind of morning dash. I won't forget this."

On July 2, Sherman's men flanked Johnston's left and the Confederate general was forced to withdraw from Kennessaw Mountain toward Smyrna. Six days later, Sherman flanked the rebels again, this time on the right by sending Schofield to cross the Chattahoochee near the mouth of Soap Creek. The last geographic barrier to Atlanta had been overcome.

The Second Minnesota had been held in reserve for most of the battle.

United under A.J. Smith

GENERAL ANDREW JACKSON SMITH received his new orders in Memphis—he was the next to be given the assignment of tracking down and defeating Nathan Bedford Forrest. His right wing of the Sixteenth Corps had reported to Memphis after the disastrous Red River Campaign. Still without a home, officially on detatched duty from Sherman's command, the Gorilla Guerrilas awaited barges to unite with Sherman in Georgia. It was not to be, not yet. They were rescheduled to head to Atlanta after first dealing with Forrest.

A.J. Smith stood with General Joe Mower on a platform watching troops pile into boxcars. It was June 22. "Soon the corps will be assembled, Joe. We'll head into northern Mississippi, Forrest's territory."

"These are good boys. They'll do the job."

"Sherman's high on you, you know. Calls you the boldest young officer in the army."

Mower's smile was barely visible on his heavily bearded face. "We have a lot of good fighters. Alex Wilkin, my First Brigade commander, is one of the best. Minnesota sent us a good one."

Mower had four Minnesota regiments in his division, the Fifth, Seventh, Ninth, and Tenth, together for the first time. Except for the Fifth, they hadn't had much experience fighting rebel forces, but that didn't mean they weren't fighters—they had all seen action against the Dakota, and after beating them in Minnesota, followed them into Dakota Territory and all the way to Yellowstone. They were hardened veterans.

"Seek and destroy Forrest," Smith told his general, "and then maybe we'll finally be able to join Sherman and be reunited with the left wing of the Sixteenth Corps."

* * *

NATHAN BEDFORD FORREST was headquartered in the small town of Okolona, Mississippi, not far from Tupelo. He stood outside his office on a boardwalk with his son William alongside.

"General Stephen Lee will be here soon, William. Smith's army is on the move. They're headed this way."

"What we gonna do, sir?"

"Wait a little, fool 'em a little, beat 'em, I hope."

An elderly woman in a long, gray, homespun dress approached hesitantly on the boardwalk. She gathered herself and looked Forrest directly in the eyes. "General, you are the last good hope we have out here. The Yankees can't beat cha. How do you keep beating them?"

Forrest smiled down at the woman. "Well, ma'am, I jest try to get there first with the most men."

"How do you know where to get to first?"

"Wherever I think the battle's gonna be fought, ma'am. I've got me a feeling right now the Yankees might be getting ready to strike somewhere along the railroad. That's why we're concentrated nearby."

"God bless you, General."

"Thank you. I need all the blessings I can get."

* * *

SMITH'S SIXTEENTH CORPS marched several days out of LaGrange without incident. On July 11, Forrest's advance forces encountered the Union forces at a hamlet called Pontotoc.

Following the fight, Smith's command continued a short distance beyond Pontotoc. They encountered a crossroads to the left going to Tupelo and the other going to the right, crossing a railroad.

Smith called up his division commander, Mower. "The rebs are watching us. I'm sure of it. Forrest plans to move ahead of us whichever turn we take. We'll take the right."

"But, General, I thought we were going to Tupelo."

"We are."

"Tupelo is to the left."

"I have a plan in mind."

The corps turned right, marched a few miles and went into camp. General Lee, now with Forrest, assumed that would be Smith's route and concentrated in front of the Union troops on that road.

Smith's forces stayed in camp all day on the twelfth. That evening he gathered his brigade commanders and explained to them, "We are not continuing along this road. I know the rebels are in force ahead of us. Come dawn, we'll march back to the crossroads and take the turn to Tupelo. We will double quick down the road."

"Brilliant, General." Wilkin reasoned. "You'll put the rebs in our right and rear trying to catch us."

Smith nodded. "We'll be entrenched outside of Tupelo before they know what's going on."

"They can't let us sit there," McMillan added. "They'll have to come after us."

"And we'll be ready and waiting," Smith concluded.

On the morning of July 13, the Sixteenth Corps put things into motion. By a rapid march, they headed back to the crossroads and took the left route toward Tupelo. The Seventh Minnesota had drawn train guard duty and marched most of the time out of the road through woods and fields, alongside the train of wagons and men. The Ninth, Tenth, and the partial Fifth marched on the road with the rest of the corps.

Once Lee and Forrest realized the ruse played by Smith, they organized to attack and head Smith off. Confederate General Buford was ordered to hit Smith's right flank. Forrest and Mabrey would assail the Union rear.

A spirited skirmish followed in a running fight that was kept up over ten miles. Rebel Brigade Commander Sam Chalmers dashed upon the federal wagon train. For a short time he held possession of the train and killed some of the mules before being driven off. The teamsters had to abandon and burn seven wagons, one caisson, and two ambulances.

Forrest launched an attack into the center of the Union line, manned by the Seventh and Fifth Minnesota. When the gray line advanced through the woods from the opposite side of the field from the Seventh, the Minnesota boys opened fire. The rebel soldiers raced like madmen across the field. The blood-curdling rebel yell screamed above the sound of gunfire.

A.J. Smith watched in amazement. "Look at 'em come!" he shouted to Mower. "They're howling and screaming like Comanches. It looks like they're in a foot race to see who can get to us first!"

"Hit 'em hard, boys!" General Mower shouted from astride his horse, just out of range on the edge of a woods.

The Seventh advanced and drove the rebels back, killing or wounding over a dozen. Then they passed an opening in the woods and came to where the Confederates were shelling the column with cannon shot.

"How'd they get cannons in there?" Mower shouted to Colonel Marshall.

"They're ours!" Marshall yelled back. "Our horses were disabled, and we had to leave 'em!"

"Keep your men in ranks, Colonel!"

"That'll be hard, sir! They're firing cannon shot at us!"

Mower watched as the men broke ranks and tried to avoid cannonballs. The general stood up in his stirrups and cried, "What are you dodging for? They won't hurt you!"

An instant later at shell ripped through Company B of the Seventh, tearing off the leg of Private George Blackwell. "Corporal," Marshall shouted to a soldier, "help him off the field!" Then he pleaded, "General, we need more men!"

"I'll send in the Ninth Minnesota. Keep the men moving!" Mower instructed. "We've gotta get to Tupelo!"

The Ninth was thrown forward and into the woods, where they formed a line and unleashed a blistering volley into the advancing rebels. Dozens threw up their arms and were driven hard to the packed earth by rifle balls.

Smith's corps reached the hamlet of Harrisburg, about a mile from Tupelo, that night. By the next morning they had taken a strong position and were entrenched. Alex Wilkin looked over the field with Josiah Marsh. "It's good ground, Colonel," he said. They were on a slight rise, at the summit of a growth of timber with an open field before them and excellent space behind for the wagons.

"Old A.J. has us ready," Marsh agreed. "We've got a line of men all along the edge of the woods both right and left of the Pontotoc and Tupelo road for about two miles. Two lines out front and one in reserve. The Fifth and Seventh Minnesota are in the center of our line."

"Are the men ready?"

Marsh squinted hard into the distance. "Yes, sir. Ammunition boxes have been sent up and down the line. Cannon batteries are placed in an excellent position to rake the open field and front, and the wagons are safe behind. All is ready."

Wilken nodded. "Sure don't look like Brice's Crossroads. I see the Ninth is in reserve."

"Three, four rods from the front. We'll be ready when needed. We always are. We're Smith's Guerillas, ya know."

Wilkin laughed. "Fight like you're in a jungle, then. They'll be coming at us soon."

General Stephen Lee surveyed the battlefield as well. Bedford Forrest stood at his side. They had reacted to Smith by forming lines with Roddey's brigade on the right, Mabry's brigade on the left, and Crossland's brigade in the middle.

"Your cavalry are some of the best infantry in the army," Lee noted to Forrest. "Today we'll find out how good they really are."

"We'll fight dismounted."

"Swing to the right first. I think they're weakest over there."

The attack did begin on the Union left. But Lyon's brigade became engaged first and was forced to fall back with heavy losses. Then Sam Chalmers's dismounted division moved forward and, after Mabry and Bell had been driven back, Rucker's brigade rushed into the fray but was also repulsed.

Alex Wilken watched from astride his horse to the rear. He proudly remarked to an aide, "They don't have a chance against us. Watch 'em fall. It's like oats at harvest time."

A moment later the brigade commander clutched his chest and tumbled from his horse. Wilken was mortally wounded.

For three hours, the Confederate forces heroically battled in the withering July heat. Some fell from exhaustion, while others were swept away by fire from the dug-in Union forces. The Minnesota troops in the center blasted into Forrest's attack. Finally they fell back, leaving dead in heaps on the battleground. It was just after noon.

Smith watched as the distant Confederates entrenched. "Should we hit them now?" Colonel McMillan asked. "There's still a lot of light."

"No," Smith mused, "there's time tomorrow. But let's make 'em pay some more. Rip up railroads and burn Harrisburg."

"Sir," McMillan hesitated. "Colonel Wilkin was killed, shot from his horse."

A hint of surprise and sorrow flashed across the general's face. "He was as brave a man as I've ever served with. Proficient in his duties and loyal to his men. It is a great loss to us."

* * *

ON THE MORNING of the fifteenth, Lee and Forrest made another attempt to uproot Smith's corps. They again smashed into the Union lines and engaged heavily for two hours with a great loss of men. At the head of his troops, Forrest mounted his horse and prepared to charge again. Suddenly he grimaced and cried out in pain.

"What's wrong?" William Forrest cried.

"I've been hit," the general announced. "My foot!"

His son looked down and watched as blood dripped from the heel of his father's right boot.

"I'll get you to the rear, sir."

Bedford Forrest, his face white, nodded slowly.

The Confederate attack at Harrisburg Crossroads outside Tupelo was over. Forrest had lost nearly 1,000 men, killed or wounded. Smith ordered a retreat to Memphis by way of LaGrange. Joe Mower countered, "Are you sure, General? Shouldn't we keep after Forrest?"

"We beat him badly, and we've ripped up miles of railroad track here. I think we've accomplished what we were sent to do."

"Are you sure, General Smith? Sherman wants Forrest's head. We don't have it."

"He's crippled. We'll get him later."

The Sixteenth Corps marched north the next day. They drove off occasional sallies by Confederate horsemen like swatting off flies. By the twenty-first of July they made LaGrange, where they boarded trains. The next day they were back in Memphis.

Once in his office, A.J. Smith soon found that Mower's concerns were real. A message was delivered from General Sherman severely castigating Smith. "You didn't follow up and capture Forrest when you had the chance," his superior admonished. "You will go back out in force and follow Forrest to the death."

This time with 14,000 infantry, including the four Minnesota regiments, and 4,000 cavalry, Smith returned to Mississippi. Nathan Bedford Forrest, unable to ride horseback, remained in Okolona tending to his wounded foot.

The Noose Tightens on Atlanta

AFTER WITHDRAWING FROM KENNESAW MOUNTAIN, Johnston's army formed a line at Zion Church. At dawn on July 4, a Union cannonade barrage spilt the pink stillness of the early morning sky. The Confederate artillery responded in kind, and throughout the day the heavens were alive with blazing fire and smoke.

The continual rumble and roar was like the sound of a thunderstorm that never ceased. Wad Carter called to his brother Tod, "It's like fireworks, like both sides are celebrating the Fourth of July."

"We need to celebrate something. I'd rather it was our independence!" Tod shouted over the roar.

Two hundred cannon kept up a duel throughout the day. It was the only fight, as cavalry and infantry were not engaged. Tod reported to General Smith, who noted, "A lot of noise and little damage. But I'm pretty sure General Johnston will have us moving."

"Do you ever get tired of it all, General?"

"The war?"

"Yes, sir, the war. I guess war in general."

"Captain, I went to school to be a soldier. Four years at Nashville Military and then a year at West Point. But then I decided maybe this wasn't for me, so I went home and went to work for the railroad. Those were good years. But when this war broke out, it was plain to me I had to follow my earlier path. It's what I believe I was meant to do. What about you? You were an up-and-coming lawyer. Already the best in Williamson County, I'm told. Is this what you want to be doing?"

"Until we are free from Yankee control, this is what I want to do," Tod replied.

"Captain, you're a quartermaster. You keep track of supplies and food. You don't have to fight. In fact, it worries me that you get yer nose a little too close to the action."

"It's hard to stay out of it."

"We all have our jobs to do. If we don't find a way to stop Sherman, it'll end badly for us, Captain. Atlanta's a key to the whole South."

* * *

JOHNSTON DID ORDER another withdrawal that night. The Second Minnesota was ordered to garrison duty at Marietta, where they camped on the beautiful lawn of ex-governor McDonald's homestead.

The Confederate Army crossed the Chattahoochee River, putting the river between its men and Sherman's. General Oliver Howard's Fourth Corps advanced on a pontoon bridge called Pace's Ferry, which was defended by dismounted cavalry. They drove off the rebels, but Howard decided not to cross the bridge because of increased Confederate forces on the other side.

The Union general determined to wait for more pontoons before forcing a crossing. Pickets and patrols on both sides of the river watched each other. Josh Owen, a private in the Twentieth Tennessee, stepped into the river to wash. A new recruit, Sam Huff, called out, "Josh, look out. There's Yankees right across and yer in full sight."

Owen smiled. "Ya got a lot ta learn. It's kinda an unwritten rule in war. This here river is a boundary, don't make no difference how big it is. We don't shoot across rivers at each other. That's jest the way it is."

He dipped his head into the stream and shook the water from his hair. Then Owen smiled and waved at the blue-uniformed soldiers on the other side. Two men waved back.

A day later, a cry came from across the river. "Johnny, O Johnny, Johnny Reb!"

A young Confederate private shouted back, "What do ya want?"

"When you gonna give up? Yer whipped, ya know?"

"We're not whipped yet, not by a long shot, and if ya think we are yer a liar and a coward!"

"Well, your General Johnston just got fired. Hood's your general now."

"Yer a Yankee liar. If you'll come out and show yerself, I'll shoot you dead in yer tracks."

"That's pretty big talk for a little boy. If others'll keep their hands off, I'll fight a duel with you."

Johnson Berry stepped out and shouted, "Billy, I don't think you should do this. But if yer set on it, here are the rules. You take yer places and fire at will across the river at each other. Shoot until one or both of ya are dead."

The two were better talkers than they were shots. They both missed their first shots. Then they fumbled and groped as they hurriedly tried to load and fire again. Six times they missed each other. On his seventh shot, the Union soldier's bullet found its mark, and young Billy crumbled to the ground dead.

"So, which was right?" a soldier asked.

"Maybe both," Josh Owen replied, "maybe neither. I guess we'll find out when they tell us."

The Rise of Hood

JOE JOHNSTON WAS A CAUTIOUS COMMANDER. John Bell Hood had urged his general to be more aggressive many times during the Atlanta Campaign. But Johnston, outnumbered at least two to one, continually reacted to Sherman's flanking maneuvers with timely withdrawals.

Now he was running out of time and space into which to withdraw. Crossing the Chattahoochee meant that the Army of Tennessee had left the last major water barrier before Atlanta.

Hood had done more than just urge a more aggressive approach to Johnston. He had also bypassed official communication channels and sent letters to government officials in Richmond castigating his commander's conduct of the campaign.

President Jefferson Davis, growing very alarmed at the situation in Georgia and after reading Hood's letters, decided to send his military advisor to Atlanta to personally interview Johnston.

General Braxton Bragg had previously led the Army of Tennessee, from Corinth to his defeat at Chattanooga, after which he had been replaced by Johnston. The change had a dramatic impact on his men, most of whom respected Bragg for his fighting spirit but despised his harsh treatment of his army.

As their army tried to hold off Sherman, now just miles from Atlanta, Bragg met Johnston at a house taken over for the occasion. Bragg sat at a desk across from Johnston. His dark eyes were piercing and restless. Bushy eyebrows and a grizzled, white-flecked beard gave him an untamed, some suggested ape-like, look.

"General Johnston," Bragg began, "President Davis is very concerned about the state of things here around Atlanta. What's your assessment?"

"I've done the best I could under the circumstances. I have less than half Sherman's men, and the Union Army is closing in."

Bragg responded, "Your tactic of continual withdrawal has brought Sherman to the doorstep of Atlanta. What you've done isn't working. We'll lose Atlanta."

"I don't know that anyone could hold it, given the circumstances and advantages the Union has. We're dug in behind earthworks and will fight like hell if they attack."

"We've received communication from some of your generals that you were urged to attack and refused to do so."

Johnston's face flushed a cherry red. "General Bragg, I did what I thought was prudent to succeed."

"All you're doing is losing land to Sherman," Bragg snapped. "The best thing you've done is get shot at Fair Pines, allowing Robert E. Lee to take command of the Army of Northern Virginia. General Johnston, General Lee is in much the same predicament facing Grant as you are with Sherman. Yet Lee has inflicted serious casualties on Grant by going on the offensive while you retreat and seldom engage. Lee's actions have saved Richmond. Similarly, Atlanta must be preserved for the Confederacy. The federal election grows near. If we still hold these two cities on Election Day, it'll go bad for Lincoln. I believe the Peace Party and McClellan will triumph."

"I'm to be relieved, aren't I?"

"What do you think? I'll let you know after I've completed my interviews."

Bragg stood tall and lean with the stature of a warrior. He perfunctorily shook Johnston's hand and directed the general out of the room.

As he left the house, Johnston encountered John Bell Hood, crutch under his right arm, entering the house. The commander glared at his subordinate with fire in his eyes and silently walked by.

Bragg greeted Hood warmly and seated him in the chair Johnston had just left. Bragg took his seat and regarded the officer across the table. Hood was tall and thin. His light-blue eyes were set in a pale face. He had a blond, tawny beard that extended well beyond his chin. It was said that his eyes shined with a glow in the light of battle.

Bragg asked, "How are you holding up, General? You're starting to look like prints of Don Quixote I've seen."

Hood laughed shyly. "I'm doing fine."

Bragg held up an envelope. "You've made some interesting comments in letters to President Davis. In these letters you say you and General Wheeler repeatedly urged General Johnston to be more aggressive."

Hood responded directly. "Sir, I've found General Johnston to be ineffective and weak-willed. I have, General, so often urged that we should force the enemy to give us battle as to almost be regarded reckless by the officers high in rank in this army, specifically Johnston and Hardee, since their views have been so directly opposite from mine."

"There are other generals, including General Hardee, who have expressed concerns that we have now retreated to Atlanta without an offensive measure. President Davis is concerned and has directed me to review our options here and make a recommendation to him."

"We should attack," Hood asserted. "I regard it as a great misfortune to our country that we failed to give battle to the enemy many miles north of our present position. Please say to the president that I shall continue to do my duty cheerfully and strive to do what is best for our country."

"I had considered Hardee, but I found him hard to deal with when he served under me before," Bragg said. "It seems the time to be a little reckless is upon us. I was a little hesitant about your age, only thirty-three, but you've packed a lot of experience into those years. You know how to fight and how to lead men."

Hood rose, standing as straight as he could on one leg and a crutch. "I'd salute you if I could," he told Bragg. "But are you sure the timing is right to change commanders?"

"We're running out of time, General. This can't wait."

Hood nodded. "Then I'll do everything in my power to save this country."

* * *

BRAGG QUICKLY RETURNED to Richmond to confer with President Davis. They met in the "Confederate White House," where Davis had a small office off his once-opulent living quarters.

Davis stood behind his desk. His tall, slender frame was bent with fatigue. His sunken cheeks framed a short, gray chin beard, but his eyes blazed bright as he addressed his military advisor. "We can't lose Atlanta, General Bragg. Foundries, factories, munitions plants, and supply depots have all sprung up there. The population has doubled to 20,000. One in four work in war production making uniforms, ammunition, and train rails, and it's the last railway hub we have. Its granaries supply Lee at Petersburg. It must be held."

"Then you need to replace Johnston with Hood," Bragg declared. "I was of the opinion before I went to Atlanta, and I'm more convinced today. Johnston has not been aggressive, and a calamity looms before us."

"What is the state of things?" Davis inquired.

"Johnston had two more defensive positions built between Kennesaw Mountain and the Chattahoochee River. He told a senator on July first that he could hold off Sherman for two months. It's been just over a week, and Sherman has crossed the river and gone through his defenses.

"Now we're entrenched behind earthworks surrounding Atlanta. Sherman's within five miles of the city. The Atlanta-to-Montgomery rail line has been cut. The line to Augusta is in great peril at Decatur. We only have one railroad line left, the Macon and Western, to keep us supplied from south of town. Something must be done to break the hold Sherman has on us. Only Hood can do it."

Davis stared intently at his desk top as if hoping an answer would magically appear. "General Lee is not of your opinion," he relayed. "He says that while Hood is aggressive, he's too reckless. All lion, none of the fox, that's how Lee summed up Hood." He thought a moment. "I'm going to telegraph Johnston," Davis decided. "I want to know his plan of operations. His future will depend on his answer."

On July 16, an aide brought the president's inquiry to Johnston. The general grabbed a scrap of paper from his desk, wrote on it and directed his aide to have the message sent to Davis. He had jotted in firm sentences, "My plan must depend upon that of the enemy. We are trying to put Atlanta in condition to be held by the Georgia militia, that army movements may be freer and wider."

In Richmond, Davis read the telegram and turned to Bragg. "General Johnston suggests an intention to give up Atlanta. That's the final straw. We will replace Johnston with Hood. See to it. We can't just sit and wait. We must take the fight to the enemy."

Johnston's demotion was conveyed to him late in the afternoon of July 17. The general read the dismissal and turned to an aide. "I'm not surprised by this," he said. "Call my commanders. I wish to speak with them."

Joe Johnston met with his division and corps commanders at a campsite looking down on the Chattahoochee.

Hardee, Cheatham, Cleburne, Clayton, Bate, Maney, Stevenson, Hindman, and Walker gathered around their general. Notably absent was John Bell Hood.

"Gentlemen," Johnston began, "the Union pontoons are set. Howard has crossed the river and outflanked us. We have no choice. That's why I've ordered a withdrawal to south of Peach Tree Creek. We're abandoning our river line."

"General," Patrick Cleburne remarked, "we're almost to Atlanta. We can't lose any more ground."

"I know. Gentlemen, it has always been my plan to isolate a Union command and hit it hard when we have near parity in numbers. We'll have that opportunity when the Yankees cross Peach Tree Creek. While they cross and before they erect barricades on the opposite shore, we have a chance at them. But I have one other comment. I will not be leading you in this battle. President Davis has seen fit to remove me as commander of the Army of Tennessee. General Hood will now lead you. I've conveyed my plan to him and he'll do as he likes with it."

Frank Cheatham sadly shook his head. "With Bragg advising him, I'm not surprised at the president's decision. But I don't agree with it. General, you have saved this army and kept it viable time after time. This has been a tough campaign. We've been fighting Sherman for four months straight, nearly every single day. But not once was our line broken. Not once were we routed off a battlefield. Your strategic retreats in the face of overwhelming odds have kept this army whole and enabled us to strike back. We've hit the Yanks hard and our men are still with you, loyal and ready to fight more."

Cleburne, his Irish eyes blazing, agreed. "The order must be remanded! It's dangerous to change the commander of this army at this particular time. We need to tell President Davis."

Hardee's face was flushed red with anger as he spoke out. "This will be a disaster. Bragg was bad enough. He treated the men like dirt. Hood will lead us into Hell with no way out. I'll resign before I serve under him."

Johnston sighed. "Thank you. Yes, General Bragg was a tough disciplinarian, but he's devoted to our cause. Apparently President Davis wants a more forceful approach. He'll get it from General Hood, although I consider it unwise. And you can't resign, General Hardee. We need you."

* * *

MEANWHILE, PROTESTS CAME to General Sherman about risking the safety of civilians, including women and children. He replied, "War is war and not popularity seeking." Sherman's tactics were fortified when Clint Cilley brought some men to his headquarters.

Clint addressed the commander inside Sherman's large wall tent. "Sir, General Smith sent me. I've brought six men with me. They've escaped from

Andersonville, the rebel prison camp not too far from here. You need to see them, sir."

Sherman followed Clint through the tent flap into bright sunlight. The general's face paled at the sight before him. The six men were walking skeletons. Through their filthy, ragged clothing, the outlines of bones and joints could be plainly seen.

"My God," he cried. "What have those animals done to you?"

"They didn't have no food, Gen'r'l," the tallest of them replied in a voice just above a whisper. "They jest kep' sending in more pris'ners, but not more food."

"How many are there?"

Another man croaked, "I heard a reb officer tell somebody there was 'round 30,000. But the graves be fillin' up."

Sherman's eyes blazed as he looked at Clint. "Captain, this puts complaints about shelling and burning their towns in perspective. The men at Andersonville must be freed. I'll send troops out as soon as practicable."

The Battle of Peach Tree Creek

EORGE THOMAS APPROACHED General Sherman's tent. It was actually one of Thomas's, but he had given it to his commander. He nodded at a sentry, who disappeared into the tent only to re-emerge with Sherman.

"Well, Cump," Thomas began, "our suspicions were correct. Johnston has been let go. Hood now commands the Army of Tennessee."

A smile lit up the general's face. "Pap, they couldn't have given us a better present if they'd wrapped it up with a bow. Johnston was good—cautious, but he had to be. Hood will make mistakes, and we'll make him pay. This is just what I wanted. We'll fight them on open ground, on anything like equal terms instead of being forced to run up against prepared entrenchments."

"Schofield and McPherson know him pretty well."

"I know, and I'll confer with them more about him. But you were his teacher."

Thomas wrinkled his nose. "He'll be brave and reckless. You're right. He will make mistakes."

"We're all across the Chattahoochee." Sherman explained, "I'm going to split us into three columns. You and the Army of the Cumberland on the left will move in from the north. You'll cross Peach Tree Creek and advance directly on Atlanta. I want Schofield with the Army of the Ohio and McPherson with his Army of the Tennessee to move along to the east. They'll cut Confederate supply lines. McPherson will take a wide arc and cut Atlanta's last rail link with the upper South. I've instructed him to send Dodge into Decatur to pull up the track."

Thomas considered the plan. "I'll have to cross at several locations on the river. I'll be vulnerable while crossing."

"I'm confident you can make the crossings," Sherman counseled.

"Are you going to try to flank him? I don't think he'll react the way Johnston did. Hood will stand and fight, not withdraw."

"Then we'll smash him."

* * *

CLINT CILLEY PEERED at a map on the table before him. A flickering lantern offered dim light. He turned to General Schofield and remarked, "So they want us up here to the east, toward Decatur. Can Thomas get through and cross the creek?"

"Old Pap is a cautious one. But if the path is clear, he'll take it, all the way to Atlanta. But there's a two-mile gap in the lines between us and Thomas. Most of it is swamp. It concerns me a little."

"What about your old roommate? What will Hood do?"

"He's not as smart as Johnston. He'll waste a lot of men trying to stop us. Men he can't afford to lose. Where is your old regiment?"

Cilley chuckled. "The Second Minnesota is behind us on Governor McDonald's plantation, camped out on a nice, soft, green lawn and doing depot and supply duty. They won't be in the fight."

"Well, Professor," Schofield smiled, "it seems the Minnesota boys are doing all right without their instructor."

"I taught them mathematics, not war. The fighting we all had to learn."

"It got you a medal of honor at Chickamauga."

"I was too scared to run. Somebody had to keep the boys fighting or Thomas, our Rock of Chickamauga, would have been tossed aside like a pebble."

* * *

ON THE NIGHT of July 19, Hood met with his corps commanders. Alexander P. Stewart, known as A.P., who after a stint in the army had been a mathematics and philosophy professor, was trim, with a dark mustache and chin beard. His quiet demeanor belied his fighting nature. Stewart had been named corps commander after Polk was killed. His men called him "Old Straight."

Hardee was a forty-nine-year-old veteran who had served from 1838 in the United States Army until the war started, when he switched allegiance to the Confederacy. His brown, gray-tinged hair was cut short, in contrast to a bushy mustache and chin beard. His claim to fame was *Hardee's Manual of Tactics*, which had become a bible for training soldiers. Quarrels with Bragg had made him controversial in some circles.

They sat around a glimmering campfire, with Hood doing the talking. "Tomorrow," the commander began, "at one in the afternoon, I want us to begin at the right and attack in echelon by division. The Yankees have some men across Peach Tree Creek, but not all. The rest will follow, but those across have not yet adequately fortified.

"Everything on our side of the creek must be taken at all hazards. Scofield and McPherson are toward the east. Cheatham and Wheeler will hold them off. We must drive Thomas, while he is isolated, to the west, toward the Chattahoochee."

"Kind of like General Johnston wanted. Hit 'em while they're apart and can't help each other," Hardee commented.

Hood swallowed hard. "There are elements of General Johnston's plan at work here. Cheatham and Wheeler's divisions should be able to hold up Schofield and McPherson while you crush Thomas. General Hardee, you will hit him from the right with three divisions. Ensure that your right flank maintains contact with Cheatham's division. General Stewart, with two divisions you will attack Thomas from the left. We have a narrow window of opportunity during the crossing and before completion of defensive works by the Yankees."

"By echelon?" Hardee asked.

"Yes, the first division on your right will advance first. Whose division is that?"

"Bate's," Hardee answered.

"After it has gone 150 to 200 yards forward, the next division must advance. Each division will follow as soon as the unit on its right has advanced the same distance."

Stewart considered and then spoke slowly. "The plan is sound. The Yankees' position invites attack, some of 'em on the north bank, and some on the south. No strong barricades and men crossing in between. Cut off from the other corps."

Hood stood and leaned heavily on his crutch. "If we strike hard, we can wreck half of Sherman's army before the rest of them can respond. But we must be audacious."

"And lucky," Hardee murmured.

* * *

AS ONE O'CLOCK NEARED, Tod Carter waited on a ridge alongside General Thomas Benton Smith. The Confederate Army was formed up in the ruins of an old farm field. Many were in a stretch 400 yards wide and half a mile long. On the edge of the field, about 300 yards away, was a twisting, torturous creek. Just beyond the creek ran a narrow strip of woodland from the west. Then the ground was open until another strip of woods to the east.

Tod commented to his general, "Not much open land here. The timber gets pretty thick."

"Just ahead of us. Not much on that ridge."

"But the closer ridge is heavily wooded."

"Captain, if the plan works, it won't make any difference. We'll hit 'em in the river and before they get dug in over here."

"It's almost one, General, and the Yankees are crossing. We better be ready."

A messenger galloped up the ridge toward Tod and Smith. He saluted the general and informed him, "General Hood's compliments, sir. The Yankees comin' from the west are gittin' here faster than he thought. Wheeler is outnumbered ten to one. We gotta shift the whole corps to new ground to match the Yankees."

Smith turned to his adjutant. "Captain Carter, spread the word. We have to change our position. Send Cheatham to aid Wheeler."

One of the first men Tod encountered was his friend, Sergeant Jim Cooper. "Jim, we've got to change up. I'm off to tell Cheatham that Wheeler needs him."

"Aren't you supposed to be tending to supplies and not riding around a battlefield?"

"That would be a waste. I've got Rosencrantz." He patted his black stallion's neck. "Best horse in the army. Sometimes General Smith needs me to deliver dispatches or messages."

"You take care, Tod," Cooper said sternly.

Tod laughed, "Don't worry."

Hood's whole army had to shift as Hardee's and Stewart's corps, ready for battle at 1:00 p.m., spent the next ninety minutes marching to new positions. By the time they were finally set, Thomas's men had all crossed Peach Tree Creek. The movements caused Hardee to lose contact with Cheatham's command.

Hardee, on the right, advanced about 3:15 p.m. But Bate's division, in the lead, by chance fell into the gap in the Union line between Thomas and

Schofield. The division included Smith's brigade and the Twentieth Tennessee. Tod Carter would mainly be a spectator to the battle.

General Walker's division was next in line to advance in two rows. They encountered Newton's division of Union marksmen. Musket and cannon fire blasted into the Confederates. "Charge 'em, boys!" Walker shouted.

"Keep hitting them!" Hood commanded as his men repeated charges for nearly three hours. They were joined by a third division, Maney's, and managed to overlap Newton's right flank until Union troops held the line and pushed the Confederates back. Fierce fighting raged where the rebel attack stalled. Hardee turned to an adjutant and shouted, "We need our reserves. Tell Cleburne to move his division up!"

The adjutant raised his voice above the din and cried, "Hood just ordered Cleburne to help Cheatham. McPherson is heading this way. Cleburne's gone!"

Hardee shook his head. "Then we can't hold them!" All along the line, Hardee's forces were driven to the rear.

Then Stewart's corps with Loring's division in the forefront joined the attack. In ferocious fighting on the Confederate right, rebel forces pounded at the Union line. Scott's brigade, left of Loring's, burst through and overran and captured much of the Thirty-third New Jersey, who were in advance of Geary's division of Union soldiers.

As Geary's men blasted into the charging Confederates, Scott's men fell back from the onslaught of lead missiles that raked into them and mowed them down. But on the other flank, another crisis erupted for Thomas's men. Rebel General Edward Walthall's division stormed ahead with three brigades. Alabamans charged up a ridge along Collier Road and overran Geary's right. Three regiments of Ohio and Pennsylvania men broke and ran like rabbits before the onrushing Confederate blitz.

But the Union line reformed and stabilized, and the men from Alabama were pushed back. Walthall's force then drove like hellions through the smoke, fire, and lead that buzzed all around. They managed to capture a portion of the Union's main line.

Suddenly a massive Union counterattack and enfilading fire from both sides drove the rebels back, and the Confederate attack fell apart. It was just after 6:00 p.m.

* * *

THAT NIGHT, HOOD ORDERED his forces to abandon the outer defenses around Atlanta and concentrate on the inner ring. A rise of ground beyond the ring, north and east of Atlanta, was still held by Confederate forces. Wheeler's cavalry, after a fierce fight through the afternoon, had withdrawn in the evening to a treeless eminence called Bald Hill. The troops dismounted and dug in.

On another nearby elevation, Sherman ordered artillery atop the hill to fire down into Atlanta. Townspeople who once felt isolated from war now found it had come to their doorstep. Hundreds fled the city and ran south as cannonballs smashed into the courthouse and rail depot.

Patrick Cleburne's division joined Wheeler late that night, and the Irishman assumed command of the defenses. At eight in the morning, Union General Blair's forces attacked the hill. Throughout a morning filled with blazing cannon and raining canister, the battle raged at Bald Hill. For a time, position of the rise alternated like a children's game of King of the Hill.

Finally, Union artillery gained a foothold on the hill and, with control of the high ground, drove Cleburne back toward Atlanta. Throughout the afternoon, Union forces strengthened their possession.

* * *

FARTHER TO THE EAST, McPherson's army was near Decatur. Cheatham and Wheeler had stalled both McPherson and Schofield, but the Union forces were now moving toward Atlanta. In front of Hood's headquarters tent, the commander of the Army of Tennessee gathered his corps leaders on the evening of the twenty-first. The elaborate Confederate defensive line included a number of artillery emplacements that covered the avenues of approach to Atlanta.

"They're trying to take Atlanta from the east," Hood proclaimed. "I always knew they would."

"They're shelling us from right in front," Cheatham observed. "That seems more urgent. We have lost the high ground. Now McPherson can advance the whole Army of the Tennessee toward Atlanta. And we lost 2,500 men yesterday, General Hood. They are irreplaceable."

A thunder of hooves alerted the officers as a scout galloped up to Hood and jerked his horse to a halt.

"General, sir," the out-of-breath rider gasped. "McPherson is coming, but he's up in the air, unsupported. He's left Decatur behind him with his baggage train."

Hood snapped, "Hardee, I want you to march around McPherson's left flank, then strike his rear. Wheeler, your cavalry will capture or destroy the baggage train. We have a chance to duplicate Jackson's flanking maneuver at Chancellorsville. We'll make them Yankees pay. Decatur is a prize city on the railroad to Atlanta, and we need to keep it."

"When do you want us to advance, General?" Hardee inquired.

"Now. I want your corps to march through the night around the Union left flank and surprise 'em in the morning."

"That's a six-mile march, sir. It'll be a tough go. But we'll be up to it."

"General Cheatham, hit the Union front. We're going to save this city."

* * *

General Sherman met with General Thomas in his headquarters tent. "I was informed that the enemy had withdrawn in front of McPherson and Schofield," Sherman explained. "I inferred that they were about to evacuate Atlanta. But Hood's inner defensive line is still strong. He has no intention of withdrawing. So I'm going to implement a plan I outlined to Grant last April. We will cut all Atlanta's railroad connections to the Confederacy."

"Starting at Decatur?" Thomas asked.

"Yes. I've ordered McPherson to send Dodge there to pull up tracks tomorrow."

Within the hour, General McPherson entered Sherman's tent atop Copen Hill. "General," McPherson pointedly began, "I've got some problems with your order."

"Oh?" Sherman raised his eyebrows. "Explain."

"My scouts tell me that large Confederate forces have been seen moving south, and I fear they will attack my left flank. You have left me vulnerable there."

Sherman's brow wrinkled in thought before he answered. "I think your concern is unwarranted, but I'll delay implementing my order until one o'clock tomorrow afternoon. If you haven't been attacked by then, you won't be." The general paused, his voice softening. "Jim, be careful. Don't take chances. You've got men to do that. You're the best I've got."

McPherson smiled. "Don't worry, sir, we'll handle the rebs just fine."

* * *

In the twilight, Confederate forces moved out. But despite Hardee's spirited urging, the pace was much slower than either he or Hood had expected.

He sent a message back to Hood informing his superior that he could not possibly attack early in the morning. Hood responded that Hardee should assault as soon as he was behind McPherson.

Wheeler's cavalry extended beyond Hardee and soon approached Sherman's supply line at Decatur.

* * *

GENERAL JAMES MCPHERSON rested astride his horse and surveyed the field to the west and Bald Hill. It was near noon, and Hardee's men were finally nearing attack position. The order from Sherman instructing him to direct Dodge to rip up tracks hadn't arrived, but the sound of battle to the southeast alarmed McPherson.

"I don't like this," McPherson observed. "General Dodge, I'm concerned about our left flank. Take your Sixteenth Corps down there and bolster the left. I'll take my corps to the high ground up there."

"Do you really think they'll attack us? I thought they were holed up outside of Atlanta."

"Hood doesn't stay put and listen to the sounds of battle. That's not a thunderstorm. I'd mortgage the farm that he's coming after us."

After Dodge was out of sight, Sherman's order arrived. McPherson folded it, placed it in a pocket and spoke to his orderly. "Too late, things have changed."

Meanwhile, to the rear, Wheeler's cavalry rode like demons toward Decatur. Near the town they encountered General John Sprague, commander of the Second Brigade, Fourth Division of the Sixteenth Corps, and attacked his force on the Fayetteville Road.

Sprague's men put up a spirited battle as the Union general ordered all supply and ordnance trains out of Decatur. As the Union troops stampeded out of the city, Wheeler's forces rode in. The town was theirs, but most of their prize had been removed.

Hardee finally launched his attack after noon. Two of his divisions ran into Dodge's reserve force and the battle was on. One unit was Bate's division, including Tyler's brigade, commanded by Thomas Banton Smith with Tod Carter. In conjunction with Cheatham, the Confederate forces formed an "L" as they slammed into McPherson's corps. Hardee's attack formed the lower part, while Cheatham's men were the vertical. Bald Hill, east of Atlanta, became the focal point of the fighting along with a smaller hill next to it.

General Patrick Cleburne conferred urgently with Cheatham. "Look, General, they've fortified the hills, but they've left the valley between the hills unfortified and unprotected, no breastworks."

Cheatham peered intently and reasoned, "They think they can enfilade down on us from both hills if we go there. But the undergrowth is thick. We have a chance."

"Let me send General Walker to hit their right. My division will follow into the trees between the hills."

"Do it," Cheatham commanded.

A savage struggle erupted around Bald Hill. Walker and his Georgians battled up the hill in fierce hand-to-hand fighting. Finally Walker himself gained the Union breastworks, where he was instantly cut down by musket fire.

Cleburne's division passed between the Union lines and cut them in two. The ground trembled as if trying to repulse the savage depredation from it. Smoke, fire, and lead flew through the steamy, hot Georgia air, burning and ripping into men on both sides. Battle flags, Union and Confederate, became intermingled in the maze of mayhem as their bearers became entangled with each other.

As cannon and shot rained into them, Cleburne's men stormed toward a hill to gain the Union breastworks. A courier shouted, "Take the hill, move to the left and charge!"

In front of them Cleburne drew his sword, pointed at the hill and yelled, "Follow me, boys!"

The rebels routed Union soldiers from their defenses, but cannon fire from atop the hill stymied the Confederates. Exhausted but still standing, they paused to catch their collective breath. Then General George Maney rose up and commanded, "Go forward and take that battery! Shoot down and bayonet the cannoneers! Take their guns!"

Cleburne added vehemently, "You heard what General Maney said, boys! By the eternal God, you have got to take it!"

The ragged and battered Confederate line surged forward, up the steep sides of the hill in the face of thousands of firing muskets and dozens of cannonballs hurled with devastating force.

Screams emanated from thousands of throats as the Confederates slammed into the Union defenders of the hill. Heat from the shot caused rebel uniforms to smolder with smoke. Skin blistered and faces blackened with gunsmoke, the Confederates raced like demons from Hell into the blue line. Officers on both sides drew swords and sidearms as they braced for hand-to-hand pandemonium.

Two miles to the north, Cheatham's troops had broken through the Union lines at the Georgia railroad. Sherman responded with twenty artillery pieces at his headquarters at Copen Hill and shelled the Confederates.

Fighting continued to rage around Bald Hill. General McPherson shouted to an orderly, "Come with me! I need to see what's happening and where we need to restore our lines!"

The two headed into the firestorm. Blindly, they rode right into the midst of a mass of advancing Confederates.

"Surrender!" a soldier shouted.

McPherson smiled, tipped his hat, and then wheeled his mount and roughly dug his spurs into his horse. The animal bolted ahead as the general tried to ride through the rebels. A shot ripped into McPherson, and he tumbled heavily to the ground. The general was dead.

About 4:00 p.m., Cheatham's corps broke through the Union front. Then other Union forces joined the fray as Sherman's massed cannon thundered and Logan's corps poured in to stop the assault. The Confederate onslaught screeched to a halt and then wilted under Logan's counterattack. The Union line was held. It was just after dark on July 22.

When Wheeler, still holding Decatur, learned that Hardee's assault had failed, he abandoned the town and headed back to Atlanta with his cavalry. The railroad at Decatur would soon be in Union hands.

* * *

BACK IN HIS DEFENSIVE WORKS around Atlanta, Hood surveyed the dramatic events of the day and penned a missive to President Davis. "The federal forces tried to capture Atlanta today, but our valiant soldiers held them at bay. They came at us from the east, and we still hold the ground here. We didn't lose an inch of what we had before the battle."

He handed the dispatch to Tod Carter, who had been sent to report by General Smith. Tod, his face streaked with sweat through powder-blackened stains, glanced at the letter and pronounced, "Sir, we've lost over 5,500 men. They're whittling us down pretty good."

Hood blazed with pride. "And each of our men is equal to three of theirs, so it's about even."

* * *

On Copen Hill, a solemn cadre of officers gathered around General Sherman. His eyes glistened as he peered down at a sheet of paper cradled in his hands. "It's hard, gentlemen. Losing General McPherson is a great loss. He was a fine man and a great soldier. It's hard for me to express my opinion of his great worth. These are a few sentiments from my official report."

Sherman began to read. "I feel assured that every patriot in America, on hearing this sad news, will feel a sense of personal loss, and the country generally will realize that we have lost not only an able military leader, but a man who, had he survived, was qualified to heal the national strife which has been raised by designing and ambitious men."

George Thomas mumbled softly, "Hear, hear."

Sherman cleared his throat and continued. "General Howard will replace Jim McPherson as commander of the Army of the Tennessee."

John Schofield, with Clint Cilley alongside, asked, "Do we attack again? They expect us to continue from the east."

Sherman replied, "It was never my intent to attack Atlanta from the east. We will now besiege the city and shell it daily. We will level it if we have to. Allow civilians to evacuate if they so wish."

"What about their supply line?" Thomas inquired. "They still have a rail line to the south from Macon and the rail station at Lovejoy."

"I don't want a long siege here. My plan is to bring them to their knees by sending cavalry south of town to cut their lines," Sherman proclaimed. "We've cut three of the four supply lines leading into Atlanta. Rousseau's brigade has been tearing up the Montgomery and West Point Road, and Garrard's just in from Covington.

"Schofield, I want you to send your Army of the Ohio cavalry, under your friend, George Stoneman, to the southeast from Atlanta, while McCook's cavalry of the Army of the Cumberland will move to the southwest. My written instructions," he handed a sheet of paper to Schofield, "are that they should leave Decatur by the twenty-seventh and cut the remaining rail line between Atlanta and Macon. They should then join forces at Lovejoy Station on the twenty-eighth. I want them to rip up at least five miles of track and telegraph. Then they are to proceed west to liberate the thousands of our men held prisoner at Camp Ogelthorpe near Macon and Camp Sumter at Andersonville."

The general added, "I've seen men who escaped—barely shadows is all that's left of them. It's past time to do something about the men still there."

"General Stoneman will be pleased, sir," Schofield responded. "He spent a year behind a desk in Washington. He wants to fight."

"Yes." Sherman hesitated. "In fact, it was Stoneman who asked for this assignment and particularly urged he be allowed to free the prisoners, but in my instructions to him I make it plain that he must let caution be his guide. He must focus on breaking up the railroad. He should not make the long ride to Andersonville unless he is assured of success. He must heed this order."

Schofield looked at Clint Cilley. "General, if it'll set your mind at ease I'll send my adjutant, Captain Cilley, along to help advise General Stoneman."

"Fine," Sherman concluded. "This needs to work, and the alternative is a siege. That's especially true if what I'm planning for General Howard doesn't pan out. We've got to take Atlanta, but it's too strong to assault and too extensive to invest. That's why I'm sending out Stoneman and McCook."

Stoneman's Raid

FOR SEVERAL DAYS, UNION FORCES continued to lob cannon shot into Atlanta from the high ground to the north. On July 28, Sherman decided to attack from the west, after failing to take the city from the north or east. His cavalry units were already skirting south of Atlanta bound for Lovejoy Station.

He sent General Oliver O. Howard and the Army of the Tennessee to move on an arc from the left wing to the right to cut Hood's last rail line between East Point and Atlanta.

Hood anticipated Howard's maneuver and sent two corps, one under Stephen Lee and the other under Alexander Stewart, to intercept and destroy the Union force at Ezra Church Crossroads, two miles west of Atlanta. Lee's corps was to stop Howard and keep the way open, and Stewart's was to follow up and hit them with a counterattack from the right.

But Howard knew what to expect from Hood, as well. "I know him from West Point," he informed Sherman. "Hood will think he can surprise us with an attack. It's his only chance against our superior numbers. When he comes, we'll be ready for him."

When Hood tried to intercept the Union Army, he found it dug in behind breastworks and rails. Lee launched a series of disjointed attacks. As Stewart's force came up, Lee convinced him to join his attack instead of moving to the right flank. "They're about ready to break," Lee argued. "With you, we can snap their line!"

Even with Stewart, without the element of surprise the Confederates found it impossible to defeat a force dug in and greatly outnumbering the attackers. Instead of continuing the attack, Lee's and Stewart's forces had to entrench. Yet, there was a measure of success for the Confederates: the Union soldiers were kept off the rail line. Now only the cavalry forces were left to destroy the railroad.

However, once again Hood suffered great losses: 3,000 irreplaceable Confederates to only 600-some Union soldiers.

Back in Atlanta, shelling from north of town continued to rain down on the populace. Streets were pocked with holes from cannonballs; some buildings were shattered and in ruin. While some residents fled to the south, many remained, some the victims of Yankee fire.

* * *

HOOD STOOD BEFORE his officers with a newspaper in his hand. He grimly related to them, "Our newspapers are optimistic. This is from the Atlanta paper, now published in Macon. 'Sherman will suffer the greatest defeat that any Yankee general has suffered during the war. The Yankees will disappear from Atlanta before the end of August.'"

Hood placed the paper on a table and leaned on his crutch. "I hope we can accommodate their optimism. The preservation of this city can only be secured if we keep our supply line to the south open. We must do it!"

"Sir," General Wheeler commented, "my scouts tell me that Stoneman's and McCook's cavalries are both heading south, likely to Lovejoy. Garrard is with Stoneman, but his 3,000 men had a hard ride from Covington, and I suspect both men and horses are tired. McCook is on an arc from the east and Stoneman from the west."

"I'm aware of that, General. I want you and Red Jackson to follow and catch them. They must not be allowed to destroy the tracks at Lovejoy Station. It's our last remaining supply line. At least one line must remain open from Macon."

"Sir, one more thing," Hardee added. "We must keep the rail open, but we've lost around 15,000 men. Reports are that Sherman's losses have been less than half that. The odds are already greatly against us. We can't afford these losses."

"We must pray that God is with us. That's one reason why we must hold the rail line. We may have to—God forbid—use it to evacuate this town. But President Davis put me in command to hold here, and it is still my intention to do just that."

* * *

CLINT CILLEY HAD JOINED George Stoneman's cavalry on July 27 as they passed near Atlanta after leaving Decatur. The general was six-foot-four and powerfully built, with a lush head of dark hair and a full mustache and beard.

His sturdy frame rested lightly on a black stallion. Cilley saluted and handed Stoneman his orders.

"So," the general commented, "my friend, General Schofield, thinks I need a little help and sends me an advisor. I trust you'll do just that, Captain, and not get in the way. I've got 2,000 men of my own to keep track of and another 3,000 in General Garrard's division, but I'm pretty sure I can do it without too much help."

"No offense is meant, sir. General Schofield has complete trust in you. It was he who got you away from Washington, after all."

"I know, Captain, and I appreciate that. We're going to ride hard. And all the way we will sweep rebel bastards aside. We will take what we need and we will destroy anything of military value that gets in our way. General McCook is of the same mind west of here."

"We meet up with him at Lovejoy Station," Cilley added.

"After some good work and a little fun. Then we rescue those poor souls at Andersonville."

"Remember," Clint cautioned, "the railroad is your main target."

"And if you forget to remind me, I have my aide-de-camp, here, to tell me." He gestured to a handsome, dark-haired, well-built man mounted beside him. "You know Major Myles Keough, don't you, Captain?"

"I've heard of him. Major, you were a member of the Vatican Guard, weren't you? You fought in a war for the pope. Good to have you here."

Keough flashed a bright smile. "Faith and be gorrah, I was just doin' what any fine Irish lad would do. I saw you fellas were havin' a wee bit of trouble, so I came over to help."

Clint nodded at a young black man seated on a horse just behind Stoneman. "Who's he?"

"This is Sam. He escaped from a plantation south of Atlanta. Now he's my guide. He knows the lay of the land around here. I hope he can get us to Andersonville."

Clint chuckled, "Railroads first, General, remember."

The Union force crossed the Ocmulgee River near Covington. Late on the afternoon of the twenty-seventh, Wheeler's Confederate cavalry approached and began to menace the Union column. They ran into an unexpected snag, as the Yankees had been newly armed with repeating rifles and drove back the rebels, who had single-shot rifles.

"I'm leaving you behind," Stoneman informed Garrard. "I need you to keep Wheeler occupied here and cover my rear. Besides, Sherman warned me not to overtax your tired horses. Keep the rebs busy for a while."

The next morning, Wheeler at first concentrated on Garrard's force. In this case the Confederates had numerical superiority and, despite the Yankee repeaters, were able to drive the Yankees back. Garrard's men retreated all the way to Marietta, close to Atlanta.

Wheeler watched the Union retreat and explained to officers standing around him, "I'm leaving one brigade here to watch over Garrard. Most of my command will go after Stoneman. I'm also sending a brigade to 'Red' Jackson. He's alone against McCook to the west."

* * *

STONEMAN'S CAVALRY, accompanied by two pieces of artillery, continued south toward Monticello, twenty-three miles from Covington, with the Ocmulgee River a few miles to their right. No property was destroyed, although horses and some personal possessions were confiscated from private citizens.

Stoneman had intended to march down the east side of the Ocmulgee before joining up with McCook at Lovejoy Station. He was shocked and dismayed when scouts reported there were no bridges over the muddy stretch of the river between Monticello and Macon where he planned to cross. On July 30, they continued the march until they reached the small town of Clinton, about fifteen miles from Macon.

"Well, Cilley," he called to Clint, "this puts us in a bit of a pickle. My scouts tell me there's no ford. We can't cross here and I can't get to Lovejoy. The next ford is too far away. We'll lose too much time. I'm not going to ride back to Sherman and tell him we couldn't do anything. I'm going east a bit to see what damage we can do. Then I'm going south and back east to Macon to liberate our boys there and at Andersonville."

"Those aren't exactly your orders," Clint reminded him.

"Sometimes you have to do what's within reach," Stoneman replied.

In bright sunlight along the river, Stoneman met with his officers. "Since we can't cross the river, I'm going down to Macon. We'll bypass Lovejoy and keep going south. Meanwhile, I'm detaching 100 men from the Fourteenth Illinois regiment under Francis Davidson."

"What do you expect to gain from that, General?" Clint inquired.

"Gordon, just ten miles down the road, is an important railroad junction. I want Davidson to destroy all the stations and water tanks from Gordon to the Oconee River and on their arrival there to burn any bridges. We'll do our own rebel taming as we head to Macon. We should never be more than a half day or less apart."

"Do you mind if I ride with them?" Clint asked.

"Have at it, boy! Just don't get hurt. Schofield wouldn't like that."

* * *

THE NEXT MORNING two forces were on the move, Stoneman's going south and Davidson's just ahead to Gordon. By afternoon Major Davidson, accompanied by Clint Cilley, had led his Illinois mounted troops along the tracks near the small town of Gordon.

Clint cocked his head and listened intently. Then he dismounted and knelt to place his ear on the track. "Train coming," he announced. "And close!"

Davidson shouted, "Back from the track, boys! Get into the brush and stay down. I don't know what's on the train!"

Boxcars loaded with Confederate militia rolled past with a loud *clickety clack, clickety clack.* "Stay down! Let 'em pass!" Davidson cried.

Directly behind was a passenger train that whirled past, following the militia.

"What do you think, Captain?" Davidson asked as the caboose rolled out of sight.

"I think they're heading to Milledgeville, the new state capital. They're going east."

"I believe you're right. They're not going to Gordon. Men," he shouted, "let's ride into town and do what General Sherman wants done!"

With that order, 100 men mounted up and galloped into Gordon. Once in the hamlet they immediately began to wreak havoc and destruction. Like a gang of vandals, they smashed windows and set fires. Clint, astride his horse, watched.

First Sergeant Francis Adams rode up to Davidson and shouted, "That big building down the street!" He pointed. "It's a warehouse and looks to be full of bacon, meal, flour, and lots of furniture!"

"Burn it!" the major ordered.

In minutes, flames flickered and then roared, consuming the entire building as if it had been slipped whole into a blast furnace. Billows of thick, black smoke hid the sun and turned afternoon into evening.

The railroad town had nearly 200 cars and engines on side tracks. "Set 'em on fire!" Davidson bellowed above the mayhem of shouting men and screaming horses. "The cars, the car shed, and any buildings having to do with the railroad!"

The men went about their task with relish. They tossed burning torches on rooftops of buildings and onto boxcars as the conflagration mounted in heat and intensity.

Sergeant Adams approached his major with a sweaty, smoke-stained, bedraggled older man in tow. He pushed the man ahead, and the townsman glared defiantly at the Union officer.

The sergeant explained, "This fella's the town postmaster. He stood in our way and tried to keep us from burnin' the post office. Even tried to take up a rifle. He's just lucky we got to 'im before he could shoot!"

"You mean *you* were lucky!" the man snapped.

"Whadda we do with 'im?" Adams asked.

"What's yer name?" Davidson asked the prisoner.

"Walker."

"Well, Mr. Walker, we need a guide to get us to the next town. You can save your life by helping us."

"I'm not helping any damn Yankees with anything!"

"Sorry to hear that, Mr. Walker. Sergeant, shoot him."

As his captor leveled his rifle at him and cocked it, Walker's eyes grew wide with alarm. "All right, take it easy," he implored. "I'll show you were Griswoldville is."

"Glad you're seeing reason, Mr. Walker. After the next town, we'll let you go. Unless you lead us astray, at which time the sergeant here will finish what he was starting to do."

"Kin I least git back my money and watch?" the man pleaded.

Davidson looked at his sergeant. "What did you take?"

The sergeant held up a bag. "About 11,000 in Confederate dollars and a gold watch." He dangled the timepiece in his hand.

The major reached down and took the watch. He examined it and stuffed it in his pocket. "Well, the watch might be worth something, but the money is trash. Throw it in a fire. Then get this fella a horse. You got a guide."

"I've got a guide?" Adams repeated incredulously.

"Yes, Sergeant, you. I'm sending you and a squad to Griswoldville with Mr. Walker. Tear up track along the way and do what damage you can in the town. I'm taking the main body on to the Oconee River and then down the left bank to Macon. You should be able to catch up with us on the way there." He looked at Clint. "Captain Cilley, do you want to go with the squad or the main force?"

"I think General Schofield would like me to stay with you, sir. You're rejoining General Stoneman."

"All right," Davidson said. "Sergeant Adams, get yourself a squad, twelve men, grab Walker and head out."

Adams saluted, "Yes, sir!"

Once their targets were blazing and destroyed, the rest of the blue-clad troops were ordered to mount up and hit the trail. "There's another town ready for us, boys!" Davidson urged.

Davidson rode alongside Cilley. "So," he said sarcastically, "how does Schofiled's errand boy like fighting again?"

"I've done plenty of fighting, Colonel."

"That's right. You were one of the heroes at Chickamauga, weren't you? You helped Thomas make his stand?"

"I did my part. I was sent to the general with a dispatch. On the way, I ran into our boys in retreat. I knocked over a reb, took his flag and stopped our boys from running. They followed me back into action."

"Well, Cilley, maybe you'll get a chance to lead us to glory, too."

The Illinois cavalry trotted out of Gordon. As soon as the raiders had left, the townspeople, largely in hiding during the attack, turned out en masse, men, women, and children. All at once, they went to work battling the fires.

"Did you need to destroy the town? Wouldn't just the tracks have been enough?" Clint asked Davidson.

The major replied, "Like General Sherman says, 'War is all hell.'"

* * *

WORD OF THE ATTACK on Gordon spread down the track ahead of Adams and his squad of raiders. They were in no rush, anyway, stopping occasionally to tear up tracks as they went along.

But ahead of them, skirmishers formed up to hold off the Union raiders. Trace Cole spotted a lone defender and snapped off a shot at him. Suddenly the way in front of the squad erupted in gunfire.

"Too much firepower up there," Adams observed. "Cole, did you see how many?"

"No, Sergeant, but it's pretty hot down that road."

"Okay. Walker," Adams turned to his captive. "Find us another way."

The postmaster nodded reluctantly. "March 'round the road. 'Bout a mile and a half away we'll hit it again on the other side."

"This town have anything to mention besides it's a railroad town?" Adams asked.

"Pistols," Walker answered. "They've got a pistol factory."

When sound of the shooting reached Griswoldville, a train of twenty-seven cars had been backed out of town. It was standing on the track when Adams's squad emerged from cover.

The Union soldiers leveled their rifles at the train crew. "Get everyone out of the cars," Adams ordered. "And unhitch the engine."

As the passengers assembled alongside the train cars, Cole Trace reported to his sergeant, "There are at least a dozen Negroes who were on board."

Adams considered this. "Tell 'em to get any private property they have off the train. They can go wherever they want. Then have the men set the cars on fire. There's a downgrade into the town. Have the boys give the last car a good push."

Within half an hour the cars were ablaze and headed slowly down the track into town. The inferno rolled along and was nearly consumed by the time it reached Griswoldville and didn't ignite any cars at the station.

The raiders remained behind with the engine. Adams gathered his squad and ordered, "Empty most of the water from the engine boiler and fill the furnace with wood. I want steam."

"Whatcha gonna do, Sergeant?" Cole wondered.

"We're gonna get the engine steamed up and ready to go. Then I want the throttle set wide open. We'll send her speeding into town."

"Sarge," a private asked, "then why take water out?"

"I don't want the engine to go a long way. Just a short way, fast. Less water, less weight, faster engine. Mr. Walker, I've got one more little task fer ya. Then you can go."

"What?"

"Hold the throttle open. You can jump off once it gets going."

Fear flashed across the man's face. "I won't."

Adams took out his pistol and leveled it at Walker's chest, "You will."

Soon afterward, the engine was deemed ready. Walker climbed on board and pushed the throttle as far as it would go. As it started to churn down the track, Walker leapt from the engine and tumbled, rolling on the ground. In moments the locomotive was roaring down the track to Griswoldville.

It entered under a full head of steam, black smoke billowing from the smokestack. The wheels were a blur of sound and fury. Ahead was the burnt-out train on the track. The engine violently smashed into the rear car, slicing through and splitting it in two, with pieces flying like chaff on either side of the track. Two more cars were blasted off the rail line by the hurtling steam-powered missile. Its steam supply exhausted, the engine creaked and rolled to a stop.

"Boys," Adams announced, "I think we've done about all we can. It's time to mount up and find Major Davidson."

* * *

MEANWHILE, DAVIDSON'S main body of raiders had ridden to McIntyre Station No. 16, where they tore up a small portion of track. They repeated their task at Emmet Station No. 15 and burned a 700-yard bridge across the Oconee River. They moved farther along the road to Toomsborough, where they destroyed half a mile of trestle work, burned a large brick depot filled with supplies and destroyed a flourmill and sawmill.

Leaving the railroad on the left and passing right of Milledgeville, Davidson continued in pursuit of Stoneman to join Capron's cavalry, from which his hundred men were detached. The major looked behind with a satisfied smile. They had burned trains, loaded cars on sidings, machinery, supplies, trestles, and a bridge. Things had gone pretty well, he thought, even if they hadn't gotten to Lovejoy Station with McCook.

* * *

WHEELER'S SCOUTS in the area had been watching Davidson's movements. They feared he was advancing on Milledgeville and notified their commander. Reinforcements were sent north from Macon to defend the town, as was a telegram alerting them of Union movements nearby. The newly named state capital only had 120 defenders.

Late in the afternoon of July 29, Stoneman's army left Clinton. Scouts were sent ahead down the Lite N Tie Road, Capron's and Biddle's brigades close behind. Silas Adams's Kentucky brigade brought up the rear with the pack train and were sent on a more direct route to Macon. At 10:00 p.m., Adams ran into Cobb's scouts and a sharp skirmish ensued. Stoneman sent men to the right to aid Adams. They succeeded, after accidentally firing briefly on fellow Union soldiers. Order on the right was restored, and Adams got within five miles of Macon by dawn on the thirtieth.

By daylight Stoneman's left wing had gotten within nine miles of Macon, just behind Adams. A Union scout rode out of the misty early morning to his general. "Sir," he reported, "the rebs are up ahead. Looks like a skirmish line at a place called Dunlap's Farm. There's a hill on the property. Behind that they have earthworks and behind that is a river."

"So," Stoneman considered, "after we bust through them, there's nothing to stop us from heading right into Macon."

"Just one thing, General: there's no bridge. Seems it washed out last spring. You can't get into Macon from here."

"Blast! Not another missing bridge!"

"'Fraid so, General."

"So we can't reach the Macon Western Railroad, either. The way to Atlanta is still open unless McCook took care of it at Lovejoy, on the other side of the Ocmulgee."

"The line to northern Virginia, the Central of Georgia, runs right through the Dunlap Farm," the scout said.

"That's the one we've been able to damage some. But I still wanted to get the Atlanta line."

By 6:00 a.m., Capron had joined Biddle to unite with Stoneman's troops, only a mile and a half from the city. As the general conferred with his brigade commanders, two guards approached with a middle-aged woman walking between them. She was dressed in a brown homespun dress and carried herself with shoulders held back and head erect.

Stoneman turned and tipped his hat to the lady. Her escort announced, "We found her just walking up to us. She says she wants to talk to you."

"Yes, ma'am, what can I do for you? It's not safe to be taking strolls out here."

"I'm Mrs. Dunlap. Our farm is right ahead between you and Macon. I'm begging you to not fight a battle on our home ground."

"Mrs. Dunlap, we'll avoid it if we can, but I can't promise anything. Circumstances dictate the flow of a battle."

"Please, try."

Myles Keough's eyes twinkled as he interjected, "General, you need a headquarters house for the fight. Why don't cha be taking over the Dunlap house?"

"Quite possible," Stoneman answered.

"No!" the woman exclaimed in alarm. "You'll shoot up my house!"

"Ma'am," Keough soothed her, "it's just the opposite. If the general is in the house, we won't be shooting at it. Now, if your lads get close, they might be hittin' it. But the general would have left by then."

Mrs Dunlap sighed. "I'll leave the door open." As she turned to leave, the woman stopped and informed the Union officers, "You might be interested that the prisoners at Fort Ogelthorpe are gone. Three hundred were all moved out."

"Where?" Stoneman snapped.

"I don't know, Andersonville, maybe."

"Then we'll find them. Good day, Mrs. Dunlap."

The Battle of Sunshine Church

G ENERAL STONEMAN CONTINUED DOWN the left bank of the Ocmulgee River toward Macon on the Clinton Road. A distant rattling of rifle shots sounded, and Stoneman grimaced. "They keep trying to bother us. Seems like the closer we get to Macon, the more shooting there is. But they're too scared to get close enough to do any damage."

"Gen'r'l, sirs," Sam suggested, "I'm thinkin' we be gittin' close ta Macon. They be waitin' for us 'n' they be good shots."

"Sam, they won't be able to stand against us. We'll sweep away their re-serves and militia like chaff in a granary. They've got a railroad bridge we need to take down. How far to Macon?"

Sam wrinkled his brow in thought. "Mebbe five miles."

"Dinner in Macon tonight, Sam. I'm buying."

* * *

CLINT CILLEY, once Adams's squad rejoined Davidson, decided he had mis-judged his timing when he rode off with the raiders. He had promised General Schofield that he would watch over Stoneman and needed to return to his duty.

Davidson's force was still engaged in depredations of the countryside as they moved to rejoin the regiment. Clint had announced that he was heading out on a more direct route to Stoneman. After his request for an escort was denied, Cilley set out alone.

* * *

THREE MILES FROM MACON, Stoneman's column ran into a heavy line of Confederate skirmishers. The Union soldiers pushed forward into blistering gunfire, and the rebels fell back behind a strong line of earthwork fortifica-tions that encircled Macon.

Fort Hawkins had once stood near where the earthworks were situated, but the old War of 1812 fort was gone. Disuse and the needs of farmers had led to its disintegration, except for one blockhouse that survived from a corner of the former structure. A battery of field artillery had been placed at the blockhouse, and from a watchpost on top, Confederate officers surveyed the field and watched the movements of Stoneman's cavalry.

Stoneman assumed a rout was eminent as the rebels fell back. "Charge into 'em, boys!" he yelled. "Push 'em all the way into the river!"

Major General Howell Cobb, General Joe Johnston, and General Alfred Iverson gazed out at Stoneman's approach while an artillery officer stood near them. Before them stretched the earthworks. Beyond that was a low hill and a farmstead, pocked and torn with rough, uneven ground. A railroad track ran through the farm field.

Cobb had positioned his men at the fortifications with the river to their rear. Skirmishers out front would retreat back to the earthworks once the shooting got heavy.

Joe Johnston, late the commander of the Army of Tennessee, had been sent to Macon as an advisor. He offered to Cobb, "Interesting choice to have your men fight behind earthworks with the river behind them."

"General, these men are green—militia, reserves, and townsmen. I want them to stand and fight. It's harder to run away if you have to swim a river."

Johnston nodded. "Good thinking."

"I can't believe it, General," Iverson exclaimed. "The Yankees are comin' in just like you said they would!"

After a sharp clatter of gunfire, the vanguard of rebel marksmen fell back behind the earthen barricades.

"Stoneman can't help himself," Cobb replied. "Now just you wait. Captain." He looked at the artilleryman and asked, "are you sighted in and ready?"

"Yes, sir, this is a fine vantage point."

"Then let 'em have it!"

"Prick and prime!" shouted the officer to his gun crews. "Now, fire!"

From the blockhouse came a thunderous roar. Canister shot ripped into the charging Yankees, cutting them down.

Union soldiers hit the ground, clinging to it as if they wished they could pull it over themselves like a blanket and hide. "Shoot!" an officer screamed. "For God's sake, give it back to 'em!"

From whatever cover they could find, or lying in the open, the blue line blasted back. Stoneman ordered Colonel Robert Smith to unlimber his two artillery pieces and hit the blockhouse.

After several futile attempts, Smith reported to Stoneman, who was ensconced in the Dunlap house. "The terrain's too rough, and there's that hill! I can't get my guns in position to fight back!"

Stoneman paused and peered ahead. "Can you hit the town?"

"Any particular target?"

"No, Colonel, just into the town. Can you do it?"

"Yes, sir, but we'll hit civilians."

"Shoot into the town."

Instead of firing on the enemy arrayed directly in front of them, the two three-inch rifled parrot guns lobbed shot into Macon. Judge Asa Holt stood on the porch of his fine, white-columned house on Mulberry Street. He watched as artillery shot slammed into buildings and scattered women, children, slaves, and other noncombatants.

With alarm, he saw a cannonball ricochet off the packed-sand sidewalk in front of his house and bounce toward him. Holt dodged to the side as the ball crashed through one of his porch columns and into his house.

He opened his door and saw the missile had smashed through his parlor and now rested in his hallway. "Jeanie!" he yelled for his wife. "Are you all right?"

Holt was greatly relieved when she appeared, pale and shaken, but untouched by the cannonball.

Union troops kept up fire and pressure, but the Confederates on the hill and from the earthworks held firm. Keough rushed to his commanding officer to urge, "We've got to fall back, General, their line is too strong!"

Reluctantly, Stoneman answered, "You're right. Bugler, sound the retreat."

As the Yankees fell back, a wave of cheers and chilling rebel yells echoed from the city. Stoneman called for his officers. Keough and his senior brigade commanders, Biddle, Capron, and Adams, joined him in his house headquarters.

"Gentlemen," Stoneman announced, "their resistance was unexpected. They fight a lot better than any militia and reserves I've ever seen. Yet, we don't need to take Macon. We've damaged track leading to it. Our main goal lies past the city, Andersonville. Sam," he turned to his black guide, "I want you to find us another way across the Ocumulgee River. Since we can't use the Macon Bridge, we'll bypass the town to the prison camp."

"Yessuh, General, I'll try. Least we don' hafta go up that hill. They calls it Dunlap."

"General Stoneman," Capron spoke with alarm in his voice. "This is fool-ish. We need to get back to Sherman. Your orders were to rip up track and only go to Andersonville if the rest of the mission was successful and not to try this unless you were assured of success. We have no such assurance."

"Colonel, I have the assurance of the men I command. We can do this." He paused and smiled. "Besides, don't you want your name in the history books?"

"I'd like to keep my name off a tombstone for a while."

* * *

IN THE BLOCKHOUSE from old Fort Hawkins, Howell Cobb and Joe John-ston evaluated the situation before them. Their artillery officer announced triumphantly, "We've got 'em, General. They'll be hightailing it back to Sher-man fer sure."

Johnston looked thoughtful and replied, "I don't think so, Captain. I'm bettin' they regroup and try to go around us. I think Stoneman wants to get to Andersonville. He thinks the Camp Ogelthorpe prisoners are there, too."

"But we still have 'em here," Cobb said smugly.

Johnston chuckled. "But if Mrs. Dunlap did her job, Stoneman thinks we sent them to Andersonville. What do you think, General Cobb?"

"I'd sure like a crack at them out in the open. Look what those devils did to Macon. It was wrong to bombard the town, just wrong."

"How well do you know this area?" Cobb asked Alf Iverson.

He smiled. "Like the back of my hand. I was born at Clinton, not far from here. I know the woods, farms, ravines, and roads all over this part of Georgia."

"If Stoneman was going to bypass Macon and move to Andersonville, do you have a good idea what route he'd take?"

"I'm pretty sure he'd head south and then around Macon. He'll get strung out. It's over fifty miles to the prison camp."

"Then take your cavalry and cut him off. Find a position between Macon and Sherman and dig in."

* * *

CLINT CILLEY HAD RIDDEN hard to the west, knowing Stoneman was on his way to Macon. He had managed to avoid Confederate patrols, having to outrun one. In the early morning of July 31, he found Stoneman's camp south of Macon.

He rode into a dispirited, bloodied cadre of soldiers resting alongside a road. Occasional bursts of rifle and cannon shot from Confederate lines in their front continued to harass them.

Near the front of the column, Clint rode into an assemblage of officers. They stood off to the side, their horses nearby. Stoneman looked up as Clint approached. "So, you've come back to us. Where's Davidson?"

"On his way to join you, sir, but he's pulling up some track along the way. The raid was successful. What happened to you?"

"Macon was well defended, and we couldn't get through to them. Even if we had, the bridge to the city was out."

"Where are you going? Andersonville?"

"That was the idea. But we've run into a strong force of rebs blocking our way. We managed to push them back some, then they pushed us back. We've been skirmishing since sundown."

"Captain," Colonel Capron added in a slow and weary voice, "we've been in our saddles almost continuously for five days and nights. It's two hours to dawn and our first real rest."

"What's the plan?"

Stoneman looked at his officers. "We've been discussing our options. We can't get to Andersonville. There's a strong Confederate cavalry in our front. So, we go back the way we came. We head north, hit the Clinton Road and head for Atlanta."

Colonel Biddle commented, "They'll try to cut us off."

Stoneman responded, "We leave at dawn and we move fast. We can't let them cut us off. Can you find us a way out of here, Sam?" he asked his guide.

"I'll do the bestest I can. But it ain't gonna be easy."

Just before dawn, Stoneman's hungry, tired, and disconsolate troops mounted their horses and headed back north. Horace Capron's brigade led the way through the mist of an eerily quiet morning. They arced past Macon on their left and headed north. Parties of escaped slaves viewed them as saviors and followed behind the army.

Everything broke loose in the early morning. Gunfire in the rear from pursuing Confederate cavalry pushed the Union force ahead of them. The Union troops fought their way in a running fight toward the Clinton Road. Once there, Stoneman was amazed at what lay before him. A strong force of Confederate soldiers was dug in and waiting on a ridge outside the small town of Round Oak. Nearby was a white clapboard church, a sign in front of which proclaimed it "Sunshine Church."

"How'd they get here so fast? We should have beaten them here easily!"

Clint reasoned, "You lost time heading south at first. You should have headed back right after your attack on Macon failed."

Stoneman shook his head. "We're in for a tough fight. But we can cut our way through."

Colonel Adams surveyed the land and surmised, "They've got the good ground, the ridge. We've got a maze of ravines, woodlands, and little hills to fight through."

"With Confederate cavalry behind us," Stoneman reminded him. "Atlanta and Sherman are ahead of us. North, that's where we have to go. Get your boys ready. We're making a charge."

On the ridge, Colonel Alf Iverson couldn't help but smile. A major alongside him praised, "Great maneuver, sir, you've headed 'em off. They got nowhere to go but to our guns."

"It's good to know shortcuts. See the men are ready, Major. Stoneman will be coming."

Soon a fierce battle raged through the ravines, hollows, and ridges around Sunshine Church as Stoneman's force surged forward. Clint Cilley watched near the rear of the attack with Stoneman. At first their attack seemed favorable as the rebel force dropped back, only to surge forward as reinforcements joined them from the north.

Iverson greeted his new troops from Milledgeville. "You're a Godsend!" he exclaimed to their commander. "Stoneman can't stand against us now!"

"Cobb sent us to Milledgeville when he thought the Yanks were going there, Colonel. It turns out they didn't, but it put us in position to help you out."

"We needed you," Iverson said gratefully. "Now I've got 1,300 men. Deploy your men to Stoneman's rear. We still hold the ridge in his front. It's time to hit those Yankees with everything we have and close the trap on them. Those cowards have been fighting women and children. Let's see how they stand against men."

The fight became even more ferocious as the Confederate forces closed like a vise on the Union army. All hell broke loose as they clashed with cannon fire and screaming horsemen armed with sabers and thundering horses neighing with fright. The escaped slaves scattered in terror-filled flight. As night fell on July 31, a defeated army congregated on a hill in the tangled terrain.

A disconsolate Stoneman looked over the ashen, fatigued faces of his officers. Keouh stood beside him with brigade colonels Biddle, Adams, and Capron. Clint Cilley watched from off to one side. The general addressed them, his voice weary. "The rebs are all around us. We're low on food and ammunition. We're outnumbered with only 2,100 troopers. They must have twice our number. But we have a chance, if we can take it."

"What's that, General?" Biddle wondered.

"Two brigades, Capron's and Adam's, will fight their way out of here. Cut through them to the north and keep running till you get to Sherman."

"What about you and the rest?" Clint inquired.

"I will cover your retreat with my Army of the Ohio, most of Biddle's brigade, as long as we can hold this hill. Captain Cilley, you will accompany Colonel Adams."

"I was ordered to stay with you," Clint countered.

"Now I'm ordering you to leave. You will."

"General, this is madness," Capron argued. "You'll get cut to pieces. Fight your way out with us."

"Sometimes a part must be sacrificed to save the whole. That is what I will do. I'll make my stand here with 600. They'll beat me, but at least it'll be worth something. Adams, you've got about 800 and Capron, 700. Take Smith with his Kentucky brigade, too. Fight like hell and keep moving."

"General . . ." Clint began.

Stoneman looked at him with resignation. "Look, I can barely ride, anyway. Four days in the saddle with hemorrhoids is more than I can handle."

Capron added, "Davidson is still out there with a hundred."

"If you find him, bring him along with you. "

Capron turned to Adams and Smith. "Let's head northeast and resupply at Athens, then head west above Atlanta where Sherman is at Marietta."

Adams looked down at a map spread upon a camp stool. He placed his finger on a small dot near Athens. "Here, we'll link up at Rutledge Station. We both should be able to get there by late tomorrow afternoon, even taking different routes. Then we hit Athens together."

"It's seventy miles and our men are tired."

"Horace, I'm guessing we'll both have incentive to move fast," Adams countered.

"You're sure about this?" Adams cautioned as he looked at his commander.

"More sure than ever. We are hopelessly outnumbered," Stoneman proclaimed. "It's still light. Get going. You can resupply at Athens. Then, if you can, destroy the armory and any government works there."

The two brigades charged off the hill with sabers swinging in the late afternoon sun. The rebel soldiers were surprised and slow to react at first. Confusion reigned as Stoneman's men dismounted and launched a spirited onslaught into the Confederate ranks. Uncertainty was mirrored in the rebel response as some headed after Capron and Adams, while most tried to hold back Stoneman. The small Yankee band fought valiantly as they pulled through twisted undergrowth that ripped and slashed their flesh. The gray-clad force even fell back at first.

Then Keogh raced to Stoneman's side. "All is lost, General, the enemy is behind us. They've got our horses and nothin' in God's green earth be stopping 'em."

Stoneman shouted to an aide, "Raise a white flag! Bugler, sound retreat! Keogh, spread the word! It's every man for himself, escape if you can!"

At the foot of the hill ran a small creek, which formed into a quicksand bog. In attempting to cross this quagmire, about half of Stoneman's force was captured. Miraculously, in the fading light about 200 escaped. George Stoneman was not among them.

General Iverson himself placed the Union general under arrest. "Well, General," he advised Stoneman, "this is a really something. I don't think anybody's caught a major general in the whole war. This is something to write home about."

"I expect me and my men will be treated with respect," Stoneman said.

Iverson's eyes hardened. "You will be given quarters for the night. In the morning your disposition will be carried out."

McCook's Raid

GENERAL EDWARD MCCOOK'S CAVALRY of 3,600 troopers of the First Division of the Army of the Cumberland had been sent southwest of Atlanta. This included a provisional division under Colonel Tom Harrison, whose men had just returned from an exhausting raid to Alabama. "Only use them as reserves," Sherman had urged.

While Stoneman ravaged towns to the east, McCook's force was to sever communication and supply lines in the west. He was to link with Stoneman at Lovejoy Station, thirty miles south of Atlanta, and then move on to Andersonville to liberate the prisoners there.

They crossed the Chattahoochee River on a pontoon bridge erected at a ferry and reached Palmetto, twenty-five miles southwest of Atlanta. There, McCook's men cut the Atlanta and West Point Railroad. On July 28, they captured and burned over 1,000 Confederate supply wagons at Fayettevillle.

Like Stoneman, McCook seemed to condone and even encourage the destruction of private property. They began riding on an arc nearly forty miles west of Lovejoy Station, and early on the morning of July 29, his raiders reached the Lovejoy rendezvous point twenty-three miles south and east of Atlanta. But Stoneman was nowhere in sight.

McCook, a thirty-one-year-old Ohioan, sat astride his horse and tugged at his bushy mustache on an otherwise clean-shaven face. "I wonder where Stoneman is," he said to his adjutant. "He should have been here by now."

"What do you plan, sir?" his assistant asked.

"We'll bide our time here by ripping up track on the Macon and Western. This is the main line left to Atlanta. If Stoneman doesn't show soon, we'll re-cross the river and head back to Sherman the way we came, a strategic retreat."

When the Army of the Ohio cavalry failed to appear, McCook's column turned northwest toward Atlanta.

168

The Union Army had ripped up over two miles of track, tore down several miles of telegraph wire, and pounced upon Confederate supply wagons, burning hundreds of them. In the process, they also killed 800 mules and captured 400 prisoners.

Pursuing Confederate cavalry under General Red Jackson collided with McCook's force just west of Lovejoy. After a sharp skirmish, the Union cavalry continued a westward retreat on the Lower Fayetteville Road. There they encountered several hundred of Joe Wheeler's horsemen, who had joined the chase from Decatur and hit the rear of the Union line.

McCook told his men, "We're outnumbered. Sweep west toward Newnan, it's the only path left open to us. We'll make a stand there!"

The Union forces raced through the night with the rebel troopers thundering along behind them. The rear-most Union regiment returned fire from horseback as Confederate gunfire savaged them from behind.

Shots echoed through the clear night air, with explosive flashes at places like Whitewater Creek and Shake Rag. Racing as if chased by banshees, McCook's force pounded thirty miles over the hard road until early on the morning of July 30, when they galloped up to Newnan, Georgia, a small "hospital" town forty miles south of Atlanta.

A regiment of Indianans from McCook's advance guard charged over a hill and into the town. They were shocked to find a trainload of Confederate soldiers sitting at a depot ahead of them, blocking the road.

Confederate General Philip Roddey, with 550 dismounted Alabama cavalrymen, had been forced to stop at Newnan that night because the track up ahead had been ripped up at Palmetto, McCook's work from a couple days earlier.

Roddey's startled men grabbed their weapons and opened fire on the Yankee intruders. Roddey ordered the train engineer to blast an alarm from the train whistle.

Kate Cummings, a nurse just leaving a hospital for Confederate soldiers, froze as she stood alongside the street and watched. She knew she should be fearful for her life, but she couldn't get her feet to move. Her eyes locked onto the dramatic scene before her.

Then she screamed with joy. Galloping into town down two different streets came Wheeler and 700 men. McCook's troops beat a hasty retreat from the town. General McCook's eyes grew wide as he surveyed the coming onslaught. He shouted to one of his officers, "Colonel Croxton, find us a road to get around this town to the south!"

As the Union troop moved below Newnan, Wheeler divided his men. He cried, "Colonel Ashby, take 200 men down LaGrange Street and out on the Corinth Road. There you can intercept the head of the Yankee column. I'll take the rest of my command and hit their flank!"

Wheeler waited in Newnan until Ashby could get into position. When a flurry of gunshots echoed in the distance, the Confederate general rushed three miles southwest of town to the intersection of the Ricketyback and Corinth roads. As Ashby's men ambushed McCook's advance guard, the rest of Wheeler's command struck the Union column's flank.

McCook's men were pushed into twisted, tangled woods south of Ricketyback Road. There they reformed and started to push back, straddling the road. The fighting continued back and forth across the Ricketyback.

Wheeler stood in his stirrups as his line wavered for an instant. He raised his sword, pointed at the Yankee position and shouted, "Bugler, sound the charge!" As the first notes cut into the air, Wheeler screamed, "Charge! Follow me!" and bolted on his horse, slamming into the blue-clad soldiers and forcing them off the road. Then Wheeler's army formed a huge horseshoe and moved in on them.

McCook, believing he was surrounded, lost his nerve. "We're completely surrounded by an overwhelming force!" he cried to his men and officers as they dismounted to fight on foot, one cavalryman holding four horses as three others fired their carbines.

The general kept repeating, "What shall we do? What shall we do?" Beseechingly, he looked up at John Croxton. "Look," he said, "you take command. Do the best you can."

The fighting continued to seesaw back and forth as roots and vines grabbed the men like hidden fingers and tripped them. While the Union forces were sustaining heavy casualties, 1,400 Confederate reinforcements joined Wheeler. Charge after charge steadily pushed McCook's men back farther into the woods.

In late afternoon, during a lull in the fight, McCook gathered his officers together. "Is this all?" he asked, looking at his subordinates.

"We've lost some," a major answered, "and we're running out of ammunition."

McCook paused, shook his head, and announced with a heavy heart, "The situation is hopeless. I see no recourse but to surrender."

Colonel Jim Brownlow of the First Tennessee Cavalry turned bright crimson and snapped, "Gentlemen, you can all surrender and be damned. I'm going out with my regiment."

John Croxton echoed, "I'm with Brownlow. We've been pretty hard on the rebs and civilians during this raid, and they aren't going to be too kind to us. I don't want to end up in Andersonville, and I don't want to see any of my troops there. Let us try to fight our way out."

Others expressed similar sentiments. McCook sighed, relenting. "All right, try to cut yourselves through their lines."

Dozens of their dead and wounded were left behind, as were all artillery and ambulances, as McCook's men mounted their horses and pushed south. With Confederates in pursuit, they crossed Sandy Creek by a rise of land called Brown's Mill. There McCook summoned some resolve. "This retreat must be protected!" he demanded. "Colonel Dorr, your Iowa boys have to hold 'em off. Then follow us!"

Dorr and his 500 men of the Eighth Iowa Cavalry fought a delaying action as McCook's column disappeared in the distance. Then, just as he was about to order a retreat, Dorr's escape route was cut off. His whole regiment surrendered. It was 5:00 p.m.

Red Jackson was left behind to gather up McCook's cannons, ambulances, and hundreds of prisoners. Wheeler chased the fleeing Union forces until dark. Then he dispatched several detachments to continue the pursuit while he went back to Newnan, where he was greeted by a thankful populace. The owner of a fine house on LaGrange Street invited the general inside to rest. He sat down at a desk, spread out his maps and fell asleep.

Into the evening and the inky pitch of night, three large columns of frightened, tired, and hungry Yankees fled desperately for the Chattahoochee River. Some made it. The Fifth Iowa and Second Kentucky reached William's Ferry and used three old canoes, with their horses swimming alongside, to reach the far shore.

A few miles downriver, Brownlow's column reached Hollingsworth Ferry. A search for a ford or a ferryboat came up empty. Many urged their horses into the water and tried to swim across. Scores were still crowded onto the riverbank early the next morning, when Wheeler's Fifth Tennessee and Third Arkansas Cavalry swooped in and captured over 100 of them.

General McCook's column, 1,200 men, raced down the road to Corinth, then galloped toward Philpott's Ferry. They reached the Chattahoochee about 11:00 p.m., almost nine miles below Franklin, Georgia.

"Sir," a young lieutenant reported to McCook, "there's no ferryboat. But there's a slave boy here. He knows where they sunk it. It's at the mouth of New River, a few hundred yards upriver."

"Get crews working on it. We've got to get it floating and fit to take men and horses across."

Working quickly, the Union soldiers managed to refloat the fragile vessel. Soon horses and men were being plied across the river. Many made it, but in the early morning dawn, Wheeler's Fifth Georgia cavalry were silhouetted on a rise overlooking the landing.

From the shore, the Yankees rattled sporadic gunfire up the hill. The Confederate cavalry stampeded down the hill with reckless abandon to the water's edge. All the stranded Union raiders were captured, along with several hundred horses and mules.

Joe Wheeler galloped up and shouted at his subordinate, "We had 'em! How did so many git across?"

"They worked through the night, sir, looks like they got a boat afloat." Sheepishly, the officer looked away and added, "Resting, sir, the men were very tired."

"They had all day to rest today!" Wheeler snapped. "By thunder, you let most of 'em get away!"

"We got near half, sir," the soldier answered defensively.

Wheeler's cavalry herded 1,250 enlisted men and thirty-five Union officers into Newnan. A two-story cotton warehouse became their prison until the Palmetto line was repaired and they could be shipped to prisoner of war camps in Macon and Andersonville.

While McCook's force desperately fought to escape Wheeler, Stoneman's brigades, led by Capron and Adams, faced similar predicaments. Leaving Stoneman to cover their retreat, the two brigades fled separately, their flights a mayhem of pounding hooves, screaming horses, gunshots, and flashing sabers. Confederates, intent on taking Stoneman's Hill, weren't ready to launch a pursuit, especially when Union troops under Stoneman came at them.

General Iverson soon addressed the need to change tactics. While continuing to deal with the Yankees on the hill, he sent Colonel William

Breckenridge's cavalry from the Army of Tennessee after Capron and Adams. He ordered a "spirited pursuit of those Yankees who are running away."

The next morning, General Iverson assembled his Union prisoners at Sunshine Church. Six hundred stood under the guard of Confederate soldiers. Stoneman, Biddle, and Keogh had been held captive apart from their men and were led before them by armed guards. A lone tree in the churchyard starkly displayed a noosed rope fastened to a limb.

General Iverson strode purposefully up to the officers. He proclaimed in a voice loud enough to be heard by men in the ranks, "General Stoneman, I have no sympathy for your situation. You invaded noncombatant communities, ravaged the countryside, and fired artillery into residential areas of Macon. These are war crimes."

Yells of "Hang 'im! Hang 'im!" arose from the Confederate soldiers.

Iverson paused and let the cry swell as it washed over them from the impassioned rebels. Stoneman paled and his lips trembled. He stared at the rope on the tree. Then the Confederate general raised his hands palm down for silence.

"But that rope isn't for you, General Stoneman. While I'm very tempted to wrap it around your neck, my superiors have other plans for you. You will be confined, along with your colonel and major, in a secure location. The rest of your men will be transported to Andersonville. Ironic. isn't it?

"Oh, there will be one hanging," Iverson continued. "Captain, bring him out."

The officer dragged from concealment a slight, sad, shackled form and pulled him to the tree. It was Sam, the young black guard who served as Stoneman's guide.

Stoneman shouted, "Leave him be! He's just a boy. All he did was show us the way!"

Iverson responded, "He is an escaped slave who has chosen to aid our enemy. Too many are running away and following your armies. I'm setting an example. Hang him, Captain!"

Sam sobbed pathetically as Confederate soldiers stood him on a stool and wrapped the noose around his neck. In an instant the boy was dead, swaying slowly from the tree limb.

"That was barbaric!" Stoneman cried. "You'll pay for this!" Then his eyes swept past the hanging tree to the assembled Confederate soldiers. "Where are the rest of your men?" he inquired of Iverson.

"That's all there are, Colonel, 186 of the finest sons of the South!"

Stoneman paled and reached out to Keogh for support. "One hundred and eighty-six? But you surrounded us, and we had 2,000."

Iverson shook his head and smiled. "You only thought you were surrounded. We fooled you, sir. You were never surrounded or outnumbered. There were more of us at times, but never anything close to your numbers."

Stoneman's eyes glistened as he fought back tears. He collapsed in total defeat.

* * *

THE TWO UNION columns under Capron and Adams raced away through the night, aiming for Rutledge Station near Athens and the needed supplies there. Capron pressed northeastward, pushing his men hard throughout the night and next day. They passed over the Milledgeville Road to Eatonton and Madison. Adams urged his force north as well, toward Rutledge Station, the rendezvous point. All the while, Kentucky regiments under Breckenridge nipped at their heels.

Capron's waited a short time at Rudledge Station for Adams, not knowing that Adams's route had taken his men on a road via Eatonton to Madison, ten miles east of Capron's position and nearly forty miles from Sunshine Church. Both forces rejoined north of Madison, where they camped for the night—but not before destroying anything of value to the Confederacy in the towns they passed through.

Early on the morning of August 2, the two commanders met. "I'll continue on ahead, to Athens," Adams informed Capron. "Watkinsville is just ahead, then it's less than ten miles north to Athens. Let me get underway first."

"I like that," Capron agreed. "You demonstrate below the town. Take Smith and his Kentucky cavalry with you. I'll take up a detached position, then rejoin you to force a crossing at the bridge over the Oconee River at Barber Creek, just below the town."

"Good," Adams concurred. "One other thing. Let's let the people of Watkinsville know that the war has come to them."

* * *

IN ATHENS, Mary Ann Cobb and other members of the Soldier's Aid Society were in the town hall on Market Street. A half dozen women were tearing cotton sheeting into bandages.

One asked, "I wonder when the Yankees will come. It's so frightful just waiting."

"Have you heard from your husband?" another woman asked Mary.

"A telegram arrived from General Cobb. The Yankees have been driven away from Macon. Our boys are in pursuit of the Yankee raiders, but I don't know what way they're heading."

A woman peered out into the street. "There's a commotion outside. Something must be happening!"

Suddenly, Mary's slave boy, Israel, burst into the room. "Mas' Howell, he wants to see Mistress!"

Mary Cobb immediately put down her work and hurried outside, where she was met by her breathless son. "The Yanks are at Watkinsville. They're looting and burning the town. A scout reports that they are marching toward Athens."

"What are we to do?" Mary asked.

"Stay calm and get organized, men and women both."

Men and women delved into a beehive of activity. Contrary to the confusion that reigned during a couple of earlier false alarms, the reaction of Athens's citizenry was solemn and resolute. No bells rang or alarms sounded. Men went to breastworks ready to fight.

Two hundred and fifty workers came armed from the Cook and Brother Armory. Three companies of home guards commanded by James White, John Billups, and Stephen Elliot Jr. also answered the call to arms. Mechanics, mill workers, college professors, newspapermen, old men, and boys who had never seen combat gathered at the town hall and shouldered their muskets, walking canes, and umbrellas.

As they headed down Lumpkin Street, an old gentleman near the front shouted, "If the Yankees git into Athens, it'll be over the dead bodies of every last one of us!"

They reached Barber's Creek, just south of Athens. Lieutenant Elliot's company continued across a bridge and deployed as skirmishers. Some planks were removed from the bridge, making it more difficult for a Union crossing. Other militiamen plunged into trenches that slaves had previously dug into the hillsides overlooking the Watkinsville Road. Behind them, two bronze howitzers were posted by Captain Lumpkin in a small earthwork.

Just as the militia and defenders took position behind earthworks, eighty blue-clad horsemen crested the ridge across the creek about 800 yards away. Nervous fingers caressed triggers as men took unsteady aim at the horsemen.

The Home Guard captain held his sword high, looked to his gun crew and, with a slash, lowered his blade.

The howitzers roared and blasted shells onto the distant ridge. A ragged staccato of shot burst from the defenders' line. Most knew that at that distance their targets were out of range.

Union Colonel Smith watched as his exhausted Kentucky cavalry scattered. He turned sadly to his aide. "They want no part of an entrenched force. We don't have the ammunition to take it, anyway, and there's no way we can get across what's left of the bridge. Move them out of range. We'll detour around Athens on Mars Hill Road. We should be able to hook up with Adams. He's close."

Near the river bridge, by the Middle Oconee River, the Athens Home Guard units blasted the weary Union troops with deadly fire. Adams looked to Cilley. "Smith has to pull back. Where's Capron? He said we'd meet here."

"I'm sure he's coming, sir!"

"Well, we can't stand here any longer in the face of this artillery. We'll follow the west bank of the river to the northwest. Maybe we'll find Capron."

* * *

CAPRON'S LOCAL GUIDE deviously misled his column and kept them away from Adams. With Breckenridge's cavalry still baying at his heels like a bloodhound on a scent, Capron broke off his planned attack and headed down the road to Jug Tavern instead. Failing to find Capron, Adams headed off on another route.

The Capron force, dead tired and barely able to remain in their saddles, lurched ahead to the northeast. Colonel Capron's eighteen-year-old son, Osmond, road alongside his father. "Where's Albert?" he asked, regarding his older brother.

"He's riding toward the back. It's better not to have you two together. Your mother hasn't forgiven me for letting you ride with me, anyway. If anything happens to either of you, she'll never forgive me."

"It's war, Father. Albert and I know the risks."

Osmond turned in his saddle and gazed at the forlorn following band. Many sagged in their saddles, heads bobbing, fast asleep. Occasionally someone would tumble off and thud onto the ground, only to scramble to their feet and mount up again. "It's been four days since anyone has had more than a few hours' sleep," he observed.

"I know, son. I figure we've ridden 'bout fifty-six miles in twenty-four hours. Up ahead is a little village called Jug Tavern. We'll water the horses there and then head on to another little town just down the road, King's Tanyard. Scouts tell me it'd be a good spot to rest the men. I can give them two hours' rest. Then we've got to move and find Sherman."

Once at King's Tanyard, Capron's men collapsed in exhaustion. Many didn't even bother with blankets or tying up their horses. They simply dropped where they stood, like dead men. Their colonel and his son found some soft grass beneath a tree and fell fast asleep. To the rear, dozens of runaway slaves camped around a flickering fire.

Just before dawn on August 3, Breckenridge's Kentucky rebel cavalry slipped around Capron's pickets in the darkness and suddenly rose up. They hit the slaves first, plowing into them, riding over the runaways, shouting and shooting. Then the rebels burst through Capron's bivouac, scattering everything before them. Blasts from muskets lit up the early morning.

Officers sprang to their feet and tried to rally sleepy and confused Union soldiers. But it was a futile effort. Rather than stand and fight, most men took to flight in panic.

A stampede mentality swept over them as the Union soldiers remounted and galloped over a bridge on Mulberry Creek. But that span was never meant to sustain the weight of so many horses and men. The bridge collapsed, and many tumbled down to drown in the creek below.

Capron had awakened with a start at the sound of unearthly yells and screams. Pistol shots ripped into tree leaves all around. He shook Osmond and yelled, "There's nothing we can do but run! Stay by me!"

"Where's Albert?"

"I don't know. He'll have to fend for himself. You're with me! Get on your horse!"

Osmond bent down to heft his saddle.

"There's no time to saddle!" his father shouted. "Slip in the bridle and let's go!"

Bareback, father and son burst through the explosive darkness of early morning. Bullets clipped all around as they thundered through the dark forest. They raced down to the bridge and found it gone.

"Father, what can we do? They're all around us!"

"Find a way to escape. Osmond, I'm near sixty years old. I couldn't last at Andersonville, and it'd be your end, too. I'd rather take a bullet than linger in that hellhole of a prison."

"They came this way!" a voice shouted in the gloom. "A man and a boy!"

"We'll find 'em," echoed back voices from seemingly all around.

Capron put his finger to his lips and whispered, "Osmond, we can't ride through them, and we can't stay here like this. The horses are jumpy and will attract attention. We've gotta dismount and start the horses without us. Hopefully the rebs will follow the sound of the animals."

With that, both men jumped down and swatted their mounts, who galloped off through the brush.

"Over there!" a man shouted as others raced in the direction of the horses crashing through the brush.

"See anyone?" a voice inquired.

"Not here," a woman's voice answered. "But there are Yankees all over. Keep lookin'."

Horace and Osmond Capron lay flat on their backs in the oozing mud, covered by brush. Voices of men, women, and children could be heard at intervals as they scoured the woods looking for Union soldiers. Barrels of rifles and shotguns, even the hats and bonnets of the searchers flashed before them.

"Osmond, quietly slip into river. We'll swim for it."

The two slunk into the muddy ooze of the river bottom and swam upriver. Silently, they cut into the cool water and beyond the search parties. Adams's force reached Sherman largely unscathed the next day. Capron lost 450 men, including his son, Albert. Most were sent to Andersonville.

Over the next several days, small remnants of Capron's command found their way to the Union lines. On August 7, the colonel, with his son and five other men, reached Sherman's lines at Marietta on foot.

Sherman was sitting on a camp stool conferring with officers when an escort brought the refugees to him. His jaw dropped as he viewed the men before him, ragged, their clothes tattered, dark circles around their eyes.

"My God, Capron, is that you!"

The colonel saluted, "Yes, sir, what's left of me."

"What happened to you all?"

Capron relayed the actions of the past week: the early destruction of the railroad lines, McCook's failure at Lovejoy Station, Stoneman's failure to link up with McCook, the disaster at Macon, the loss at Sunshine Church and subsequent race to the north by his and Adams's men with another failure at Athens, and his own narrow escape with his son at King's Tanyard.

Sherman shook his head. "Colonel Adams is here. He gave me his report. I've never been a great advocate of cavalry, and you have given me more cause than ever to be cautious about its use. This is the greatest cavalry blunder and defeat of the entire war. Now we have no choice but to do something I abhor. We will have to besiege Atlanta. I just hope it doesn't take months. I don't want another Vicksburg or Petersburg."

"We cut railroad lines," Capron proclaimed defensively.

Sherman snorted. "The rebs have already fixed them. The line to Macon still runs to Atlanta. Prepare for a siege."

Back to Forrest

O
N JULY 31, A.J. SMITH's Gorilla Guerrilas boarded trains to transport them into Mississippi from Memphis. They were 4,000 cavalry and 14,000 infantry strong in pursuit of Nathan Bedford Forrest. The Confederate general was still in Okolona, tending to his foot wound that kept him from riding horseback.

The Minnesota regiments, riding in boxcars, traveled through LaGrange, Grand Junction, Holly Springs, and Waterford toward the Tallahatchie River. Jimmy Dunn rocked and bumped along, standing next to Levi Carr.

"I hear Grant traveled this same route in the Vicksburg campaign," Jimmy announced. "He planned to attack from the south."

"But Van Dorn demolished his supplies at Holly Springs and Grant had to call things off," Carr said.

"Too bad Grant tore up some tracks and blew up a bridge on the way back north. We'll have to do some fixin'," Jimmy surmised.

They reached the Tallahatchie, eighteen miles south of Holly Springs, and attempted to cross the river next to a ravaged bridge. Mule skinners snapped whips, sounding as sharp as cracks of thunder, when ragged musket fire greeted them from the underbrush on the river banks. Willie Sturgis joined Jimmy and Levi as members of the Fifth and Seventh Minnesota thrashed over the river and returned fire.

"Well," Willie proclaimed, "we drove 'em off. Now the rest can cross."

Jimmy squinted into the fading sunset. "Gettin' dark. I 'spect they'll cross over tomorrow. Let's get ourselves into camp."

As night fell, the Minnesota boys attached their shelter halves and lit campfires. Soon coffee was simmering in pots and chunks of salt pork were being roasted from bayonet points.

"Do ya think we'll catch 'em this time?" Will Hutchinson wondered.

Sergeant Chris Chapman of the Seventh responded, "We got A.J. Smith, not Sam Sturgis. If anyone can catch Forrest, it's A.J. We almost got him last time."

"In a way you did. Forrest is shot, crippled up, I hear," Jimmy added.

Levi Carr seemed perplexed. "I'll believe that when I see it."

A loud boom was followed almost instantly by an explosion and a flash as a cannonball tore into the earth and burst into flames, creating a shower of earth and rock.

"Cannons!" Chapman yelled. "Hit the ground, boys!"

As Union soldiers dived for cover, a series of blasts reverberated from across the river.

"Six-pounders!" the sergeant yelled again. "At least a half dozen!"

In the noise and confusion, men scrambled for cover. Mules, bellowing and screaming to get away from the shells, galloped down a wooden corduroy road. Some teams pulled wagons, careening and thundering over the rough road.

A short time later the cannons ceased firing, and the sounds of soldiers moving away from across the river became apparent.

"I wonder why they're goin'?'" Jimmy asked.

"They were makin' things darn unpleasant for us," Levi commented, "and we didn't have nothin' ta throw back at 'em." He listened intently. "It shore sounds like they're gone. We might as well turn in for the night."

The next day, Colonel Marshall solved the mystery when he made an announcement to the encamped Minnesotans. "We captured a Texas captain. I asked him why they stopped shelling us last night." The colonel paused for effect, then continued. "He replied, 'We heard you bringing heavy artillery down to the river, and we got out of the way.'" Marshall grinned. "It was our mules and their wagons that scared the rebs away. Huzzah for the mules!"

The soldiers laughed and burst out in a chorus of "Huzzah! Huzzah! Huzzah!"

Smith decided to continue following Grant's 1862 rail route from Holly Springs to Oxford, knowing that his men would have to repair tracks and a bridge as they endured sporadic Confederate gunfire.

* * *

SAM CHALMERS'S CONFEDERATE cavalry dug in and harassed Smith as best they could. But it wasn't enough. Forrest rode by carriage into Oxford, where he conferred with Chalmers. He hobbled to a bench in Oxford Square and motioned for his officer to sit beside him. His brother, Colonel Jesse Forrest, stood nearby.

Forrest didn't mince words. "We're outnumbered, battered, and bruised, including me."

"What should we do, General?"

"Well, we can't fight such a large force head on."

"What, then? Smith is fixed to join Sherman after he finishes with us, General Forrest."

Forrest sat in contemplation. Then his face lit up. "We can get Smith to move away from Sherman and out of northern Mississippi."

"How?"

"We'll go up north first and attack Smith's base of operations. Memphis!"

"We . . . attack . . . Memphis?" Chalmers asked, slowly.

"It'll be the last thing them Yankees would expect us to do. They've been in control of the town most of the war with no problems. I'll take 2,000 cavalry troops and hightail it from Oxford to Memphis by way of Panola County, Mississippi. You stay back here, hold your own against Smith by pretending you've got more men than you've got."

"How do I do that?"

"Make noise, ride around in circles with the same men, harass 'em some more. Smith will never know our movements in this area. I think it'll work."

Chalmers smiled. "That's why they call you the wizard."

"Memphis is my hometown, ya know. Hey, Jesse," he called his brother, "how 'bout we go home and visit family?"

"But your foot?" Chalmers asked. "How can you ride?"

"I've tried some," Forrest said. "I kin git by with one foot in the stirrup and my bad one out."

* * *

SMITH'S ARMY FIXED TRACKS, rebuilt the Tallahatchie Bridge and kept an eye on what they supposed to be Forrest's men around Oxford. In mid-August, heavy rainstorms delayed work and turned the road into a muddy quagmire.

Patrols were sent out in search of Confederate forces, but only small numbers of rebel soldiers were encountered. Occasional skirmishes erupted with Chalmers's men as Union soldiers readied the way to Oxford.

Meanwhile, Forrest closed in on Memphis. On the night of August 20, his cavalry was poised outside the city limits. In thick fog, the general limped to a camp stool and sat before his son William and brother Jesse. "It's all set. We can't capture the city. I know that. They've got near 6,000 men there, three times what I have. But we can fool 'em. They got no idea we're here. I've talked to my officers. We have three objectives: capture Union generals Washburn and Hurlbut, release our boys from Irving Block Prison, and cause Smith to be recalled from Mississippi."

"How will we enter the city, sir? Where do we attack?" William inquired.

"Attack?" Forrest chuckled. "We don't attack. Look at this pea soup we're in. We'll just ride right by their pickets. Tell 'em we're a Union patrol and we've got rebel prisoners. They'll invite us right in. Then we divide up and do what we came to do."

* * *

At 4:00 A.M. on the morning of August 21, Forrest rode at the head of a column of 1,500 Confederate cavalry. They trotted slowly down the main road leading to Memphis. Near the city limits Union guards, rifles at the ready, blocked the road.

"Who are you? What are you doing here?" a sergeant demanded.

Forrest, his diembodied voice coming from the dark and fog, replied, "Patrol sent out by General Hurlbut to capture Confederate prisoners. I've got a few hundred rebels here for Irving Prison."

The sergeant turned to his patrol. "Sounds right. I know they've been rounding up rebs." He turned back to Forrest. "Pass through."

Once they entered Memphis, Forrest screeched, "Now, boys, send 'em ta Hell!"

Even with just one spur kicking, his horse launched into a gallop. The silence of the night was shattered by galloping hooves, gunshots, and shouts. The raiders split into three groups to pursue their separate missions, firing at Union soldiers all the while.

A Confederate officer smashed down the door of Union General Stephen Hurlbut's quarters. But at the first sound of gunfire, the general had escaped.

Forrest trotted on his horse into the lobby of the luxurious Gayoso House Hotel, seeking other Union officers and General Cadwallader Washburn. His men smashed through door after door in search of their prize. A captain strode up to Forrest and handed him a new Union general's uniform. "It's Washburn's, General," he announced. "It's all of him we could find."

The Union general had gotten away by running down an alley dressed only in his nightshirt. He found refuge at Fort Pickering.

Union soldiers barricaded at the State Female College next to Irving Block Prison and stalled Forrest's attempt to break in.

After two hours of fighting, Forrest ordered a withdrawal. He left Memphis at the cost of thirty-four men, but he cut telegraph wires leading to the city and took 500 prisoners and large quantities of supplies, including many horses. Under a flag of truce, he sent back Washburn's uniform.

Hurlbut, from a house where he sought sanctuary, watched Forrest and exclaimed, "There it goes again! They'll supersede me with Washburn because I could not keep Forrest out of western Tennessee, and Washburn cannot keep him out of his own bedroom!"

Raid at Oxford

ON THE MORNING OF AUGUST 22, A.J. Smith's Sixteenth Corps was strung out for six miles on the road leading to Oxford, Mississippi, where Forrest was said to be headquartered. The Fifth Minnesota was once again acting as rear guard. The Seventh marched into Oxford behind General Smith.

Smith, accompanied by Joe Mower, First Division commander, rode into the Oxford town square. There they were met by three official-looking men. Smith and Mower dismounted and approached the three.

"Welcome to Oxford, sir," the older of the men greeted. "I'm the mayor, and these are councilmen."

"Thank you," Smith answered. "I'm General Smith and this is General Mower. It's awful quiet here. Where are the people?"

The mayor looked around at the quiet streets and empty buildings. "They all left when they heard you were coming, General. They didn't have a good experience with Grant in '62."

"All right," Smith continued. "Where is General Forrest? We hear that he has headquartered here."

The mayor tried to suppress his emotions but couldn't contain a smugness that flashed across his face.

"Haven't you heard, sir? General Forrest has gone to Memphis. He raided there yesterday."

"What!" Smith exploded. He snapped to a nearby aide, "I want verification."

"That might be hard, General," the mayor commented. "The telegraph to Memphis has been cut."

"Try!" Smith snapped again.

As the aide hurried away, Mower turned to Smith. "That could be why things have been so quiet around here. Sure, we had some fighting that bogged us down, but nothing like we expected and no Forrest."

"So," Smith surmised, "we weren't fighting a large Confederate cavalry or even Bedford Forrest. Blast! He tricked us and now we have Confederate armies on two sides."

In a few minutes, the aide returned. "General Smith, the mayor's right, I couldn't get through to Memphis, but I did reach one of our nearby outposts. Forrest was in Memphis. He burned some government buildings, killed or captured about 500 and generally caused damage and havoc. There's more, though. It seems Jubal Early has burned almost all of Chambersburg, Pennsylvania."

Smith's face burned a deep crimson as his emotions flashed between embarrassment at Forrest's trickery and being appalled at Confederate destruction in Memphis and Chambersburg.

"Mower," he snapped, "make 'em pay! I want Oxford burned. Start right here in the town square with the courthouse."

The Oxford mayor exclaimed with alarm, "No, General! That's wrong! These people did nothing!"

"You've harbored Forrest. That's enough. General Mower, place these three under arrest. I don't want them getting in the way."

"What about the army, General Smith?" Mower asked.

"We have enough in town now to do the job. Leave the others on the road, in formation."

The scene quickly turned to absolute chaos as officers lost control of Union soldiers bent on revenge and retribution. Flames and smoke rolled from the courthouse. Soldiers broke into homes and plundered, carrying away mirrors, rocking chairs, vases, articles of clothing, bedding, books, and whatever else appealed to them.

After looting houses, the rioting soldiers, more like a mob, set them afire. Chaplain Elijah Edwards of the Seventh Minnesota appealed to Colonel Marshall. "Sir, this is outrageous. Is there no sense of decency?"

"Apparently not today, Reverend," Marshall observed. "At least most Minnesota boys are back on the road in ranks."

Soldiers began to sweat and cough in their mission of ruin as the smoke grew denser and the flames more intense. Chaplain Edwards watched with disgust as a lone horseman galloped down the street, clattering through the suffocating smoke. The horseman flung an empty whiskey bottle, smashing it on the street, while he held before him a grinning skeleton he had stolen from a doctor's office.

"Drunk!" Edwards spat the word out like it tasted bad. He looked around at other soldiers as they took swigs from liquor bottles.

"He's not the only one," Marshall said sadly. "It seems they found the taverns."

The rest of the army was strung out along the Holly Springs Road for six miles. Sergeant Willie Sturgis spat onto the dusty road and called to Jimmy Dunn and Levi Carr.

"Well, boys, we've been sittin' here for near two hours. What do ya s'pose is tyin' things up?"

"I don't know," Jimmy responded. "Maybe Gen'r'l Smith found old Forrest and they's talkin' things over."

"Naw," Levi rejoined. "If'n Smith runs inta Forrest, they won't be doin' no talkin'. Fact is, we'd be up there fightin'."

"Looky here," Willie announced, "here comes Captain Bishop. Maybe he knows somethin'."

The captain of the Fifth Minnesota strode to where his company lingered along the road. "Men," he shouted, "General Smith ordered the boys up front ta do some burning in Oxford. Seems that General Forrest left us here and raided Memphis. Smith is a bit put out about that and is taking it out on Oxford."

"How long we gonna sit here, Captain?" Will Hutchinson asked.

Bishop considered. "Not much longer. It's not that big a town. I expect we'll move out directly."

Eventually, late in the day, the order came to move out. When the column passed through Oxford, they did so under a canopy of flames. Jimmy looked to Levi. "There's hardly nothin' left. No businesses, no supply depots, warehouses, no courthouse."

"And hardly any houses," Levi concluded.

"Look there!" Jimmy cried. "There's a church in the square, looks untouched."

Willie Sturgis announced to his friends, "I heard the captain talkin'. That's an Episcopal church, and there's a few houses here and there that didn't git burnt. They've got a university here. Smith ordered ta leave that alone, too. It's bein' used as a hospital for both armies."

As the army marched north out of Oxford toward Memphis, the citizens of the Mississippi town returned. Aghast at the destruction, one man kicked an empty whiskey bottle from the street.

"Drunken cowards! That's what they are!" the man proclaimed. "It musta taken a drunk to lead 'em. There he goes, 'Whiskey Smith.'"

Atlanta Falls

SHERMAN BROUGHT IN HIS TOP subordinates to consider his next move after the failure of the Stoneman and McCook raids. John Schofield with his aide Clint Cilley, along with Oliver Howard and other officers, listened as their commander outlined his plans.

"Our siege is underway, but they have thirteen miles of defenses. This will take months, as I feared it would. Howard, you failed to break through at Ezra Church. Schofield, you spent the first week of August trying to cross Utley Creek. Your delays didn't allow you to exploit the rebels' position, and now we're entrenched before the Confederate main lines."

"It was the abatis, sir," Schofield acknowledged. "We couldn't get through their defenses, but they couldn't get by us, either. Fire was hot on both sides."

"It's behind us now," Sherman responded curtly. "It all is. The battles to get here, the raids on railroad lines, the siege. We've tried them all and here we sit. If we don't do something soon it might be over."

"What do you mean?" Schofield wondered.

"The election. If Lincoln loses and McClellan wins, our new commander-in-chief may very well end this war on Confederate terms."

"Do you think taking Atlanta could change the election?"

"It could. We can't just sit here and wait to find out. I'm sending you out on a flanking movement to the west. We had the right idea before, it just didn't work then. We must cut the railroads to Atlanta. We starve them out. With no food or supplies, Hood can't hold the city."

Hood had the same goal regarding Union supplies. Wheeler and his cavalry raided into northern Georgia to destroy railroad tracks and supplies destined for Sherman.

At Dalton on August 14, Wheeler attacked a Union garrison and demanded its surrender. During the ensuing fight, the Union forces withdrew to fortifications on a hill outside of the town. The outnumbered Yankees held on until after midnight, when Wheeler called off his attack. At five the next morning, the Confederates withdrew.

While Wheeler was to the north, Sherman sent General Judson Kilpatrick to raid rebel supply lines. He hit the Atlanta and West Point Railroad on the evening of August 18 and tore up a small area of tracks. On the way to Lovejoy Station on the Macon and Western Railroad, Kilpatrick hit Jonesborough's supply depot on the rail line. Large amounts of supplies were burned there on the night of August 19.

On August 20, Kilpatrick's raiders reached Lovejoy Station. As they began their destruction, Patrick Cleburne's division appeared and a fight raged into the night. Fearing encirclement, Kilpatrick ordered a hasty withdrawal north. The Yankees escaped, leaving behind destroyed Confederate supplies and ruined track. Within two days, the rail lines were again operational.

Sherman was clearly frustrated when he met his corps commanders, Jefferson C. Davis, Oliver Howard, John Schofield, John Logan, and David Stanley. "We keep hitting them on raids, cutting their lines, ripping up tracks, and then they just rebuild them and things keep going the way they were before. If we can just permanently destroy Hood's lines, he can't survive. Atlanta will be ours."

"Yes, sir," Davis agreed. "But how?"

"We go all out. I'm sending six of our seven infantry corps on another flanking movement to the west, along with a couple corps of cavalry. I want the whole railroad ripped up between Rough and Ready and Jonesborough. How many men does Hood have there?"

Howard answered, "About 25,000, as near as our scouts can figure."

"We can put 70,000 against them."

"We should roll over them, General."

"We had better."

* * *

TOD CARTER WAITED at Lovejoy Station. Colonel William Shy of the Twentieth Tennessee stood at his side. "What have you heard from General Smith, Captain? Are we just gonna sit here?"

"Orders are coming. But I've heard that the Yanks are coming from the west, a lot of them. Hardee is ordering a two-corps assault, with Stephen Lee to stop 'em. Cleburne is leading Hardee's corps, so the general can direct both corps. We stay with Cleburne."

"Well, we stopped 'em at Utley Creek."

"And they want us to stop 'em at Lovejoy. If we don't, it's all over for Atlanta."

* * *

ON AUGUST 31, Oliver Howard entrenched two corps on the east side of the Flint River near Jonesborough. Logan's Fifteenth Corps dug in on high ground facing east and the Macon and Western Railroad. The Sixteenth Corps, now led by Thomas Ransom, formed a right angle connected to Logan's right facing south. Blair's corps was in reserve.

Hardee ordered Cleburne north on the left from Lovejoy Station to attack the federal line held by Ransom. Stephen Lee's corps was to make a secondary attack on the right against Logan's line.

But as Cleburne's corps, led by Mark Lowrey, turned north toward the Union lines, they were surprised by Kilpatrick's dismounted cavalry. From behind fence rails a continuous fusillade of shot ripped into the Confederates from Spencer repeating rifles.

Lowrey broke off his attack against Ransom. Instead of retreating, he directed his entire division against the Union cavalry. Thomas Benton Smith's brigade, with Tod Carter at his general's side, was in the thick of the fighting as they pushed the Union cavalry off the field.

An order came to pursue Kilpatrick across the river. Tod spoke urgently to Smith. "Shouldn't we finish what we were sent to do? Drive off Ransom."

"Lowrey wants to press them over the Flint River. I hope it works."

But General Stephen Lee mistook the firing between Lowry and Kilpatrick as the main assault and attacked well before Cleburne's troops had actually gone into action with Ransom. Lee ordered a frontal assault that was vigorously led by J. Patton Anderson. At nearly the same time, Lowrey was stopped by Giles Smith's division west of the river.

From the federal lines, General Logan watched Anderson bravely lead his men forward, holding his hat high on the point of a sword. Then Union fire cut the Confederate officer down. Logan shook his head. "Such a waste," he commented sadly. "That was a brave man and a great soldier."

Heavy fire drove Lee's forces back. The ground behind them was littered with the dead and dying. Hardee accosted Lee. "Turn your men around, sir! Renew the attack!"

Lee looked back and shook his head. "My men are in no condition to do so. Our casualties are too heavy."

In Atlanta, John Bell Hood received word of the action at Jonesbourgh. He quickly scribbled out a message to Hardee, then turned his ashen face to an aide. "We couldn't dislodge the Yankees. Lee's corps must retreat tonight into Atlanta's defenses. I fear they'll make a direct attack on the city. Get this dispatch to Hardee."

On September 1, Sherman brought up the Fourteenth Corps under General Jefferson C. Davis to assault Hardee's line north of Jonesbourgh. Stanley's Fourth Corps had been busy destroying the Macon and Western Railroad near Rough and Ready. They ripped up the rails, heated them over burning ties and then wrapped the rails around trees, forming "Sherman's neckties." Sherman now called Stanley's force into his line.

Hardee had met with his commanders during the previous night. He entrenched his lone corps in a north-south defensive line parallel to the Macon and Western line. Cheatham's division took the left, Bate the center, and Cleburne took the right on the line.

Thomas Benton Smith, in the center with Bate, observed to Tod, "Cleburne's division wraps around to the east. We have a salient centered on the railroad."

"We're getting pretty thin, General Smith."

"Calling Lee's corps to Atlanta didn't help. We need them here."

"And Hood needs them there."

"Well, Captain, it seems we're long on needs and short on what's needed."

* * *

At 4:00 P.M., Stanley's corps had still not arrived on the battlefield. Sherman ordered General Davis, "I'm not waiting any longer for Stanley. We have numbers on Hardee now anyway. I want you to take the salient."

Smith sent Tod to the apex of the salient, where Daniel Govan's brigade held. "Colonel Govan," Tod instructed, "this spot must be held. General Smith wants you to understand the importance of it."

Govan's face twisted up as if he had just sucked on a sour lemon. "Boy, we are badly outnumbered. But tell General Smith we'll fight 'em till we can't fight no more."

Davis sent a brigade of U.S. regulars into the breach. Tod joined Govan's force as they huddled behind their entrenchments and opened fire on the attack. The blue line broke and fell back.

"That wasn't too bad," Tod reckoned.

"They're just warmin' up. The next attack they'll be more serious," Govan cautioned. "You better git back to Smith while you can."

Tod mounted his horse and raced back to his commander. Just as he did so, Davis positioned three of his divisions for an assault, Absalom Baird leading the center. Union troops with fixed bayonets pounded into a wall of Confederates. The struggle erupted into hand-to-hand combat. In the heat of late afternoon, sword and bayonet slashed through smoke-filled air. Sweat and blood marked the face of nearly every man as the rebels desperately clung to the slice of land they held.

Then the center snapped and Baird's men poured through. Surrounded, Govan dropped his sword and surrendered. Nearly 600 of his men laid down their arms in hopeless resignation.

Hardee, watching the wreckage of his center, cried out to his three re-serve brigades commanded by Vaughn, Lewis, and States Rights Gist. "We have only one hope! They can't roll up our line on the east. If they do they'll destroy our entire corps. Stop them! I don't care how, just find a way!"

Vaughn slammed directly into the breach and plugged the gap. Lewis and Gist extended the northern Confederate line east to protect the far right and prevent the federal infantry from decimating the rebel line. As darkness fell, the Confederate line, battered and crippled, still held. The tenacious de-fense by the three brigades allowed Hardee's corps to retreat south in good order to Lovejoy Station.

Hood was left no choice when word reached him of the defeat at Jones-bourgh. "General Lee," he informed his corps commander, "our supply lines are finally cut. There will be no fixin' 'em. Sherman is closing in, and we have to save this army. Leaving the city is the only way."

On the night of September 1, Hood evacuated Atlanta. He ordered any-thing that might be useful to the Union forces be destroyed. Eighty-one rail cars filled with ammunition and other military supplies were set aflame. As the cars exploded and the inferno reached its flaming fingers into the sky, buildings caught fire, and the storm of combustion raged through the town.

Miles away, Clint Cilley watched the yellow-orange glow in the night sky. Occasional explosions reverberated in the distance. "General Schofield," he said, "they'll never forget this night."

"And neither should we, Captain Cilley. It's the night Lincoln's presi-dency was saved and a big nail set in the coffin of the Confederacy."

The next day, Union troops marched into the smoldering ruins of At-lanta as Hood slipped past federal forces at Jonesborough en route to Lovejoy Station, where they would spend most of September.

Sherman telegraphed to Washington, "Atlanta is ours and fairly won."

Chasing Sterling Price

STERLING PRICE WAS A BIG MAN. He stood over six feet tall and weighed 290 pounds. His wavy, light hair was always combed and parted. The former governor of Missouri had opposed secession of his state but changed positions because of what he considered overly aggressive actions on the part of Union officials who took over the Missouri militia at Camp Jackson. Price felt that rendered Missouri a vassal and not a state.

He had fought in early battles in Missouri and Arkansas, including as the victor at Wilson's Creek. But petty disagreements with Benjamin McCullough, another general at the battle, led to a division rather than a union of the Confederate forces when the fighting ceased. Their continual bickering and failure to work together led to General Earl Van Dorn's taking over all command.

Then losses followed at Pea Ridge, Iuka, and the second battle of Corinth. Van Dorn was replaced by General John Pemberton. Frustrated, Price went to Richmond to air his grievances and request a return to Missouri. He was granted an audience with President Davis, but the outcome was less than Price hoped for.

Davis listened to the Missourian's complaints and then curtly cut off Price.

"General, you opposed secession in the first place. You quite actively opposed the formation of the Confederacy. You have been a burr under the saddle of other Confederate generals. I question your commitment to the cause."

"Mr. President," Price countered, "that is certainly not my intent. I simply believe that a much better job needs to done in the West."

"Van Dorn, McCullough, and Pemberton have tried. Now we have Kilby Smith, one of our best in command."

Price puffed up. "I have experience in three wars now, the Mormon, Mexican, and this one. My accomplishments have been second to none. Send me back to Missouri in command."

Davis paused and tried to remain composed. He couldn't. "General Price," he snapped, "you are likely the vainest man in this army. I will send you back to Missouri, but not in command of any troops."

"Sir, that is a mistake. What will I do?"

"You'll wait until I decide what to do with you."

* * *

PRICE WAS PLACED in command of units fighting under Kilby Smith in the West. He was ordered from Arkansas to Shreveport during A.J. Smith's Red River Campaign. Dick Taylor requested that Price join him to the south to fight A.J., but Kilby Smith was convinced that Nathanial Banks would take Shreveport if Price and his men were sent away.

Once the Union threat had disappeared, Price met with Kilby Smith with a plan of his own. "I want to retake Missouri," Price proclaimed. "I'm convinced Missourians will rise up to support us if Confederate forces move back into the state."

Smith looked hard at the big man before him. "What do you propose?"

"Let me invade Missouri. I can retake it for the Confederacy and at the very least imperil Abraham Lincoln's chances of reelection."

"What forces would you require?"

"I can put together 12,000 cavalry and fourteen cannon. Give me as many infantry brigades as you can afford. Also, we have guerilla bands in the area, Bloody Bill Anderson, William Quantrill, who can wreak havoc with railroad and wagon transportation. They can even disrupt traffic on the rivers. I have three division commanders: Fagan, Marmaduke, and Shelby. I plan to travel in three columns, twenty miles apart, to St. Louis."

Smith considered. "Well, Fagan is an Arkansas politician with little military training, General Marmaduke is West Point trained, but your best man is Joe Shelby. He's smart and tough. Listen to him. You have a plan that has a chance. Be careful with the guerillas, General, they can be hard to control."

"I hold William Quantrill in high regard," Price responded. "I have great appreciation for the hardships he and his men have endured and the contributions they've made to our cause."

"You've convinced me. You're clear to raid into Missouri."

In early September, Price's force was on the move. But not with infantry. Smith had changed his mind. The Confederate raiders were cavalry and cannon. Kilby Smith had decided not to invest heavily in this venture, and Price's entourage was a ragged lot. Most of the troops were clothed in tattered rags, and several thousand were barefoot. Many were without canteens, cartridge boxes, or other military issue. They carried water in jugs and stuffed cartridges in their shirts and pockets.

They didn't have tents or blankets, and arms consisted of an endless variety and caliber of rifles and muskets. A consistent ammunition supply for the army was nearly impossible.

* * *

FOLLOWING THEIR ENGAGEMENTS with Bedford Forrest and the destruction of Oxford, Mississippi, A.J. Smith's Sixteenth Corps continued on to Memphis. There the Third Division boarded boats to join Sherman. The First Division, with the four Minnesota regiments under Joe Mower, remained in Memphis waiting their turn to head south, as well.

On September 12, a clerk onboard Smith's steamer handed him a telegraph message. Smith read it and turned to an aide. "It's from Sherman in Atlanta. It says, 'I have been trying for three months to get you and Mower to me, but am headed off at every turn. General Halleck asks for you to clear out Price. Can't you make a quick job of it and then get to me?' So," Smith concluded to his aide, "we turn around and head back to Memphis. But let's get Mower moving now."

The general unfolded a map on a deck table and scrutinized it for a moment. "Get this message sent to Mower. He is to take the First Division down the Mississippi to the White River in Arkansas, and then up that to Duvall's Bluff. We'll go by boat to Jefferson City and meet up with Mower at La Mine Bridge."

"Can't Rosecrans handle it?" the aide wondered. "He's got command of the Department of the Missouri."

"Well," Smith speculated, "Old Rosie had an encounter with Price at Iuka. Even though we won the battle, Price gave him all he could handle. I'm guessing Rosecrans is a bit skittish that Price is heading his way, and he has a right to be. He only has 6,000 men in St. Louis. I hear he's begging for reinforcements. Price likely has designs on our supply stores in St. Louis. Grant, who is . . . shall I say, skeptical of Rosecrans's ability, wants to make sure Rosie doesn't skedaddle and leave St. Louis. So, the guerillas are set on Price's trail."

* * *

WHILE INFANTRY PLODDED after them, the Confederates had reached Missouri. When they crossed the Missouri line, nearly a quarter of Price's ill-supplied force was without rifles or muskets. Joe Shelby had been ordered to round up any Confederate deserters he could find along the way and had collected 3,000 of them. On September 26, the three columns converged on Fredricktown, not far from St. Louis.

Price met with his commanders in a confiscated farm house just off the trail. "Gentlemen," he began, "an entrenchment of Union soldiers lies between us and St. Louis. They are garrisoned in Fort Davidson at a place called Pilot Knob. We will destroy the Yankee force there and then continue on to St. Louis."

Joe Shelby looked at Price with questioning eyes. "General Price, how many Yankees are at Pilot Knob?"

"Scouts report about 1,500."

"And," Shelby continued, "We've been told there are about 6,000 soldiers in St. Louis. Our goal is the city. We can take it in one day. It would be wrong to bother with a small garrison when St. Louis could easily fall. We get delayed here and that would give the Yanks time to reinforce."

"That's a dangerous tactic," Marmaduke warned. "We would be leaving an unmolested federal garrison to our rear as we move north."

"It's only fifteen hundred men," Shelby rejoined.

"That's why we shouldn't leave it," Fagan countered. "We can take it easily and then move on St. Louis without concern."

"Once we turn west again we'll have plenty of concerns," Shelby added. "There will be Kansas and Missouri militia in our front, Union cavalry behind us, and A.J. Smith's boys are out there trying to cut off an escape to the south. We have to move quickly."

Price rubbed his smooth chin. "I agree with generals Fagan and Marmaduke. We can make short order of Pilot Knob and still hit St. Louis in good shape. Shelby, you move northwest to Irondale and destroy the St. Louis and Iron Mountain Railroad. Our other two divisions will attack Pilot Knob. General Marmaduke, is your whole division here yet?"

"Still approaching Fredricktown, sir. They'll be here shortly."

"Catch up to us. Fagan, you're to move north and then on Pilot Knob."

Shelby protested one more time. "General Price, the fort is on the floor of a valley surrounded on three sides by commanding hills. It is so situated that we'll have to cross a few hundred yards in the open to reach it. Get artillery up on the hills. That's how to take it."

"General Shelby," Price replied, "we will continue as planned. The die is cast."

* * *

UNION GENERAL Thomas Ewing sent two companies of infantry out from Fort Davidson to patrol roads leading to Fredricktown. The battle began when they ran headlong into Fagan's advance troops. Ewing sent artillery and all the cavalry he could muster to reinforce his patrols. Repeated attacks drove the Union soldiers back into the fort as darkness fell.

The next morning, Fagan, now joined by Marmaduke's men, dismounted and headed into a gap on the floor of the valley between a low mountain, Shepard, to the rear and Pilot Knob. Throughout much of the morning, heavy skirmishing slowly pushed the Union forces back. Confederate troops suffered severe losses with little gain. Eventually the Union patrols were overwhelmed and forced back to rifle pits, which extended from the walls of the fort.

Price knew he had Ewing bottled up. He called on Colonel Maclean, who had an animosity-filled personal relationship with Ewing, to present surrender terms to the Union general. Then Price turned to his artillery commander. "Bring our cannons up on Sheperd Mountain. If the Yankees decide to keep fighting, we'll pour shot into 'em."

Maclean rode across the valley floor under a flag of truce into the fort. A short time later he rode back to Price. Red-faced, he addressed his general. "Ewing turned down surrender. He says, 'Come and take us.'"

"Wait till the cannons are set. He won't be so confident."

A messenger rode up from the mountain. "Captain Wilson's compliments, General. He says one gun became disabled trying to get it up the mountain. Federal artillery hit it. The gunner was killed. It will take considerably more time than planned to get into position."

Maclean snapped, "Forget the cannons. We should hit 'em head on."

Price thoughtfully considered his options, then announced, "All right, a frontal attack it is. We have the men to do it. Prepare the men to attack."

For an hour, an unearthly silence swept over the valley. In the fort, General Ewing peered out at the open space before him. He turned to his artillery officer. "You've done well shooting up at the rebs on the mountain. But they'll be coming from out there, across the valley now. Switch from maximum elevation to ground level in your sighting. I want half-inch lead balls in canister shot."

Ewing then ordered his men assembled. He stood on the walkway on the fort wall and shouted down to his men, "The rebs will be coming soon. They'll likely make a charge over the open plain before us. Riflemen, line the walls. There's not room for everyone on the walls. I want others to tear cartridges, load rifles and pass them up to be fired again. The rest of you, get in the rifle pits outside." Before them, 9,000 Confederate soldiers crouched, waiting in the shadow of the mountain.

At two o'clock, cannons shattered the eerie silence as they opened up on the earthen fort. Then waves of dismounted Confederate cavalry poured into the open. They formed long columns three ranks deep and slowly moved toward the fort.

In Davidson, Ewing urged patience. "Hold your fire, boys," he cautioned his riflemen. But the time for caution was past regarding his cannons. "Artillery! Prick and prime!" he ordered. "Now, fire!"

The big guns roared. At a short distance across a flat plain against a massed enemy, they couldn't miss. Like a giant sickle, they swept through as the attacking force crumbled to the ground. Columns of dense smoke rose hundreds of feet about the walls.

When the Confederates were 500 yards from the walls, Ewing unleashed his riflemen. Three hundred men lining the top of the walls poured unstinting fire at the advancing rebels. With loaded weapons being handed back up almost as fast as the spent ones were handed down, the shooting never stopped. Soon it became difficult to see the gray-clad army through the dense clouds of gunsmoke.

At 200 yards, the southern brigades blasted their first volley and, like a crazed mob, burst into a desperate charge. Fire leapt from the muzzles of gun barrels at the fort. Union soldiers could only see the legs of Confederate soldiers below the smoke. The gallant gray lines relentlessly pushed forward. But in the face of an onslaught of lead and death, they stopped at about thirty yards and slowly fell back.

Their officers shouted, praised, swore, and beat at them with the flats of their swords, urging their men to regroup and charge again. They reformed and swept forward into the sheet of death before them. This time some managed to gain the dry moat surrounding the fort. Union gunners, with artillery shells fused as grenades, leaned over the walls and tossed them into the huddled Confederate soldiers.

Just a few yards from the fort the blood and confusion overwhelmed Price's soldiers, and they finally turned and ran. As the smoke cleared, the Confederates streamed away from the fort. Soon the result became apparent. For 500 yards on all of the three sides under attack, the ground was covered with dead and wounded men in gray. Then, as if trying to erase the horrific scene, the skies open up and rain washed over the field.

* * *

THE CONFEDERATES' FRONTAL ASSAULT on the earthen structure resulted in 1,000 Confederate casualties. The Union commander blew up the fort's powder magazine during the night and escaped with his command after suffering fewer than 100 casualties. Price was left with a hollow victory that crippled his military goals.

His losses at Fort Davidson made a raid into St. Louis impossible. From Pilot Knob, Price began a western swing away from St. Louis. Union soldiers were rapidly reinforcing the city. Price ordered his army west to Jefferson City, where he planned to inaugurate a Confederate governor, who was riding with him. They found the capital city to be heavily fortified and turned west toward Kansas City.

* * *

A COUPLE DAYS into Mower's campaign after Price, while the Confederates were approaching Pilot Knob, the Union supply officer met with Colonel Hubbard and Lieutenant Colonel Will Gere. The two officers sat on their horses, rain dripping off the brims of their kepi caps. The supply news was not good. "The food they issued us at Little Rock is bad, sir."

"What do you mean?"

"The food in the supply wagons, all of it, is moldy. The bread is decayed."

"What can we do?" Gere demanded. "It's rained two days straight and the men are drenched. Now it gets even worse."

"Cut rations, live off the land and pray," Hubbard replied.

* * *

JIMMY DUNN MARCHED alongside Will Hutchinson through a steady rain in a cypress swamp. "This ain't so bad, Will. If it wasn't rainin', we'd be complainin' about the knee-deep water and how miserable it is. Being wet all over seems more normal."

Will shook his head. "Only a real optimist like you would think like that. We've bin goin' miles through this. Trippin' on roots, watchin' fer snakes, gittin' ate up by mosquitos."

"And when we get to a road," Levi Carr called out, "the rain has washed it down to a rocky bed."

"Another thing," Will suggested. "Don't ya think it's kinda funny that here we are, infantry, chasin' a cavalry?"

Jimmy shivered. "That don't bother me as much as headin' out in summer uniforms. It's downright chilly out here."

"It was hot when we left Memphis," Levi noted.

"It wouldn't be half bad," Will complained, "if they hadn't given us moldy food." The men were on half rations, ten days of food for a nineteen-day march.

The nights were even worse. The men, who were cold, sore, weary, drenched, and suffering pain from hunger, collapsed on soggy ground. Levi leaned against a log and held up a foot. The ragged remains of a shoe fell apart in his hand. "Don't that beat all," he mumbled.

Levi gazed at the soldiers before him. A couple had struggled to their feet. One was trying to start a fire to maybe heat some water for coffee or their new dinner fare, beech leaves. Jimmy sat across from Levi, gnawing on the bark of a sassafras tree branch. All their uniforms were in tatters. Some were more naked than clothed.

First Lieutenant John Bishop and Major Tom Gere, looking nearly as pathetic, came upon the men from Company B. Will Hutchinson was on his knees, working with a tinder box and prayerfully blowing onto faint embers.

Jimmy asked the officers, "How far we go today?"

Gere answered, "About twenty miles. The road was better today."

"Where we goin'?"

"Cape Girardeau."

"How far from Brownsville is that?"

"About 335 miles, Jimmy."

"We're movin' pretty fast, Major."

"We're trying to intercept Price. Some days we get behind because of the terrain and only make seven or eight miles. We've gone twenty-five to thirty on good days."

"Major," Levi grumbled, "there ain't been no good days on this march. Not a one."

Gere looked at Bishop, who responded, "I'm sorry, but it isn't getting better. We're here to tell you that rations have to be cut to one third."

The men groaned and cussed, but Jimmy grinned in spite of his misery. "Don't get so down, boys." He bit off a chunk of bark. "This is getting more tasty every day. I just think like I'm eatin' a turkey leg."

"God be praised!" Will shouted as a couple of flickering flames erupted from the fire he was trying to start. "We'll get something warm soon!"

As the boys clapped and cheered, Gere and Bishop turned and walked away to deliver their gloomy message to other soldiers. "They're good men," Bishop said.

* * *

THE NEXT DAY, the division set out in a steady light drizzle. Miserable as it was, it was a welcome relief from soaking rain. General Mower rode at the head of his men, wearing a rain slicker and wide-brimmed hat. A couple of scouts rode up with a cadaverous-looking man who, even though he wore dirty and ripped clothing, had the appearance of a prince compared to the soldiers.

"This here is a local," a scout informed his general. "We found him jest up ahead."

The scrawny, middle-aged man spat a brown streak through yellow-stained teeth and looked at Mower.

"What were you doing up ahead?" Mower asked.

"Huntin' squirrels and anathin' else that happens by."

"You seen General Price?"

"Who dat?"

"General Price. The Confederate cavalry. Have you seen them?"

"What be a Con-fed-rat?"

"Confederates!" an exasperated Mower snapped. "The army fighting the United States to form a new country!"

"There's a war goin' on? Where? I ain't seen nobody up here."

"I don't believe this," the general mumbled to his scout.

"These are backwoods folks, sir. Lots ain't ever been more than a few miles from home. They don't know what's going on over the next range of hills, much less where the fightin' is."

Mower shook his head in disbelief. "Thank you, sir," he acknowledged the man before him. "Let him go," he ordered his scouts. "We'll learn nothing from him."

They passed east through Pocohantas, Arkansas, and Poplar Bluff and Greenville, Missouri, before reaching the river at Cape Girardeau on October 5. In nineteen days, they had averaged eighteen miles a day and traveled over 335 miles. After suffering their greatest endurance test of the war, they boarded boats and traveled on to St. Louis, where they found Price had attacked Pilot Knob.

From there Mower's division, in transports, went up the Missouri River toward Jefferson City. As Price continued to raid eastern Missouri, he was pursued by Pleasanton's cavalry and the Union regiments in boats. The river journey was not a leisurely cruise, however. Low water left the transport frequently mired on sandbars and mud. Troops would then jump into the river to lighten the load and raise the boat. To their relief, the regiments boarded a train for the final stage to the bridge where Smith awaited them.

The La Mine Bridge had been put out of commission several times throughout the course of the war. Thus, it marked the end of the line for the railroad. But it was there that the First Division was reunited with the Third and A.J. Smith.

* * *

ON SEPTEMBER 27, the day Price attacked Pilot Knob, there had been rebel success in another part of Missouri. Bloody Bill Anderson and thirty guerillas had split off from Quantrill. They had been striking isolated garrisons and outposts, murdering and scalping teamsters, cooks, and other unarmed personnel. Anderson's band of cutthroats, including brothers Frank and Jesse James, rode into Centralia. There, the Confederate guerillas burned a train, robbed its passengers and shot in cold blood twenty-four unarmed Union soldiers heading home on furlough.

Three companies of Union militia gathered and chased Bloody Bill and his men out of town, but Anderson quickly rounded up 175 allies from other bands and wheeled around to charge into the pursuing militia. Only twenty-three of the 147 Union militia survived the onslaught. Those wounded and not killed outright were finished off with shots to the head.

* * *

STERLING PRICE CONTINUED to cut a swath of destruction across his home state as he raced toward Fort Leavenworth and Kansas City, but his cavalry numbers continued to decline as a result of desertions, disease, and battlefield losses. Union forces drove hard in pursuit.

From La Mine Bridge, A.J. Smith's guerillas left on October 18 on a grueling march of 175 miles, averaging nearly thirty miles a day. They pushed Sterling Price west toward Kansas City and the Union forces of Alfred Pleasanton's cavalry and Sam Curtis's Kansas militia. Smith ordered a forced march from Sedalia in hopes of catching Rosecrans's cavalry. They marched until midnight, when the exhausted men began to drop out in squads. Soon there was almost no army at all on the trail. When Colonel Marshall of the Seventh Minnesota reached the appointed campsite, only his adjutant and one other soldier were with him. It took until noon the next day for the army to come back together. They resumed the march, hearing of a fight at the Little Blue River south of Kansas City. By the time they got there, the fighting was over and Price was moving south.

Union cavalry and militia were coming up behind Price. From October 20 to October 28, a series of battles and skirmishes were fought east and south of Kansas City. Union forces hammered Price from behind and in front. Smith's guerillas closed escape routes, except one along the border all the way back to Arkansas. Price took it as Smith closed on him.

A.J. spoke to his brigade commanders. "Price is close. It's been a long and hard chase. I promise you a shot at him soon."

Excitement rose in the tattered ranks of Union soldiers when they reached Hickman Hills on the Blue River. Jimmy Dunn excitedly proclaimed to his friends, "This here is where the trails west start: the Santa Fe to the south, the California to the west, and the Oregon Trail farther north. We know the West. We fought Indians. Maybe we're goin' west again."

"I don't think so, Jimmy," Will Hutchinson responded. "Last I heard, Sherman still wants us in Atlanta."

A message from Rosecrans awaited Smith at the trail junction. He read it in the presence of Lucious Hubbard and other regimental commanders. "General Rosecrans has a directive for us. He says, 'You are essentially on General Price's rear. Matters are now in hand. If Price continues to the Kansas state line you will halt pursuit and return to St. Louis.'"

"Don't that beat all," Joe Mower proclaimed. "All this and we'll likely never get to fire a shot at Price."

"Maybe if we move fast enough tomorrow we can catch him," Hubbard suggested hopefully.

"Then try to run him down," Smith said.

The chase continued the next day. Smith's guerillas crossed the Blue and Little Blue rivers and finally caught sight of Price's cavalry in the distance. They chased him down the Kansas state line to near Harrisonville, Missouri.

Price was driving his cavalry hard to the south. His raid into Missouri was over.

Jimmy Dunn watched with Will and Levi. "Looks like Price is livin' up to his nickname."

"'Old Skedad,'" Will said. "The greatest skedaddler in the Confederate Army."

"Rivaled only by our own 'Old Rosie,'" Levi added sarcastically.

Smith received an order to call off the pursuit. The threat was over, and his foot soldiers weren't going to catch the horse soldiers, anyway. Rosecrans delivered an order for Smith to march back across the entire state to St. Louis. On October 30, they set off east.

* * *

PRICE TRUMPETED SUCCESS to Jefferson Davis. He boasted, "I have marched 1,400 miles from beginning to end. This is far more than any other Confederate army. We tied up Union troops that could have been fighting in the East and we tore up Union railroads and confiscated or destroyed much Union property."

President Davis saw it differently. He responded, "It was a greater disaster than any other southern advance into Union territory. You started with 12,000 men, picked up thousands of recruits along the way and returned to Arkansas with fewer than 6,000. Organized resistance in Missouri appears to be over."

Unorganized resistance was also dealt a blow. In spite of some successes, the fighting had wrecked most Confederate guerilla bands and killed their leaders. Bloody Bill Anderson was dead, and William Quantrill had set out on a mission to assassinate Abraham Lincoln and met his end in Kentucky.

After Atlanta

HOOD AND HIS ARMY OF TENNESSEE started September near Lovejoy Station while Sherman camped near Atlanta. After a truce to allow Atlanta civilians to leave, Hood began to move his army to a new base at Palmetto, Georgia, about twenty miles due west of Jonesborough and still south of Atlanta. By September 21, his cavalry and infantry were both encamped there.

Hood had formulated a plan to move north to cut off Sherman's supply line to Chattanooga. His plan needed confirmation, and the man with the authority to do it was on his way. President Jefferson Davis was coming by train from Richmond. On a wet and soggy afternoon, September 25, Davis arrived at Palmetto.

When the president stepped out on the rail station platform, he was met by Tennesseans from Cheatham's division. Tod Carter, with his friend Jim Cooper, watched as the ramrod-stiff leader paused and gazed at the hundreds assembled before him. He shouted, "Be of good cheer, for within a short while your faces will be turned northward and your feet pressing the soil of Tennessee."

Davis met Hood with an icy glare and silence. Hood ushered the president into a house that had been secured as his headquarters. Davis spoke deliberately to his commanding general. "I am disappointed that Atlanta was lost. I was assured you would hold it after I replaced Johnston with you."

"We did the best we could, Mr. President. Sherman had too much for us to overcome."

"Now what do you propose?"

"To move north with my whole army. I can't trust this to our cavalry alone. We can cut off Sherman's lines to Chattanooga and Nashville."

"There's some logic to that, General Hood. It would be futile to attack the army that just beat you."

"Yes, but when Sherman moves into the open we can fall on his exposed rear and grind him up."

"You've got to do better, General Hood. Just operating in Sherman's rear is not enough. I want a plan going forward that's more than that. You must force Sherman into the open and annihilate him."

"I need more men."

"Another fifteen to twenty thousand will be joining you from Kilby Smith."

"I have another request, sir."

"What?"

"I want General Hardee removed from my command. In three of the four battles for Atlanta, Hardee was in command, and in each case was late in executing attacks. Cheatham can take his corps."

Davis sighed. "As you may know, when I replaced Johnston with you, Hardee asked to be transferred. I will do as you request and also send General Beauregard to advise you."

"Where will you send Hardee?"

"South Carolina eventually, but for now, leave him here. Get me a more detailed plan by tomorrow."

The next day, Davis spoke upon a hastily erected platform to a crowd of concerned citizens. The slim, gray-haired leader rubbed his goatee as he looked over the sun-splashed crowd. The president knew he had to give them hope. "I have good news!" he proclaimed. "We can turn the tables on Sherman. General Forrest is already on our roads in middle Tennessee. General Hood's army will soon be there as well. The Yankee army will have to retreat or starve. Sherman's retreat will be more disastrous than what happened when Napoleon retreated from Moscow."

* * *

LATER THAT DAY, Hood and Davis met again. Davis was blunt. "What the hell do you propose to do next?"

Hood outlined an expansion of what he had offered to Davis the previous day. This time the president concurred, and that night Hood met with his division commanders, Cheatham and Stewart, to explain the agreed-upon plan.

The three were hunched around a flickering campfire as Hood explained, "We can't take Sherman head on. I 'spect he's gonna march though Georgia."

"How do you propose to stop him?" Stewart wondered.

"I don't. We're going north."

"What?" Cheatham exclaimed. "Why would we go in an opposite direction?"

"To turn Sherman topsy-turvy. We cut his supply lines up north from Chattanooga. We cut his communication. Maybe we can even force him out into the open, where we can hurt him some. We can take back Nashville; it's not heavily garrisoned. Better yet, our way is clear to the Ohio.

"From there we could move into Kentucky and then head east to help Lee. Sherman either has to let us go or disrupt any march through Georgia. He'll have to turn north himself or reduce his force by sending a corps or two after us. I'm sure Grant won't let us wander off alone."

"You've got a lot of maybes there. But we're running out of options," Cheatham replied thoughtfully. "And we don't have the manpower to beat him in a pitched battle."

"It just might work," Stewart concurred. "Do you leave any behind?"

"At Lovejoy we have militia and Wheeler has 10,000 cavalry. That should keep Sherman occupied while we head north. I'm leaving General Hardee behind with Wheeler."

"What will Hardee say to that?" Cheatham wondered.

"It doesn't make any difference. You will take over his corps."

Cheatham's face flashed foreboding and then determination. "I'll do my best, General."

"Good," Hood concluded. "We head north up the road to Altoona."

On September 29, the Army of Tennessee was on the move.

* * *

IN HIS CAMP outside Atlanta, William Tecumseh Sherman was savoring his victory but also planning his next step. Oliver O. Howard, the one-armed, Bible-thumping, right-wing commander of the Army of Tennessee and its left-wing commander, General Henry Slocum, along with John Schofield and George Thomas, listened intently.

"This war can only come to an end," Sherman surmised, "if the South's strategic, economic, and psychological capacity for warfare are decisively broken. I propose a scorched-earth policy. We will march across Georgia in a wide swath from here to Savannah. These people are traitors. I want to cut a band through this state that will be evident fifty years from now."

"What about our supply and communication lines?" Thomas asked.

"We will have none. We will live off the land. Foragers will spread out and take what we need from farms and the countryside. We will destroy the railroads as well as the economic and agricultural infrastructure of Georgia as we travel. We will march in two wings, one under Howard and the other under Slocum. Kilpatrick's cavalry will support both.

"But if you want to know the truth, it's not so much ripping up railroads and destroying property that I'm enamored of. People all over the North, the South, and even Confederate sympathizers in Europe will be confronted with proof positive that the game is up.

"There is also another objective. Grant and Lee are stagnated outside of Richmond. After we reach the sea, we'll head north. This will put us in Lee's rear. The threat will cause him great consternation."

"What does Grant think?" Slocum asked.

"General Grant and President Lincoln both have reservations, but I have offered my firm belief that this is best. I'll get a final word from them soon."

"Let me add my reservation," Thomas said. "Leaving our supply line concerns me."

Clint Cilley strode purposefully into the camp. "General Sherman, sir, I have a dispatch for you."

Sherman read the dispatch, then looked up and smiled. "It seems that General Hood has left Palmetto and appears to be heading north toward Tennessee. That means he's virtually leaving me to do whatever I want."

"It looks like Wheeler's cavalry and some units under Hardee have been left behind," Clint added.

"They'll be like flies to swat away."

Schofield wondered, "What if Hood heads for the Ohio?"

Sherman laughed. "Maybe I should send him rations to help him along."

"Sir," Clint added, "I have another dispatch, this one from General Grant."

Sherman ripped open the dispatch and read with disgust washing over his face. "General Grant orders us to pursue Hood. Secretary of War Stanton and General Halleck also appear vehemently opposed to my plan. They ask, how I can leave the Confederate Army free to roam about at will, gobbling up hard-won Union garrisons in Tennessee or even Kentucky, possibly as far as St. Louis or Chicago. Blast it! They don't understand."

"Maybe later, Cump," Howard consoled his commander, "or maybe we crush Hood out in the open."

Sherman, his face flushed red as a hot iron, simply shook his head in disgust.

Then he peered at Thomas. "In light of Hood's movement, I do recognize the need to anticipate where he may be heading. General Thomas, you will take the Fourth and Eighth Corps and head north. I want you, personally, to go to Nashville and establish headquarters there. Send the two corps, under command of General Schofield, into northern Alabama and southern Tennessee to watch out for Hood. I'll see that reinforcements are sent to Nashville. Grant and Lincoln willing, the rest of us will chase Hood."

Thomas peered intently at Sherman. "May I make a request for reinforcements?"

"Certainly, what do you have in mind?"

"Smith's Sixteenth Corps. You've had them traipsing all over Missouri and Arkansas after Price. They marched through Louisiana fighting Dick Taylor. Isn't it time to bring them back to the East? I'll need them in Nashville."

"Pap, I've been trying to get them down here. Every time I issue an order to that effect, something turns up that demands they be sent elsewhere."

"I want them," Thomas asserted firmly.

Sherman sighed. "And just like every other time, I'll send them elsewhere, this time to you in Nashville. But not Joe Mower. You can have Smith, but I'm taking Mower. Hopefully, we'll make short work of Hood."

Chasing Hood

JEFFERSON DAVIS MADE A SERIES of speeches to public audiences. It wasn't always pleasant as he traveled among soldiers and the people. Shouts of "Give us General Johnston back!" and "Git us more men!" echoed after the president as he rode along.

After Davis's decisive meeting with Hood, the Army of Tennessee was lined up for a review. Pine torches lit the podium area as members of the presidential entourage followed his address with remarks of their own. F.R. Lubbock, Governor of Texas, was sure that soldiers from Texas would be glad to see him. As Davis reviewed the troops, Lubbock approached soldiers in the ranks, supposing they were from the state.

But Lubbock had stopped one regiment to the right of Texas. He stopped his horse in front of Cleburne's Irish Regiment, smiled, doffed his hat and announced, "I'm Governor Lubbock of Texas."

He waited a moment, anticipating a cheer, and then heard a shout in a thick Irish brogue, "An' who in the bloody hell is Governor Lubbock?"

The governor turned his horse and galloped to catch up with Davis and his party. He sped right past the Texas regiments.

On September 27, Jefferson Davis left for Richmond. The fate of the Confederacy and the Army of Tennessee was solely in the hands of John Bell Hood. On September 29, Hood began his push north. His army had increased to 44,403 men, and he expected still more from Kilby Smith.

The Confederate forces went about their task with fervor and delight. At three different places on the Chattahoochee River, the gray columns of the Army of Tennessee crossed over on pontoon bridges.

General Red Jackson had been left with a portion of Wheeler's cavalry. His raid at Marietta, Georgia, severed the rail line there—Sherman's supply line to Chattanooga and Nashville was gone.

The three corps of infantry marched on and by nightfall on October 2, were fifteen miles from Palmetto. They had increased in numbers and now were increasing in resolve and confidence as they pushed ahead like a tidal wave.

Tod, his brother Wad, and Jim Cooper sat before a campfire in the fading light of evening. The sun had set, and a pink glimmer was all that remained of the daylight.

"Heard from home?" Wad asked.

"No. I hope all is well." Tod looked pensive. "I haven't been home since the war started. I'd really like to see the place again soon. Three and a half years," he mumbled. "A lot's happened since I've been home."

"We're going north, Tod. You heard President Davis. He said we'd have the dirt of Tennessee under our feet soon. Sure thing. Maybe we can pay a visit when we get close."

"I hope we can, Wad."

"Tod," Jim said tentatively, "I've got family in Franklin, too. If you get a leave, see if you can get me one, too. I'd like to go with you."

"I'll ask. I don't know if they'll let me go."

Nearby they heard a chorus of voices singing, "The Girl I Left Behind Me."

"What's that?" Wad asked.

"Let's find out." Tod said.

The pair walked in the direction of the singing. It was at the camp of the Irish Brigade, and they were serenading General Cleburne, who stood before them in humble repose. The handsome thirty-six-year-old officer with a wiry build tipped his hat, revealing a thick shock of reddish hair. Cleburne brushed tears from his cheek as he listened.

I'm lonesome since I crossed the hill
And over the moor that's sedgy
Such lonely thoughts my heart do fill
Since parting with my Betsey
I seek for one as fair and gay
But find none to remind me
How sweet the hours I passed away
With the girl I left behind me

After the last line slowly drifted away, Cleburne spoke, tears glistening in his eyes. "I be touched, men. Thank you for the fine singing. You've made me think of my dear Susan, to whom I be betrothed."

He cleared his throat and continued, "I want to say some things to you about how proud it is I am of you. You came here from the emerald isle. You didn't have to get into this war, but you did. I be thinking that you saw what I saw. That the plight of the South is quite like the plight of Ireland. That the mistreatment of our homeland by the British despots is similar to what the Yankees are doing to those of us in the southern states."

He paused and his voice rose. "If we fail in our cause, the South will find itself trampled and downtrodden. If this cause, which is so dear to my heart, is doomed to fail, I pray heaven may let me fall with it."

The Irish erupted in a boisterous cheer. Tod turned to Wad. "Inspiring, isn't he?"

"Makes me proud," Wad murmured. "Who is Susan?"

"From what I hear, Cleburne was best man in the wedding of General Hardee. He fell in love with the maid of honor, and they are engaged. She's the daughter of a wealthy plantation owner from Alabama."

Wad smiled. "Isn't General Hood engaged, as well?"

"Yes," nodded Tod. "From what I'm told, though, the courtship has not gone smoothly. But for now, the ardent campaign of General Hood has been successful."

* * *

THE NEXT DAY, Hood's army continued along the Western and Atlanta Railroad tracks. Sherman had garrisoned rear guard troops at little stations along the way. On October 4, General A.P. Stewart's corps hit Big Shanty, north of Atlanta, where they destroyed a dozen miles of track and captured Union prisoners.

Marching on to Ackworth Station, Stewart had similar results. Hood was then informed that Allatoona Station had a rich store of Union supplies. He met with General Samuel French. "They've got a million in rations there," Hood said. "I want you to take your division. How many men do you have?"

"Three thousand."

"Take them into Allatoona and destroy the rations. They only have rear guard garrisoned there. You shouldn't have any trouble."

But when French reached Allatoona on October 5, he discovered that Sherman had rushed General John Corse by rail to Rome and then over to

Allatoona. After finding the Union forces dug in, French sent a note telling Corse, "You are surrounded, and to avoid a needless effusion of blood I call on you to surrender your force at once."

Corse read the note and sent one back reading in part, ". . . we are prepared for the 'needless effusion of blood,' whenever it is agreeable to you."

Back in Atlanta, Sherman received word of Corse's plight and knew that he must take the unwanted path of following Hood instead of marching to Savannah. He called to General Slocum, "I'm leaving your corps to guard Atlanta, with 60,000 men. I'm going after Hood. I've got Thomas and Schofield up in Tennessee, so General Cox will command the Army of the Ohio, Stanley has the Army of the Cumberland, and Howard will keep the Army of Tennessee. We'll maintain a forced march to aid Corse. It is absolutely necessary to keep Hood's army off our main route of communication and supply."

Meanwhile, at ten in the morning, French attacked Allatoona. The station was on a mountain pass that the railroad ran through, and the hamlet had only a few houses and the Union depot. Several redoubts ringed the station, manned by Union infantry and artillery.

French's force overwhelmed the redoubts in vicious hand-to-hand fighting. Outnumbered three to two, Corse ordered his men into the remaining redoubt in the center. There they held off the onslaught.

At this time, Sherman's force reached the crest of the mountain and looked down at the fight. Sherman remarked, "Look at this view. We can see back to Big Shanty and for fifteen miles to Allatoona, even with the smoke of rebel campfires and burning railroad ties. Listen, you can hear the sound of cannon down below.

"General Cox, get between Hood's main force and French down there in Allatoona. Burn houses or brush along the way so I can follow your advance. I'm going straight to Allatoona to support Corse."

French had captured the Union supplies and ordered parties to burn them. With disgust, they reported back to French that the matches wouldn't light and they couldn't set anything on fire.

At noon, one of the Confederate general's signal officers reported that a message had been intercepted from Sherman. "It's a message to Corse," the officer relayed. "It says, 'Hold on, I am coming.' And federal infantry is moving up behind us on the tracks."

"Well, I'm not going to be trapped between Corse and Sherman," French stated. "We'll withdraw back to Hood." French had suffered 799 casualties, twenty-five percent of his division.

By 3:30 p.m., French's division had reformed and was marching southwest to Hood's army, fifteen miles away. Corse sent a message to Sherman. "The fight was ferocious. I suffered 707 casualties, thirty-five percent of my command. I am short a cheekbone and an ear, but am able to whip all hell yet."

In actuality, Corse had only received a scratch. When Sherman arrived, he looked over Corse, tugged the "wounded" officer's ear and said, "Well, Corse, they came damned near missing you, didn't they?"

In a cold, hard rain, Hood pushed his men on the trail at four o'clock the next morning. He passed over battlefields of the previous May, bones from horses, fresh graves, wreckage from equipment, and splintered trees destroyed by hails of lead from the spring battles.

Sherman was kept busy repairing the damage done by Hood. It took a week with 10,000 men, six miles of iron, and 35,000 new crossties between Big Shanty and Allatoona to get the trains running again.

Then Sherman lost track of Hood and telegraphed Slocum in Atlanta to be on guard in case Hood doubled back. But the Army of Tennessee had marched with blazing speed around Rome, through a gap in the mountains leading into the Chattooga River Valley and to Resaca, fifteen miles north of the Union army.

Another Union force was garrisoned at Resaca, and on October 12, Hood immediately demanded its surrender. The Confederate general added to his dispatch, "No prisoners will be taken."

Colonel Clark Weaver evaluated his situation and responded, "I have to state that I am somewhat surprised at the concluding paragraph, to the effect that, if the place is carried, no prisoners will be taken. In my opinion, I can hold this post. If you want it, come and take it."

Hood read the response and exclaimed, "What gall he has! He can't stand against us!"

At that moment a scout rode up and informed Hood, "Sherman is down the road. He's miles away yet, but he's coming."

Hood leaned back in his saddle, his brow wrinkled in thought. He turned to General Cheatham. "We've got more important things to do than to be stuck here. The Union garrison at Dalton and its railroad are ripe for the taking. It all started at Dalton, six months ago," he mused. "We'll close the circle there. I want to wreck Sherman's railroad all the way back from Resaca through Dalton to Tunnel Hill, just south of Chattanooga."

"What then, General?"

"We'll see how things play out."

"How did your meeting with Beauregard go?"

Hood flexed his bad arm, recalling the conversation of two days earlier. "He endorses my intention to wreck the northern stretch of rail to Chattanooga. Then we fall back into Georgia to Gadsden. Our excess wagons and artillery are already there. At Gadsden we will give battle to Sherman if he follows us. But if he goes off in another direction . . ." His voice trailed off.

Cheatham finished, "We follow him."

"That's what Beauregard expects, but circumstances will dictate what we do."

"Circumstances and you, General Hood," Cheatham added.

Hood's army plodded down the road to Dalton, Georgia.

Colonel Lewis Johnson commanded the Union garrison at Dalton. As with Corse and Weaver before him, Johnson turned down Hood's demand that he surrender. His force of twelve hundred watched apprehensively as division after division tightened the noose around their garrison.

Johnson surveyed his command and recognized that his situation was different from the previous garrisons attacked by Confederates. Most of his force was made up by the Forty-fourth Colored Troops.

Johnson discussed the predicament with his officers. "The rebels are not easy with Negro prisoners," he asserted. "They'll be put to hard labor for sure."

"That's better than Andersonville," a captain proclaimed.

"But Forrest is with them," Johnson countered. "At Fort Pillow he slaughtered 500 of them after they surrendered."

"That's not for sure," the lieutenant colonel countered. "We do know that Forrest treats Negro soldiers as runaway slaves."

The debate lasted over two hours. Johnson finally decided to hoist a white flag when it was reported that Cleburne's Irish Brigade was immediately in Hood's rear and overly anxious to fight.

"The Irish hate the Negroes," Johnson claimed. "In the heat of battle this could become a massacre."

"Didn't Cleburne suggest that the Confederacy enlist slaves into the army and give them their freedom?" the captain suggested.

"Yes," Johnson agreed, "and they almost kicked him out of the army over it. He made a logical argument that it came down to numbers. But he lost the discussion, and we have to surrender. Look around. We're outnumbered and surrounded, and the men we have here have not fought a battle."

Shortly after Hood's army marched into Dalton, the Forty-fourth U.S. Colored Troops were rounded up and put to work ripping up the track in the direction of Tunnel Hill. Tod Carter, standing with Colonel Bill Shy, watched the men straining in the hot sun. Most of the army joined in with the Forty-fourth, and the hard work became like play as they bent heated rails around trees or telegraph poles.

"It's like a game," Tod noted. "They learned well from Sherman. They're making their own neckties."

"But they call them 'Old Mrs. Lincoln's hairpins,'" Shy laughed.

"Hood's been riding through the division proudly claiming we flanked Sherman out of Atlanta."

"Well, Captain Carter, whatever it is, things are going right. The boys are feeling pretty good."

They tore up twenty-five miles of track stretching from Tunnel Hill to Resaca, then determined that with Sherman moving up from the south and having accomplished his goals in northern Georgia, it was time to head southwest toward the Alabama state line.

Cheatham suggested to Hood, "Why not head north now past Chattanooga? There aren't enough federal troops between us and there to stop us. We could make Nashville, and Thomas only has eight to ten thousand men there."

"General, we may do that in time. But the plan we made was to draw Sherman into the open and hit 'em. I'm stickin' to the plan."

The Army of Tennessee continued to march across frosty northern Georgia. Then Hood ordered a halt in a beautiful valley, and for two days the army rested. The general rode and walked among troops, who happily greeted him and seemed to be in a good mood.

It had been four years of fighting for many of his troops. They were worn down, and many had tattered uniforms and were barefoot. Some fortunate ones had been supplied new uniforms. All seemed excited at their prospects in spite of the loss of Atlanta.

Hood watched soldiers sitting around a campfire folding cowhide around their feet. One soldier shouted, "Hiya, Gen'r'l, not bad on the feet, iff'n ya wear the hair side in. Smells a little rank after a couple days, though."

"We'll get ya shoes in Tennessee, boys!" Hood beamed.

Buoyed by the high spirits of his troops, Hood called for a meeting with his senior officers. "Sherman is close," he reported. "He's in the open and we could give him a battle in the morning."

"How many does Sherman have?" Stephen Lee asked.

"Wheeler's scouts say 65,000."

"About 20,000 more than we have," Stewart commented.

"But our boys are ready," Hood rejoined. "As ready to fight as I've seen them."

"Thousands don't even have shoes," Cheatham pointed out.

"All right!" Hood snapped in exasperation. "I'm ready to head into battle. I need to know if my commanders believe there is a least hope of victory!"

"They've got 65,000 tough veteran troops, Sam," Cheatham cautioned. "Our boys might have the spirit, but I don't think that's enough."

Lee shook his head. "It would be suicide."

Hood stood up, leaning heavily on his crutch. "Is there anyone here who at least thinks there's a chance of winning?" He glared at his officers, most of whom stared wordlessly at the ground.

"Well," Hood snapped, "we can't expect to win a battle if we go into it with officers who don't think it can be won. We sure can't entrench. Sherman would just repair the railroad and get all the supplies he needs while we're cut off. We'd be trapped here. Get away from me. I've got to figure this out. I'll have a plan in the morning."

At sunrise, Hood called his officers together again. The early morning rays glistened off the golden fall leaves still clinging to trees in the forested valley. Hood stood with his crutch, his back to his officers as he surveyed the beauty before him. Then he turned to face his men.

"I want you to know I'm disappointed in you. But we won't be attacking Sherman. I have had another plan, and now we will implement it. We will march to Gadsden, then Tuscumbia by Florence. We will wait there and be joined by Forrest. Then we will march into Tennessee. I hope to eventually establish our line in Kentucky. Schofield will be between us and Thomas at Nashville. We outnumber Schofield, and we can beat him before he can join Thomas. After that, we move on Nashville, beat Thomas, and resupply there. More men will join us as we march through Tennessee and Kentucky. We can threaten the Ohio River Valley and Cincinnati. We'll even have Grant looking over his shoulder at Petersburg."

Cheatham spoke slowly, "Well, there's a lot of 'ifs' in that plan. But I vote for it. It's worth a try."

Stewart nodded. "I'm on board."

Hood looked over the men before him. "Objections?" he asked. No one stirred, and the general continued. "All right, then we have a plan."

* * *

AN ANGRY AND FRUSTRATED Sherman kept pursuing Hood but couldn't quite catch the Army of Tennessee. Anger grew in him like a hot fire as he passed through the wake of destruction left behind by the rebels.

He glared at generals Cox and Howard. "Look at this! Wreckage all around. We can't get to Hood, and we're back in north Georgia. Back where we started six months ago."

Howard offered hopefully, "Hood's not far off. We can catch him."

Sherman replied crisply, "You think so? The lightness and celerity of his army convinces me that I can't possibly catch him on a stern chase. Now he's crossed into Alabama and seems to be heading for Gadsden. It's October seventeenth, and I'm tired of this wild goose chase. I'm halting the army right here, in sight of the Georgia-Alabama border. I'll resume my entreaties to Washington to let me move through the bowels of the South to Savannah and leave these traitors something to remember for a lifetime."

Cox asked, "Have you heard from Grant or Halleck?"

"No one has answered my plan to march to the sea affirmatively. But I know one thing: I'm done trying to catch Hood, and we're going back to Atlanta."

* * *

THE ARMY OF TENNESSEE marched with a spring in their steps down the beautiful valley of the Chattanooga River. The red, gold, and rust colors of autumn splashed the landscape as if sprinkled from an artist's palette.

Songs broke out from the ranks as rumors spread that after being resupplied in Gadsden, the army would turn north and cross into Tennessee, homeland for half of them. Pierre Beauregard, of diminutive stature and French heritage, was waiting when Hood arrived at Gadsden. For the second time, Davis's hand-picked advisor met with the rebel general.

Hood went over his plan with Beauregard, but his advisor was not convinced. "I've received word from President Davis. He thinks you should have kept after Sherman and should still take after him."

"What happened to 'pressing the soil of Tennessee'?" Hood countered. "That's what he told the boys at Palmetto."

"I'll help you if I can," Beauregard said, "but I'll need some convincing."

After two days of discussion, Hood's plan was approved. Then he ran into a snag. "General," Hood reminded Beauregard, "I'll need at least half of Wheeler's cavalry. I need them to watch my flanks. The rest can go south to bother Sherman."

"No, General Hood, I must insist, all of Wheeler's cavalry must return south to trouble Sherman. But I will give you the use of another cavalry division."

"Whose?"

"Nathan Bedford Forrest."

"You're giving me the Wizard of the Saddle? All right, I'll take him."

After that conversation, Beauregard interceded with Jefferson Davis and got him to sign, reluctantly, on to Hood's plan. Word quickly spread through camp that many were heading home. Great cheers burst from the throats of men who were eager to set foot on home soil. Soon the army was on the march to Guntersville, where they planned to cross the Tennessee River.

The soldiers marched as if on a lark. They were well fed, and many had been issued new uniforms and even shoes. Best of all, they were marching home. But then things started to go bad. Forrest was not at Guntersville. Scouts informed Hood he was still 200 miles to the northwest, between Jackson and Johnsonville.

Their cavalry was near Kentucky and couldn't get across the river there because rain had flooded it. The stream was too deep and swift for horses to cross.

Hood bitterly complained to the scout, "Tell Forrest I need him. I can't even cross the river here if I don't have cavalry watching my flank and guarding against an attack. This will set us back. Thomas might get reinforced before we can get to Nashville if we have to delay."

The scout sadly repeated, "There's a flood. Gen'r'l Forrest can't cross."

Hood fumed and then replied, "We'll head west to Florence and Tuscumbia. Tell General Forrest to meet us there."

It was a hard march west. Morale that had been high at the prospect of crossing the river into Tennessee fell like a rock as they journeyed toward Florence, Alabama.

Bill Shy complained to Tod Carter, "The march is bad enough. But there's little food for the men. No meat for three days. It's getting so bad that two ears of parched corn a day is a feast."

"We're doing the best we can. Sometimes not much is the best we can do. It wasn't easy laying hands on what little corn we found."

Shy looked around. "The scenery has changed, as well. It was fun traveling through the valley. It was all like a beautiful painting. And now . . ." He paused. "We're marching through what the Yankees left behind. Burned out farmsteads, no livestock, and hardly any people. It's forsaken."

On October 30, Hood's army entered Tuscumbia and nearby Florence. General Thomas Benton Smith rode into the town alongside Tod. All were shocked at what they saw. The magnificent plantations they had passed earlier were now in ruins. Many of the buildings in the town were burned-out shells. In lots all over the city, pairs of chimneys stood as stark reminders that houses had once stood there.

"Damn Yankees!" Smith exclaimed. "Why do they make war on civilians?"

"*Vexilla regis prodant inferni,*" Tod replied.

"What?"

"'Forth go the banners of the king of Hell.' In other words, Sherman. This is his handiwork."

"I believe Sherman's instrument here was General Dodge. It was his troops that marched through here."

Tod's face flashed crimson. "The same Dodge who hanged Sam Davis!"

"Did you know him?" Smith asked.

"Davis's family and mine did business. Smyrna is only about twenty miles from Franklin."

Smith's face grew grave. "They'll put up a statue of Sam Davis some day with his last words on it."

"Yes, 'I'd rather die than betray a friend,'" Tod quoted solemnly.

The Army of Tennessee went into camp near Florence to await the arrival of Forrest's cavalry and to resupply the troops. On November 6, Hood sent a telegram to President Davis reviewing his army's movements and the plan to cross the Tennessee and advance on Nashville.

Davis's reply caused consternation. Hood sought out General Beauregard. "Listen to this! Here's what our president wants now. 'You should keep after Sherman. If you keep his communications destroyed, he will most probably seek to concentrate for an attack on you. But if, as reported to you, he has sent a large part of his force southward, you may first beat him in detail, and, subsequently, without serious obstruction or danger to your rear, advance to the Ohio River.'

"General, we can't do both," Hood continued. "Sherman is now over a hundred miles away. We might finally be ready for a pitched battle, but not at the two-to-one odds we face against Sherman. Morale would plummet if we headed south to fight him. The majority of this army wants to go home, to Tennessee. They'll fight like hell up there."

Beauregard seemed perplexed. Then he answered, "Send a dispatch to the president expressing those sentiments. I'll back you with a telegram of my own."

He sent a message informing Davis that he would not countermand Hood's plan. Beauregard explained that the weather was inclement and the state of the railroads going south were such that Hood couldn't overtake Sherman anyway. He added that if Hood's forces moved east, it would leave Alabama open for Thomas to take.

Hood's proposal was not altered, and he continued to await Forrest's arrival. A pall fell over the camp on November 9. Word came to Hood that Abraham Lincoln had been re-elected president. McClellan had captured the electoral votes of only three states.

Davis telegraphed Beauregard and expressed his dismay over the election results. "If only Hood and Johnston had not lost Atlanta, this could have been different. Hood did have a chance to redeem himself at Guntersville. Even though I had apprehensions about his plan, if he had crossed the river there and driven toward Nashville, he could have beaten Thomas. McClellan and the Peace Party might have won then."

Beauregard bowed his head and said softly, "But he didn't cross at Guntersville."

* * *

SHERMAN CONTINUED an exasperating correspondence with Grant, Halleck, Stanton, and Lincoln. He sat on a camp stool on a frosty late October night in front of his tent. His camp was between the two wings of his army.

Wrapped in an old army overcoat, Sherman poked a stick into a weakly flickering campfire and tried to stir it into life. In fading light, he re-read messages from a handful of telegrams. Halleck asserted that while Atlanta had been taken, he hadn't destroyed Hood's army. "And now," Lincoln's top military advisor wrote, "you want to abandon the mission altogether and go off in a different direction."

Grant, still unconvinced by Sherman's plan, telegraphed, "Do you not think it is advisable now that Hood has gone so far north, to entirely ruin him before starting out on your proposed campaign? With Hood's army destroyed you can go where you please with impunity." An implied order followed. Sherman should go after Hood again.

In desperation, Cump had responded to Grant, "If I could hope to overhaul Hood, I would turn against him with my whole force. Then he would retreat to the southwest, drawing me as a decoy away from Georgia, which is his chief object. No single army can catch Hood, and I am convinced that the best results will follow from defeating Jeff Davis's cherished plan of making me leave Georgia by maneuvering. I regard the pursuit of Hood as useless."

The next morning, Sherman continued to his command post between his divided armies. While enduring the bumping and swaying of his railroad car, he penned a follow-up response to Grant. "If I turn back, the whole effect of my campaign will be lost. I am clearly of opinion that the best results will follow my contemplated movement through Georgia."

Cump Sherman's day brightened considerably when he read his commander's reply. "I do not see that you can withdraw from where you are to follow Hood, without giving up all we have gained in territory. I say, then, go on as you propose."

On November 2, his world brightened even more when a message arrived from Lincoln for Sherman, echoing Grant: "Do as you propose." Sherman's incessant requests and entreaties to put his plan in motion had finally paid off. On November 15, the 300-mile March to the Sea began. The Second and Fourth Minnesota regiments fell into line with 60,000 other soldiers to head to Savannah. They marched out in gleaming sunlight. A band stuck up the song "John Brown's Body" and the tune spread through the ranks. General Sherman commented, "I never heard the chorus of 'Glory, Glory Hallelujah' sung with more spirit or in better harmony than with a 60,000-man chorus."

* * *

IN TUSCUMBIA, ALABAMA, a day later, a similar celebration occurred. Cheers, songs, and playing bands greeted Bedford Forrest and his men as they rode into town. Hood enthusiastically greeted Forrest at his headquarters.

"Are you ready, Forrest? Now that Lincoln has been re-elected, two things may happen. Either we'll be fighting another four years, or we've gotta win the peace."

"I'm ready to be of service, General Hood."

"Did you resupply from Yankee stores at Johnsonville?"

"Not much. We engaged them on November fifth. The Union general set his transports on fire. Before we could extinguish them, the blaze spread to the depot. Most ever'thing burnt up."

"Too bad. Rest your men, but don't get settled in too much. Within a week we'll be moving north."

Hood conferred with Cheatham, Stewart, Stephen Lee, and Forrest. He listened to a report from his commissary officer. "It's been difficult, but we've pulled together rations for twenty days," the officer related. "Our supply line is tenuous. We had to transport on two railroads and then travel over fifteen miles of bad roads to Tuscumbia. All the way, heavy wagons were pulled by undernourished horses and oxen. But we made it."

"Excellent," Hood responded. "I'll see you're written up for it in my report."

Lee remarked, "I've heard that Sherman's army is marching east from Atlanta."

"Most of them. This will not change our plans. I always expected Sherman to head for the sea. Even if we wanted to, he's too far away for us to head him off now. We will continue with our alternative strategy."

"Which is?" Cheatham wondered.

"After we cross the Tennessee, we'll move north in three separate columns: Cheatham on the left, Lee in the center, and Stewart on the right. General Forrest, your cavalry will aggressively screen our movements. You know the rest, we take Nashville and continue to the Ohio."

"When do we come together?" Cheatham asked.

"We unite at Mount Pleasant, Tennessee, and then move on to Columbia."

On November 21, after three weeks at Tuscumbia, the much-anticipated crossing of the river into Tennessee took place. They crossed over on a floating pontoon bridge into a raging snowstorm with the wind howling from the west.

Once over the river, the Army of Tennessee, accompanied by Forrest's cavalry, was on the loose between the state line and Nashville. Only two corps commanded by John Schofield stood between Hood and an under-manned Nashville.

* * *

A JUBILANT AND DETERMINED Sherman continued with his plan to drive to the east. He reviewed with his commanders, "It will be as I instructed before we headed after Hood. We march in two columns, one wing under Howard, the other under Slocum, Kilpatrick's cavalry in between. We started out with a couple of weeks' rations, when that's gone we live off the land and we head to the sea."

"What's the opposition?" Slocum inquired.

"It looks like Wheeler's cavalry and some militia."

"So ten, maybe 20,000 at most against over 60,000."

"They can't stop us, General Slocum, and Hood is traipsing off into Tennessee. Thomas is to wait in Nashville for reinforcements and he's ordered Schofield to delay Hood until more troops arrive. A.J. Smith is on the way to him."

On November 22, the first fighting of the expedition burst out at Griswoldville between Kilpatrick and Wheeler. On the same day, Slocum's wing hit Milledgeville. The state capitol was unceremoniously evacuated by the governor and legislature. Small battles and skirmishes continued. But the great army rolled inexorably toward the sea.

* * *

LATER THAT DAY in Nashville, George Thomas received word that Hood was marching north to Tennessee. Thomas hurried off a dispatch to Schofield in the field. "I believe that Hood is moving to Columbia, Tennessee. You are to retreat north with your two corps and beat the Confederates to Columbia."

Thomas had stationed one division each at the cities of Murfreesboro, Decatur, and Chattanooga. His corps at Nashville was mostly made up of untested, green noncombatants. His hopes rested on the Twenty-third Corps under Schofield and the Fourth Army Corps under David Stanley, with the former in overall command.

Schofield moved quickly, with the knowledge that delay would allow Hood to cut his army off from Nashville. Although harassed by Confederate cavalry, the Union Army reached Columbia before Hood on November 24. The Union troops dug in and fortified. Schofield told his adjutant, Clint Cilley, "I'm going to rely on you in the days ahead, Major. We need to keep lines of communication open with all my commanders. I trust you to keep me informed and deliver the messages I send promptly and efficiently."

"Whatever you want, sir. I'm ready to serve."

Leaving Missouri

AFTER LETTING STERLING PRICE go at the Kansas state line, the Sixteenth Corps of A.J. Smith traveled south to Harrisonville. With the knowledge that Price was retreating south and no longer a threat, the Union forces went into camp to rest for three days.

In rags, dirty, and bloodstained, the men huddled around campfires and gratefully ate food delivered from the town. Jimmy Dunn patted his stomach. "It was gittin' lonely. Sure good to have somethin' in it."

"Short term," Levi Carr complained. "Now we turn east. We still will be short rations."

"How far is St. Louis?" Jimmy asked.

Will Hutchinson wrinkled his brow in thought. "'Bout 300 miles. We can make it in fifteen to twenty days, dependin' on how hard they push us."

"We've been pushed pretty hard," Levi snapped. "For nothin'."

Jimmy shook his head in disgust. "All that marchin', eatin' wood, freezin', soaked to the bone. For what? We never did catch up to Price. Closest we got was to see the dust his horses kicked up."

"But he knew we were on his tail," Will offered. "We made him keep moving. It's like chasin' a fly around the cabin with a swatter and he flies out a window before ya git him. It got away, but it knew I was after him and he won't be around to bother me no more."

"But we had 'em and Old Rosie stopped us," Jimmy complained.

Levi puffed up like a rooster. "Wait till we git ta St. Looey. I got a rope with General Rosecrans's name on it. Nobody should be able to put us through what we bin through and not answer for it."

"Watch how ya talk," Will admonished.

Levi replied defensively, "Well, it's true."

* * *

ON OCTOBER 30, as Price escaped south, the Sixteenth Corps turned to the east and back to St. Louis, 285 miles away. The first days of travel were over flat, easily traveled terrain, blessed by mild weather. Then the rain hit them.

The temperature turned bitter cold and the march continued over alternately muddy and frozen roads. On the left of the column was the Missouri River, its water level too low for boats. On their right was a railroad line with no cars to carry them.

Still in tattered, ragged clothing, the men sought some protection by wrapping hole-filled blankets over their shoulders.

Jimmy exclaimed, "This is like Minnesota. It can't get no worse!"

Willie Sturgis pointed skyward. "Don't be so sure. There's snow comin'."

On November third and fourth as they marched back through Sedalia they were hit by a snowstorm, rare at that latitude. But it came—heavy, cold, and wet. It collected as the army marched. Then a brisk wind from the north whipped it into a blizzard. Men without shoes wrapped anything they could find around their feet. They trudged ahead, with shoulders hunched and their bodies leaning into the cold wind. Soon the snow was a foot deep, the brilliant whiteness stained red by the bleeding feet of marching men. It didn't let up until the next day.

"Hang in there, men," Lieutenant Bishop urged. "You're Minnesota boys. You can handle snow! You can take whatever rebs or Mother Nature has for you!"

"I'd rather be a Florida boy today," Jimmy called, "thanks just the same!"

They were on the trail eighteen days, marching sixteen of them. They averaged eighteen miles a day, finally reaching Benton Barracks in St. Louis on November 15. The army was at half strength.

The men collapsed in the barracks, over-fatigued, cold, and nearly naked. A.J. Smith found a dispatch awaiting him from General Sherman.

"Well, Mower," he informed his division commander, "you are to join Sherman outside of Atlanta."

"What about you and the rest of the army?"

"I am to proceed immediately to Nashville with my guerillas. Three divisions; 9,000 men."

"Immediately?"

Smith tossed the order in a basket. "To me, immediately means right after these men are fed, clothed, and rested. I will not leave this city until my men have recovered from one of the most arduous and senseless campaigns in this war. They deserve proper clothing and a few days' hearty food."

"It was even worse than the Red River Campaign," Mower agreed.

"Certainly more pointless."

"Who's replacing me if I'm to join Sherman?"

"Arthur McArthur."

"He's a good man."

Smith adjusted his wire-rim glasses and remarked, "One thing. I understand the men are taking great offense regarding General Rosecrans's order keeping us out of the fight with Price. I've heard there's grumbling about a lynching of our general. While I doubt anyone is serious, I want strict orders given that our troops stay away from Rosecrans's headquarters."

True to his word, A.J. Smith spent the next few days badgering, coercing, and demanding until he received the needed supplies to equip his army. When satisfied that they were rested and ready to go, Smith allowed them to board the steamer *W.L. Ewing*. On the twenty-fourth of November, they began the trip to Nashville.

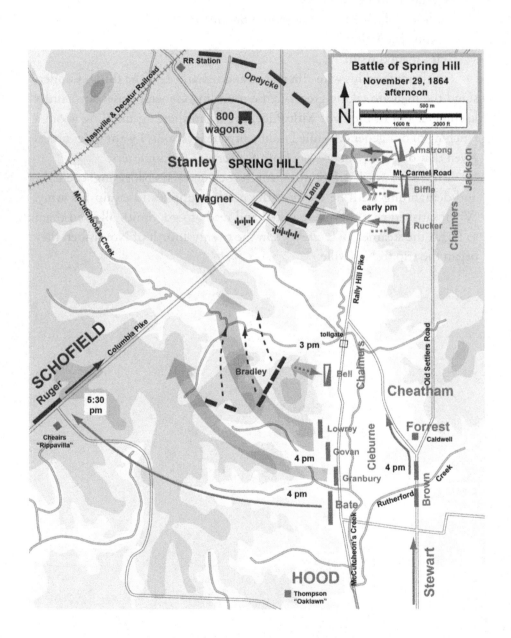

Battle of Spring Hill
November 29, 1864
afternoon

The Race to Spring Hill

HOOD ANNOUNCED TO CHEATHAM and Stewart that Schofield was to the northeast at Pulaski. "We need to move fast and outflank him. Schofield will have to fight us or run back to Nashville. Either way, we'll get him. We outnumber him. If he stands and fights, we'll beat him. If he tries to run to Thomas, we'll run him down."

Twenty-five miles to the northeast, in Pulaski, General John Schofield conferred with his adjutant, Clint Cilley. "Hood's crossed the Tennessee. I fear that he might try to cut us off from Nashville by getting between us and the Duck River crossing at Columbia."

"Do you think so?" Clint asked. "What if he swings around and attacks us here at Pulaski?"

"Possible. Thomas has ordered us to prepare for either possibility. We'll keep the army here for a couple of days and hopefully divine what Hood's up to."

Schofield turned and looked out over the campground of his 28,000-man army. Stocky and balding with a bushy, black beard, he looked older than his thirty-three years. When he had arrived in Pulaski he had taken command from General Stanley and organized his army's defenses.

He looked back at Clint. "I just hope that Thomas doesn't dawdle. Whatever Hood does, we need to react quickly. Pap wants us to fight at Pulaski. I don't know if that's the right move."

For a couple more days, the Union Army stayed in camp while Schofield planned and debated what he should do. Then a scout from James Wilson's cavalry brought an urgent message from his general. "Hood is on his way to Columbia. In fact, he's closer to it than we are."

Schofield launched his army into a desperate day-and-night forced march. He was determined to reach Columbia before Hood. Losing the race

229

would cut him off from Nashville. They hit the Lawrenceburg Pike just outside of Columbia only a few miles ahead of Hood.

Hood's corps led by Stewart, Lee, and Cheatham had traveled separately, slowed by bad weather and bad roads. After sixty miles they came together at Mount Pleasant on November 26, close to Columbia. But Schofield was already there, digging in and fortifying across the Duck River.

Hood established his army in a position across from the Union forces. The Confederate general was welcomed at Hamilton Place, the mansion of the late General Lucius Polk, located just outside of Columbia.

A steady stream of visitors came to the stately mansion, including Governor Isham Harris, General Cheatham, and many other high-ranking officers. As things took shape for the impending battle, Mrs. Polk arranged for day-long festivities. Bands played and food was served to her guests.

While Hood and his officers partied, Schofield stood behind breastworks constructed on the far side of the Duck River. The river and the town of Columbia were in front of the Union army. He complained to Clint Cilley, "I hope this is what I'm expected to do. All I know for sure is that we're supposed to delay Hood. But my instructions from General Thomas are unclear, and our communications system is full of problems."

"Why won't the War Department let us have the cipher to decode telegraph messages?"

"Because, Major, they trust only the telegraph corps with ciphers. I can't get any timely information from Thomas regarding what to do or when to do it. The one clear order I have is to hold back Hood while Thomas waits for Smith to get to Nashville. So that's what I'm doing."

* * *

SAM HOOD DIDN'T have to worry about orders reaching him. He was pretty much on his own now. On the night of November 27, after partying at another mansion, he met with Stephen Lee, Bedford Forrest, and Frank Cheatham. They gathered in a house in Columbia, where Hood outlined his plan while a snowstorm whipped up tiny icy missiles outside.

"General Lee, you will demonstrate in Schofield's front. Fire cannons to make it look like you're massing for an assault. Meanwhile, I'll take the main force and move three miles east of town. Our engineers have secretly been constructing a pontoon bridge. We'll use the bridge to cross the Duck River behind Schofield's left flank to the rear. Lee, while you blast away in front, we'll get behind him. Then we head pell mell for Nashville. We'll either beat Schofield there or he'll have to outrun us. Once we get to Nashville, we hit 'em hard. Spies have spread the word there amongst our sympathizers to storm key parts of the city once we begin the attack. General Forrest, I expect Wilson's cavalry to cause problems for us at the bridge. We need you to take care of them."

"As you wish, General," Forrest replied.

"It looks like a good plan," Cheatham agreed.

Hood beamed. "I think it's worthy of the great Jackson, himself."

That day, while other officers were fêted by Columbia gentry, Patrick Cleburne rode by St. John's Chapel, a church built by Leonidas Polk. Cleburne paused there to admire the green ivy that covered the brick walls. Set in a magnolia grove was a neat graveyard with clipped green grass.

Cleburne turned to his aide. "It is almost worth dying for, to be buried in such a beautiful spot."

On the morning of November 28, Tod Carter stopped by General Thomas Benton Smith's tent. His commander had just finished shaving, a bit of white lotion still smudged on his cheek. "Captain," he said warmly, "good morning on such a fine day."

"Good morning, General," Tod shuffled a little and then began tentatively, "Sir . . . I was . . . wondering . . ."

"Wondering what? Don't be afraid to ask me. What do you want?"

"I haven't been home, sir, not since the war started. Franklin is less than twenty-five miles away. I'd like to see my family. Could I go in advance of the brigade and see them?"

Smith leaned over a camp desk and scratched a short message on a scrap of paper. Wordlessly, he handed it to Tod. It read:

Headquarters Tyler's Brigade in the field near Columbia,
Tennessee, November 28, 1864
Tod Carter, Aide-de-Camp, has permission to go in advance
of this command to Franklin.
By order of T.B. Smith, Brig. Genr'l, commanding.

"How about my brother, Wad, and Jim Cooper?"

Smith considered. "Cooper can go with you. I don't want to send two brothers off together. It would be bad if something happened. Tell Wad I'll see he gets time once we pass through Franklin."

Mounted upon his stallion Rosencrantz, Tod rode with Jim Cooper on a long and tedious trail running from Columbia to Franklin.

"Yanks still hold Franklin," Jim commented. "How will you get home?"

"You've seen our place. The Carter farm is on a hill on the edge of town. The Yanks are in the town. I'll be in and out, and they'll never even know I was there."

"It's even easier for me. My family is miles from town."

"I miss my bed," Tod said. "I'm tired of sleeping on cold, hard ground."

"I miss my ma's cookin'."

"Jim, home cooking is like going to heaven. You've never had a breakfast like my father makes. Sausage, bacon, and ham straight from the smokehouse. Fresh-laid eggs. Biscuits. We gotta ride faster, Jim, my mouth's starting to water."

It was a rough ride through the day. By late afternoon, the sun was already dimming in the west. Tod and Jim saw a cabin off the trail. Smoky tendrils from a chimney gave promise of warmth and maybe a meal.

As they rode into the yard, a man stepped off the cabin porch. The ominous click of a musket being cocked sounded in the gloom.

"Hold on, sir!" Todd shouted. "We're friends."

A grizzled, middle-aged man spat a steam of tobacco and grumbled, "That depends on what side yer on, don't it? You're wearin' uniforms. You deserters?"

"No, sir," Tod replied. "We've been given permission to go in advance of the army. I can show you." He pulled out the paper from his commander.

"Put that thang away. I kain't read."

"Do you have any food? A place to sleep?"

"Fresh hay in the barn." He pointed behind his cabin. "Ya gotta be careful, Yanks are all around here. Kain't let ya in the house, case they come by. I'll bring some warm grub to the barn."

"Thank you, sir,"

"Much obliged," Jim added.

The two men bedded down in the sweet-smelling, soft hay. After about an hour the barn door opened and the space glowed from the light of a single lantern. Tod squinted in the sudden brightness. Then his eyes focused on a beautiful image. A lovely young woman stood before them, dressed in a long black robe. She held a wicker basket in one hand and the lantern in the other.

"I told Jake I'd bring you some food," the woman said as she handed the basket to Jim.

"Who are you?" Tod inquired. "You're not his wife."

The woman smiled softly. "No, I'm not. I travel this road some, going to Nashville and Smyrna."

"Thank you, ma'am," Tod said. "Isn't it kind of dangerous for a woman to be alone, traveling these roads at night?"

"Usually I have an escort. He's in the cabin with Jake."

"Tod," Jim stated, "she must be a courier."

The woman laughed. "And who are you?"

"Just two soldiers going home to Franklin for a short visit."

"What's your name, Captain?"

"I'm Tod Carter, and this is Jim Cooper."

"Carter. I've heard the name. I think my father mentioned it, and I know my . . . the family of a good friend of mine did business with Carters."

"Who are you?" Tod asked.

"My name is Mary Kate Patterson. My father is a doctor."

"Who was your friend's family?"

"The Davises from Smyrna."

"Tod!" Jim exclaimed. "Don't you realize who this is? She's Sam Davis's friend. The one who arrived just when they were hanging him." Jim looked at her. "I'm right, ain't I, ma'am?"

"Yes, Sam Davis was my friend."

"He was a real hero," Tod commented softly. "He gave his life when he could have saved it with just one word."

"He wouldn't give up his friends to save himself. That's how he was," Mary Kate explained. "What are you doing here? Where is your army?" Her tone became business-like.

"General Hood is coming up from Columbia," Tod said.

"The Yankees still have Franklin, and Thomas is waiting for reinforcements in Nashville," Mary Kate informed the men. "A.J. Smith's corps is getting close. I have a message to deliver to our loyal friends in Nashville. You two be careful and stay out of the way."

Tod walked over to Mary Kate and took her hand. "I'm sorry for what you've been through. You be careful. This is dirty work for a lady."

Mary Kate nodded. "We all serve the Confederacy in different ways. I carry dispatches. The Yankees leave me alone. They've seen me plenty. I just smile and wink at them. You, they won't take so lightly. Watch out."

* * *

HOOD ROSE EARLY on the morning of November 29. A heavy, cold mist draped over the town and river. A light sprinkling of snow remained on the ground. The general dressed, drank a cup of hot coffee and waited as his horse was led to him. Two soldiers helped him up into the saddle and then strapped him in.

Hood looked down. "Thank you, boys. I was a much better horseman when I had two legs."

The general joined Cheatham as he led his troops down a path for three miles to Davis Crossing, where the bridge had been built. As they neared the bridge, the stillness of the early morning was shattered by the sound of cannons.

"Lee's doing his job," Hood noted. "Now we get across."

The chill of early morning evaporated as a warm sun beamed down on the Confederate advance. Twenty thousand men had reached the far side of the Duck by mid-morning. Invigorated by the sun's warmth and the explosion of fall colors, unencumbered by artillery left with Lee, they turned straight north to Spring Hill.

The previous day, Schofield had been in a quandary in his position behind the Duck River. His telegraph operator, the lone holder of the cipher needed to translate messages, had deserted. General Wilson had informed him that he had discovered from captured Confederates that Hood was laying a pontoon bridge to the east and would cross soon.

The last message delivered from Thomas instructed Schofield to move his troops to Franklin to form a line of defense on the Harpeth River instead of the Duck at Columbia. Thomas was sure that A.J. Smith's arrival with the Sixteenth Corps was imminent and they would join Schofield at Franklin.

"Cilley," Schofield reasoned, "If Wilson is right and Hood is trying to flank me, we've got to beat hell back to Spring Hill before he gets there. But what if he isn't going there? What if it's a trick? Once I get this army moving north, Hood could cross the river and crash into us from the rear, though they're still in our front. How do I know if it's just a division or Hood's whole army?"

Throughout the night, Schofield fretted and wondered what to do. He cursed the deserted telegraph operator. He cursed General Thomas for not giving him clearer instructions. Then morning came and Lee opened up with his cannons. Near dawn, word came from Clint that Hood was indeed crossing the Duck. Schofield knew he had to act.

He called in General David Stanley. "Take two divisions and get to Spring Hill. It's about twelve miles, a little less than half the distance to Nashville. Take all the wagons and reserve artillery. We need to keep them out of rebel hands. Leave Kimball's division up the road a piece to guard against any flank attack by Hood. You'll travel on the Columbia Pike. Hold the crossroads at Spring Hill. We need to pass there to get to Franklin."

It was 8:00 a.m. when Stanley began his mission to Spring Hill with 5,500 men. About 20,000 stayed behind with Schofield. He had to outrace Hood.

Forrest's cavalry had been busy. Wilson's troops had tried to attack as Hood crossed the river, but Forrest's troops rode like devils into them and scattered Wilson's force. They were ten miles away before they stopped.

Then, after leaving a small force behind to watch over Wilson, they galloped to Spring Hill, hoping to beat Stanley there. But the Union soldiers, running part way, got there first, kept control of the Colombia Pike and drove back the Confederate horsemen. Hood ordered Forrest to hold a position northwest of the town. Forrest continued to fight there until his men were out of ammunition. It was one o'clock in the afternoon. Forrest called for more cartridges and powder and held on.

James Chalmers, one of Forrest's division commanders, pushed back a throng of Union cavalry near the edge of a woods. They came upon strong Union breastworks manned by a mass of Union infantry and retreated back to their lines.

When Forrest returned, he spied Yankee cavalry back on the boundary of the trees. The general rode to Chalmers. "Why don't you drive those fellows off?"

"There's federal infantry behind those fortifications."

"Chalmers, I think you are mistaken. That is only a small cavalry force."

Reluctant to contradict the Wizard of the Saddle, Chalmers replied, "All right, I'll try it."

He reformed his cavalry and yelled, "Forward, gallop!"

It was a bloodbath. As Chalmers's troops charged into the trees, rifle and artillery fire burst from the Union breastworks. Horses tumbled; men flew through the air. Arms, legs, and heads were ripped off. It was over in an instant. Only a few rebel cavalrymen were unharmed, including Chalmers.

The Union soldiers stared in astonishment at the wreckage strewn before them. They didn't bother with the small band that retreated. Chalmers rode back to Forrest, who had observed the carnage. "They was in there sure enough, wasn't they, Chalmers?"

"Yes, sir." Chalmers tried to stifle his sarcasm. "That is the second time I found them there."

* * *

AT 3:00 P.M., Hood's main force topped a rise overlooking Spring Hill, two miles away. He watched as the last of Schofield's wagons traversed Columbia-Franklin Pike into the village. He noted that Stanley had erected defenses on three sides of the little town.

Hood immediately sent for generals Cheatham and Cleburne and gave them orders. He also told them General Stewart was close by, and he would have him rush his men to the front.

Hood established his headquarters in the mansion Oaklawn, the beautiful, white-columned brick home of Absalom Thompson. From there he ordered General William Bate, "I want you to take your division toward the Columbia Pike and sweep toward Columbia."

"Yes, sir," Bate replied, "but General Cheatham ordered me to form up at Spring Hill on Cleburne's left."

"Who commands here?"

"You do, General," Bate said, chagrined. "We'll head to the pike."

Neither bothered to tell Cheatham of the change. As the general watched Cleburne move into position, Bate's division followed as expected. Both divisions disappeared as they headed down a rise. Cheatham couldn't see Bate head west toward the pike.

John C. Brown's division of Confederate infantry appeared, and Cheatham instructed them to head to the right of where he expected Cleburne to be. "We've got 'em now," he told Brown. "We have a front of Bate on the left, Cleburne in the center, and you on the right. I don't think they've got much more than 5,000 in the town. If Hood commits his whole force here, we have 25,000."

Brown added, "That doesn't include Lee's men."

"It's a big moment for us. We can't lose it," Cheatham added.

* * *

ALSO AT ABOUT 3:00 p.m., Schofield, back in Columbia, concluded that Hood was not going to attack him there. He left a division under General Jacob Cox and with three brigades, headed up the Columbia Pike toward Spring Hill.

* * *

CLEBURNE'S DIVISION of 3,000 men made an echelon attack from right to left at about 4:00 p.m. with three brigades led in order by Lowrey, Govan, and Granbury. Cheatham expected Cleburne to drive north into Spring Hill. Hood's intention was to use this formation to sweep toward the turnpike and then wheel left to intercept Schofield's vanguard on the pike. But he didn't observe Union troop movements south of town.

Cheatham, watching from a knoll, heard the rattle of rifle fire signaling that Cleburne was engaged. Bradley's Union brigade, south of the village, blocked his path. The stair-step echelon formation wasn't very effective against Bradley's fortified Union position on their right and left, and allowed only Lowrey's brigade to engage them at first. Fierce fire from the Union line stalled Lowrey, who dashed over to Cleburne. "There's a federal regiment left on the field that's about to attack me!"

Cleburne instantly raised his hand as if he were going to snap a whip. He shouted, "I'll charge them! Govan, I'll personally lead the brigade forward!" He wheeled them into a northern alignment on Bradley's right flank. The Union line was a semi-circle south and east of Spring Hill. Cleburne led his force, splashing over Rutherford Creek. It was about half an hour from sunset.

There, Cleburne encountered Forrest. His dismounted cavalry had been fighting all day, and the men and the general were exhausted. Cleburne removed his hat, waved it back at his infantry and shouted, "Let's get some Yankees, boys!"

The outflanking of the Union position by Lowrey and Govan broke the line, and Bradley's men fled toward Spring Hill in disorder. Cleburne's charge pushed the fleeing Yankees right to the edge of town. But there, Cleburne's two brigades were stymied short of the turnpike by Wagner's fierce artillery fire.

Cheatham expected Bate to follow in, not knowing Bate had been moved by Hood. The general moved Brown's brigade to the right of Cleburne. Then a courier from the Irish general raced to Cheatham. "Gen'r'l Cleburne says he ran into a strong entrenchment of federal troops. They mauled him, sir. He says they need to halt."

"Brown has crossed Rutherford Creek, he's moving to Cleburne's left. Tell the general to stay put until he hears the sound of Brown's guns. That's the signal for another attack on Spring Hill. Forrest will be on Brown's right. I'm sending Gist's brigade as well."

But that didn't happen. Gist didn't arrive, so Forrest didn't move into position. Brown, informed that Union troops were on his right and front and that Forrest was not to be seen, didn't order an assault. Therefore, Cleburne did not resume his attack.

Night fell on the battlefield with the Union still in control of Spring Hill, and Hood's forces in position to the south. Farther south, just off Columbia Pike, Schofield was encamped. In the evening, Lee left his position in front of Columbia and used the pontoon bridge to hurry to Spring Hill. At 10:00 p.m., the remaining Union force under Cox raced up the pike to find Schofield.

Hood was livid when he confronted his officers. First he accosted Cleburne. "You should have been able to smash those Yankees. What happened?"

"I ran into heavy fire. I thought I had Bate on my left, but he wasn't there. I was to wait until Brown engaged."

"I ordered Bate to that position," Cheatham said.

"I ordered Bate to the pike," Hood explained.

"You didn't tell me. I ordered him back."

"Brown," Hood asserted, "you were supposed to charge when Forrest opened fire."

Brown rejoined, "Forrest didn't open fire. I was told Stewart's entire corps was being rushed to my right flank. I waited for them. They never came. Besides, Cheatham came to my position and said to call off the assault."

"That's not true," Cheatham countered. "I never got to that position. A courier told me that General Hood wanted to see me."

Stewart interjected, "A courier brought me orders that I was not to cross Rutherford Creek and that I should wait for further instructions."

Hood countered, "My order was for you to cross the creek."

Forrest joined the back and forth. "I was to fire when Gist arrived. Gist didn't. I was 'bout out of ammunition, anyway."

"Enough of this!" Hood thundered. "You all have excuses for what should have been an easy assault. General Cheatham, I never ordered you to call off the assault. The fact is, no decisive all-out assault was launched by anyone. We lost one big chance, but we still have a golden opportunity. At least we have 'em trapped and the road is blocked. We must not let Schofield through, and tomorrow we take Spring Hill. It's still within our reach to achieve all our goals, including moving on Nashville."

As the meeting concluded and Brown walked past, Hood stopped him and spoke in a confidential tone. "General, there's those that say you were drinking during the battle, and that's why you didn't act."

"That's a damn lie," Brown retorted. "I heard some of your generals did stop by the mansion for refreshments during the battle. But not me."

Hood reddened. "There should have been no time for 'refreshments' for anyone and you better not have been there."

Brown looked away. "Just stopped by once to get another horse."

"Maybe it was your horse that was drinking," Hood concluded sarcastically.

It was now past dusk, and Hood had ordered Stewart, "Move north and get across the pike."

A guide who lived in the area led Stewart into the darkness. For several hours they fumbled about, finally encountering Forrest's headquarters. There, a messenger from Cheatham's staff delivered news that Hood now wanted Stewart to form on Cheatham's right, next to Brown's division.

Stewart questioned Forrest, "This is strange. Why would Hood send us a message by Cheatham's staff and not his?"

"Where would this position you?" Forrest wondered.

Stewart's brow creased in thought. "This will take us away from the pike and not across it. Besides, it'll take all night."

"Bivouac your men," Forrest suggested, "then let's head off to Hood and see if we can figgur this out."

Hood's officers' meeting had adjourned to the Absalom Thompson mansion, where many of the generals debated and discussed the events of the day over fine whiskey provided by their host. Cheatham, Granbury, Cleburne, Walthall, and others indulged heavily in the amber fluid.

"Where's our fine commander?" Cleburne asked.

"I believe his wounds and ailments are giving him some trouble," Granbury said. "He's upstairs self-medicating."

"Laudanum?" Cheatham questioned.

Granbury shrugged. "His wounds pain him," he replied simply.

Cheatham stood on slightly unsteady feet. "I believe the lovely Jesse Helen Peters is awaiting me," Cheatham announced. "I must not disappoint her." He firmly grabbed the banister and strode up the stairs.

When Stewart and Forrest arrived, they were told that Hood was upstairs, asleep.

"Wake him up," Stewart snapped. "We've got to get something straightened out."

The two generals were escorted into Hood's bedroom. Hood, still in bed wearing a nightshirt, asked groggily, "What is this all about?"

"General," Stewart cut to the quick, "did you change your mind? Did you send orders for me to form up on Cheatham's right?"

"Yes, I did."

"But General Hood," Stewart objected, "this will take us away from the pike."

Hood waved his hand to dismiss them. "Let the men rest where they are tonight. We'll finish the fight in the morning."

As they were leaving, Hood asked Forrest, "Can you throw a barricade across the pike?"

"My men are exhausted and out of ammunition. We were in the saddle for nearly twenty hours today. But we'll try."

The Trap Fails to Spring

SCHOFIELD'S 20,000 INFANTRYMEN marched as quietly as they could on the Columbia Pike. Thousands of flickering Confederate campfires glimmered near the edge of the road. A Union officer spied an encampment not far from the road and halted his troops. As he investigated, he saw a horseman in the dark. "Whose division is that on the left?" he asked.

"General Cleburne's," came the answer.

"All right," replied the officer as he galloped back to his men.

The night was dark, no moon, only stars in a clear sky. The Union Army was told to move at a steady pace. But when wagons and artillery broke down, the road clogged and traffic stopped.

A colonel rode up, put his finger to his lips and ordered that no one should speak above a whisper as the broken-down equipment was fixed or discarded off the road. Around midnight they reached Spring Hill and watched the shadows of Confederate soldiers as they moved around their campfires.

For hours, the Union force snaked through the Confederate lines. They bypassed Spring Hill and continued past it toward Franklin. One lone Confederate private managed to get through to Hood in the mansion, where the general was asleep.

"Gen'r'l," he tried to alert his sleepy commander, "the Yankees, they's movin'. The pike past Spring Hill is filled with 'em."

Hood ordered Cheatham to investigate and to fire on anything moving on the pike. Cheatham instructed General Ed Jackson to observe the pike. Jackson, grumbling after being awakened from a sound sleep, headed out to the road. He reported that he saw nothing.

Forrest's division of cavalry under Red Jackson did confront Union infantry on the pike about midnight. Massed Union troops drove off the cavalry.

Schofield's whole army disappeared into the night. Hood had lost another opportunity to upend the Union force. Riding alongside his commander was Clint Cilley. Schofield leaned over and addressed Clint. "I want you to go on ahead. I sent Captain Levi Scofield with Cox directly to Franklin. Tell Scofield, my engineer, to place divisions in defensive positions as they arrive. Tell him I expect our defenses to be in place when I get there."

Clint saluted. "Yes, sir." He spurred his horse and galloped down the pike into the night.

* * *

THE NIGHT OF NOVEMBER 29, Tod Carter and Jim Cooper reached Winstead Hill, about two miles from the Carter house. At the foot of the hill on the west side of the Columbia Turnpike was the home of Green Neeley, a friend of the Carter family.

It was late and Tod didn't want to ride up to his house in the dark, not knowing who might be keeping guard, so they stopped at his neighbor's. Neeley greeted them warmly and brought some hot stew and bread to his guests, who ate heartily.

"This is great, Mr. Neeley," Tod said between slurps of stew, "and tomorrow morning I'll be eating breakfast in my father's house."

Tod and Jim slept in the house that night, curled up in army blankets.

In the early morning hours, a fleet of boats carrying Smith's guerillas arrived in Nashville.

* * *

SAM HOOD AWAKENED on the morning of November 30 and soon discovered that his world had turned upside down. Dawn was just breaking when Hood arose, eagerly expecting to resume the battle. He had gone to bed knowing that Schofield was nearby but was confident his path on the pike to Franklin was blocked.

His adjutant gave him news that infuriated him. "Sir, the Yankees are gone!"

"Gone? What do you mean, gone?"

"Their camp is empty, sir, they are nowhere in sight. They must've passed on the pike during the night."

"Impossible. We had them in a trap, just waiting to spring it!"

"They're gone," the adjutant repeated.

Hood slammed his crutch onto the floor. "Breakfast was scheduled for my officers at Cheair's mansion. By God, I'll get to the bottom of this there!"

The general silently fumed as his generals arrived at the mansion, located on the pike near Spring Hill. He waited until they were seated and food was being served before he lashed out. He stood at the end of a long dining room table, glared at those assembled and loudly exclaimed, "Schofield is gone! Right under your noses! His army, over 20,000 men, simply marched by you in the middle of the night. How did this happen?"

Stewart exclaimed, "Sir, you moved me away from the pike!"

"I moved you onto the pike," Hood corrected.

"A soldier warned you around midnight, didn't he?" Cheatham asked Hood. "Then you had me investigate. General Johnson said no one was on the pike."

"There wasn't," Ed Johnson claimed. "Either Schofield had already passed or there was a break in his lines, but I didn't see anyone."

"It all started yesterday," Hood countered, "when Cleburne's division didn't finish the attack."

It went back and forth, shouting, finger pointing and recrimination. Accusations of drinking, womanizing, and dereliction of duty and worse were espoused. Hood ranted, "This was destined to be the best move in my career as a soldier. It came to naught because of you!"

Stewart claimed defensively, "They had good ground. They were dug in behind breastworks."

"Breastworks!" Hood was livid. "Are you telling me that an army after a forward march of 180 miles is still unwilling to accept battle without breastworks? If that is true, I have grave concerns about this army. Are you really unwilling to charge breastworks?

"I count six opportunities you had to close the pike," he continued. "None of them happened! Forrest, you had the first chance, the attack on Spring Hill in the morning. Cleburne could have smashed Stanley's troops, and Bate could have headed off Schofield on the pike. Brown, when you didn't act, a general assault on Spring Hill was not put in motion. Cheatham failed to have Johnson, or anyone else, close off the pike last night, and Forrest, you had a chance at Schofield late last night north of town. They escaped you. Schofield escaped all of you!"

Brown leaned over to Cleburne and whispered, "Well, Pat, Hood's as wrathful as a rattlesnake this morning, striking at everything."

Prelude to Battle

THE ARMY OF TENNESSEE hit the Columbia Pike in an ugly mood. Now they were chasing Schofield knowing full well that they had had him bottled up, but somehow the cork had come out of the bottle.

The mood of the army didn't match the brightness of the sunny, late November day. The countryside was lush, and a panorama of fall colors exploded around them. Passing along the pastoral environs, they were greeted by encouragement and cheers from ladies, old men, and young boys who lined the fences and fields.

Hood led Stewart's corps in the vanguard of the march. Cheatham was next, followed by Stephen Lee, who was racing to catch up from Columbia.

"Yankees bin running down the pike like rabbits!" an elderly farmer shouted.

It might have encouraged the men in the ranks, but their officers were still frustrated, bitter, and at odds with each other.

Pat Cleburne was down the column, riding with Brown. Cleburne had on a new gray uniform and his favorite old kepi-style cap. He turned and said to Brown, "John, Hood's trying to blame me for what happened yesterday. I won't have it. I didn't order a second attack on Stanley because I was ordered to let you go first and you never did."

"I couldn't," was all Brown would say.

Cleburne looked silently at Brown, his handome thirty-seven-year-old friend, and continued riding.

Brown found words. "Hood was just frustrated. Don't let it bother you."

"It does bother me. It hurts me deeply. When this is over I shall demand a full investigation of what happened at Spring Hill. Hood is the one responsible for this mess, and he should own up to it."

As a courier rode up and delivered orders, Cleburne concluded, "We will resume this conversation at our earliest convenient moment."

* * *

AT 3:00 A.M. THE NIGHT before, the vanguard of Schofield's army reached Winstead Hill, just south of Franklin. Tod and Jim Cooper slept soundly and didn't hear as the army passed.

Unencumbered, General Cox and his army had outpaced everyone and reached Franklin before any other units arrived. Cox surveyed the town from the outskirts and saw an imposing brick house located on a low hill away from the town proper to the south. Believing that Schofield was still several hours behind him, Cox rode to the house.

All was dark and quiet. The inhabitants of the home were sleeping. Cox's aides pounded loudly on the wooden door and a sleepy, elderly man opened it. "What's this all about?" he asked. "It's four thirty in the morning."

Cox announced directly, "I'm a Union general, and we have need of a headquarters building. I have decided to use your house."

Alarmed, the man responded, "But I have three families here, mostly women and children."

"What's your name, sir?"

"Fountain Branch Carter."

"We will try not to overly disturb you or your family. But we need this place. How many are here?"

"Seventeen. Should we leave?"

Cox considered. "No, you should be all right here. My men will leave you alone."

Clint Cilley rode into the Carter yard just as Branch Carter stepped back inside his house. Cox turned expectantly to Clint. "Have you word from General Schofield?"

"He wants Captain Scofield to prepare defenses. He's on his way and Hood is behind him."

"Major, we'll get things ready here soon. But my men are exhausted. I can't order them to dig trenches in this condition. We need a few hours."

"General Schofield is anxious. I expect he'll be here before long."

"I've spoken with Captain Scofield. We know what to do. Some defenses remain from a fight here last year."

The exhausted staff of General Cox was soon sleeping on the Carter house's floors and porch. His troops camped behind the house. After riding through the night himself, Clint wrapped himself in a blanket and fell asleep leaning against a tree trunk.

Within the hour, Schofield arrived. He flung open the Carter house's door and shouted, "Cox, where are you?"

The sleepy general rose from the floor near the kitchen fireplace, his full head of hair disheveled. Cox ran his hands down both sides of his full-bearded face. He saluted, "Right here, General."

Schofield stared at him with bloodshot eyes. "I've ridden around the town," he announced breathlessly. "The Harpeth River is swollen and the pontoons aren't here. The county bridge is gone, and we can't cross at the ford. We are trapped in this town, and Hood is on his way. Where's A.J. Smith? General Thomas said he would be here."

"Smith has not arrived yet, General Schofield. The last I heard, Thomas is still waiting for him."

Schofield gazed heavenward in disbelief. "What more can go wrong? All right, here's what we do. I'll tend to the crossing. We need to fix the bridge and get our wagons across. Get Scofield and get breastworks and other defenses ready. I expect Hood this afternoon. General Cox, I'm putting you in command of the Twenty-third Corps. Hold back Hood at all hazards until we get the bridges repaired."

Schofield turned as Clint entered the house. "Major, head back down the pike. I need to know how close the rebs are."

* * *

As CLINT RODE back toward Winstead Hill, he encountered a lone rider approaching in the dim light of early morning. Apprehensively, he fingered the handle of his holstered pistol as the rider grew closer, then reined in his horse as they came alongside each other.

"Good morning. A little cool this morning for a ride. Do you have business in town?"

Tod pulled close the coat he had borrowed from Neeley, hiding his uniform. "I've got some family down there. I'm just going for a visit. I farm a piece back there."

Clint peered through his glasses. "You don't look much like a farmer."

"And you don't look much like a soldier, but you're wearing a blue uniform."

"You got me there. I probably look more like a teacher. That's what I was."

"Lots of other fellas with blue coats down there?"

"Quite a few and more to come."

"Well, I don't want to get in the way." Tod tipped his hat. "Nice to meet you. Maybe I'll run into you again sometime."

"Maybe, if the war don't get in the way."

The two riders continued on, in opposite directions.

* * *

CLINT RODE ON past Winstead Hill, where he met the rest of Schofield's approaching army. He knew that Hood was somewhere behind them and that Wagner's division was in between with his artillery unit, trying to delay the rebel army. Clint continued down the pike.

* * *

TOD WAS DETERMINED to get his home-cooked breakfast. Jim Cooper had ridden to his family's farm, and Tod had gone on the Franklin Road. The Carter house was in sight, and all was quiet and serene as Tod neared it. Things hadn't changed much in three and a half years. The sturdy brick house looked the same. In front stood the smokehouse, office and, over across the pike, the cotton gin.

Tod paused at the garden gate, between the smokehouse and office, with his hand on the latch and thanked God that he was home. Tears of joy filled his eyes. Tod wiped them away. "What would Moscow think?" Tod muttered to himself. "A soldier crying at the door."

Then he saw his sister, Fanny, come onto the porch. Shock, not joy, swept over her face when she saw her brother. She frantically waved Tod away and mouthed, "Go back."

He looked at her silently and questioningly, then turned and walked back to where Rosencrantz was tethered. Fanny would not have acted as she did unless there was danger. Tod knew he had to leave. Breakfast would have to wait for another day.

* * *

THE HARPETH RIVER was deep and, with the heavy rains, swollen. Deeper and faster than normal, the river was not wide, but it was treacherous. Franklin sat in the valley of the Harpeth. The river bordered much of the eastern and northern parts of the town before it took a twisting turn north, almost forming a semi-circle on Franklin.

Three roads ran into the town: Carter's Creek Pike to the west, Lewisburg Pike to the east, and, in the center, the Columbia Pike, which passed between the Carter house and cotton gin. The Nashville and Decatur Railroad skirted the eastern edge of town.

Schofield went to his telegraph operator first thing in the morning. The general was pale and agitated, impending dread etched on his face. He hadn't seen Wilson or his cavalry since Forrest had run them off at Spring Hill. He scribbled out a message to Thomas: "I do not know where Forrest is. Wilson is entirely unable to cope with him."

"I hope this gets through," Schofield told the operator. "My last one to Thomas didn't."

The message did get through, setting up a desperate correspondence between Franklin and Nashville.

Schofield sent to Thomas, "The 15,000 fresh troops under A.J. Smith must have arrived by now. Please send them to me."

Thomas replied, "The first just arrived by steamboat and cannot be dispatched to you that quickly. I do not want you to risk too much. I send you a map of the environs of Franklin. Can you hold off Hood for three more days?"

Schofield returned, "Three days. I don't know if I can hold him three hours. I cannot prevent Hood from crossing the Harpeth whenever he may attempt it. I am satisfied that I have heretofore run too much risk to hold Hood in check. The slightest mistake on my part, or failure of a subordinate during the last three days, might have proved disastrous. I don't want to get into such a tight place again."

By mid-morning, most of Schofield's army had trudged into Franklin. Wagner's divisions were still on rear guard duty, shepherding in the last units. They were exhausted, hungry, and in need of sleep. But there was little time for rest. Work had to be done.

Meanwhile, Cox and Captain Scofield were frantically working 20,000 men to construct a defensive line in the other half of the semi-circle enclosing Franklin. Using the Harpeth River as an anchor at two points, the line stretched over two miles from where the Harpeth entered Franklin at the southeastern boundary of the town to where it made its swing to the north.

The line ran directly in front of the Carter house, which formed the southern periphery.

A barricade in front of the house was being feverishly constructed by hundreds of men. Along the two-mile front, breastworks sprang up. They were particularly strong on the southern boundary of the line in front of the Carter house.

There, a four-foot-wide, two- to three-foot-deep trench was dug. Behind that was an earthen wall topped by wooden fence rails four feet high, then another trench three to four feet deep in which defenders could stand and aim their weapons through head log gaps at the top of the wall.

About 200 feet behind the main works, less in some places, was a 150-yard retrenchment line. Made of earth and rails, the low mound was intended to be a traffic barrier and not a full-fledged defensive earthwork. The Carter house was sixty feet behind this second line, just off Columbia Pike to the west. Southeast of the pike, just in front of the main line from the cotton gin east, was a thicket of Osage orange shrubs. These were sharpened and pointed outward to act as abatis. Along the main line to the southwest was a locust grove, beginning west of the Carter house. The trees there were also cut, sharpened and used as abatis.

The weak point in the line was where the pike entered the town. The road needed to be kept open to allow for wagon traffic, so a barricade was placed across the pike. Batteries of cannon, four near the cotton gin on the main line east of the pike and four on the west side by the smokehouse, were ready to support Union forces.

The Carter house itself was Cox's headquarters, the main parlor his nerve center. Schofield met with him there shortly after noon. "General," Cox began, "we're about ready for them. I believe the Carter Hill is the key to any strong system of defense in front of the town and that the line from the cotton gin as a salient to the knoll near the riverbank must form our line of battle on the left flank."

"What about the pike coming in?"

"It's our weak point. But it's strongly barricaded."

"Good. I like the looks of what you've done. Cilley just reported back to me. He says Hood could be here about one o'clock this afternoon. Wagner has been holding them off all day. He left Columbia at six this morning."

Cox continued, "I've got Wood's Fourth Division and Wilson's cavalry north of the Harpeth to watch for any flanking movements. General Stanley has ordered General Wagner to hold Winstead Hill until nightfall."

"That's impossible," Schofield interjected. "Wagner can't hold them off. I'll have him throw up defenses on either side of the pike about half a mile out. Fire a few rounds and then fall back to the main line. Cilley," he turned to Clint. "Deliver that message."

"Are the bridges fixed?" Cox asked.

"Almost. Soon we'll start moving the wagons over. If Hood hasn't attacked by six, I'll move the whole army out to Nashville. I'll make my headquarters on Figures Hill in Fort Granger. They've got some big guns up there, three-inch rifles, to throw some shot into them."

* * *

AS CILLEY PREDICTED, about 1:00 p.m. the first Confederate units reached Winstead Hill. Per orders delivered by Clint, General George Wagner had placed two brigades, one on either side of the pike, on a ridge a half mile from the main line. John Lane and Joe Conrad were commanding.

There had been a third brigade, commanded by a short, curly-haired Dutchman named Emerson Opdycke. When ordered by Wagner to dig in with the others, Opdycke blanched. "That is ridiculous, General Wagner," he said. "I will not do it. The risk is too great. All day my men have had Forrest nipping at their butts. They're tired, and I'll have none of this."

"We can do it!" Wagner proclaimed proudly, his goatee quivering. "We saved our troops with rear guard action from Columbia. We were first to Spring Hill, saving the day again, and now we are last to leave Spring Hill, rear guard again. These are great boys! Have faith in them!"

"General, this is fool's work. The position is untenable, and I will not let my men face it. We have been fighting, climbing over fences, passing through woods, thickets, and muddy cornfields and we are entitled to some relief."

Wagner gave up. "Well, Opdycke, fight when and where you damn please; we all know you'll fight." Then he turned and rode off toward Franklin. Opdycke and his division followed, where they took up a reserve position behind the Carter house.

* * *

TOD HAD HURRIED back up Winstead Hill during the early morning, riding until he found advancing Confederate columns. He sought out Tyler's Brigade and General Thomas Benton Smith. "You're on leave, Captain," Smith noted. "You don't have to be here."

"General, the Yankees are in my house. They're in my yard. They're all over Franklin. I want to lead a charge to get them out of there."

Inside the Carter house, the patriarch, Branch Carter, prepared to move his family into the basement, including Moscow and his four young children, the four Carter sisters, two slaves, and five members of the neighboring Lotz family. There were twelve children under the age of twelve.

Little eight-year-old Alice McPhail, Branch's granddaughter, tentatively crept down the stairs into the cellar. "I'm scared," she whimpered to Branch. "The Yankees are coming. What's gonna happen?"

Her grandfather placed his big, worn hand atop her head of curls in a comforting gesture. "It'll be all right, Alice, it's safe down here. Look, we've put rope rolls in the basement windows. Bullets can't come through the stone walls or the windows. And look, we've got food."

A hole had been dug in the middle of the north cellar floor. All the meat from the smokehouse, potatoes, lard, and big sacks of ground meal were stuffed into the hole. Wooden planks were nailed over it, bricks set on top and a big table put over it all.

"See, Alice," Branch assured her, "the Yankees will never find it."

* * *

JUST AFTER 1:00 P.M., Hood rode up Winstead Hill. The vista of the Harpeth Valley spread out before him. The ground was still a lush green and flat for a mile and a half to where a low ridge bisected the Columbia Pike. Beyond that, another half mile away, the Carter house stood upon a low hill. Bedford Forrest rode beside Hood as they headed down the crest to a linden tree, the only tree in sight.

"Beautiful, isn't it?" Hood said admiringly.

"Sure is, Sam, except for one thing. That long blue line up there spoils things."

"General Forrest, we can't let them reach Nashville. This afternoon we've got to make a final effort to overtake and rout the enemy. Drive them right into the Harpeth. We can't hope to get between Schofield and Nashville. Even if we cross the river after them, there isn't enough distance for us to divide them before they reach the city."

"What do you propose?"

"We attack them. I'll send Stewart's column to the east toward the Lewisburg Pike. Cheatham will lead his column over Winstead Hill. Bate will move left through a gap close to the Carter's Creek Pike on the western edge of town."

"Charge the breastworks? You can't be serious."

"I'm very serious. It can be done."

"Look, give me one strong division of infantry with my cavalry and within two hours' time I will agree to flank the federals from their works. I could march east to the Harpeth, cross over and swing around against Schofield north of Franklin."

"No," Hood countered. "I want you to put your cavalry on both flanks. If the assault proves successful, you can complete the ruin of their army by capturing any attempting to flee to Nashville."

"I'll do what you order. But I want you to know I don't agree."

Frank Cheatham, after hearing of Hood's plan, approached the general. "Sam, I don't like the looks of this fight. The federals have an excellent position and are well fortified. It will be a desperate chance if we attempt to dislodge them."

Hood said, "I would prefer to fight them here, where they have only eight hours to fortify, than to strike them at Nashville, where they have been strengthening themselves for three years and more."

While his men were ascending Winstead Hill, Pat Cleburne had been enjoying a game of checkers with his staff. He had drawn a board on the ground with his staff and used colored leaves as chips.

Then word came to him of Hood's plan to assault the Union barricades. He and General Brown hurried to Harrison Mansion on Columbia Pike, where their general had established a headquarters.

Earlier, Cleburne had observed the Union line through field glasses. He made only one simple remark: "They are very formidable." Now, with his general, he was direct. "An assault on the Union lines will involve a terrible waste of life. Order a flanking movement. Turn Schofield out of his entrenchments."

Brown supported Cleburne, but Hood was adamant. "The country around Franklin for many miles is open and exposed to the full view of the U.S. Army, and I cannot mask the movements of my troops so as to turn either flank of the enemy. If I attempt it, he will withdraw and precede me into Nashville."

Frustrated and depressed, the two rode off to issue orders to their men. Govan, one of Cleburne's division commanders and a friend from Arkansas, met his general. "What's wrong, sir? You look like you've lost your best friend."

"I'm afraid I'm going to lose a lot of friends. Hood told us we have to carry the Union works at all hazards. Look," he pointed to the north and Franklin, "see the heavy breastworks, the bayonets, the guns."

Govan mounted his horse and prepared to ride away. He stopped and looked back at his friend. "Well, General, few of us will ever return to Arkansas to tell the story of this battle."

"Well, Govan, if we are to die, let us die like men."

Around 2:00 p.m., as the rest of the Army of Tennessee prepared to attack, Forrest brought two divisions across the east bank of the Harpeth River. He headed north with 3,000 men. Forrest had divided his command, as ordered by Hood, and sent Chalmers to the west on Hood's left flank.

Wilson, with 6,000 men, was waiting for Forrest. For the next several hours a cavalry battle raged east of Franklin and the Harpeth. The two-to-one odds eventually wore Forrest down. That, and a shortage of ammunition, caused Forrest to recross the river.

Battle of Franklin
November 30, 1864
Actions after 4:30 pm

0 50 m 100 m 150 m
0 0.05 mile 0.1 0.15

N

Harpeth River

Loring
Scott
Adams
Lewisburg Pike
Nashville & Decatur RR

Featherston

STEWART

French Walthall
Cockrell Sears Reynolds Quarles Shelby

120 IN
63 IN
128 IN
1 OH
5 MO
G
112 IL

Stiles

Cox

Casement
Gin
Cotton
124 IN
6 OH
65 IL
65 IN
5 TN

16 KY, 12 KY, 8 TN (3 Cos)
100 OH Bty
104, 6 OH Bty

Granbury Govan Lowrey
Cleburne

Columbia Pike

Reilly
Lotz
House
Carter
House
175 OH
20 OH Bty
retrenchment
72 IL
Bty
Bty

Gordon
Strahl
Brown

Opdycke

Ruger

Bridge's Bty
Strickland
44 MO
111 OH
& 24 MO
107 IL
193 OH
129 IN
183 OH (2 Cos)
present-day Natchez St.

Locust Grove
abatis

Gist
Carter

Moore
23 MI
118 OH
80 IN

Johnson
(S.D. Lee)

7 pm

7 pm

Deas
Manigault

Smith Jackson
Bullock Bate

Sharp
Brantley

Kimball
Grose

Carter's Creek Pike

CHEATHAM

Chalmers

Courtesy of Hal Jasperson.

The Battle of Franklin

BY MID-AFTERNOON, THE SUN WAS ALREADY dipping toward the western horizon in the mostly cloudless November sky. The Army of Tennessee was moving into position. Bate's division, with Tod Carter, was assembled at the foot of Winstead Hill at 3:00 p.m. They were ordered to take ground to the west until they cleared Brown's Division and Pilot Knob, where they were to turn left. When they reached a house near the Carter's Creek Pike and passed through Mrs. Bostick's yard with General Thomas Benton Smith's brigade to the west, they would be in a straight line to the Carter house.

As they waited at the foot of the hill, Jim Cooper found his friend. "Tod, what are you doing here? You're still on leave."

"So are you, Jim."

"Yes, but I'm in the infantry. I'm supposed to be here when a battle's fought. You're an assistant quartermaster. You don't have to fight this battle. Stay out of it."

"Jim, the Yanks have built breastworks across my father's farm. My home is being overrun by Union soldiers who are using it as their headquarters. No power on Earth can keep me out of the fight. *Aut vincere aut mori.* Either to conquer or die."

Clint Cilley had left Schofield at Fort Granger and delivered a dispatch to Cox at the Carter house. He observed the officers and men in and around the house. It was a warm, hazy afternoon and the men were relaxing on the porch and green grass of the lawn. They grew silent while they watched with foreboding as lines began to form two miles away.

A half mile closer to the hill, Lane and Conrad watched the Confederates form their regiments into lines. Tension and anxiety grew as the 3,000 watched the panorama before them swell to over 20,000 men.

Music from the Confederate brass band suddenly echoed from behind the rebel lines. The sweet sounds of "Bonnie Blue Flag" and "The Girl I Left

Behind Me" somehow seemed out of place. More than one grizzled veteran soldier wiped a tear from his eye as he listened to the plaintive melodies.

Soon Union troops countered with band music of their own, as "Yankee Doodle" and "The Battle Hymn of the Republic" burst forth from their lines.

Then the strains of "Dixie" brought the Confederate soldiers back to the moment. They swelled with pride and anticipation. When the music stopped, a deathly silence hung over the field. Men broke out in a cold sweat. It was time. Then at 4:00 p.m., an artillery shot arced through the sky as daylight faded and the sun settled into a bank of dark clouds. The shell clipped Carter's porch roof and blasted into the yard. The fight had begun.

Counting heads in the cellar, Moscow shouted, "Where's Lena, where's my girl?"

The nearly twelve-year-old girl was nowhere to be seen. Bullets began to ricochet off the brick. Moscow raised the cellar door and shouted for his daughter again. Lena appeared in the arms of Clint Cilley, clutching a doll closely to her chest. "I had to get my baby. She was in the trunk upstairs."

Clint grimly handed the girl down. "She was running around. I thought it best to deliver her to you."

Moscow nodded his thanks and pulled the girl down the stairs, where he held her close. Outside, another round from a Confederate cannon shattered the smokehouse. The children gathered around the women and began to cry.

A half mile in front of the Union line, Wagner's two divisions readied themselves. They had tried to throw up breastworks, but with only two picks and two shovels it was difficult. Men dug with their hands, trying to find a chunk of wood, a clump of roots, anything to aid in the defense.

George Wagner was watching his two divisions from the Carter house. Having fallen from his horse, he rested on a crutch as he stood alongside Captain Scofield. The orders given Wagner to "give the men a few volleys and then fall back to the works in good order" had not been passed on to Logan and Conrad. He had ordered them to "stand and fight."

The Union regiments along the main line grew tense in expectation as they watched the distant Confederates begin their advance on Wagner's men. Across the main line of breastworks from the Union, left to right on the Carter property, was the Eighth Ohio battery, just east of the cotton gin. Then, where the line angled back toward the pike and the house, the 104th Ohio waited.

At the weak point on the pike, a Kentucky battery was primed and ready. From there down the line to the west were the Fiftieth Ohio and Seventy-second Illinois, located in front of the house. Then came the 111th Ohio with the Twenty-fourth Missouri, stationed behind the locust grove abatis. Next came the 107th Illinois, 129th Indiana, 183rd Ohio, Twenty-third Michigan, 118th Ohio, and the Eightieth Indiana, which had Carter's Creek Pike on its immediate right.

The retrenchment line behind them consisted of the Forty-fourth Missouri, a regiment of new recruits who had never seen battle. To their right was the 183rd Ohio. To their left, next to the smokehouse, was the Twentieth Ohio Battery.

Hearts quickened up and down the line as the rebel assault moved toward them. As they came ever closer to the small, beleaguered band on the ridge, a staff officer from Conrad's brigade galloped back to Wagner. "Sir!" he shouted with unmistakable fear in his voice. "The enemy are forming in heavy columns, we can see them distinctly in the open timber and all along our front!"

Wagner, sitting atop the main barricade and resting on an elbow, stared directly at the officer. "Stand there and fight them," he commanded. Glaring at Scofield, he raised his voice. "And that stubbed, curly-headed Dutchman, Opdycke, will fight them, too."

Scofield knew what Cox had ordered and corrected, "But, General, the orders are not to stand, except against cavalry and skirmishers, but to fall back behind the main line."

Wagner did not respond. Later, as they watched the troop movements in their front, other officers gathered around Wagner. Then another courier wrenched his galloping horse to a stop before the general.

The rider implored Wagner, "The enemy are advancing in heavy force. They will overlap our two brigades on both flanks. You must move them. They can't remain there any longer!"

"Go back, and tell them to fight—fight like hell!"

The horseman turned pale. "But, sir, they'll be overwhelmed. Hood's entire army is coming!"

Wagner slammed his crutch onto the ground and glared. "Never mind! Fight them!"

As the rider galloped back to the front, Wagner took a flask from his pocket and took a long pull.

"What are you drinking?" Scofield demanded.

"Water, boy, just water."

"It sure doesn't smell like water."

Near panic was setting in on the ridge. A captain was handed an order delivered by an orderly. It read, "Hold the position to the last man, and have the sergeants fix bayonets. Any man not wounded who should attempt to leave the line without orders should be shot or bayoneted by the sergeants."

A sergeant beseeched the captain, "What can our generals be thinking, keeping us out here?"

One private turned to a comrade as they watched the Confederates march with precision.

"It looks like they're on dress parade, Bobby. Don't they look fancy, swords and bayonets flashing in the sunlight?"

"Look there, Sammy!" his friend exclaimed. "They're movin' into close order now! The lines are closin' up!"

The sergeant pleaded with his captain once again. "There's enough of 'em comin' to swallow us up. For God's sake, let us get behind the works."

The captain responded, "Sergeant, keep your place, and not another word."

As the sun dipped lower, a chill swept over the Union brigades in spite of the still-warm temperatures. Bobby looked over at Sammy. "I feel like the icy fingers of Death himself just touched me."

* * *

SAM HOOD TOOK his place against the single tree at the base of Winstead Hill. Staff had placed blankets on the ground for him to sit on as he rested his back against the tree. His view presented him a magnificent spectacle. In the fading but still bright sunlight, a band had struck up again. Twenty thousand men marched over the flat plain toward the ridge in perfect order, formed for battle. Stewart was to the right, Cheatham in the center, and Bate was swinging to the left.

As Stewart's corps formed up, an officer in Sam French's division shouted to a regiment the famous line from Lord Nelson at Trafalgar: "England expects every man to do his duty."

A sergeant in the formation rejoined by shouting back, "It's damned little duty England would get out of this Irish crowd." A roar of laughter swelled from the ranks. Then they moved out.

A hundred flags waved in a gentle breeze. Generals, with swords unsheathed, directed their forces onward. A haze hung over the field.

Cannon had been blasting long range from both sides. Then the order to charge electrified the rebel regiments. A blood-curdling yell emanated from 20,000 throats. The crack and rattle of musketry joined the cacophony of a symphony from Hell.

States Rights Gist ordered a charge in the center. He mounted his horse, removed his hat to wave and encourage his men forward. He disappeared into the haze and smoke. Gist's horse was shot out from under him. He drew his sword and rushed forward, leading his brigade. Then he clutched his chest and fell. A bullet had pierced his heart. He was the first Confederate general to die that day.

Cheatham's and Stewart's corps swept over Lane's and Conrad's brigades like they weren't even there. Union soldiers tried to stand and fight, many getting off four or five rounds before a raging wall of fire from thousands of weapons fired nearly simultaneously swept them away.

Union defenders shot and reloaded so rapidly that some burned their hands on rifle barrels. Hand-to-hand fighting ensued, and then came the cry, "Fall back!"

A couple thousand Union soldiers who were left standing or hadn't already run made a dash for the works a mile and a half away.

Like boys chasing rabbits across a field, the Confederate regiments sprinted after the fleeing, blue-clad soldiers. Their cry echoed from officers behind them, "Into the works, boys! Follow them into the works!"

At the main line breastworks, cold sweat beaded on the brows of defenders as they watched a horde of blue and gray running straight at them. "Start shooting at 300 yards!" a captain commanded.

"At what?" a soldier cried. "That's our own men coming right at us!" The first from Logan and Conrad reached the breastworks, leapt the trench and scrambled up over the barricade. Many were wounded. Many were hit and dropped dead on the other side as they tried to make it to safety. As they rushed pell mell toward their main line, Yankees tossed away knapsacks, blankets, muskets, and anything that could slow them down.

Bill Kessy nimbly avoided some objects and jumped over others as he dashed toward the breastworks. After leaping the trench and flying over the head logs, he dropped, exhausted, on the other side. A private grabbed his hand in admiration. "That was amazing. How'd you do it?'

"I was inspired by 10,000 bullets," Kessy replied breathlessly.

Pat Cleburne flowed across the plain with his division. He spotted an aide, I.H. Magnum, who was positioning an artillery battery. "It's too late for artillery!" he bellowed. "Go on with Granbury."

Cleburne then galloped off to where Govan's men were preparing to charge. A few hundred feet from the breastworks, his horse went down with a thud. As the general tried to mount another horse, it was struck by a cannonball. Cleburne, waving his cap, disappeared into the smoke. Moments later, a bullet ripped into his chest just below his heart.

In the breastworks, the long line of Union soldiers waiting in the trench stood and fired a vicious volley. The onrushing line of gray, sprinkled with some blue, were sliced down as surely as if the Grim Reaper himself was swinging a scythe through them.

But another line of Confederates was behind the first and then another. Before the Union soldiers could reload, the gray horde had swept over the main line of breastworks and blasted a 200-yard gap in the Union line where the Columbia Pike ran through it.

There was a cataclysm in the Union center. The Seventy-second Illinois fell back. The Fiftieth Ohio was obliterated and the 111th Ohio fell back. Chaos reigned as the veterans in the front of the line were routed. Eight regiments of Tennesseans under General John Gordon and nine regiments of Texans under Granbury poured through the gap.

Sixty feet behind the main line was the retrenchment secondary line. The green troops of the Forty-fourth Missouri watched, awestruck, at the mayhem just in front of them. They had been placed in this backup position with the assumption that they would not be needed.

A young Missourian turned to his friend. "Toby, this is for real. Those are real bullets. These people want to kill us!"

As veterans ran past them back toward the town, Captain Scofield shouted to the Missouri soldiers, "Steady, boys, steady. Now let 'em have it!"

A withering burst came from the Union line. The charging rebels were momentarily stymied and then came on again. The Forty-fourth Missouri rose up to stop them. Hand-to-hand combat resulted. The battery of four cannon at the smokehouse proved useless at this point. The gun crews couldn't get them into position to shoot. The barrel swabs were turned into clubs.

Bate's division had wheeled west and turned at Carter's Creek Pike. At the first charge, they swept straight forward to the Carter house. Jim Cooper, riding beside his friend, cautioned Tod, "Be careful. There's a lot of open ground here. Don't start the men too soon."

But as they neared the house, Tod Carter, on Rosencrantz, looked back at the men behind him. "If you want to go home, follow me!" he shouted. "I'm going home!"

With sword drawn and pointing as far ahead as he could, Tod led the charge in the center of Bate's advance. He galloped ahead. Then the horse plunged with a bullet in its side. As Rosencrantz stumbled, Tod flew over the steed's head. The young man had been hit nine times. He lay still on the ground, 526 feet southwest of his house. It was 5:00 p.m., and daylight had turned to dusk while the fight raged on.

From Fort Granger, General Schofield had watched the Confederate attack with alarm. "Tell 'em this," he told his adjutant. "The edges of the breach in the center are the anchors. They must be sealed off and we must regain the center."

"Yes, sir."

"And, Clint?"

"Yes, sir."

"Keep your head down."

"I tried that once in a swarm of bees, kind of like this. It didn't work."

Behind the line, Cheatham cried, "Pour into them, boys! Put human muscle in place to break the enemy!"

It became an all-out brawl in the center. Some rebel soldiers became hung up or impaled in the locust grove abatis. To the west, beyond Carter's Creek Pike and past the Nashville and Decatur Railroad to the east, fighting was furious. But it was nothing like what was happening in front of the Carter house.

A Confederate colonel, blood streaming down his face, gained the top of the breastworks. "Surrender, damn you!" he shouted. A Union defender placed his rifle barrel in the rebel's stomach and yelled, "I guess not!" as he pulled the trigger.

General Stanley hurried behind the Carter house to find Opdycke, but the "stubbed, curly-headed Dutchman" was already on his way. Seven regiments of Illinoisans, men of Reilley's reserve and the Twelfth Wisconsin under Arthur McArthur, streamed toward the front of the house.

The two sides smashing into each other at a full run, the collision of flesh, bone, steel, and wood made a sickening sound. McArthur shouted,

"Up, Wisconsin!" With his saber flashing and slicing, he aimed toward a Confederate flag in the forefront. His horse went down, and McArthur clutched his own shoulder as blood seeped between his fingers. One step after another, he continued to fight through the smoke and darkness to the flag, lit by gunfire.

He came face to face with a Confederate major holding the flag. The major drew his pistol and fired. McArthur stumbled back, a bullet in his chest. Then the Union officer lunged forward, running his saber into the Confederate's stomach. As the major fell to the ground, he fired his pistol again, striking McArthur in the knee.

In the garden, in the yard around the house, around the office and smokehouse, the desperate battle raged. Thousands of men were crammed into a space no larger than a few acres. In such close quarters, it became nearly impossible to fire and reload rifles, so they battled with the butt ends of their weapons, hoes, picks, shovels, axes, and anything they could find. One Union soldier swung a gun butt so hard at a rebel officer he nearly decapitated him.

They battled hand to hand, gouged, bit, and bayonetted each other for over an hour. Soldiers were covered with blood, some with brains and other body parts. The Confederates kept coming through the darkness, even when they couldn't see. Some regiments made up to eleven separate charges, flinging themselves again and again into the breastworks or at the office and smokehouse.

Union reinforcements came in from the flanks, and gradually and grudgingly, the rebels were pushed back. Some, wounded, exhausted, or both, were left behind. Of these, some were defenseless and wantonly executed by Union soldiers, some of whom shouted, "More killed, less to prison camps!" They shot them like animals in a pen.

In the cellar of the Carter house, Branch Carter's family huddled to escape the pandemonium above them. The sounds of racing feet on the floorboards, unstinting gunfire, and explosions from outside shook the house and caused the foundation to tremble. At times the ceiling trap door would open and frightened Union soldiers would tumble down the stairs in search of a safe haven. "Stay away from my family!" Carter warned ominously as he hefted a shotgun.

Outside, once pushed out of the yard, the Confederates of Brown's and Cleburne's divisions took cover in the trenches in front of the main line barricades. The Union troops followed and took positions in the ditch behind the breastworks. The two armies lambasted each other from one ditch to the other, just a few feet apart, with only a mound of dirt in between.

The mostly silent batteries by the cotton gin on the other side of the pike starting blasting into the rebels from the side. The angle in the line taken by the Confederates exposed them to withering fire from the flank.

Clint Cilley, having delivered orders about the edges of the gap, now stood with the battery. After the roar of cannon he heard an unmistakable pop and crack.

"What's that?" he asked one of the gun crew. "It sounds like you're hitting tree branches."

"No, Major," the man replied. "What you're hearing is snapping bones. Listen, first the explosion, then the bones."

Unable to go forward or retreat while facing deadly fire, some rebel soldiers began to signal surrender by raising their caps on rifle barrels and waving them in the air.

Watching from the rear in the murky smoke and darkness, Frank Cheatham couldn't ascertain what was happening. All he could see through field glasses was a large smoky cloud, singed by flashes of flame in the center of the field. The rattle of musketry and the roar of cannon were plain. He had sent couriers to bring back a report, but none had returned.

Hood was even worse off. From his perch at the base of Winstead Hill, all he could see was the flickering flashes of guns and the echoes of gunfire. What neither general could know was that their army was stuck in place just outside the Union works.

While they were mired in the center, Stewart's corps was still active on the east; on the far west, Bate's and Chalmer's dismounted cavalries were preparing to attack. Distance had delayed Bate and Stewart and kept them out of Cheatham's direct attack. From both the east and west, the two forces, under Stewart and Bate, slammed into the Union lines.

Sam French, under Stewart, led two brigades toward the cotton gin, 100 yards east of the Carter house. Just in rifle range, they discovered Union colonel Jack Casement standing on a parapet giving a speech. He was yelling, "Well, I want you to stand here like rocks and whip hell out of them!"

Then he turned, spotted French's men, drew two revolvers and blasted away until they were empty, at which time he jumped down with his men.

French attacked but was driven back. Walthal's men, French's right, became entangled in the Osage orange abatis. Then Walthal, whose men had become intermixed with some of Loring's on their right, tried to attack just east of the cotton gin. The space between the Union line and the river squeezed the force together and stymied their effectiveness. After six successive futile charges, they fell back.

William Loring's division, under Stewart, launched two attacks against the Union brigade of Colonel Stiles. Both times he was driven back with heavy losses. Union artillery was fired down the railway cut, and air filled with canister shot prevented any attempt to flank the blue troops there.

Confederate general John Adams galloped his steed directly onto the earthworks and grabbed the flag of the Sixty-fifth Illinois. Both he and his horse were cut down in a hail of lead. A rebel brigade fell back, only to be met by Loring. Astride his horse, he confronted the retreating men. "Great God. Do I command cowards?" he shouted.

He wheeled his horse and, in an effort to inspire his men, sat in his saddle for over a minute in full view from the Union lines. To the amazement of everyone, he rode back unscathed. But the brigade still made no progress and was withdrawn.

Bate was trying to hammer away on the far left, but lack of coordination with Brown's division led to failure. Chalmer's cavalry was fighting to Bate's left but was hidden by rolling hills, and Bate didn't make contact with them, either. When they turned at the Bostick house, Union fire raked Bate's flank. He had expected help from Chalmers and was unaware that the cavalry was engaged over the hill to the west. Both Bate and Chalmers would withdraw.

* * *

AS IT GREW LATER and night fell like a black curtain, the performance wasn't over. Hood had one more act. Stephen Lee had arrived from Columbia at 4:00 p.m., after Cheatham and Stewart had begun their charge.

Hood had ordered one of Lee's divisions, under Edward Johnson, to fight if necessary, and had sent Lee to find Cheatham to coordinate with him. It was dark when Lee finally found Cheatham. "'Use them, if necessary?' Are you serious? I could use your whole army!" Cheatham replied to Lee. "Slide your men in between Brown and Bate and hit 'em again!"

At 7:00 p.m., it was dark. Only a thin sliver of moon was on the rise when three brigades, led by Lee's subordinate, Johnson, crept as quietly as possible to within thirty paces of the Union main line. Then the sky lit up just off the left side of the locust grove. The heavens erupted as Confederates again surmounted the ditch and barricade and charged over the works.

Desperate hand-to-hand fighting again raged along the line west of the Carter house. It looked like the rebels had surprised the Union soldiers and might break through. Then sustained volleys were poured into the rebels until they fell back. It was nearly 8:00 p.m., and the slivered crescent of moon disappeared behind a cloud, as if to hide from the blood-stained field. While scattered gunshots echoed late into the night, the battle was essentially over.

The Next Day

BY NINE O' CLOCK THAT EVENING, Schofield made a decision to pull out of the slaughter pen that was Franklin. Before the battle even started, his engineers had seen to the repair of two bridges across the Harpeth, and Union supply wagons had immediately started making the crossing.

Now Schofield announced to his officers, "I'm obeying an order from Thomas that arrived just before the fighting started. We are to return to Nashville. Tell your men to move quietly."

"When?" Stanley asked.

"Now. Tonight."

"What about Hood?" Wagner asked.

"If he wants to move into the town, let him. He paid for it. We wouldn't have been here in the first place if the bridges hadn't been out."

"Couldn't we have followed the wagons out earlier?" Opdycke wondered.

"You know better than that," Schofield replied. "Hood would have been flanking us or on our tail all the way to Nashville. He could have cut us off."

By midnight, the whole army was over the Harpeth and marching to Nashville. Only the dead and wounded were left behind.

In the Carter house, the cellar door inched open as the night grew quiet. Branch Carter's head rose above the floorboards. His face paled as he viewed the horrific scene in his house. Dozens of bloody men were crowded before him. The parlor rug was soaked red in blood.

"Keep 'em down there," he told Moscow. "It's a butcher shop up here."

But the eerie silence in the cellar of a house filled with death became unbearable, and the Carter family began to emerge. The house was filled with Confederate soldiers. Moscow watched as a Confederate officer led thirty captured prisoners from the upstairs. "I found them hiding in a room up there," he announced. "They didn't fire a shot in the whole battle."

Little Alice McPhail walked through the terrors of the house onto the porch. As she breathed deeply to clear her head, the girl's nostrils filled with the acrid smells of battle. A horseman rode up. "Missy," Thomas Benton Smith asked, "is this where Squire Carter lives?"

"Yes, sir."

"Tell him Captain Carter is severely wounded. I will show him where to find him."

A party of Carter family members, with General Smith leading Fountain Branch Carter, Tod's three sisters, and his sister-in-law, headed out southwest of the house. Lanterns sliced through the inky blackness, illuminating the faces of the dead and dying. They gingerly tried to step over or around the casualties on the body-strewn ground.

They came upon Rosencrantz first. The stallion was lying cold and dead. Tod's sister, Fanny, shouted, "Here, I've found him!" Lying nearby was Tod, his wounds grievous and rendering him delirious. "Jim," he called, "you there, Jim? I can see my house. I'm almost home."

Litterbearers put Tod on an overcoat and carried him through the garden gate. They brought him into the debris of a shot-to-pieces parlor and laid him on the floor among the Union wounded left behind.

Later he would be moved to a bed in the sitting room, where a doctor probed his head and removed a bullet above his eye. His sisters remained in the room, prayerfully appealing for his recovery.

Frank Cheatham had left his headquarters when the firing stopped and walked onto the battlefield. Holding a lantern, he peered into the faces of those who had suffered in the holocaust. Big tears rolled down his cheeks as he cried plaintively, "My poor boys. What have we done to you?"

* * *

BUILDINGS ALL OVER Franklin began to fill up with the wounded and dying. Southeast of town, behind Stewart's division, was the McGavock estate, Carnton. There in the white, stately brick home with its beautiful columns and verandas, thousands of casualties would soon fill up the house and grounds.

Mrs. Carrie McGavock, the mistress of the house, worked tirelessly with doctors through the night to provide whatever aid and comfort she could. No one could know that the rest of her life would be devoted to the victims of that night.

* * *

IT WAS AFTER MIDNIGHT when Hood's three corps commanders reached their commander's headquarters alongside the pike. Hood, his arm in a sling and wearing a false leg, asked for reports from them.

Stewart replied, "We are all cut to pieces. There is no organization left except for the artillery."

"General Cheatham?"

"I went out onto the battlefield, General. I could have walked all over the field upon dead bodies without stepping upon the ground. I never saw anything like that field, and I never want to again. My division is gone."

Hood's eyes flashed, and he glared at Lee, "Are you, too, going back on me?"

"General, one of my divisions is badly cut up. But I still have two left."

"Fine. Then this is what we'll do. We didn't have much artillery yesterday. Lee can bring all his batteries up now. We will open up on the Yankees at daylight with a 100-gun barrage. Then we will charge the breastworks again at 9:00 a.m. with everything we have left."

"Charge!" Cheatham's voice raised in alarm. "General Hood, we don't have an army fit to fight. We have six generals dead: Gist, Adams, Stahl, Cleburne, Carter, and Granbury. More are seriously wounded."

Hood straightened his body as best he could. "We will attack at nine."

* * *

BUT THROUGH THE NIGHT, as Confederate officers and men grew closer and closer to the town, it became obvious that no Union troops were there, save the casualties. There would be no attack in the morning of December 1, for there was no one to fight.

Sam Hood rode with other officers to view the horrific scene. In the garden, in the yard, in front of the Carter house for a few acres, the ground was covered with dead men wearing blue and gray.

In the trench before the house, the dead were stacked seven deep. Many were frozen upright, unable to fall because of the bodies pressing against them.

In the few areas where the carcasses of horses or the bodies of men were not, the once-green grass had been ripped up by cannon and rifle shot and now resembled a plowed field. Hood found a spot which had been cleared away for him in front of the Carter house. He held his slinged arm as he sat on a stool and cried.

As Hood continued on and rode through Franklin, evidence of terrific destruction lay everywhere. Details had been busy collecting the dead. Confederate dead were laid in mass graves, trenches two and a half feet deep that stretched for a mile and a half on either side of Columbia Pike.

He continued on to Carnton and bowed his head before the six Confederate generals lying in repose on the long back porch of the mansion. "I'll see you didn't die in vain, I promise you," he said softly.

"So more will die?" a woman's voice sounded behind him.

He turned to see a pleasant-looking middle-aged woman whose face showed obvious fatigue and strain.

"I'm General Hood, ma'am."

"I know who you are. I'm Mrs. McGavock, and this is my home."

"Thank you, Mrs. McGavock," Hood said gently. "Your work here is greatly valued."

"I didn't ask for this. But I'll tend to these men as best I can. Now why don't you end this war?"

"It'll end, Mrs. McGavock. It'll end soon."

The people of Franklin were left to care for wounded, bury the dead, and repair the destruction.

Before he left, Franklin Hood issued a general field order to be read to each regiment. It read: "The commanding general congratulates the army upon the success achieved yesterday over our enemy by their heroic and determined courage. The enemy have been sent in disorder and confusion to Nashville, and while we lament the fall of many gallant officers and brave men, we have shown to our countrymen that we can carry any position occupied by the enemy."

* * *

CHEATHAM BALLED UP the order and threw it onto the ground. "Is he serious?" he exclaimed to Stewart. "By my count we had over 6,000 casualties, at least 1,700 dead. All this in three hours. What happened at Gettysburg to Pickett pales to what happened here. And Hood is claiming a victory? This was pure hell. He sent us into their most heavily defended barricades. Farther to the east and west, the lines were defended, but not as much. What was he thinking?"

"Well," Stewart answered, "based on the fiction of this field order, we may never know what he really thought."

* * *

IN QUICK SUCCESSION that morning, Hood issued orders. First, details were sent out on the field to collect loose weapons. Lists of dead officers were compiled and instructions given to his corps commanders.

Stewart, with his obliterated corps, was to cross the Harpeth and move around Franklin to Nashville. There he would camp north of the town. Lee and Cheatham were to march their divisions straight up the Columbia Pike, through the desolation and destruction, and cross the bridges on the other side of town bound for Nashville.

The route took them directly past the scene of slaughter and the trench graves. Some men couldn't look as they marched by. Others were sickened and demoralized at the site.

Before they left, Stephen Lee had questioned Hood, "Shouldn't we head south, General?"

"No. We have limited prospects, but to turn around and march out of Tennessee now would be the end of this army. We could go past Nashville and move through Kentucky to the Ohio. But we can't leave Thomas with a reinforced army behind us. General Lee, we need a decisive victory, and we can get it at Nashville."

To Nashville

A.J. SMITH'S SIXTEENTH CORPS reached Nashville about two hours after Schofield notified George Thomas that Hood had been defeated at Franklin. Fifty-nine transports with 10,461 battle-tested veterans disembarked.

Smith stepped off the gangplank into the inky blackness of the night. He stepped onto a dock and into the arms of the normally stoic General Thomas, who wrapped his big arms tightly around the slender commander.

"Thank God, you've made it. I heard you were delayed in Paducah," Thomas proclaimed.

"We were delayed and distracted many times. We even had a steamboat sink on us. But we're here, General, and glad to help."

As they walked away, Thomas continued. "I've had to piece together whatever I could find. I've had to call in units from outposts and supply garrisons. We even have Sherman's men who are recovering from wounds and illness, those he won't take on his march across Georgia. I've got eight regiments of colored troops who have no combat experience and other green recruits. It's providential that you have arrived and that Schofield beat Hood and will be here tomorrow."

"What's the plan?"

"I now believe we can hold off Hood defensively, but I still don't feel confident in going on the offensive. I don't have much cavalry. Most are in Kentucky trying to get remounts. Schofield tells me that Forrest has 12,000 cavalry. I need more time."

On the afternoon of December 2, Schofield and his army marched into Nashville.

He delivered his report to General Thomas. "Hood just charged into us, Pap," Schofield relayed. "They fought like devils, but it was a slaughter."

"What were your casualties?"

271

"It's still being counted, but it looks like only 200 killed and about a thousand wounded and a thousand captured. I don't know their casualties but the ground was littered with their dead and wounded. It has to be many thousand."

Thomas's face grew somber. "I commend you on your victory. But it's sad. Sad that so many from the South fought so valiantly and gave their lives for a cause so terrible."

Schofield replied, "Let's hope we have similar results here. Are you ready to fight them? Hood will be coming."

"Once I get some cavalry and consolidate my forces, I will be. I hope that will happen fast enough for all concerned."

Thomas had been undergoing intense pressure from Halleck, Grant, and Lincoln to act on Hood. He sent off a telegram saying he wished to delay a few days. That set off an uproar in Washington.

* * *

BACK IN FRANKLIN on December 2, Tod Carter was on his deathbed. His family gathered around as he breathed his last. Fanny's eyes overflowed with broken-hearted tears as she tenderly whispered, "You made it home, my darling brother, you made it home."

* * *

SAM HOOD WAS DOWN to about 22,000 men when he put them on the pike to Nashville. His troops were in dire need of clothing and equipment. Their threadbare, rotted uniforms would offer small comfort when the weather turned cold.

He sent off a bombardment of telegrams seeking assistance. Hood was desperate for reinforcements. He wired several requests for men from Kilby Smith in Shreveport but received no response.

Smith finally replied, "No, I will send no men to Nashville. The river is too high and we can't cross."

Hood beseeched him to use canoes. But Smith wasn't coming. The Army of Tennessee marched toward Nashville, where Hood ordered a camp established south of the town late in the day on December 2.

* * *

THOMAS RECEIVED TELEGRAMS of his own from his superiors. Grant urged an immediate attack, suggesting, "We might have to abandon the line of the Tennessee River and lose all the roads back to Chattanooga."

Grant followed with another message: "You should have ordered Schofield to attack Hood immediately after the Battle of Franklin, instead of retreating to Nashville."

Secretary of War Stanton contacted Grant, saying, "This looks like the McClellan and Rosecrans strategy of do nothing, and let the enemy raid the country."

Thomas replied that he needed time. He had no cavalry and inclement weather was setting in.

For a few days Grant waited, and then wired Thomas. "Hood should be attacked where he is," he wrote. "Time strengthens him, in all probability, as much as it does you."

Stanton and Grant began discussing the need to replace Thomas in Nashville. Grant insisted that if "Old Slow Trot" Thomas didn't act soon, he would replace him with Schofield. "There is no better man to repel an attack than Thomas. But I fear he is too cautious to ever take the initiative," he said.

Halleck continued to badger Grant to replace Thomas and not wait any longer. Grant deferred, saying, "I keep thinking of something Sherman said: 'Thomas might be slow but he is as true as steel.'"

As days lengthened to a week, Grant grew more and more frustrated with Thomas's perceived inaction. Someone was apparently feeding false and derogatory information to Grant from Nashville.

General James Steedman had just reported to Nashville from Chattanooga, and Thomas's chief of staff asked him to investigate any correspondence sent behind Thomas's back. Steadman's aide discovered a copy of a telegram from Schofield to Grant. It read, "Many officers here are of the opinion that General Thomas is certainly too slow in his movements."

Earlier in the week, a shower of ice and sleet had created a frozen morass on the roads. Thomas called his officers together and outlined his communications with Washington. He asked what they thought.

Cavalry commander James Wilson answered, "General, we have to wait until we get a thaw. My horses can't stand in this. They'll slip all over the place."

Others echoed similar sentiments before they were dismissed. The consensus was to wait for better weather. Back in Washington, Grant decided to remove Thomas, then changed his mind a few hours later and didn't send the order. Steedman brought the found telegram copy of Schofield's message to Thomas, who was shocked.

"Can it be possible that Schofield would send such a telegram?

Steedman pointed to the document. "There's Schofield's signature."

"Why would he send such a thing?"

"General Thomas, who is next in command to you and who would succeed you?"

Thomas finally understood. "Oh, I see."

It had been Clint Cilley who delivered Schofield's message to be wired to Grant. Before doing so, he asked his general, "Are you sure you want to send this?"

"Yes. Thomas has a history of indecisiveness. This is a time to be decisive. Grant and Sherman both have long been frustrated by his inability to act."

"But he always wins," Clint countered. "He hasn't been on the losing side of a battle yet when he was in command."

"And I don't want this to be the first, Major." He paused, as if pondering whether to continue. Then he did. "When I was a cadet at West Point, I got into a scrape, nothing major, it involved not adhering to some regulation. They were going to kick me out of the academy. I appealed and the court martial voted to let me stay. Thomas was one of two who voted to let my punishment stand. At the Battle of Franklin, I repaid Thomas's stern denial of clemency to a youth by saving his army from disaster, and saving Thomas, himself, from the humiliation of dismissal from command. Deliver the telegram."

* * *

HOOD HAD SENT his cavalry under Forrest and Bate's division to Murfreesboro from Franklin. They were to rip up the railroad from south of Nashville to Chattanooga. They both encountered unexpected resistance from Union forces. While Forrest, with his cavalry of 6,000, continued to demonstrate there, Bate was recalled by Hood to Nashville.

Hood had spent nearly two weeks planning and constructing defenses for the attack he knew was coming. His troops had shivered and endured in their trenches and barricades while the wind howled and ice stung their faces. The threadbare clothing had not been replaced and provided little protection from the elements.

The Army of Tennessee was deployed in an east-west line four miles long, just south of Nashville. It didn't match the seven miles of Union outer defenses of the city. The army was positioned in a convex semi-circle facing Nashville from the south. Stewart was on the left flank of Hood's line, Lee in the center, and Cheatham on the right flank.

Hood had established his headquarters at Traveler's Rest, a mansion on the Nashville-Franklin Pike owned by John Overton. As at Columbia weeks before, there were dances, parties, and dinners held, and even marriages performed. But the level of gaiety was subdued. The memory of Franklin weighed heavily on the officers and blunted their enthusiasm for fun.

On December 8, Hood met with his corps commanders in the mansion. A map was spread on a table in the dining room. Hood stood looking at the map as Cheatham, Stewart, and Lee filed in. Hood gestured for the three to sit. Cheatham began, "General, I'd like to offer my apologies for miscommunications that allowed Schofield to escape at Spring Hill."

"Accepted," the commander replied brusquely, "but that's behind us now. We have to deal with the present. This damn cold weather is slowing down our defenses, namely the redoubts, but we have time. I do expect an attack before the year is out, but not real soon. I've sent for more troops and pray someone will answer positively."

"The men are freezing, sir," Stewart added. "They're not happy and are cursing the weather, the army . . ."

"And General Hood," Cheatham finished.

"I've begged Beauregard to get us food and clothing," Hood responded. "Nothing yet."

Lee continued. "Men are getting sick, and they huddle so close to smoky fires for warmth they're getting eye infections."

Exasperated, Hood gave a sharp jab of his index finger as he pointed at the map. "Our agents in Nashvillle have been helpful. This map shows current Union defenses. Miss Patterson delivered it. See here, Fort Negley has cannon capable of hitting our lines. I've also been informed that my old instructor at West Point, 'Pap' Thomas, is under severe pressure to attack. But that won't happen until we get a break in the weather and, knowing Thomas, some time after that."

"How many men do they have?" Cheatham asked.

"Spies say about 60,000. About half are veterans and half new green recruits, eight regiments of coloreds."

"And we don't have much over 20,000."

"That's why we're building the redoubts. I'll put a battery of artillery and around 150 men in each one. Thomas will have to swing wide to get around them. We have a better chance when they're strung out like a long snake. Stewart, to your left down to the Cumberland will be Chalmer's cavalry."

"What about bringing back Forrest?" Lee suggested. "It bothers me that he's twenty-five miles away in Murfreesboro."

"He's tied up with Yanks there. It keeps the federals there and not coming to help Thomas. Gentlemen," he concluded, "when the weather turns warmer, brace yourselves."

Along the Hillsborough Pike on a north-south line along his left flank, Hood had ordered the construction of redoubts. These small earthen forts were built not only to protect the flank but to cause any attacker to have to make a wide swing around them, making attackers more vulnerable. While complaints abounded about the cold, an ice storm hit on December 9 that made the previous weather seem summerlike. The frigid air, snow, and ice stopped operations on both sides for several days.

* * *

WHILE THE ICE STORM raged, George Thomas continued communicating, sometimes multiple times a day, with Grant and Halleck. He wired, "I have done all that I can until the weather breaks. Earlier delays were caused by lack of cavalry and the need to consolidate troops. That has been taken care of." Later, Thomas added, "If you should deem it necessary to relieve me, I shall submit without a murmur."

While Grant had determined not to relieve Thomas, he was not satisfied with the response from the Rock of Chickamauga, so he wired, "If you delay attack longer, the mortifying spectacle will be witnessed of a rebel army moving for the Ohio River, and you will be forced to act, accepting such weather as you find. Let there be no further delay."

However, the deep freeze in the South continued. On December 10, 11, and 12, the temperatures didn't top twenty degrees during the day and hit zero at night. Jimmy Dunn and Willie Sturgis wrapped blankets around their shoulders and sought warmth by holding their palms over a smoky campfire.

"This is supposed to be the sunny South," Willie complained.

"Yep," Jimmy agreed. "We might as well be back in Minnesota."

"We'll be home soon enough, Jimmy. The rebs can't hold on much longer."

"I've got a girlfriend, ya know," Jimmy smiled. "Back when we were home on furlough we got together. I miss her plenty."

Willie laughed. "I'm sure Old Pap would hurry this up if he knew it was getting in the way of your romance."

Then, on the fourteenth, the Nashville sun warmed and thawed the icy ground. Grant was preparing to leave for Nashville to take over himself when Thomas wired that, with the break in the weather, he was prepared to attack.

* * *

NEARLY HALF THE CONFEDERATE Army was without shoes. If leather could be found, the men wrapped it around their feet. More likely, they were lucky to find cloth.

Jim Cooper had become a captain in the Twentieth Tennessee. He stood on the morning of the fourteenth with his young colonel, Bill Shy.

"Look," he pointed at a blood-stained path in the snow. "It's from the men's feet. They gotta get shoes somehow."

"Well, Captain," Shy drawled as he looked up into a sunny blue sky, "one's sure it's gonna warm up today. If it's warm, watch for the Yankees to attack soon and," he paused, "they have shoes."

* * *

THOMAS CALLED HIS OFFICERS together in his hotel room in Nashville to outline his plan for battle. "Gentlemen," he began, "it's taken time to combine this army, but it's done." He nodded at each man in turn as he spoke their names. "General Schofield, you arrived with your Twenty-third Corps and 10,000 men. General Wood, with 14,000 from the Fourth Corps. General Steedman brought us an assortment of 7,500. General Wilson, after some travail, has put together a cavalry of 12,000, and General Smith, we are finally blessed with your 10,500 of the Sixteenth Corps, your gorilla guerillas."

Wilson smiled. "General, we are recently armed with the new seven-shot Spencer repeaters. It was worth the wait to get these."

The stoic Thomas's face briefly creased in what some swore was a smile. "With what I have here, that puts us near 65,000 men. Hood has about a third of that, and Forrest isn't even with him, although Bate now is.

"Steedman, you will demonstrate on the right flank in the eastern sector. Your maneuver is a feint. I want Hood to send reinforcements from his left flank. Wood, hold the center while Smith and Wilson swing around in a giant pivoting movement and attack Hood's left flank in force. I think Hood expects me to get strung out going around his redoubts. But Smith, you're going to attack the outermost flank and distant forts on Hood's left first, working toward the inner forts where the majority of Hood's men are concentrated."

"What about my corps?" Schofield asked.

"You are held in reserve."

"I would like to participate in the attack."

Thomas considered and replied, "Follow after Smith, then."

That night Levi Carr, Jimmy Dunn, Will Hutchinson, and Willie Sturgis played cards around a smoky campfire. Jimmy folded his cards and placed them on the stump they were using as a table.

"Ya think we're going out tomorrow, boys?" Jimmy asked.

"Sounds like it," Willie replied. "I heard our lieutenants talkin', Gere and Bishop. They said ta be ready."

"Ya ever think that Bishop wouldn't even be here if Jimmy hadn't saved his life at Redwood Ferry?"

Jimmy looked contemplative. "Lots has happened since we fought the Sioux at Redwood Ferry. We fought a whole Indian war and then went south. I got ta thinkin', boys. Do ya know how many fights we've been in?"

Willie frowned with deep thought. "No, Jimmy, how many?"

"Well, I counted 'em up. Since the Fifth left Minnesota after fighting the Sioux, it's been almost three years. We've been on thirteen campaigns, five sieges, and thirty-four battles."

A voice sounded out of the shadows. "How old were you then, Jimmy?"

Tom Gere stepped into the dim light of the fire.

The men started to rise, but Tom held his hands palms down. "Don't bother, I'm just here to tell you that the Fifth will likely see action tomorrow. We're in McArthur's First Division in Hubbard's Second Brigade with the Ninth Minnesota."

"What about the Seventh and Tenth?" Levi called.

"Both are in McArthur's First Division with us. The Tenth is with McMillan in the First Brigade and the Seventh is in the Third Brigade."

"Lieutenant," Willie asked, "what's this McArthur like?"

"John McArthur is from Scotland. He wears a Scottish cap with no brim. He's stocky, muscular, and there's no nonsense about him. He's a fighter."

Jimmy's mouth curled upward at the corners. "Just leave it up to us Minnesota boys. We'll take care of Sam Hood by ourselves."

Gere laughed. "Don't ask for more than you can handle."

"Lieutenant," Jimmy said more soberely, "we've come a long way from Fort Ridgely, and I don't mean miles. You were just a shavetail, but you helped save the fort."

"You did your share, too." Gere looked at Will, Levi, and Willie. "All of you. Now take care of yourselves."

As he turned and walked away, Jimmy called, "Seventeen."

"What?" Gere asked.

"You asked how old I was at Fort Ridgely. I was seventeen."

"Let's all live long lives."

* * *

DECEMBER 15 DAWNED cool and foggy. A ground-hugging mist kept the Union troops back while the big guns lofted shot toward the Confederate lines. A pea-soup fog hung thick in the air as the battle began. After about two hours of salvos from artillery, the Union troops launched their ground attack at about 8:00 a.m., when Steedman began his feint on the Union left.

Steedman didn't exactly command a corps. His provisional detachment of the District of the Etowah was a collection of United States Colored Troops, garrison soldiers, stragglers, invalids, deserters, and quartermaster troops.

The 7,500 in his command would be led by colored regiments in the vanguard. They materialized out of the fog on Cheatham's front in the eastern sector of the Confederate right. Two brigades of colored troops were under Colonel Tom Morgan, and a brigade of "convalescents, conscripts, and bounty-jumpers" was led by Colonel Charles Grosvenor.

Grosvenor's brigade was to support Morgan but botched the order. Morgan rounded the right flank and moved toward the rear of the Confederate troops, not realizing that the end of the line was actually an earthen lunette manned by Granbury's brigade of Texas artillery.

Cheatham's men opened up on Morgan and decimated his brigade with heavy fire. Union soldiers leapt into a nearby railroad cut, seeking safety, but they were mowed down there as well.

The feint did not fool Hood. He kept his troops on the left in place. Anticipating an attack to the west, he moved portions of Lee's command from the center to the left.

At 10:00 a.m., Thomas's big wheel on the Confederate left began. The area with the redoubts was held by Stewart's corps. Smith's infantry and Wilson's cavalry marched out and wheeled first westward and then south.

Smith rode alongside First Division commander John McArthur. They looked over the string of redoubts along the Hillsborough Pike. "Can you take them?" Smith asked.

"Yes, I can," McArthur replied, and then rode off without another word to find his brigade commanders.

After pounding the redoubt with artillery, McArthur's First Brigade of his First Division hit the outermost redoubt, Number Five. The Tenth Minnesota, along with Wilson's cavalry, charged up the steep hillside of the redoubt.

Four smoothbore Confederate cannons raked the hillside with canister and shell. For several minutes of murderous fire and fighting, the Union troops, led by Minnesota's Tenth, scaled the hill into the redoubt and planted their flag.

Just to the north, Lumsden's Confederate batteries on Redoubt Number Four, a half mile away, opened up with four smoothbores on the Yankees who had just taken Number Five. From Number Five, the Yankees returned fire from captured cannons. The Minnesotans and other brigade troops huddled behind the earthen wall of the redoubt as a leaden storm filled the air.

For three hours the fight raged as little round missiles sizzled through the air. Dismounted Union cavalry crept closer and closer to the fort. Just after 2:00 p.m., they rose out of the grass and charged. Charles Lumsden, rebel commander, ordered, "Double canister! Fire!" The blast decimated the blue line charging them.

Colonel Jennison of the Tenth Minnesota, sword drawn, sat with his back to the wall and told his major, "The firing is intense. We can't stay here. It's either abandon the fort or charge the redoubt. What do you think?"

"I think we take that redoubt!"

With a loud cheer, the Tenth Minnesota joined the rest of the brigade and charged Number Four from the southwest.

To the northwest of the earthen fort, the Second Brigade with the Fifth and Ninth Minnesota formed up to attack.

Jimmy Dunn nervously clasped his rifle as he stood in line next to Levi Carr.

"Are you ready, Levi?"

"I'm ready, Jimmy, keep your head down."

"You too, Levi."

Colonel Hubbard raised his sword as he stood before his regiment and shouted, "Give 'em a Minnesota yell, boys! Charge!"

A roaring, boisterous cry rose from the Fifth and Ninth Minnesotans as they charged over the couple hundred yards to Redoubt Number Four.

Forty-eight Alabama artillerymen and another hundred infantrymen held on as they loosed a blistering fusillade at the Union attackers.

Jimmy raced up the embankment on the north of the redoubt, his bayonet fixed and ready. A rebel aimed his rifle directly at him. Jimmy froze for an instant and then charged on.

The rebel squeezed his trigger, but when the striker hit the percussion cap, nothing happened. Jimmy clubbed the defender alongside his head with his rifle stock and raced into the redoubt with his brigade.

As Union lines closed in around them, Lumsden and his gun crews stood fast and fired as rapidly as they could. Then suddenly, the guns went silent. They wouldn't fire. A sergeant shouted over the roar of Union guns, "Captain, the man with the friction primers has run off! We can't shoot without them!"

Lumsden took a quick look around and shouted, "Take care of yourselves, boys!"

The defenders scrambled over the fort walls and raced to the rebel lines. The Tenth Minnesota buried their flagstaff in a second redoubt.

While the First and Second Brigades of the First Division were fighting their way to victory over two forts, the Third Brigade with the Seventh Minnesota was waiting just west of Redoubt Number Three. They bombarded the earthen walls with cannon blast after cannon blast from a nearby hill.

The Seventh watched and waited for the order to attack. As A.J. Smith rode toward them, the boys of the Seventh shouted, "A.J., bring us a fort, bring us a fort!"

Smith grinned and cried, "I'll bring you a fort, and it won't be long!"

Before Number Four had fallen, Smith rode off. Colonel Marshall of the Seventh turned to his adjutant. "Listen to the cannon and musket fire. It's from Redoubt Four. That's where old A.J. is going, he's looking for Hubbard. He's leaving this one, Number Three, for us to take care of."

Moments later, the cry came to charge and storm Redoubt Number Three. The guerillas of the Sixteenth Corps raced across an open stretch and overwhelmed the Confederate defenders. As soon as they took the fort heavy fire came from Redoubt Number Two, which was but a short distance to their left, just to the east across the Hillsboro Pike.

Lead buzzed by the Minnesotans of the Seventh. As with the First Brigade at Number Five, the Third Brigade was pinned down. They could stay where they were or charge the next fort in line, Redoubt Number Two. Brigade Colonel Sylvester Hill gave the order to charge the nearby fort. As he pointed with his sword, a musket ball struck him in the forehead. He was dead instantly. Minnesota Colonel William Marshall took command of the brigade.

With the Seventh Minnesota in front, the brigade charged into Redoubt Number Two. They instantly turned the fort's captured guns on Redoubt Number One.

General Wood's Fourth Corps had been ordered to take the same redoubt. In mid-morning, he was instructed to move on Stewart's troops holding Number One and the Confederate line running east toward the Granny White Pike. By mid-afternoon, Wood still hadn't obtained his goal. Elliott's division also was stymied. General Nathan Kimball was next given the order to take Redoubt Number One.

Kimball's men charged, and when they finally reached the fort from the north, they were met by men of the Third Brigade as the guerillas streamed into the fort from Redoubt Number Two, 200 yards to the south. General Kenner Garrard's Second Division of the guerillas had aided with an assault from the west.

The fall of Redoubt Number Four had more of an effect than just silencing Confederate guns. With it out of the way, federal guns could now concentrate on the rebels behind stone walls, Lee's two brigades sent from the center of the line by Hood. McArthur's men massed and charged the wall, breaking through the rebel line and driving them back.

Wilson's cavalry of 12,000 had protected the Union right through the day. Chalmer's force of 1,200 tried throughout the day to fight behind fortifications and keep harassing Wilson. In the end, Chalmer's outmanned force was driven back and out of the battle.

By nightfall, all of Hood's redoubts had fallen. Smith's guerillas had carried the day.

Jimmy savored the victory with his friends. "I told Lieutenant Gere we could do it, and we did. Minnesota boys were in the lead all day. We were in on taking all five forts and sent Hood back eight miles."

Lieutenant John Bishop patted Dunn on the back. "You did some hot work, men. Hood's army are all east of the Granny White Pike."

"So what do we do?"

"Tomorrow we finish them off."

Thomas sent a telegraph to General Halleck outlining the day's success. Stanton, in a joyous mood, brought the news to President Lincoln, who had a much better night's sleep.

* * *

THAT NIGHT, Hood consolidated the Army of the Tennessee. Hood had moved his army into a contracted line shaped like a shallow "U," two miles south of his earlier position. His order of corps commanders changed. Cheatham went from the far right to the far right of the line. Lee, who had been in the center, was now on the far right. Stewart moved from the left to the center.

The line of defense was shortened and was anchored by two hills, Compton's on the left and Peach Orchard Hill on the right. The former oversaw the Nashville-Franklin Pike a possible escape route south and the latter was just west of Granny White Pike, another major road south.

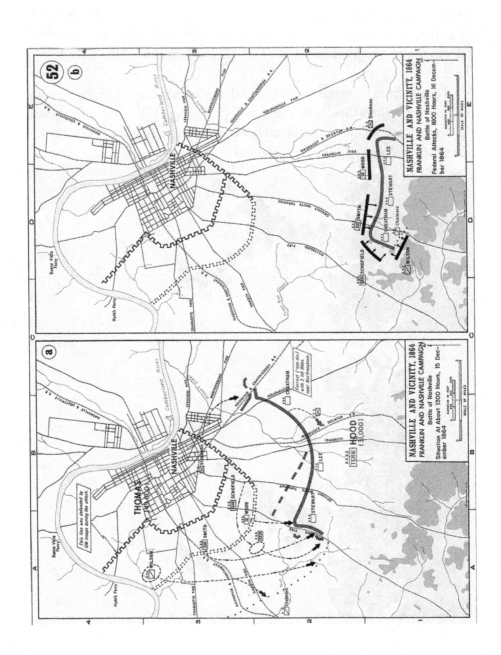

NASHVILLE AND VICINITY, 1864
FRANKLIN AND NASHVILLE CAMPAIGN
Battle of Nashville
Situation At About 1300 Hours, 15 December 1864

NASHVILLE AND VICINITY, 1864
FRANKLIN AND NASHVILLE CAMPAIGN
Battle of Nashville
Federal Attacks, 1600 Hours, 16 December 1864

Nashville

DURING THE NIGHT, FRANK CHEATHAM personally escorted General Bate onto Compton's Hill, a lump of ground south of Nashville and on the Confederate far left. He pointed out the lines of battle on the hill that had been established for Bate.

Bate didn't like the position. "It's muddy. I can't get artillery up here, and these lines are all wrong."

"I'm not authorized to change the lines. Fortify them and find a way to get cannons up here," Cheatham replied.

Bate's men worked feverishly on defenses through the night, but there were only shovels for one in ten. The defenses became low mounds of dirt and small piles of rocks. A road was discovered, and cannon were brought up to a plateau.

* * *

THOMAS ASSEMBLED his officers to lay out the next day's plan. As he stood before them, he unfolded a sheet of paper from his pocket. "I've just received a wire from General Grant," he announced. "He was on his way to visit us, but he is a few hundred miles from here and now will go no further. The general says that we need to push the enemy and give him no rest until he is destroyed. He adds that much is expected of us."

Thomas looked over the room of officers, some puffing away on cigars, and simply said, "I think we have done pretty well today."

"What about tomorrow?" Schofield asked.

"Hood has contracted his defensive line and moved it back. It is anchored by hills on both ends. Steedman, you will renew your offensive on Hood's right. Wood, continue to hold the center in place. Meanwhile you, General Schofield, and Smith and Wilson must pound them on the left and rear."

* * *

IN CAMP, Jimmy Dunn and Will Hutchinson chewed on salt pork and hard-tack. Jimmy first floated the pork in his tin cup of hot coffee. He swished it around, peering into it.

"Any extra meat?" Will wondered.

"Nope, not one little bug floated out of the meat."

"I've had times when there wuz more bugs than meat."

"Guess they're feedin' us better."

"At least we have food," Will said with approval, "not like the Red River where we ate bark."

Jimmy thought and added, "Like I wuz sayin' yesterday, Will, we bin through an awful lot."

"Yep, Jimmy, we'll have a lot of stories to tell back home."

"I don't know if I'll be able to talk much about this."

"Whadda ya mean, Jimmy? You talk to everybody. Just think of all the people in your dad's hotel you can talk to. You'll be the star of Chatfield. I bet Greg Davids from Preston will even talk about you there."

Jimmy snickered. "Do you think folks will believe what he says?"

Sure they will," Will grinned. "Everybody knows and trusts Greg Davids."

"I just hope I'm there to tell stories, Will," Jimmy said solemnly.

"Of course ya will, Jimmy. Just keep yer head down."

* * *

THE SKY OVER NASHVILLE was slate gray the next morning. The ground was ice-encrusted, the temperature cold. Soon a cold drizzle began to thaw the ground, making the mud even stickier. Hood visited his lines just after dawn. He met with his corps commanders, encouraged them, and then, just in case, "should any disaster happen to us today," gave them routes of retreat.

At 8:30 a.m., Smith's corps moved to within 600 yards of Compton's Hill and began an artillery barrage. The onslaught of cannon fire would continue throughout the morning. Smith's Minnesota troops lined up for battle. Their cartridge boxes had been replenished, and they awaited orders. They crossed a field and marched through a woods before coming in sight of the enemy half a mile away. In front to their right was the lump on the ground called Compton's Hill. In the front of the First Division, Confederate soldiers waited behind a stone wall that stretched along the base of the hill. The Fifth

Minnesota was ordered to a line of willows that skirted a ditch, where they waited for hours.

West of the hill, Schofield handed a dispatch to Clint Cilley. "Bring this to Thomas," he said. "I need more men. I think Hood may attack me."

"Do you think so, sir? The shelling seems to be pinning them down."

"I will not risk a suicide attack. Take the dispatch to Thomas."

As on the previous day, Steedman and Wood's men began with a feint on the right. They maneuvered over the slippery ground and at noon stormed through the drizzle up Peach Orchard Hill.

Georgia and Louisiana brigades unleashed fire that cut the Yankees down. Beaten back, the Union forces regrouped and charged again and again.

The U.S. Colored Troops displayed great valor. At noon, they led a determined assault on the Confederate works. They rushed into abatis forty feet in front of the rebel wall and charged en masse. Confederate general Holtsclaw watched as five separate color bearers were shot down attempting to gain his works. He murmured, "They came to die."

The courageous assault was futile, and hundreds fell from Confederate fire. The dead piled up in front of the defenders' wall. At mid-afternoon, Lee's Corps still held the hill and, most important, all pikes in the area, including the path to the Nashville-Franklin Pike.

On the other end of the line, General Schofield received instructions from Thomas to attack Compton Hill at 1:00 p.m. Thomas had explained in his dispatch, "I want pressure on both their flanks. Smith led the fighting yesterday. It's your turn today. Attack the hill."

Schofield turned to Cilley. "Look up there," he pointed at the hill. "I don't have sufficient men to storm those heights. Tell Thomas I must have more men."

Clint rode off to find Thomas.

Meanwhile Wilson's cavalry, after facing stiff resistance in the morning, finally managed to get around Cheatham's flank and move behind him. The plan was that once Wilson was in position on Cheatham's flank, Schofield should attack from the front.

Wilson sent three couriers, one after another, to Schofield with messages urging him to attack. He would not move his army. Finally Thomas sent Smith's Third Division under Colonel Moore to Schofield. It was now 3:00 p.m., and still nothing from the commander of the Fourth Corps.

Schofield sent Clint back to Thomas. "Sir," the adjutant delivered, "General Schofield's compliments, he says that to scale the hill he still doesn't have enough men. He would like General Smith's Second Division under Garrard. General Smith refused to send it. He says," Clint continued breathlessly, "that it would be a bloodbath for his men to attack such heights with artillery ringing the summit and Cheatham's men in the trenches."

At about the same time Clint was with Thomas, John McArthur had for the second time left his position on a high hill directly south of Compton's Hill to confer with General Couch, Schofield's left wing commander who was positioned to McArthur's right.

For the second time he implored Couch, "Fer God's sake, man, attack the hill before the day is lost and we have a stalemate. Join with me!"

As he had once before, Couch responded, "I can't. I have no orders to do so from General Schofield."

"Schofield be damned. He is supposed to have acted by now."

"I have no orders, General McArthur, and I won't move until I get them."

Disgusted, McArthur returned to A.J. Smith. "General, let me take over Couch's position in the line. I'll make a charge on the hill."

"Hold on for a bit. I need to make General Thomas aware of this plan."

McArthur looked perplexed and then determined as he said, "General, if I don't hear from you by 4:00 p.m., I will attack."

Smith rode off to find Thomas. He found Wilson first and the two rode to Thomas's headquarters. It was almost 4:00 when they got there. The sky was growing dark as clouds and rain continued to provide an air of gloom.

As they approached, they found Schofield and Thomas standing on a hill. The vista before them presented the whole left flank of Cheatham's army. Wilson could see his own cavalry on the left and rear of the Confederates.

Thomas was complaining, "The day is almost done and we've accomplished nothing except a bloodbath on the right, where Steedman and Wood decimated the Confederate troops."

Wilson asserted, "My men are in position and ready. You can see them from here with your glasses."

Smith then made his request. "General McArthur requests permission to immediately attack the Confederate salient in his front."

Thomas shook his head. "No, the prescribed order of attack gives the initiative to General Schofield."

"I need more men," Schofield demanded. "They can flank me."

Thomas raised his field glasses and looked toward Compton's Hill, searching for Wilson's men. Then he saw something else. "What's this? There's a mass of our troops moving out from the trees on the left. They're heading for the Confederate lines."

"What time is it?" Smith asked.

Wilson removed a round watch from his vest and replied, "Four oh five."

Smith stifled a smile, "That would be General McArthur. Apparently he grew tired of waiting."

Thomas lowered his glasses and turned to Schofield. "General McArthur is attacking without waiting for you. Please advance your line."

Less than half an hour earlier, McArthur had ridden back to Couch. The Scotsman's artillery had just opened up on the hill. He told Couch, "I'm going to attack the hill from your position. Move your men out of the way."

"On whose orders?"

"Mine."

"What about Thomas, Schofield? What about Smith? Do any of them approve of this?"

"General Couch," McArthur replied in a tone that dripped icicles, "either fight now or get your men out of the way."

Couch hesitated, then, "All right. It's on your head."

A long column of the guerillas moved by the right flank down an old wagon road into the valley and into the vacated trenches, preparing to charge the heights on Compton's Hill.

* * *

AS THE SHADOWS LENGTHENED, Hood had reason for optimism. On the right Lee had repulsed the Union attacks and routes of retreat, if needed, were still open.

Hood had sent out a message: "The commanding general takes pleasure in announcing to his troops that victory and success are now within their grasp; and the commanding general feels proud and gratified that in every attack and assault the enemy have been repulsed, and the commanding general will further say to his noble and gallant troops, be of good cheer—all is well."

Bate was not convinced by Hood's message as he surveyed his position. Hood had transferred some of his men to help Lee, and Bate's lines were stretched thin. He complained to his captain, "Our works are terrible. We have just rocks and logs thrown together. And I don't like the placement of our cannon. I fear we are not on the military crest of the hill. We are on the topical crest and won't be able to see them until they are nearly on top of us."

"General, a six-foot man could not be seen twenty yards from the front," his captain agreed, "thus making it possible for the federals to mass an attacking party within a few yards of the position and be perfectly sheltered from our fire."

* * *

MCARTHUR SENT THREE regiments of Smith's First Division guerillas, 1,000 men, for the salient angle of the hill from the northeast as concentrated fire from Union artillery ringed the hill in smoke and fire.

The order to charge was bellowed from the front. Colonel McMillen shouted at his First Brigade, "Don't cheer or fire a shot until the works are gained!"

His Tenth Minnesota on the far left of the division sprinted forward. They cheered anyway. The Ninth Minnesota, just left of the Tenth, joined them in storming the slope of the hill to their left, while the Fifth Minnesota, next in line, followed just to the west of Granny White Pike. The Seventh, just left of the Fifth, was east of the pike. A wide plain extended before the Tenth, with a low fence running through it. A sheet of lead whistled continually from the barricade.

The valiant boys from Minnesota were ordered to demolish the distant fences and to throw up slight breastworks. Once their task was completed the order, "Forward!" sounded. The Tenth led the way, battling toward enemy-held positions over ground littered with guns, knapsacks, and equipment. The Minnesotans ignored with disgust the Union boys retreating back through their lines while complaining of hunger, thirst, or exhaustion.

Their eyes were fixed on the goal before them, the formidable earthworks that stretched up and over the crest of a high hill.

The Tenth Minnesota charged across the field to the hill. The rebels opened with a firestorm of shell, canister, and musketry. The shelling hit them like iron rain, with a terrible effect. The ranks to the left were decimated, but it would take more than powder and lead to stop them.

McMillen watched as a volley flashed and went over the brigade's heads on the right. But firing on the left took a heavy toll on the Tenth. Still, fighting like devils, they charged on into the Confederate works.

Hubbard's Second Brigade and Marshall's Third Brigade were moved into position. In front of the Fifth and Seventh was a cornfield that had become a muddy mire, 400 feet of it leading to the hill and the wall at its base. It ran south, along the Granny White Pike. As the Tenth scaled the steepest part of the hill, to their left the Ninth faced lower elevations and intermingled with the Fifth Minnesota. Left of the Ninth's original position, the Fifth and Seventh slogged into the cornfield as a steady rain opened up. Colonel Hubbard, in front, was waving his hat high. Colonel Marshall, leading the Third Brigade, rode his little chestnut horse, Don, across the field with his men. In front of them to the east was a six-gun bunker in the underbrush, with Stewart's line behind a stone wall.

As the Minnesota boys charged, canister shot from the rebel bunker swept across the field. Lethal fire ripped into the assaulting regiments, causing many men to crumble into the muddy stubble of cornstalks.

Jimmy Dunn had paused at the edge of the field as he watched his comrades sink ankle deep and some knee deep in muck. He called to Lieutenant John Bishop, "Hey, Lieutenant, this ground looks like a sty. If I wanted ta slop pigs, I wouldda stayed home."

"We'll clean yer pretty blue uniform later, Jimmy!" Bishop called back.

Jimmy trudged into the field with the rest. Shot and shell from the Confederate works blasted into the field, sending clumps of mud rocketing into the gloomy, darkening sky. Musketry, cannon, and canister sliced into the advancing blue line as the soldiers struggled to charge while sinking in mud.

The flag bearer held the stars and stripes high as he plodded on toward the rebel works. A lead ball found its target and took him down. Jimmy, right behind, grabbed the flag before it had scarcely hit the ground. He found Levi Carr and cried, "Follow me and the flag, boys!"

After a few steps, Jimmy clutched his gut and tumbled into the mud.

Levi rushed to his friend, "Hang on, Jimmy!" he shouted. "I'll come back for ya."

Marshall, guiding the colors, was one of the first to the rebel wall. He spotted a rebel gunner who had just fired off a shell and ran him down. A Union private yelled, "Be careful, Colonel, don't get out front so much!"

A Confederate officer standing with his back to a wagon wheel shouted, "Hell, any man who is brave enough to ride a horse across that field will never be killed."

A moment later, Marshall jerked back in his saddle as a shot tore into his chest. Mystified, the colonel looked down at the hole in the front of his blue coat. Reaching down, he pulled out his doubled-up gauntlets, which he had placed in his front coat pocket. He shook a lead ball out of them and continued with the fight.

Bate's men were being hit in the front, sides, and rear. "Keep yer heads down!" he screamed over the cacophony of sound. "Keep down or you'll lose yer heads!" The Tenth and Ninth knew all about the military crest, and they knew their enemy didn't have it. The Tenth had started unseen at the base of the hill and fought their way up. Cannon could not be tilted low enough for the proper firing angle.

Furious hand-to-hand fighting broke out on the slopes. The Fifth and Seventh charged toward the side of Compton's Hill across the field and into the line of defense below the hill. The rebel lines broke at all quarters. Tom Gere raced alongside a flag bearer from the Fourth Mississippi. He tackled the rebel, cracked him over the head and took the flag.

Nashville spectators who watched the fight from rooftops a couple miles away claimed it looked like the Yankees poured like a cloud into Bate's Division. Jim, who was now Thomas Benton Smith's adjutant, was just below the crest of the hill when the Minnesotans slammed into it. Both armies became so intertwined in the struggle that it became impossible to tell one side from the other.

Bill Shy leapt into the brawl. He fired a shot into a scrum of blue. A return shot ripped into his head. Soon the outmanned rebels were overrun. They threw down their weapons and raced down the back side of Compton's Hill with the Union soldiers in hot pursuit. Once at the base, the rebels ran into the same problem leaving the hill as the Yankees had approaching it: mud.

As the fugitive rebels sunk into the mud, Yankee pursuers fired away. General Henry Jackson, one of Bate's brigade commanders, struggled across a marshy field as Union troops suddenly appeared behind him. As he sank in the quagmire, one of his aides urged him to remove his knee-high boots.

As Jackson struggled to pull off a boot, a voice cried, "Surrender, damn you!" They looked up and in the faint remaining light saw four Yankee soldiers along a nearby fence line.

Their rifles were leveled at the rebels.

Jackson strained to put his boots back on. His aide walked behind him and turned down his collar, hiding his general's insignia. Then the Union soldiers, rifles at the ready, approached the general as he arose and turned up his collar.

John Bishop exclaimed, "You're a general!"

Jackson replied, "That is my rank."

Bishop laughed, screamed and hurrahed. He waved his hat and bellowed for all to hear, "Captured a general, by God! I will carry you to Nashville myself!"

General Thomas Benton Smith was trying to hold his line in the face of the sweeping Union onslaught. As he drew his pistol and fired, he realized that only a small squad was still with him. His men had run away. Now surrounded, Smith ordered the squad to cease fire and waved a white handkerchief over his head and surrendered.

The stream of rebels running to the rear onto Granny White and Franklin pikes became a river. Confederate officers tried to stem the mass retreat but as the roads filled with fleeing soldiers, halting them was impossible. Rebel soldiers raced through the woods. Wagons were abandoned on clogged roads.

Sam Watkins of the Twentieth Tennessee said, "It was like trying to stop the current of the Duck River with a fish net."

A young officer who had not been in the fight rode into the fleeing mob. "Stop! Stop!" he yelled. "There is no danger there!"

A veteran soldier paused, turned and called back over his shoulder, "You go to Hell. I was there!"

The cold rain turned to snow. In the fading light, nearly all of Hood's army fled from hill to hill. From his horse, George Thomas watched the fall-colored hill as blue-clad soldiers swarmed up the slope, flags waving in the twilight. A mixture of haze and smoke drifted from the hills into the valley beyond.

Thomas watched intently as his face lit up in joy and anticipation. "Hurrah for the Minnesota boys!" he shouted. "Hurrah for the snow diggers!"

The cheers of his charging troops as they smashed through the Confederate works echoed back to Thomas. He nodded at A.J. Smith, riding alongside Clint Cilley, who had just delivered a dispatch. The commanding general commented, "The voice of the American people, General."

Hood ordered the remnants of Chalmers's calvary to keep Granny White Pike open. Thomas sent General Wilson and his cavalry to duel with the Confederate forces. Screaming horses, gunshots, and shouting men spilled together in a death struggle. In the darkness, soldiers could barely see past their horses' ears. Opponents could only be identified in the flashes of gunfire.

On the Franklin Pike, Cheatham's and Stewart's men were running for their lives. The task of protecting the rear of Hood's army as they ran away rested on Stephen Lee's shoulders.

Lee galloped among the running men. He saw a battle flag and seized it. Lee bellowed at those racing by him, "Rally, men, for God's sake. This is the place for brave men to die!"

A drummer boy began to beat the long roll, and some soldiers stopped and reformed under Lee's command. Achieving some semblance of order, they were able to delay the Union pursuers temporarily.

Thomas and Smith, with Clint, rode to where Wilson's troopers were still embroiled with Chalmers. The Rock of Chickamauga beamed at his cavalry general. "Dang it to hell, Wilson, didn't I tell you we could lick 'em, didn't I tell you we could lick 'em if the boys in Washington would only let us alone?"

Clint watched the scene of the rebel rout. He looked at the generals with him and observed, "The death knell of the Army of Tennessee was sounded at Franklin, and this is the funeral."

The ruined Confederate Army struggled in disarray down the Franklin Pike. Forrest had been sent an urgent message to return from Murfreesboro to aid Hood. He reached them on the road, too late to aid in the battle. Only Chalmer's cavalry was left to aid the retreat.

Thomas Benton Smith was being led under guard from the battlefield to Nashville. Inexplicably, Colonel William McMillen, commander of McArthur's First Brigade, drew his sword and slammed it over the defenseless Confederate's head.

As the boy general stumbled, McMillen slashed his sword twice more into Smith's head. The young officer fell to the muddy ground. Part of his brain oozed through a gash in the top of his head.

Levi Carr returned to the cornfield where Jimmy Dunn lay in the mud. Jimmy was in severe pain, shot in the stomach. Levi and Will Hutchinson carried him to rear as gently as possible to the hospital tent.

A doctor quickly examined him and explained to Will and Levi, "He's gut shot. There's nothing much I can do except give him something for the pain. He'll be gone in a couple days. We're using a building in Nashville for a hospital. You can see him there."

* * *

THE NEXT MORNING Levi Carr, Will Hutchinson, and Willie Sturgis entered a large room filled with cots, an aisle down the center. They found Jimmy near the center.

The boy managed a weak smile. "Well, they missed my head," he said softly.

"Do ya hurt much?" Willie asked.

"I mostly feel kinda numb. How'd the battle go?"

"We won, Jimmy. Minnesota boys did it," Levi asserted. "Our four regiments were the ones that went up the hill and drove off the rebels. It was us."

"I said us boys could do whatever they asked."

Willie informed Jimmy, "Lieutenant Gere, he captured a reb flag. A Mississippi one."

Will added, "And Lieutenant Bishop, he captured a reb general."

"They should both get medals," Jimmy said.

Levi said, "The regiment is pulling out. We're all going with General Thomas after Hood. I guess the folks in Washington want us to finish him off."

"We gotta go, Jimmy," Willie said softly. "Captain just gave us a few minutes to see you before we marched out."

Levi smiled. "You'll be feelin' better when we get back," he said. "We'll see ya then. Keep thinkin' 'bout that girl in Chatfield."

Jimmy looked at each in turn. "I won't be here when you get back. You all know that. Gut shot folks don't get better. They just die."

Each of the three silently shook their friend's hand and walked away.

The next day, Jimmy Dunn died.

* * *

HOOD MANAGED TO PUT TOGETHER something that resembled an army and marched south from Franklin. They traveled light, having lost most of their equipment in Nashville. Thomas, having been ordered by Grant to pursue Hood, moved his army south of Nashville.

Then a telegram arrived from Halleck, which read, "Permit me, General, to urge the vast importance of a hot pursuit of Hood's army. Every possible sacrifice should be made."

Thomas bristled but, buoyed by his success in Nashville, replied, "We cannot control the elements. Pursuing an enemy through an exhausted country, over mud roads completely sogged with heavy rains, is no child's play. Sherman took the best divisions of the army with him. I was left with a disorganized force."

Halleck issued an apology and stressed that the government had great confidence in Thomas.

Hood had planned to meet Thomas head on by forming a line at the Duck River. He believed he must do something. "We can't run forever," he told a confidant. "But the condition of this army is such that I fear Thomas would destroy it. I had my heart so set on success. I had prayed so earnestly for it—that my heart has been very rebellious."

Bedford Forrest arrived on the scene and bluntly helped Hood make a decision. He said, "If we are unable to hold the state, we should at once evacuate it." Exiled Governor Isham Harris agreed. With Forrest acting as rear guard, the battered Army of Tennessee headed south. For ten days his army maintained a grueling 100-mile retreat. Bloodied and battered, they endured an almost continual cold drizzle. They needed some luck to cross the river in Alabama.

Thomas had his own problems with weather, missing pontoons, and failure by the Union Navy to destroy a pontoon bridge. This gave Hood the luck he needed, as he used the bridge to cross. It was December 26, 1864. The only combat involved skirmishing between Wilson's and Forrest's cavalry.

Thomas called off the chase, and Hood's forces trudged into Alabama through ice, snow, and cold. As they passed south of Pulaski, Hood and his staff were riding on a narrow road and were about to push a soldier off the path. The veteran turned and began to sing, to the tune "The Yellow Rose of Texas":

> So now I'm going southward
> My heart is full of woe.
> I'm going down to Georgia
> To see my uncle, Joe
> You can talk about your Clementine
> And sing of Rosalie
> But the Gallant Hood of Texas
> Played Hell in Tennessee

* * *

THE ARMY OF TENNESSEE never fought in a major battle again. In his time in command, Sam Hood had lost 23,500 of the 38,000-man force he had inherited from Joe Johnston. At Nashville alone, Hood had lost 2,300, killed or wounded.

George Thomas listed 387 killed, 2,562 wounded, and 112 missing. A third of his casualties happened in the assault on Overton Hill. Once they reached Pulaski, some of Hood's command went east to join Joe Johnston against Sherman. On January 23, Dick Taylor took over the remainder of Hood's command.

Their erstwhile general addressed his men one last time. "My dear boys," he began. "It is my fervent hope that you will give General Taylor your full support and that you will avenge your comrades whose bones lay bleaching on the fields of middle Tennessee."

The End

THE SECOND MINNESOTA REGIMENT, commanded by Judson Bishop, had followed Sherman throughout the Georgia campaign. On April 10, 1865, they were leading the army toward Raleigh, North Carolina. After destroying a bridge, they continued ahead with Bishop and Major John Moulton in the lead.

A great wave of sound rippled toward them from the head of the army. "What's that?" Moulton wondered.

"Sounds like cheering, Major, but I can't be sure."

"Look there," Moulton pointed. "It's Clint Cilley."

Cilley trotted to them with a huge smile on his face. "Lee gave up," he announced. "Two days ago at Appomattox Court House, Virginia. Lee met Grant and surrendered."

"Hallelujah!" Bishop cried. "Is it really over?"

"Not quite," Clint responded. "Joe Johnston still has an army around here, but it's just a matter of time—days maybe, weeks at the outside."

Bishop sat back in his saddle and viewed his men with pride. "It's a great moment, not just for the Union but for Minnesota. Clint, when the war started there were scarcely 170,000 people in the entire state, about 25,000 enlisted in the army. It's amazing what they accomplished. The First Minnesota saved the day at Gettysburg, the Second with a magnificent charge up Missionary Ridge, the Third redeeming themselves after surrendering at Murfreesboro with distinguished service against the Sioux and now maintaining order in Arkansas."

Clint nodded in agreement. "The Fifth, Seventh, Ninth, and Tenth fought Indians and rebs all over the West before winning the day at Shy's Hill at Nashville. We lost more Minnesota boys on that hill then in any other battle."

"And they never stopped fighting," Bishop continued. "Since Nashville the Fourth have been with us and Sherman, and the Fifth is still fighting in Alabama. I heard they attacked Fort Blakely just yesterday."

"Even the Sixth got in on that one," Cilley added. "They were kept fighting the Sioux until they were finally garrisoned around St. Louis before getting to fight in Alabama."

"I heard the Seventh was at Spanish Fort, Alabama, too."

"They even got the Eighth down here," Moulton added. "For near four years they fight Indians and then join us here with Sherman. Hell, they marched way out to the Yellowstone first."

Bishop chuckled. "Sherman's Woodticks."

"The Ninth left Nashville for Spanish Fort, too."

Bishop considered, "Minnesota boys were there at the beginning and they're in Alabama now, wrapping up the last battles of the war. Too bad the Ninth lost Wilkin at Tupelo. He was a good man."

"That brings us to the Tenth," Cilley continued. "Since the eleventh never really fought in the war."

"Jennsion's Tenth, from Indians to the Red River to Nashville, then New Orleans, before finishing up at Spanish Fort and Fort Blakely." Bishop paused. "They made us all proud to be from Minnesota."

"Ya know," Clint wondered, "Minnesota is barely seven years old. I wonder if we will ever contribute as much to our nation's history as we just have."

Bishop shook his head slowly. "Just so what these boys did will never be forgotten. They came to a new land and offered their lives to keep it."

* * *

ON APRIL 26, 1865, Joe Johnston surrendered the Army of the South. Remnants of some Tennessee regiments mustered out for the last time. Sam Watkins stood alongside Wad Carter as they watched the army dissolve before them. They marched by a tattered, bullet-riddled rebel flag just barely clinging to a nearly shattered flagstaff and stacked their weapons alongside it.

Sam observed, "We started the First Tennessee with 1,200 men. With recruits and conscripts, over the course of the fighting we had 'bout 3,200. We had sixty-five left this morning. That's with officers. Sixty-five men."

Wad blinked back the mist forming in his eyes. "So many died, for a cause we could never win."

"Your brother, Tod, Sam Davis, Bill Shy. How might things have been different if they'd lived? Even big battles that we won, Chickamauga and Franklin, were really losses."

"Sam, our boys had spirit, they were devoted to our cause. Did we have the leaders?"

"What happened to us went a lot deeper than leaders," Sam observed. "The East had Lee, and we were lucky to have Albert Sidney Johnson, prob'ly the best we had. Bragg, Joe Johnston, Hood all had faults, but the North just had too much for us, too much of everything."

"Poor Sam Hood," Wad continued. "He got whittled down pretty good by the war and in the end even his fiancée left him. Our boys knew what the outcome might be. But they freely followed the stars and bars."

"Ya know, Wad, when ya think about it, we didn't have such good reasons ta fight at all. It was all down to splitting up our country. Right or wrong, like it or not, that is what this came down to."

"Yeah, Sam, at least one thing came out of this for sure: we will be one country."

Epilogue

I N THE FALL OF 1907, THE FINISHING TOUCHES were added to the new, magnificent Minnesota State Capitol. The classic, domed building was made of shining white marble from Georgia. The structure gleamed from a hilltop, with downtown St. Paul and the river below.

At the official opening of the building two years before, veterans of Minnesota Civil War regiments had marched up Robert Street, climbed the wide staircase leading into the capitol, and presented their battle flags to Minnesota state officials, who ordered them placed on display in the rotunda. Some of the artwork commissioned by architect Cass Gilbert was not ready to be displayed at the opening, but two years later, all was ready.

A medium-sized older man, his mustache and hair tinged gray, held a young boy's hand as they entered a large, ornate room. "See the pictures on the wall, Tommy," the old man pointed at two large murals. "They tell the story of what happened in the big war. Let's go to the big room up ahead. There are some things in there I want you to see."

The two walked through a set of wide-open double doors into the governor's reception room. Dark oak woodwork and paneling cast a rich glow, emphasized by gold molding that framed eight murals, most about seven by fourteen feet in size.

At either end of the large room were paintings that depicted the Dakota people in Minnesota. One concerned the Treaty of Traverse des Sioux and the other, the discovery of the Falls of St. Anthony by Father Hennepin. On the other two walls, with two on each side, were paintings of Civil War battles.

"Look closely at these paintings, Tommy. They tell the story of what Minnesota did in the Civil War. There weren't many of us, and we had just become a state, but we made people sit up and notice.

301

"Look there, Gettysburg, where the First Minnesota made a charge at Plum Run Creek and plugged a hole in the Union line. We lost eighty-two percent of the regiment in that charge.

"And see here, where the boys are charging up a hill. That's Missionary Ridge. And see that fellow waving his hat? That's Judson Bishop. He was a newspaperman in Chatfield when the war started, became a colonel."

"Did you know him, Grandpa Charlie?"

The older man laughed. "Know him? Sure I did, I was from Chatfield, too. But I was just twelve when the war began. Men like Colonel Bishop didn't spend much time talking to kid privates."

"You were in the war? What did you do? You were only twelve."

Memories swept over the man like a great wave, there was so much to say. But he simply replied, "I played a drum."

He nodded at another painting. "See that one? That's the Battle of Nashville. Four Minnesota regiments charged across a muddy cornfield and up Shy's Hill—they renamed the hill after a rebel captain killed there. Our boys drove the rebs right off the hill and won the battle.

"But I lost a good friend there, Jimmy Dunn." He paused and rubbed an eye. "I can still remember his smile and his laugh. Tom Gere got a Medal of Honor at Nashville for taking a reb flag. John Bishop captured a rebel general there, but Bishop would have been dead if Jimmy hadn't saved his life in the Indian War."

"You fought the Indians, too, Grandpa?"

"From the beginning, right here in Minnesota. I played the drum at Fort Ridgeley. Then I went south with the Fifth."

The man stood in the middle of the room and pensively took in each painting. He looked sternly at the boy beside him. "Four of our colonels became Minnesota governors. Clint Cilley, he got a Medal of Honor, too, but never came back. He wound up a congressman in North Carolina."

The old man paused. "Remember what you see here. This is part of our history. It's a part of who we are today."

"Won't that change, Grandpa? A hundred years from now, won't some other history be maybe more important?"

"History is the story of how we became who we are," Grandpa Charlie said. "There should always be room for other stories. But we can't change the past, and our history must always have an important place in the pages of our memories, and," he looked around, "in our historic buildings. It isn't always pretty and the stories are both good and bad. But we can't wash away what happened. The bloodstains are too deep."

The man paused, gazed around the room and whispered to his grandson, "Remember. Remember that Private Charlie Culver, drummer boy, Fifth Minnesota, joined up to fight the war that saved our country."

The boy looked up at his grandfather. "I'll remember, Grandpa. I just hope everyone does."

"Look around you, boy," the old man directed. "These paintings depict a time of glory for Minnesota boys. But most of them are gone now."

His hand swept before him at the valiant men performing heroic deeds on the paintings affixed to the walls.

"This is what's left of them, what remains of glory. Never let the memories die."

* * *

Arthur McArthur, badly injured at Franklin, survived and became the father of General Douglas McArthur, a World War II hero. General Thomas Benton Smith survived his attack by General McMillan but received a serious brain injury. He died in 1923 after forty-seven years in a Nashville insane asylum. Major Myles Keogh was released from Confederate custody after two and one-half months. He continued in military service until June 25, 1876, when he died with Custer at Little Big Horn. Clint Cilley was appointed a regional administrator for the Freedman's Bureau in North Carolina. A popular lawyer as well, he was elected to Congress from North Carolina.

Terms

Infantry Units
  Company: 100 men
  Regiment: 10 companies
  Brigade: 3 to 6 regiments
  Division: 2 to 6 Brigades
  Corps: 2 to 4 Divisions
  Army: 1 to 8 Corps
These numbers could vary depending upon the numbers of men available. Confederate and Union command structures might also vary in numbers.

Cavalry
  Troop: 100 men
  Regiment: 12 troops
  Brigade, Division and Corps
Initially, each Union cavalry regiment was assigned to an infantry division. The Confederates brigaded their cavalry together. The Union eventually adopted this organization as well. As the war progressed, both sides formed cavalry divisions. The North also formed cavalry corps, and the South later also adopted this innovation.

The basic unit of artillery is the battery, which has 4 to 6 guns, is commanded by a captain and has 4 lieutenants, 12 sergeants and corporals and 120 privates. It typically had 4 guns in the South and 6 guns in the North.

Military Terms
  Flank: the end or side of a military position
  Long Roll: a long, continuous drum roll that commanded a regiment to assemble
Abatis: A line of trees chopped down with their branches pointed out at the enemy.
Wheel: Change direction to the reverse flank.
Oblique: Crossing the battlefield in a diagonal line.

Load in Nine Times:
  1. Load
  2. Handle Cartridge
  3. Tear Cartridge
  4. Charge Cartridge
  5. Draw rammer
  6. Ram cartridge
  7. Return rammer
  8. Prime
  9. Shoulder arms

Sources

Admiral David Dixon Porter, Chester C. Hearn, Naval Institute Press, Annapolis, MD, 1996.

Captain Tod Carter of the Confederate States Army—a biographical word portrait, Rosalie Carter, 1972.

The Carter House, Battle of Franklin Trust, Franklin, TN.

"Carter House," Eric Jacobson, lecture, Nov. 2004.

Civil War maps attributed to Hal Jesperson, www.posix.com/CW.

Colonel Aytch, Sam R. Watkins, Collier Books, Macmillian Publishing Company, NY, 1962.

Guide to Civil War Nashville, Mark Zimmerman, Battle of Nashville Preservation Society, Nashville, TN, 2004.

The Life of Billy Yank, Bell Irvin Wiley, Louisiana State University Press, 1987.

The Life of Johnny Reb, Bell Irvin Wiley, Louisiana State University Press, 1987.

Minnesota In The Civil and Indian Wars 1861-1865, Vol. I, The Board of Commissioners, Pioneer Press Company, St. Paul, MN, 1891.

Minnesotans In the Civil and Indian Wars 1861-1865, Vol. II, The Board of Commissioners, Pioneer Press Company, St. Paul, MN, 1893.

"The Red River Campaign," civilwarhome.com/redriverrecords.htm.

Shrouds of Glory, Winston Groom, The Atlantic Monthly Press, New York, NY, 1995.

The Story of a Regiment, Judson W. Bishop, Newell L. Chester, editor, North Star Press, St. Cloud, MN, 2000.

U.S. Minnesota Troops & The Final Charge at Nashville, Kenneth Dugan Flies, Hiawatha Press, Eagan, MN, 2007.

CPSIA information can be obtained
at www.ICGtesting.com
Printed in the USA
LVOW03s0453150817
545055LV00001B/1/P